PRAISE FOR THESE
award-winning authors

New York Times bestselling author
Elizabeth Lowell

"When it comes to delivering epic romance and suspense,
Ms. Lowell is in a class by herself."
—*Romantic Times Magazine*

Elizabeth Lowell is "a rare romantic jewel."
—*New York Times* bestselling author
Kathleen E. Woodiwiss

New York Times bestselling author
Rebecca Brandewyne

"Rebecca Brandewyne is one of the best writers of our time!"
—*Affaire de Coeur*

"I have been reading and enjoying Rebecca Brandewyne
for years. She is a wonderful writer."
—*New York Times* bestselling author Jude Deveraux

Award-winning author
Merline Lovelace

"[Merline Lovelace's stories] sizzle
with a passion for life and love..."
—*New York Times* bestselling author Nora Roberts

"Top-rate suspense with great characters,
rich atmosphere and a crackling plot!"
—*New York Times* bestselling author Mary Jo Putney

New York Times bestselling author **Elizabeth Lowell** has won countless awards, including the Romance Writers of America Lifetime Achievement Award. She also writes mainstream fiction as Ann Maxwell and mysteries with her husband as A. E. Maxwell. She presently resides with her husband in Washington State.

Outstandingly gifted, *New York Times* bestselling author **Rebecca Brandewyne** is one of the most popular romance authors writing today. She has received countless awards and critical acclaim for her work in contemporary, historical and Gothic fiction. Rebecca's novels have been published in over sixty countries. She is an avid collector of porcelain figures, movie posters and Star Trek® memorabilia. Rebecca currently lives with her family in Wichita, Kansas, where they sometimes chase tornadoes—for fun.

Merline Lovelace spent twenty-three as an air force officer, serving tours at the Pentagon and at bases all over the world before she began a new career as a novelist. When she's not tied to her keyboard, she and her own handsome hero, Al, enjoy traveling, golf and long lively dinners with friends and family. A *USA Today* bestselling author, Merline is known for her mainstream military thrillers and her historical novels for MIRA as well as her category romances. Merline can be reached by e-mail through the Silhouette/Harlequin Web site at http://www.eHarlequin.com or at her own Web site, http://www.merlinelovelace.com.

ELIZABETH LOWELL
REBECCA BRANDEWYNE
and
MERLINE LOVELACE

At the **Edge**

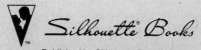

Published by Silhouette Books
America's Publisher of Contemporary Romance

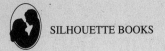 SILHOUETTE BOOKS

AT THE EDGE

Copyright © 2002 by Harlequin Books S.A.

ISBN 0-373-48485-2

The publisher acknowledges the copyright holders of the individual works as follows:

DARK FIRE
Copyright © 1988 by Two Of A Kind, Inc.

WILDCAT
Copyright © 1995 by Rebecca Brandewyne

RETURN TO SENDER
Copyright © 1998 by Merline Lovelace

This edition published by arrangement with Harlequin Books S.A.

® and TM are trademarks of Harlequin Books S.A., used under license. Trademarks indicated with ® are registered in the United States Patent and Trademark Office, the Canadian Trade Marks Office and in other countries.

Visit Silhouette at www.eHarlequin.com

Printed in U.S.A.

CONTENTS

DARK FIRE
Elizabeth Lowell

Prologue

"You want me to do *what*?" Trace Rawlings asked, raising dark eyebrows.

The man called Invers sighed and rubbed his palm over his thinning hair. "You heard me the first time."

"I've been back in Quito for less than an hour," Trace pointed out. "That damned Polish orchid hunter you sicced on me was the genuine article. He was after orchids, period, and he would have taken on hell with a bucket of water to get to them."

Invers tried to look sympathetic. He failed. He needed Trace too badly to be diverted by something as useless as compassion.

Trace swore under his breath and glared at the small passport photo Invers had given to him. A woman's face stared back at him. Cynthia Edwinna Ryan McCall had black hair, midnight eyes, skin as fine as expensive porcelain, a remote expression and a father who could make highly placed American embassy officials sweat bullets.

"Hell," Trace muttered. He looked up, pinning Invers with a jungle-green glance. "After this, we're even."

Invers let out a rushing breath. "We'll be better than even, Trace. I won't forget this, believe me."

Trace grunted.

"She'll land in a few minutes, so we'll have to be quick. The passport is issued in the name of Cynthia Ryan. She won't tell anyone who she really is. Also, she doesn't know that her father has been in contact with us.''

"Does it matter?''

Invers rubbed his palm over his head again, a sign of his unhappiness. Silently he wondered just how much of the story he could tell Trace before the other man would throw up his hands and back out. To anyone who didn't know Big Eddy, the whole story would sound preposterous. To anyone who did know him, the whole story would sound like what it was: preposterous but all too true.

"You ever meet Big Eddy McCall when you were in the States?'' Invers asked cautiously.

"No.''

"Um. Well. Ms. Ryan doesn't get along with her father. Not surprising. Nobody really *gets* along with Big Eddy. You *go* along with him or you go under. Nothing personal, you understand. That's just the way he is. A real steamroller.''

Trace grunted again. "What about her?''

"Ms. Ryan? Oh, she must be at least as stubborn as he is. More stubborn in some ways. Every man her father has picked out for her has been thrown back in his face. He's finally given up on marrying her off.'' Invers paused as though struck by a new thought. "By God, that's quite an accomplishment. I think she might be the first human being ever to say no to Big Eddy and make it stick.''

"So?''

Invers rubbed his head again as he gave Trace a sideways glance. Everything Invers had said so far was technically true. Big Eddy had given up on marriage for his daughter. He had not, however, given up on the idea of grandchildren. He wanted an Edward Ryan McCall IV to be born as soon as possible. One of his sons had produced a grandchild. That wasn't enough. Big Eddy wanted about a dozen other grandkids as backup for life's nasty little surprises. That was where his daughter came in. Big Eddy had finally figured out that a woman didn't have to be married in order to have children.

Invers didn't think Trace was ready to hear about that part of Big Eddy's proposed deal. In fact, Invers doubted if Trace would ever be ready to stand at stud for Big Eddy, much less to find out that it had been Raul's idea in the first place. It was the better—indeed the only—part of valor to tell half-truths to Trace and to let Big Eddy believe what he wanted to believe about the man he had ordered Invers to hire. And never to mention Raul at all.

"Um. Well. Big Eddy's daughter goes by the name of Cindy Ryan and is in business with a woman called Susan Parker. That's where you come in."

Trace arched his eyebrows again. It wasn't like Invers to loop around a subject eight times before getting to the point.

"Ms. Parker comes to Quito several times a year to buy cloth," Invers continued. "This time her native buyer didn't show up, so she hopped a bus over the Andes to go looking for him."

"Did she find him?"

"No. She won't, either," Invers added with uncharacteristic bluntness. "When he wasn't buying cloth he was smuggling emeralds out of Colombia. He stiffed one of his connections and hasn't been heard from since."

Trace shrugged. "It happens."

"Yes. Well. Ms. Parker hasn't been heard from for ten days, either. Not officially, that is."

Green eyes focused on Invers with startling intensity. "And unofficially?"

"Unofficially she is the pampered guest of *Señor* Raul Almeda," Invers said. "*Señor* Almeda would like her to remain for a while longer. That's why his shortwave radios are all on the fritz."

Trace hissed an obscenity that Invers chose not to hear.

"From all indications, Ms. Parker isn't burning down the house trying to leave," Invers said.

The left corner of Trace's mouth kicked up slightly. Raul was a good friend as well as a connoisseur of elegant women. Raul was also very well connected to the government of Ecuador, which was why Invers looked so unhappy at the thought of displeasing him.

"So what's the problem?" Trace asked. "Is Ms. Parker's family worried about her?"

"She has no family, but apparently she's rather close to Ms. Ryan, who is flying to Ecuador to find out what happened to her partner."

"I still don't see the problem. Just tell Big Eddy's daughter that her friend is shacked up with every woman's dream lover."

"I suggested a similar solution to *Señor* Almeda."

"Raul didn't go for it?"

"No. He can be rather, um..."

"Autocratic," Trace said flatly. "He was born too late. He should have been an emperor."

Invers, being a diplomat, chose not to point out that Raul was descended from French, Spanish and Inca royalty, and ruled his immense land holdings like the tyrants his ancestors had been. A benevolent tyrant, granted, but a tyrant nonetheless.

"In any case," Invers said smoothly, "we all want to avoid any suggestion of an, um, incident. We can't have Ms. Ryan running around raising an embarrassing hue and cry for Ms. Parker. If we tell Ms. Ryan that Ms. Parker is quite happy on the Almeda *hacienda*, Ms. Ryan will want to talk to her. Then we'll have to tell her that the radio isn't functioning at the moment and won't be functioning in the near future. I don't think Big Eddy's daughter will find that explanation, um, acceptable."

Eyes closed, Trace went over all that Invers had said. And more importantly, all that he had not said.

"You're quite certain that Raul's latest captive is a happy captive?" Trace asked, focusing on Invers with an intensity that made the other man long to be elsewhere.

"As of five days ago, yes."

"Do you have any indication that Ms. Parker or Ms. Ryan are involved in smuggling of any kind?"

"No, thank God," Invers said fervently.

"Then what is it, precisely, that you want me to do?"

"Allow Ms. Ryan to hire you to 'find' her friend. Take your time getting to the Almeda *hacienda*, and—"

"How long?" Trace interrupted.

"Four or five days. A week at most. *Señor* Almeda isn't known for the duration of his, um, enthusiasms."

Trace smiled slightly but said only, "Stalling shouldn't be a problem. That early storm made a mess of the mountain roads."

"It disrupted communications, too," Invers added without missing a beat. "Be sure to point that out to Ms. Ryan."

"No problem. Hell, it's the simple truth."

"There is no such thing as a simple truth," Invers muttered beneath his breath.

Trace smiled rather grimly. "Anything else?"

"Don't reveal that you know Ms. Ryan is Big Eddy McCall's daughter. And be very, very certain that Ms. Ryan doesn't know you have been hired by her father. Otherwise she'll walk out on you and try to hire another guide. That would make things exceptionally, um, difficult for the embassy."

"Have I been hired by Big Eddy? I thought I was just doing you a favor."

Smiling blandly, Invers offered Trace one-half of a very complex truth. "Big Eddy requested of the embassy that we hire the best man in Ecuador to guide and protect his daughter while she's here. She would, after all, make a tempting kidnap target. You'll be paid one thousand American dollars a day for your, um, efforts."

Trace's green eyes narrowed. "That seems excessive."

"Big Eddy is excessively rich. Think of it as combat pay," Invers added, smiling thinly.

"Are you really expecting someone to grab her?"

"No. But face it, Trace. I'm not sending you on a picnic. Any woman who can stand up to Big Eddy could teach stubborn to a Missouri mule."

"I'm hardly known as a pushover," Trace pointed out.

"Yes. I am well aware of that fact."

Invers smiled and silently wished that he could go along with Trace and Cindy Ryan. It would be worth considerable inconvenience to find out who taught stubborn to whom.

Chapter 1

Good work, Invers. It saves a lot of wear and tear on the hunter when the prey walks right into the trap, Trace thought sardonically as he watched the tall, raven-haired woman weaving through the smoky bar toward him.

At that moment Trace was ready to accept any break Lady Luck was passing out. He had left Invers less than twenty minutes before. No time to shower, shave, change clothes or do anything else in the way of recovery from the past six weeks of trying to keep J. Ivar Polanski, orchid collector extraordinaire, from killing himself or someone else while pursuing living baubles to adorn spoiled rich women such as the one crossing the crowded room right now.

Not that Cindy Ryan needed any decoration, Trace decided as she came a bit closer. The face-only photograph hadn't done her justice. She had the kind of figure that made a man...restless.

"Mr. Rawlings? I'm Cynthia Ryan."

The voice was a husky contralto that made every one of Trace's masculine nerve endings stir. His physical response irritated him. So instead of responding immediately, he sipped at the fine Scotch that the waitress had put in front of him a few moments earlier. Without saying a word he let the smoky, intimate taste of the liquor expand through him like a kiss from the kind of woman he had always wanted and never found. Only after the taste on his tongue had dissipated to a shimmering echo of heat did he look up.

At that moment Cindy found herself hoping she was mistaken and that this man was not Trace Rawlings. It was all she could do not to step backward when his cool green eyes focused on her. The man lounging at the small table with his long legs stretched in front of him wasn't what she had expected to hire. She couldn't believe that this man with his stained khaki bush clothes, scarred boots and a dark, three-day stubble on his heavy jaw, was the guide the American embassy had enthusiastically recommended that she hire. Could this be the bilingual backcountry genius who had no peer in Quito, Ecuador or anywhere else up and down the South American Andes?

"Trace Rawlings?" Cindy repeated, knowing her voice was too husky, too skeptical, and unable to do anything about it. The man was frankly unnerving. He radiated the kind of relaxed, clearly undomesticated presence that people associated with cats stretched out in a patch of sunlight. Big cats. Black jaguars, for instance. Dangerously handsome, dangerously powerful, dangerously sleek, danger-ously...*dangerous.*

"That's me."

Trace's voice was a perfect match for his appearance. The resonances were deep, predatory and compelling. Nerve endings Cindy didn't know she had stirred and shivered in dark response.

"Do you have any identification?" Cindy asked finally, frowning as she looked Trace over once more.

Her opinion hadn't changed since her first glance at him. There was nothing reassuring about Trace Rawlings, and Cindy very much needed reassurance right now. Susan had been missing for ten days, and Susan, whatever her quirks, was not the type to vanish without leaving so much as a note for her friend.

Trace felt his irritation turn into a razor edge of anger at the dubious looks he kept getting from Big Eddy's snooty daughter. Coolly Trace gave Cindy precisely the kind of once-over she had just given him.

"ID?" he asked softly. "Sure thing." He turned and called to the bartender in machine-gun Spanish and instantly was answered in the same way. "Anything else?" Trace asked indifferently, reaching for the Scotch once more.

"I beg your pardon?"

Someday, you'll do just that, princess—and mean it, Trace thought with a surge of purely masculine emotion as he sipped the aromatic golden liquor. *Snotty rich girls who go slumming in the wrong places tend to get men knifed in back alleys.* And beneath that thought was another: *God, if Cindy's partner is half as sexy, no wonder Raul wanted to sabotage the radio, lock all the doors and drop the keys into the nearest sacred well.*

"You wanted ID. Paco vouched for me," Trace said carelessly. "We've known each other for years."

"But I don't understand Spanish."

Trace shrugged. "Tough taco, princess. It's the language of the day around here."

Cindy's black eyes narrowed. When Trace focused his attention once more on his Scotch, she fought a sudden, sharp struggle with her temper. Normally she would have been the first to find humor in the situation confronting her, but nothing was normal for her right now. She was tired, had a screaming headache from Quito's ten thousand feet of altitude and was worried about Susan.

In no way did Cindy feel like catering to the irrational male whims of a lean, dark, down-at-the-heels American who had gone native.

"Well, Tarzan, put this in your taco," Cindy drawled. "Invers at the embassy told me that a man called Trace Rawlings has been known to hire himself out...if the price is right. So I guess I'll just have to start naming figures. When the price is right, Trace Rawlings will stand up and be counted."

Only the fact that Cindy had been raised by a steamroller disguised as a father, and had an older brother whose temper was frankly formidable, gave her the courage not to turn and run when Trace looked up at her. There was a long silence while she returned him stare for glare.

Slowly Trace smiled.

Cindy felt tiny shivers chase up and down her spine. If she had believed she could outrun Trace, she would have sprinted for the door right then. But she knew she couldn't outrun him, so she didn't even try. Trace was acclimatized to Quito's staggering altitude, but lack of oxygen would bring her down before she had taken thirty steps. There was no choice for her now but to dig in right where she was and brazen it out the way she had always done with her father.

Besides, Susan was somewhere out in the wilds alone, and this was the wild man who could find her.

"One hundred dollars a day," Cindy said, her voice too husky, almost breathless.

Trace's cold green eyes looked Cindy over again in a very leisurely manner, admiring all the velvet curves and alluring shadows, noting with a kind of distant surprise that she had made no effort to enhance or even to announce the feminine bounty beneath her clothes. The off-white jumpsuit she wore was loose and wrinkled. The belt around her waist could have been tightened several more notches without cutting into tender flesh. She wore flat sandals rather than heels, which would have emphasized the sway of her shapely hips. Her toenails were bare of polish. So were her fingers. If she wore makeup, it didn't show in the bar's dim light.

Maybe that's why Big Eddy keeps picking out men for her—she's so rich she's never bothered to learn all the little tricks and traps poor girls use to get men interested.

"Two hundred."

Trace flicked another disparaging glance over Cindy and went back to his Scotch. *The most important thing I'll teach her is that there are some things money can't buy—and Trace Rawlings is right at the top of the list.*

"Three hundred."

Angrily Trace wished that he had told Invers to go spit up a rope. But Trace hadn't been that smart. Instead he had promised to keep an eye on Big Eddy's obviously spoiled daughter. In order to do that Trace had to appear to be hired by her...which meant she would think she had bought him.

Combat pay. And I'll earn every nickel of it.

Trace shrugged again. His pride could take it. He had suffered far worse blows and survived. And he owed Invers.

"Four hundred."

Trace stretched, bringing his long arms and large hands high over his head. Cindy measured his size and length and realized with a sudden curious weakness in her knees that she was within his reach.

"Five hundred," she said in a rush.

"Princess, you just hired yourself a guide."

Cindy looked at Trace and wondered how Red Riding Hood would have felt if she had hired the Big Bad Wolf to guide her through the terrors and traps of the forest.

She would have felt the way I do now. Scared!

"All right." Cindy took a deep breath, telling herself she was relieved to have hired a guide, wishing she believed it. "My friend and business partner, Susan Parker, came to Quito to buy native weavings. But she doesn't speak Spanish so she has a native buyer who meets her in Quito and turns over all the cloth from the various native villages on his circuit. You see, we have clothing boutiques on both coasts of the U.S., and Susan is a designer, and we...never mind, that's not important," Cindy said, realizing that she was babbling but unable to stop completely. Trace was too unnerving. She wanted to run but she couldn't, so the next best thing was to finish hiring the jungle cat, find Susan and get the hell away from those disdainful green eyes.

"Susan arrived in Quito ten days ago," Cindy said quickly. "Pedro, the native buyer, didn't show up. She called me and said she was going to check the villages on Pedro's circuit. That was ten days ago. I haven't heard from her since. She hasn't checked out of the hotel, but she hasn't been in her room since she asked directions to the bus. The clerk wrote them for her in phonetic Spanish so she could say them correctly."

Trace reached for the Scotch. "Bus? Phonetic Spanish?"

"She doesn't drive or speak Spanish. She was born in Manhattan."

Trace grunted. "Let me see if I have this straight." He finished off the Scotch and looked at Cindy with heavy-lidded eyes. "Your friend doesn't speak Spanish, doesn't drive and is somewhere out in the boondocks looking for a native known to her only as 'Pedro.'"

Scarlet stained Cindy's cheekbones. Put that way it made Susan sound as though she had the IQ of a toothbrush. That wasn't the case.

"I assure you, Mr. Rawlings, Susan is an accomplished traveler. She speaks neither Arabic nor Chinese, yet she has traveled extensively—and alone—in the Middle East and China."

Trace grunted. "Then why are you worried about her?"

"She always leaves me an itinerary. When that isn't possible she calls every few days. Never less than once a week. It has been ten days since her last call."

"Maybe she found Pedro or some other native and holed up with him for a little slap and tickle." Trace let his glance rove over Cindy's body again. "It happens, you know."

"Not to me," Cindy retorted instantly.

"But you're not the one who's lost, are you?"

"Mr. Rawlings—"

"Yes, Cindy?" he interrupted.

The casual use of her first name didn't escape Cindy. Trace was flatly stating that he was in control of the situation and she was not.

"For five hundred dollars a day I expect a little less insolence, *Trace.*"

"Say it again, princess," he murmured.

"What?" she said scathingly. "Your name?"

"No. Insolence. You put just the right amount of nose into it," Trace added, brushing the nail of his index finger beneath his nose in a mocking gesture. "You learned that at a fancy finishing school, I'll bet. Pity they didn't teach you something useful, like good manners."

Cindy felt another wash of heat over her cheekbones and made a desperate attempt to get a grip on her fraying self-control. She told herself she was feeling emotional because of the altitude, the worry, the lack of sleep…anything but the fact that she hated seeing masculine disdain in Trace's cold green eyes. She closed her own eyes, hoping that the stabbing, screaming pain of her headache would be calmed by darkness.

No such luck.

"Mr. Rawlings, I don't have the time or energy to play word

games with you." Cindy opened her eyes. "My friend is missing. I was told you were the best man to find her. I have met your price. Could we just get on with it?"

"Oh, you've got plenty of time to play games," Trace said, signaling for another drink. Against his better judgment he used his right foot to shove out a chair for Cindy. "Sit down before you fall down."

Trace spoke over Cindy's shoulder to the waitress, who was approaching with his Scotch. Cindy understood just enough of the Spanish to be irritated by what he had ordered for her.

"I'm old enough to drink," she said.

"Dumb enough, too, I'll bet."

"Is that the voice of experience speaking?" she asked, looking pointedly at the Scotch Trace had just picked up.

"You'd better believe it, princess."

The whiplash of Trace's voice snapped Cindy's attention back to his face. Not for the first time she realized that he was not a man whose looks inspired a gentle glow of comfort in a woman. Without glancing away from Cindy's pale, strained expression, Trace raised his voice and called out again in rapid Spanish. Two more rounds of Scotch materialized with dazzling speed, accompanied by a warm bottle of Coke.

"Drink up," Trace said, gesturing to the liquor and simultaneously snagging the bottle of Coke in one big hand, taking it out of her reach.

Cindy looked warily at the Scotch. "Why?"

"Right now your head feels like someone buried a hatchet in it, your stomach has a sour disposition and walking across the room is like going up a flight of stairs. It's called altitude sickness. If you want to make it worse, have a shot or two of liquor. Have it on me. The sooner you drink, the sooner you'll know that I *am* experienced in this territory. You aren't. I may be a peon, but you need me, princess. The quicker you get that straight, the better off you'll be."

Cindy sat down and looked away from the jungle-green eyes staring at her, labeling her, dismissing her. The pain in her head doubled suddenly, making her breath catch. The airline flight attendant had warned the passengers that altitude sickness wasn't uncommon for the first few days in Quito. The best advice was to rest as much as possible, eat lightly, drink juices and take aspirin for the headache. If you didn't feel better after a few days, you were supposed to go to a lower elevation.

And stay there.

Sighing, Cindy put her elbows on the table and massaged her temples. "Sorry to disappoint you, Mr. Rawlings. I like my headache just the way it is. No additives necessary. So drink up. My treat." When the silence had stretched to the point of discomfort, she grimaced. "The first village on Susan's list was Popocaxtil. Do you know it?"

"Yes."

"How long will it take us to get there?" Cindy lifted her head and unflinchingly met Trace's green glance. "Don't try to talk me out of going with you. If Susan is hurt or needs help, I want to be there for her."

"Is she your sister?"

"No."

"Your lover?"

Cindy's jaw dropped. She tried to say something but no words came out.

It was Trace's turn to sigh. There went the obvious explanation for the fact that a woman who looked like Cindy—and was rich into the bargain—was neither married nor, if Invers were to be believed, interested in men at all.

"Women have been known to prefer women," Trace pointed out calmly.

"Having met you I'm beginning to understand why!" Cindy pushed the two shot glasses of Scotch away from her with a sweep of her slender hands. "How far is it to Popocaxtil?" she demanded.

"It depends."

"I'm waiting breathlessly. On what does it depend?"

"The weather," Trace said succinctly.

"When I landed an hour ago, the weather was just fine."

"You were lucky. The rainy season is early this year. The area around Popocaxtil had a hell of a storm four or five days ago. Part of the main blacktop road washed out. As for the last fifteen klicks of the dirt road to the village..." Trace shrugged. "It will be two, probably three days before the road will dry out enough to be passable."

"Klicks?"

"Kilometers."

"Oh. Fifteen kilometers is about seven miles, isn't it?"

"Close enough."

"That's not very far."

Trace's very dark eyebrows were deeply arched to begin with. When he raised one of them in a silent show of skepticism, he appeared almost diabolical.

"That depends," he said.

"On the weather?" Cindy retorted.

"You're learning."

"We'll just have to tough out the weather. I can't sit around here waiting for—"

"Princess, I just got back from six weeks of camping out in the lowlands," Trace interrupted. "If you think I'm going to spend the next two days winching my Rover out of bogs instead of relaxing and soaking up some of the joys of civilization while the mountain roads dry out, you're nuts."

"I can't believe I'm hearing this. Susan might be lost and afraid and hurt and all you can think about is having a Scotch?"

"Don't forget a hot shower," Trace suggested softly.

"Why not? You apparently did, along with a shave and clean clothes!" Cindy made a sharp gesture with her hand. "Never mind. There's no sense in appealing to your better nature. I doubt that you have one. Seven hundred a day and we leave right now."

Trace picked up his second Scotch, held the glass against the table light and admired the liquid's fine color. "No."

The refusal was so soft that it took a moment for it to register on Cindy.

"Eight hundred," she said angrily.

"No."

"Nine!"

"Princess, there are some things money can't buy. I'm one of them. If you need my help, ask. Don't wave money."

"Ask? *Ask!* What do you think I've been doing?"

"Demanding or buying."

"Instead of begging?" Cindy suggested icily. "Haven't you learned yet, Tarzan? All begging gets you is sore knees." She pushed away from the table and stood, ignoring the hammer blows of pain in her head. "Fortunately I won't have to wear my knees out on your masculine ego. I don't need you. I'll check out the villages myself."

"How? You don't speak Spanish, much less any of the local Indian dialects."

"Neither does Susan."

"Look where it got her."

"I'm planning on it!"

Trace laughed derisively. "Sure you are." He glanced at Cindy's pallor, at her lips drawn flat with pain and at the fine trembling of her hands. "Go back to your room and lie down, princess. I'll pick you up Thursday morning at your hotel at dawn."

Cindy spun on her heel and walked out, neither looking back at Trace nor aside at any of the interested patrons watching the tall *gringa* stalking away from the bar. She was furious with herself for handling Trace so badly and furious with him for being such an unbending, overweening s.o.b., and furious with life for putting her in a situation where her father's money—which she would never have touched for any reason less urgent than Susan's disappearance—couldn't even buy a decent guide.

Smiling coolly, Trace watched Cindy leave. He had been rough on her and he knew it, but it had been a cut-and-dried case of self-defense. He had been caught flat-footed by her, his dropped jaw flapping in the wind. Nothing in Invers's briefing or in the picture Trace had been given of Cindy had even hinted at the real woman. Quick, intelligent, vital, with black eyes whose clarity and enigmatic depths challenged a man. And she had something more, something Trace had dreamed about but never found.

Beneath that cool exterior Cindy McCall burned with the kind of passionate, dark fire that a man would kill for. Or die for.

Trace had felt an answering fire licking through his body. It was still there, burning, urging. He ignored it now as he had ignored it in Cindy's presence, knowing that to give in was to hand himself over to his sensuous combatant without a murmur of protest. He wouldn't allow that to happen.

The smile on Trace's lips curled higher as he realized that he was probably the first man ever to say no to Ms. Cynthia Edwinna Ryan McCall. It must have been a salutary learning experience for her. At the very least, in the future she wouldn't look down her nose at Trace Rawlings with such fine disdain. She needed him. It would be a pure pleasure to hear her admit it.

Smiling, Trace sipped at his Scotch.

He was still smiling Thursday morning when he drove over to pick up Cindy, only to discover that she had rented a Jeep and set off down the highway for Popocaxtil on Tuesday.

Chapter 2

Cindy stared at the smudged, rumpled map again. If she were right, she was definitely on the road to Popocaxtil. If she were wrong, she was one lost puppy.

She looked dubiously through the cracked windshield at the so-called road, which was a raw gash that wound up and down and sideways across the shoulder of a mountain whose top and bottom were hidden in clouds. The dense forest of the uplands had given way to an equally dense cover of brushy plants. The road had remained the same...awful. She hadn't seen a road sign since yesterday.

The one nice thing was that Cindy's headache had finally gone. She didn't know whether she had become accustomed to the thin air or the road had really dropped more in altitude than it had subsequently gained clawing its way back up the mountain. All she knew for certain was that her headache had departed, and for that blessing she was profoundly grateful.

Again Cindy looked from the map to the road. Hers were the only vehicle tracks to mark the rutted, overgrown track since the last rain.

"I'm not lost," she said aloud, wishing it didn't sound so much like a question.

"You're not lost," she answered herself firmly.

She heard the conversation with herself and muttered, "I'm going crazy."

"No, you're not," she retorted immediately. "You just like to hear English spoken after days of incomprehensible Spanish."

"Really? That makes me feel better. Know something? I like you."

"It's mutual."

"Maybe I *am* going crazy."

"No, you're just stalling. You don't want to go back to wrestling with the Jeep."

"You're right."

The paved road Cindy had started out on had been no treat once Quito's environs had been left behind, but compared to the secondary and tertiary roads she had encountered since then, the paved road had been a miracle of modern engineering. Her whole body ached from fighting the Jeep over the rain-greased road.

Sighing, Cindy leaned forward and turned the ignition key. The engine started immediately, a fact that continued to surprise her each time it occurred. To be diplomatic, the Jeep had an aura of experience about it. To be factual, the Jeep looked as though it had been through the wars, all of them, beginning with the Crimean and progressing right on through Vietnam.

Despite that, the vehicle seemed quite hardy, if Cindy discounted the tires' distressing tendency to flatten at inconvenient moments. Not that any moment would have been truly convenient. The first flat had occurred yesterday, after only a few hours on a detour to bypass a washout on the main paved road. She had barely begun to wrestle with the jack when a boy who looked too young to be out in the world on his own had walked by, seen her distress and stopped to help her.

The language barrier proved to be irrelevant. A flat tire by any other name was still not round. The boy had simply handed his baggage into Cindy's keeping and had proceeded to whisk off the tire, put on the spare and watch with fatalistic good humor as the tire promptly sank onto its own rim. The spare had been as flat as the other one.

The boy had pried both tires off their rims, patched the inner tubes and pumped them up, using tools from the battered box that was bolted in the cargo area of the Jeep. Then he had put all the pieces together again, giving Cindy two good tires. During the entire process she had stood in the cool drizzle and held the boy's precious baggage—a burlap sack containing two monumentally unhappy piglets—and watched what he was doing very carefully. The patching procedure was simple. Find the leak, clean the area to be patched, apply sticky stuff to the patch and the patch to the tire, hang on tight to everything and count to fifty-eight thousand while two piglets achieved operatic heights of despair within the burlap bag.

Even the memory of it made Cindy laugh aloud. She wished she had a picture of herself holding a sack with two bouncing pigs in one hand and an umbrella in the other hand, while rain ran in rivulets from her chin and elbows as she leaned over and braced herself against the Jeep in an effort to keep the boy dry during a sudden shower. But if she had had that picture she would have traded it for the one she really wanted, that of a busload of natives standing in the muck up to their ankles as they argued and gesticulated robustly about the best way to free her Jeep from an entanglement consisting of uninjured but outraged livestock, a pile of kindling that could have filled a church and enough mud to build the Great Wall of China.

Still grinning at the memories, Cindy eased the Jeep from the verge back into the road. And it was *into* rather than *onto* the road. The ruts were twin and sometimes triplicate trenches filled with water. The water looked either brown or gunmetal gray, depending on the angle of the sun through the dispersing clouds.

No matter how hard Cindy tried, it was impossible to keep the Jeep's tires entirely free of the ruts. At least there was a bottom to the ruts, she consoled herself. She wasn't at all certain she could say the same about the puddles of water that lurked in low places along the sides of the road. When there was a side to the road, that is. Sometimes there was nothing but a long, long drop into a valley.

Water was everywhere, trickling from each crease and crevice on the steep mountainside. Early that morning the trickles had been creeks and streams, but the runoff had slowed dramatically as the rains diminished in the highlands. The thought cheered Cindy as much as the sunshine streaming between banks of clouds. Soon it would be actually warm instead of nearly warm. Soon the Jeep's canvas roof would stop drooling water down her left shoulder. Soon she would turn a corner and see a tattered Popocaxtil sunk happily into the mire. There she would be able to find food and water and, best of all, word of Susan Parker.

If this were, indeed, the road to Popocaxtil.

It took every bit of Cindy's concentration to enable her to pick her way over nature's obstacle course at a rate slightly faster than that of a three-legged burro. With every yard she progressed she silently thanked her brother Rye for having forced her to learn unwanted skills. Years ago he had insisted that she learn to drive his rugged ranch road in the Jeep he kept for winter transportation. She would never again tease him about his rustic taste in road surfaces. After her experience in Ecuador she would be able to drive Rye's ranch roads at eighty miles per hour blindfolded.

The Jeep's front tires were grabbed by ruts at the same instant that the wheel was wrenched from Cindy's hand. She downshifted for more power, grinding the gears heartlessly. Rye had neglected to show her the finer points of speed shifting or double clutching, a fact that she regretted now. At the time, however, she had thought it outrageous enough that he had insisted she learn to drive primitive roads in a vehicle that lacked an automatic shift. And then she had had to learn to change a tire in the bargain. She had given Rye a steady line of smart remarks while he tutored her, but the next time she saw him she would gratefully go down on her knees in the ranch yard and kiss his dusty boots in thanks for his foresight.

Crunching and groaning, the Jeep clawed out of the deep ruts. Even on flatter ground, the vehicle wanted to lunge to the right. Cindy found a relatively firm spot, stopped and climbed out to see what was wrong. With a sinking heart she realized that the right front tire was a mere shadow of its former rotund self.

"Damn!"

Swearing at the tire wouldn't get it changed. Nor was Cindy's vocabulary extensive enough to make her feel better. Muttering, she went to the back of the Jeep, unbolted the jack, shoved it under the chassis and started leaning on the jack's lever.

What had taken the boy mere minutes to accomplish took her nearly half an hour. Finally the flat tire rose far enough above the mire for her to be able to reach all the lug nuts holding the wheel in place. She grabbed the lug wrench and leaned. It popped off, nearly sending her face-first into the mud. She put the wrench back over the lug nut and leaned again.

Nothing happened.

Cindy leaned harder and then harder still. She had never considered herself an Amazon, but she couldn't believe that she was too weak to remove a simple lug nut. After all, the boy who had helped her yesterday had been her height and he hadn't had much trouble changing a tire. Finally she jammed the lug wrench in place, held onto the Jeep, and jumped onto one arm of the cross-shaped tool, using the weight of her whole body to force the nut to turn.

Five jumps later she managed to loosen the first lug nut. The rest of them weren't as easy. By the time Cindy had dragged the wheel off, rolled it to the back of the Jeep, swapped it for the spare and gotten the spare screwed into its new home to the best of her ability, she was dirty, thirsty, hungry and exhausted. After she put away the tools she sluiced off the worst of her dirt in a rain puddle. The cool, murky water tempted her almost unendurably.

"Don't be an idiot," Cindy told herself as she licked dry lips and wiped her hands on her dirty jeans. "All you need to really make your day is the local version of Montezuma's revenge."

Wearily Cindy pulled herself into the Jeep's rump-sprung seat, started the engine and crept forward, praying that no other tire would flatten. She wasn't going to take time to patch the ruined inner tube right now. In truth, she was afraid that she wouldn't be able to pry the tire off the wheel rim, much less put it back together again.

The next hour was uneventful. Then Cindy came to a steep curve where the road had a pronounced outward slant toward the valley, which was a breathtaking two thousand sheer feet below on the right. Suddenly all four wheels began to spin as the Jeep lost traction in the greasy mud and began to slide sideways inch by inch toward the drop-off. She clung to the wheel and fed gas gently, wondering if forward momentum would get her past the slippery spot before gravity pulled the Jeep into the abyss. Just as she reached for the door handle to jump out, one front wheel finally found good traction and pulled her up and around the dangerous curve.

Over the shoulder of the mountain a long, narrow valley opened up. The surrounding forest had been cut or burned fairly recently, giving the valley floor a ragged, mottled look. Only very small trees and modest bushes grew along the road. There wasn't a drop-off or a curve in sight. After what Cindy had been through, the road looked beautiful.

"Hang on, Susan, wherever you are. I'm coming. Not fast, but I'm coming."

Feeling much more cheerful, Cindy drove down the gentle incline into the valley...and sank right up to her bumpers in mud.

"Gracias," called the man to Trace.

As Trace waved in acknowledgement, the man gunned his rattle-trap truck, lifted a rooster tail of dirt into the air and shot around a muddy spot where the main road had washed out. Trace wound the forward winch cable he had used to free the man's truck and climbed back into the big, battered Land Rover. He had covered the distance from Quito to this point in record time, despite the washouts, and every inch of the way he had wondered if he were on a wild-goose chase.

Even after Trace had seen a place on a washout detour where a vehicle had pulled over to change a flat, he hadn't been convinced that the small footprints in the mud had belonged to Cindy. A woman, yes. The disdainful princess? Maybe, but not very damned likely.

Trace hadn't really believed that Cindy had set off alone for Popocaxtil until he had turned off the main road onto the dirt road. At a tiny village where he had stopped for food and water, he had heard the epic of a bus, a Jeep, a mountain of kindling, assorted livestock— and *una Americana muy hermosa* who had black hair, a warm smile and no Spanish to speak of.

Trace hadn't seen Cindy smile, but he doubted that there was more than one beautiful American woman who was traveling the backcountry alone in a Jeep, asking in fractured Spanish along the way for a village called Popocaxtil.

Certainly someone had recently been along the dirt track he was driving. That someone was getting a cram course in four-wheel skills, if the abundance of wallow and skid marks were any indication. At first the Jeep had hit all the bad spots in the road as though it were guided by a perverse sort of radar. As the kilometers went by, Cindy—presuming it was, indeed, Cindy who was steering the Jeep— had learned how to keep the vehicle from getting high-centered between the ruts. She had also learned that the rut-puddle you know is a lot safer than the puddle at the side of the road. Presumably she had also learned to feed gas evenly and firmly in the boggy spots to prevent digging in or fishtailing all over the place.

Now, if only it would rain.

With the cynical eyes of a man who has found answers to questions most people would rather not even ask, Trace measured the clouds. If it didn't rain before sunset he would be surprised. If it did rain, it wouldn't amount to much.

Too bad. A good rain would wash her right out of the game and into my arms.

The phrasing of his own thought made Trace's mouth flatten into a hard line. He had spent two very restless nights thinking about Cindy Ryan's cool intelligence and taut, warm curves. The combination fascinated him even as it challenged him. It also irritated him unreasonably. He was old enough to know his own mind and body very well, but the depth of his response to the lush Ms. Ryan was something new.

And the jungle had taught Trace that new was a synonym for dangerous.

Frowning, he drove on. A few minutes later the road divided. There were no signs to mark towns or directions. The main dirt road went to the left. The fresh tracks he was following went to the right. In the distance, the road began snaking up the steep side of a mountain.

"She must have been born under a lucky star," he muttered, wondering how Cindy had known to take the right-hand fork to Popocaxtil. Nothing about the road announced it as a likely candidate for anything but a dead-end logging track.

Ahead, lightning danced among the lowering clouds. Suddenly Trace wasn't so sanguine about rain washing Cindy into his arms. If she didn't know enough to pull over, park and wait out the storm, a good rain might wash her right off the mountain. The people who had made this road had neither known nor cared about grading the surface so that an out-of-control vehicle would slide into the mountainside rather than into the abyss. The road had been graded—if it had been graded at all—with rapid drainage in mind. Every slant led downhill. The farther up the road, the longer the downhill drop to the valley below.

As the afternoon wore on, Trace drove the Rover with near-reckless speed. The track became worse with every foot it climbed up the uninhabited mountainside. He paused only a few seconds at the spot where the Jeep had had its second flat. A single glance told him that there was only one set of footprints this time. Any tire changing that had been done had been done by the princess herself. One corner of his mouth curved up at the thought of how muddy she must have been by the time she had finished.

Then Trace wondered which one of Cindy's men had taught her to change a tire, and what else he had taught her to sweeten the lesson.

Trace pushed the thought away and concentrated on the road, which had dwindled until it required every bit of his skill and coordination, not to mention occasional applications of pure strength, just to keep the Rover pointed in the right direction. When the road pitched up suddenly, and simultaneously wrapped out and around a tight curve, he saw the broad marks left by Cindy's Jeep as it had slid sideways closer and closer to the lethal drop-off on the right side of the miserable road.

"Christ," Trace hissed between his teeth as he saw how close Cindy had come to disaster. "It's time someone put a leash on that high-nosed little…"

Trace's voice died as the Rover breasted the small ridge and he saw the burned-over valley spreading out below. A few hundred yards away, in the center of a deceptively smooth-looking stretch of road, a Jeep was buried up to its fenders in mud.

Smiling rather grimly, Trace let in the clutch and started toward the prey he had finally run to ground.

Chapter 3

Cindy didn't even notice the Rover cautiously working its way toward her. At that particular moment she wouldn't have noticed anything less impressive than a magnitude eight earthquake. She was bent over, panting and red faced, hopping around on one foot in the muck while she tried to force the broken-handled shovel into the muddy mess with her other foot. The point of the whole exercise was to ladle enough of the goo from the vicinity of the front tires so they could find the traction necessary to pull the Jeep out of the bog.

There was more gluey mud lying in wait than Cindy had the muscle or tools to remove. After more than an hour of shoveling she doubted that she was going to get the job done by herself. Unfortunately, there wasn't much hope of help. The surface of the road hadn't seen a wheeled vehicle since the last hard rain. If there were any native pedestrians about, they hadn't passed her way lately. Not so much as a footprint marred the deceitfully smooth surface of the bog ahead of the Jeep.

With a muttered word of disgust, Cindy watched the hole she had just made with the shovel slowly fill up with goo. She propped the slippery, much-too-short handle of the shovel against the Jeep and decided there was no help for it, she would have to go for more shrubbery. Wiping her hands on equally muddy jeans, she released the cable on the winch that was attached to the Jeep's front bumper.

Rye hadn't spent much time showing her how to work his Jeep's winch, but she had remembered enough to get the thing unlocked and started about an hour ago. Trial and error had refreshed her memory after that.

The first time Cindy had wrapped the cable around the skeletal trunk of a burned tree, she had confidently expected to winch the Jeep out of the mud. She had figured it would take a lot of power, so she had given the winch everything available. For a few moments the cable had whined taut and the Jeep had indeed crept forward. Then the tree had exploded into charcoal and the cable had snapped back toward the Jeep with enough force to make the air whistle.

After that Cindy had gone back to shoveling until her hands had stopped shaking. Then she had attempted to use the winch again. All that had been within reach of the cable had been tree skeletons even more frail than the first one she had tried to use. In the end she had settled for the vigorous green bushes and saplings that had grown up since the fire. The first bush she used the winch on instantly leaped out of the mud and bounded toward her. The second and third bushes did the same. None of the shrubbery had held long enough to move the Jeep forward so much as an inch.

The bushes had other uses, however. Cindy had discovered rather quickly that their branches could be beaten into smaller pieces with the shovel and then pushed under the Jeep's wheels to make a sort of rough mat that gave more traction than straight goo did. That was how she had managed to move forward a whole fourteen feet. At the present pace she would be out of the bog by nightfall…of next week.

Putting that unhappy thought from her mind, Cindy slogged over to the nearest shrub with the broken shovel in one hand and the cable hook in the other. Kneeling, using the shovel, she pushed the end of the cable around the base of the bush until she could grab the hook with her free hand, put it over the cable and stand up. As she turned to go back to the Jeep, she spotted movement on the road.

At first Cindy thought that the vehicle slipping and slithering half on and half off the road was a mirage coming toward her. When it came to a halt fifteen feet away—just before the point where her Jeep's wheels had sunk in to the fenders—she recognized Trace.

He was smiling.

Normally Cindy would have been the first one to laugh over the picture she must have made with mud up to her eyebrows and greenery sticking to unlikely parts of her anatomy. Unfortunately her reaction to Trace hadn't been normal from the first word they had exchanged. Suddenly Cindy was furious with Trace, with the Jeep, with the muddy road, with the world in general and Ecuador in particular; but most of all she was furious with herself for caring that she looked muddy and foolish in front of Mr. Trace Insufferable Rawlings.

When the Rover's door opened, Cindy turned her back on Trace and put the winch into motion with a vicious jerk. The bush fairly jumped out of the soil and raced toward her. She stopped the winch, lifted the shovel and began beating on the shrub until it had flattened out enough for her to release the hooked end of the cable without having to stand on her head in the muck to do so.

"Aren't you a little old for mud pies?"

The deep, amused male voice did nothing to cool Cindy's temper. She turned and slowly looked at Trace from the ground up. His lace-up jungle boots were scarred and clean where they rose above the mud. His khaki pants were clean, dry and tucked into the tops of his boots. Though loose fitting, the pants managed to convey very strongly the masculine power just beneath the cloth. His belt was wide, worn and fastened around a lean waist. An astonishingly big knife—more of a sword, really—was sheathed at his waist. His shirt was khaki, clean, dry, long sleeved, with cuffs rolled up just far enough to reveal tanned skin and a sheen of black hair stretched over sinewy arms. His hands were strong, long fingered and very clean. The black hair on his forearms was thickly repeated in a rich cloud that curled up from the open neck of his shirt. He had shaved since their last meeting. Somehow the clean, heavy line of his jaw was more intimidating than the careless masculine stubble had been.

Cindy looked no higher than the sensual lips curving beneath the black swath of Trace's mustache. The triumph and amusement in his smile made her own lips flatten. She told herself that she was a big girl, that she could take whatever teasing Trace dished out without losing her temper and making the situation worse by saying something.

And then she discovered that she was wrong. With a sense of mingled horror and pleasure she heard herself say, "I'm too old for a lot of things, Tarzan."

Cindy's black glance sweeping back down Trace's body hinted that he was foremost among those objects she had outgrown. Without another word she turned her back on him and resumed flattening the uprooted bush and stuffing it beneath the leading edge of her left front tire.

"You know, an intelligent girl like you should have figured out by now not to bite the hand that is going to feed her. But since you haven't, I'll be glad to deliver a little remedial instruction."

"You're too kind," she muttered, chopping viciously at the bush.

"I know. I also know if you'd been reasonable a few days ago instead of being a high-nosed princess who didn't know any more about men than to throw money at them, you could have spent the past two days doing your nails and have ended up no farther from Popocaxtil than you are now."

Cindy went very still. Slowly she released the shovel because she didn't trust herself not to take a swing at Trace with it. Part of her was appalled that she had even thought of it. Another part of her was appalled that she hadn't followed through. Three days ago she would have sworn that she knew herself through and through. Trace, unfortunately, brought out depths in her temperament that had remained blessedly hidden until she met him.

She knelt and began cramming brush around the tire by hand. Trace offered advice on the best type of greenery to use until she lost patience.

"Are you going to help get the Jeep out or are you just going to stand around and make noise?" Cindy asked without looking up.

"I'm waiting for a request. A nice one."

For an instant the world went an odd shade of reddish black in front of Cindy. Too many memories. Too many useless requests.

"Would you please," she said in a husky voice, *"go to hell?"*

Trace's green eyes narrowed as though he had been slapped. For a minute the only sound was that of soggy brush being rammed into the mud. Then came the distinct sucking sounds of Trace's boots as he walked back to his Rover. Cindy didn't look up. She simply continued blindly stuffing twigs and leaves and stems into the mud, furiously refusing to give in to tears or to memories, telling herself that she had come this far without Trace, she could go the rest of the distance alone, too.

The door to the Rover opened quietly and closed with emphasis. Trace sat back on the comfortable bench seat of the Rover and stretched his legs onto the passenger side of the floorboards. Confident of the outcome, he waited for Cindy to get tired of chewing on her pride, swallow hard, and ask him for the help she so clearly needed. Her learning when to ask for help—and how to ask for it— would make the rest of the trip a lot easier on both of them.

Trace had no intention of fighting Cindy every inch of the way while they 'searched' for her crazy friend. Not only would continual fighting be stupid, it could be dangerous. There were times and places in the wilds where questioning instructions was a fast way to get into deep trouble. If he said jump, she would have to learn to jump. If she needed help, she would damn well ask for it. That was the only way to ensure that she didn't put both of them in danger with her foolish stubbornness.

Combat pay. Well, you sure called it, Invers, you s.o.b.

A curse hissed between Trace's teeth. All fights between Cindy and himself would be won and lost right here, right now. She had chosen the battleground, the weapons, and the stakes—her pride. The only thing that remained for Trace to do was to accept her surrender so that they could get on with the farce of combing the wild country to find a woman who wasn't lost.

From Trace's vantage point in the Rover he could see the churned mess behind the Jeep. Twigs and slender branches with bruised and shredded leaves stuck up every which way on the sides of the deep ruts the Jeep had left. Idly, then with growing understanding, Trace's eyes followed the various trails Cindy had left through the mud as she had attached cables to bushes and dragged them to the Jeep.

The shattered remains of a charred tree raised Trace's dark eyebrows. *I hope that little fool didn't have the winch at high revs when that trunk came apart.*

Yet an uneasy prickling along Trace's spine every time he looked at the ruined tree told him that was precisely what had happened. Rather grimly he wondered if the crack in the Jeep's windshield was old history or if the glass had given way from a recent hit delivered by a dangerous, whipsawing steel cable.

The longer Trace looked at the area immediately around the Jeep, the clearer it became to him that Cindy had been mired in place for a long time. Incredibly enough, and despite her demonstrable lack of expertise in such situations, she had managed to get the Jeep to move forward a few feet. Grudgingly Trace gave her credit for not sitting with her clean hands folded in her lap, waiting for a knight in muddy armor to rescue her.

Stubborn and resourceful, but that won't get the Jeep out of the muck. Even if it would, there's no way that soft rich girl is going to have enough strength to make mud pies much longer. Hell, it's a miracle she hasn't given up by now. She's got to be exhausted.

Fifteen minutes, Trace reassured himself silently, watching Cindy kneeling in the mud next to the front end of the Jeep. *Half an hour, max. Then she'll wise up and give up and do what she should have done in the first place—ask me for help.*

Trace was correct in his assessment of Cindy's reserves of strength. The past few days had exhausted her. Doing without food or drink so far today had been the final touch. She was running on adrenaline alone, supported by the rushing chemical wave of fury that came each time she looked up through the black, tangled curtain of her hair and saw Trace all dry and clean and comfortable, lounging in his Rover while he watched her crawl around in the muck.

Cindy winched another bush out and began beating on it with her shovel. When it came time to remove the cable from the mangled bush, her fingers were uncooperative. They insisted on trembling and tangling and slipping when they should have held firm. It was a good five minutes before she was able to retrieve and rewind the cable. Finally she picked up the shovel again and used its edge to smash and gnaw the bush into smaller pieces. One by one she shoved those pieces in the mud around the front tires.

Past experience had taught Cindy that she would need at least one more bush rammed into the muck before there would be enough traction for the Jeep. The prospect cheered Cindy considerably. Maybe this time she would get completely free of the bog and get on with looking for Susan. Even though the rational part of Cindy's mind kept insisting that Susan was an experienced traveler who had a positively feline ability to land on her feet no matter what the circumstances, the irrational part of Cindy's mind kept whispering about all the disasters that could befall a woman traveling alone in a foreign country.

For instance, Susan could have hired a guide like Trace Rawlings.

The surge of adrenaline that followed upon the heels of seeing Trace still ensconced within the dry, clean comfort of the Rover served to push Cindy through the mud, cable in one hand and shovel in the other. She was running out of conveniently placed bushes. On her hands and knees, and finally on her stomach, she maneuvered the cable until steel encircled the base of a bush. Slowly she slogged back to the Jeep, fired up the winch and reeled in the bush.

The bruised leaves of this particular bush smelled like the worst kind of swamp. Even more depressing, the five-foot-long branches were unusually springy, which meant that breaking each stick took twice the whacks with the shovel that an ordinary shrub would have. Finally, however, Cindy had the bush beaten and chopped into use-able portions. Wearily she set aside the shovel, picked up a clump of vile-smelling greenery and began cramming it into the muck in front of one tire.

Trace looked at his watch for the thirtieth time in as many minutes. A half hour gone and Cindy didn't look much worse off than she had before. Obviously she was tired. Just as obviously, she wasn't going to give in. His lips flattened into a hard line beneath his dark brown mustache as he remembered what Invers had said: *Any woman who could stand up to Big Eddy could teach stubborn to a Missouri mule.*

Teeth clenched as tightly as her hands, Cindy trudged back toward the side of the road, dragging the winch cable in one hand and the shovel in the other. All that kept her from going down on her face in the mud and staying there when she hooked the cable around a bush was a bone-deep determination not to knuckle under to a man again, because once she did, she would lose more and more and more of herself until there was nothing left and she was just a shell standing and watching Jason walk away from her, taking her innocence, hopes and belief in herself with him.

But I learned from that, Cindy told herself firmly. *After Jason left I told Big Eddy to go directly to hell and to take his dreams of a dynasty with him. Then I changed my name, closed all the McCall expense accounts, and left home.*

Since then Cindy had not taken one dime from her father. She would speak to him as long as the subject of men, marriage or babies did not arise. If she didn't like what she heard—and she usually didn't—she would turn around and walk away. The kind of pride, intelligence and courage it had taken for Cindy to walk out on uncounted millions and make a life for herself was often labeled "character" when it occurred in men. When it cropped up in women, the labels applied were a good deal less flattering.

They were nothing, however, to the names Cindy called Trace as she fumbled around pushing more brush into the mud.

Trace looked from his watch to the muddy woman and mangled bush. His green eyes narrowed in a combination of irritation and grudging approval as the time registered.

Forty-seven minutes.

Absently Trace knuckled the hinge points of his jaw, trying to loosen muscles clenched in outright rebellion against sitting and doing nothing while a woman worked herself into the ground right in front of his disbelieving eyes.

She has to learn that I'm valuable to her or we're going to end up in big trouble in the cloud forest.

Somehow the lesson seemed less important to Trace at the moment than it had before.

Yet cold reason told him that the lesson was more important than ever. Cindy simply must give him a measure of control over their

lives in the cloud forest. She had proven herself to be far too determined an individual for Trace to even consider fighting with her over
every little aspect of the expedition.

If she would drive herself to exhaustion rather than admit that she
needed his greater strength, to say nothing of his expertise, what
would she do when an important issue arose, such as running for
cover from a storm rather than continuing to drive on a road that
would go from difficult to dangerous with the first good rain? What
if he told her not to question some natives about Susan—and there
were some natives in the backcountry who definitely should *not* be
questioned—and she went ahead and asked questions anyway, endangering everyone with her stubborn certainty that she could do
everything herself, and do it better?

Trace kept repeating that line of reasoning as he watched Cindy
through hooded eyes, silently willing her to give in at least long
enough to rest for a time.

She didn't. She simply kept after the task of freeing the Jeep with
a tenacity he could only admire. Yet the more he watched, the less
he could bear it. She was overmatched. He knew it even if she didn't.
He found it too painful to see her working her heart out when he
knew that eventually she would fail.

But Trace forced himself to watch the uneven contest between
woman and bog. If Cindy could drive herself beyond all reason, the
least he could do was to witness the brutal cost of her learning this
particular lesson.

For both of them.

It would have been difficult to say whether Cindy or Trace was
more relieved when she finally fumbled the last bit of brush into the
mud and climbed into the Jeep.

At first it was enough for Cindy just to sit behind the wheel. Not
to be bent over in the mud was sheer heaven. Besides, in the Jeep
she was beyond the reach of the puddles. Their winking, reflective
surfaces had been tormenting her with visions of drinking and drinking cool water until she was satiated.

"Not to mentioned drinking at the same time hundreds of miscel-
laneous and unpronounceable microscopic beasties that would make

you so sick you'd be afraid you *wouldn't* die,'' Cindy reminded herself wearily. "No water for you until you're out of the bog and have time to boil up a quart or three."

Sighing, Cindy wiped her muddy hands on her muddy slacks and reached for the ignition key. Her hand trembled visibly. She closed her eyes and willed herself to be strong for just a bit longer. The Jeep would get free this time. It had to. She was too tired, too hungry and much too thirsty to do it all over again.

As always, the Jeep's engine fired up the first time. Cindy wiped her palms on opposite shoulder blades—the cleanest patches on her shirt—and gripped the wheel. Carefully she let in the clutch and fed gas. The front wheels slipped, spun, skipped, and finally bit into the mess of mud and shrubs. The Jeep lurched forward a few inches, slewed off to the right, found traction again, leaped and then swerved off to the left side of the road. The vehicle measured its own length in untouched muddy road, bucked, wallowed, whined...

And settled up to its fenders once more in the bog.

The sight of Cindy slumped over the steering wheel was too painful for Trace. After a single glance he looked away. Her posture stated her defeat more clearly than any words could have. He had won, she had lost...and the taste of victory was muddy on his tongue. He reached for the Rover's door, wanting to save Cindy the walk over to his vehicle to ask for help.

The Jeep's door popped open at the same instant as the Rover's. Cindy got out, sank calf-deep, and slogged to the front of the Jeep. It took her a long time to unlock the winch and drag the cable toward a big, particularly lush bush on the edge of the road. Though the bush was on the same side of the road as the Rover, Cindy didn't even glance toward Trace.

He closed his eyes, then opened them again. Nothing had changed. Cindy hadn't admitted defeat.

What is it with you, princess? Why is it impossible for you to give me a fraction of an inch? Would you ask me for help if my bank account was as big as yours?

Since the bitter questions never left Trace's mind, no answers came.

Cindy staggered, slipped and went down on her hands and knees. She stayed that way for a few moments, head down, beaten but unbowed. Slowly she pushed herself to her feet. Trace swore steadily, savagely, but he knew defeat when he stared it in the face. He could not force himself to sit and watch Cindy work until she fainted from exhaustion.

And that was what it would come to.

Nor would the bitter lesson have accomplished anything useful. Quite obviously the princess would drop dead in her muddy tracks before she lowered herself to ask for anything from a peon like Trace Rawlings.

So let her drop.

Trace didn't bother to answer his silent inner snarl. The sentiment was only the last defiant cry of the vanquished, and he knew it. There were some people he could have watched dispassionately while they drove themselves beyond exhaustion, but Cindy wasn't one of them. Bitterly cursing his weakness every step of the way, Trace closed the distance between himself and Cindy, who was almost up to the robust bush she had chosen to sacrifice beneath the Jeep's front wheels.

Just as Trace caught up to Cindy, she screamed chillingly and lashed out with the broken shovel at a snake that had been concealed within the bush.

Chapter 4

An instant later Trace slashed through the snake with his machete. Even as the big knife flashed past her, Cindy spun away from the bush in an effort to flee that was as reflexive as the trapped snake's strike at her had been. But Cindy went no more than a step before she discovered that her body was trembling too much for her to do more than sway on her feet. Trace held her upright with his left hand while he finished off the snake with the machete in his right hand. Only when he was quite certain that the reptile was dead did he sheathe the lethal blade, grab Cindy and carry her back to the Rover.

"Didn't anyone ever tell you that snakes don't make special allowances for stubborn princesses?" Trace demanded, his voice loud and rough with the adrenaline that was still pouring through his blood. Cindy had come within inches of dying, and while she was probably too naive to know it, he wasn't. "It's a damn good thing you got lucky with the shovel or that big 'two-step' would have nailed you on the first strike and you would have gone two steps and died. Do you understand me, princess? You would be d-e-a-d, *dead*. Where do you think you are—Disneyland? Didn't you even think to look for poisonous snakes?"

Cindy bit her lower lip and struggled to control the shudders racking her body in the wild aftermath of fear. "Rye always t-told me if

I made p-plenty of noise, s-snakes would leave before I ever saw them.''

''That doesn't mean you can close your eyes and braille your way through an Ecuadoran cloud forest,'' Trace snarled, wondering who the hell this Rye was. ''Use your head! It's too cool, wet, and overcast for reptiles to be particularly lively right now, so the two-step felt trapped by you and it lashed out to protect itself. Thank God the snake was too sluggish to be any more than half-speed on the strike. You were lucky. Very, very damn lucky.'' Trace's arms tightened around the muddy, womanly weight in his arms. ''But don't push it, princess. God has better things to do than to watch out for stubborn princesses.''

''G-go to—''

''Hell,'' Trace interrupted impatiently, finishing Cindy's sentence for her. ''You keep recommending the place to me. Perhaps you would like to join me there?''

He yanked open the passenger door of the Rover and slid in, still holding on to Cindy. When she struggled as though to get off his lap, Trace's arms tightened.

''Not a chance, princess. I came so close to putting you at the very top of my private list of midnight regrets that I'm not letting go of you for awhile. God, I can hardly believe you're alive,'' he said in a raw, husky voice as he smoothed his cheek over the tangled silk of Cindy's hair. ''That was too close. Much too close.'' He felt the sudden shudders of her body and shifted her until he could cradle her in his arms. In a much more gentle voice he murmured, ''It's all right. Go ahead and cry. You're safe now.''

Cindy sensed as much as felt the caress of Trace's cheek over the crown of her head. She didn't cry despite the burning of her eyes and the ache of her throat. She had learned long ago that crying, like begging, was a waste of time and energy. What was going to happen would happen and neither her tears nor her pleas would make a bit of difference in the outcome.

She took in and let out a long, shaky breath and then another and another until she gradually relaxed across Trace's lap, her cheek on his left shoulder, her left hand tucked beneath his chin, her palm resting in the warm nest of hair that pushed up through his open collar. When he began to stroke her hair and spine with slow sweeps of his right hand, she sighed and shut her eyes, absorbing his comfort as if it were a balm.

Close up, the signs of Cindy's fatigue were all too obvious to Trace. Beneath random smears of dried mud, her skin was very pale, almost translucent. It was the same for her lips, nearly bloodless. Her eyelids showed dark lavender shadows of exhaustion. The slender lines of her hands were blurred by mud and the random cuts and scrapes that came from changing tires and winching bushes out of the ground. Her loose cotton clothes looked as though she had been packed in a mud bath and left to steam for an hour. Her blouse clung to her like a brown shadow. Her hands were smeared with mud, and so were her feet.

All in all, Trace had never seen a woman half so sexy to him...nor had he ever felt half such a heel.

The realization shocked him. It was utterly irrational. No sane man would prefer a muddy lap full of mulish stubbornness to the perfumed, practiced allure of the women he had known in the past, would he? No, of course not. No sane man would let himself in for the kind of grief a spoiled princess would inevitably deliver to her lover, would he? No, of course not. No sane man would....

Cindy sighed and snuggled fractionally closer to Trace's body, distracting him from his interior catechism on the subject of masculine sanity. Her breath stirred the hair below his throat and the distinctive, male flesh between his legs stirred in answer. He fought the nearly overwhelming impulse to pick up Cindy's hand and kiss her muddy little palm.

I've gone nuts.

Trace closed his eyes. It didn't help. It just made his other senses all the more acute. He felt the taut, full weight of Cindy's breasts resting against his chest, the rounded sweetness of her hips cradled between his thighs, the delicate touch of her breath and fingertips softly tangled in the hair just below his collarbone. He could also feel with razor clarity the heavy, deep beat of his own blood and the surging heat filling his loins, filling him.

Princess, what would you do if I peeled you out of those muddy jeans and unzipped my pants and fitted you over me like a hot velvet glove?

Trace's heartbeat doubled at the thought. His eyes snapped open. Very carefully he lifted Cindy from his lap and slid out the Rover's door, muttering something about getting her gear from the Jeep. Mud squelched and sucked at his boots all the way to the Jeep. He grabbed the two small suitcases from the back and tucked them under one arm. A folded tarp, mosquito netting and a sleeping bag went under the same arm. There was nothing left in the cargo area of the Jeep but the battered toolbox that had been bolted to the floor.

The front—and only—seat of the Jeep didn't offer much more in the way of supplies. Purse, empty canteen and a paper bag with a few discarded food wrappers were the only things Trace found. He grabbed the purse and canteen and went back to the Rover.

Cindy sat on the passenger side of the bench seat, watching Trace and wishing that he were in the car with her again. She could still feel the imprint of his hard body and the gentle, reassuring sweeps of his hand over her. She hadn't felt so cherished since the months after her mother's death, when Rye would hear his little sister crying in the night and come to her room and lift her into his arms, rocking her until she fell asleep once more.

"Anything else?" Trace asked, looking into the clear, black eyes that watched him with surprising intensity. He felt an urge simply to stroke Cindy's tangled raven hair once more. The effort it took to control the impulse shocked him.

"Just the radiator water and gas cans," she answered.

Cindy's voice was somewhere between husky and raspy, as though her scream of fear had made her hoarse.

"They'll be okay for now," Trace said. "Do you feel strong enough to steer the Jeep while I winch it out of the muck?"

She blinked slowly, trying to focus on his words instead of on the sculpted line of his lips. "That's all? Just steering?"

Trace nodded.

Mentally Cindy took stock of herself. She had never been a tenth so tired. On the other hand, everything still worked, after a fashion.

"I can handle it," she said, as much to herself as to Trace.

Cindy started to climb out of the Rover, only to feel Trace's hard arms sliding beneath her knees and around her back once more. She made a startled sound as he lifted her from the Rover's bench seat and walked over to the Jeep as though she weighed no more than one of her soft-sided suitcases. He looked down at her surprised, mud-smudged, yet still elegant face. Beneath his dark mustache, one corner of his mouth kicked up slightly.

"I asked you about steering, not walking," he explained.

Trace saw the slow curving of Cindy's lips, felt the subtle changes in her body as she relaxed against him, and wanted to laugh in triumph and howl with frustration at the same time.

"A man of your word, is that it?"

As Trace looked down at Cindy again, all the laughter left his face.

"Yes," he said simply.

For a long moment she stared into his intent green eyes. At that moment he reminded her oddly of Rye, the only man who had never failed her trust. Slowly she nodded.

"All right," Cindy said in a husky murmur. "I'll remember that."

Just as Trace reached the Jeep, Cindy spoke again.

"Trace?"

"Hmm?"

"Thank you."

"For this?" he asked, lifting her a bit higher.

"No. I mean, yes, but...the snake," she said simply. "Thank you."

Trace's mouth flattened out and his arms tightened around Cindy in unconscious protectiveness. "No need to thank me. You got in the first shot."

"Luck. The snake was twice as long as that miserable shovel handle."

Cindy watched as the powerful man holding her closed his eyes, concealing their jungle green behind a dense thicket of nearly black lashes. They were the only hint of softness in Trace's suddenly bleak face.

"Don't thank me. I'm the fool who nearly got you killed."

"That's ridiculous. You didn't put the Jeep in the bog or the snake in the bush."

"I should never have allowed you to drive out of Quito," Trace said flatly.

"What do you mean, *allow*?" she retorted. "You had nothing to do with it. I rented the Jeep the same way I drove it—by myself!"

"And look where it got you."

Cindy looked up into Trace's narrowed green eyes and swallowed hard. "Into your arms?" she asked weakly.

Unwillingly Trace smiled even as he slowly shook his head. "Up to those sweet lips in mud, that's where," he muttered, outlining the curves of her mouth with a glance that revealed frank male hunger. "I can pull you out of the mud with no problem, but after that you might find yourself in bigger trouble than you were before."

Before Cindy could answer, Trace dropped her into the driver's seat of the Jeep and strode away. She watched with a mixture of envy and admiration as he maneuvered the Rover through the mud and into position with matter-of-fact strength and skill. The Rover had two winches, one in front and one in back. When the vehicles were roughly lined up Trace used the rear winch cable to attach the Jeep to the Rover.

The bigger, wider tires on Trace's vehicle spun through the fresh layer of storm-deposited silt to the older, more solid road beneath. The Jeep lurched forward, startling Cindy. She did her best to steer, but knew that it was the much heavier Rover and Trace's skill that were doing the real work. Together the two vehicles churned through the low stretch of the road and up the muddy incline on the opposite side.

The whole process took about three minutes.

Furiously Cindy's hands clenched around the wheel, wishing it were Trace's throat. He had barely gotten his boots dirty yanking the Jeep out of the bog, yet he had sat on his rump and watched her work her hands raw poking brush into the mud.

Waiting for her to ask him for help. *Nicely.*

It was just as well that Trace kept on driving rather than stopping to disconnect the two vehicles. Cindy was far too angry to pay much attention to details such as steering or clutch or accelerator. She was too furious to do anything but grit her teeth against the scream of pure rage that was trying to claw its way out of her throat. Her temper wasn't improved when a village appeared no more than ten minutes farther down the road.

"Damn him!" Cindy said with aching force. "*Damnhimdamnhimdamnhim!* If I had known, I could have walked here in half an hour!"

The object of Cindy's wrath divided his attention between the road ahead and the Jeep behind, towing Cindy to a spot just in front of the local cantina. As he parked, several old men looked up from their comfortable positions around a canted table. Cindy watched Trace walk over to the men before she got out and walked stiffly to the front of the Jeep. Without looking at Trace she began tugging at the cable, trying to release the Jeep.

"Leave it," called Trace. "We're not going anywhere today."

"Speak for yourself," Cindy muttered beneath her breath.

The next thing she knew her hands were being yanked away from the cable.

"I said leave it."

Cindy stared at Trace in mute, seething defiance.

"This is Popocaxtil," he said. "You wanted to come here, remember?"

She transferred her glare to his throat.

"Something bothering you?" Trace asked calmly.

"You. You're despicable. You knew you could get the Jeep out in a matter of minutes, but you let me work until I was cross-eyed."

Trace waited.

"And you knew all along that Popocaxtil was close by!"

It was more of an accusation than a question, but Trace answered anyway.

"Yes."

"But you didn't tell me!"

"You didn't ask." He looked at the high color that rage had brought to Cindy's mud-smudged cheekbones and inquired softly, "Anything you want to ask me now, princess?"

Trace waited, but Cindy simply turned away, dragged herself into the Jeep once more and sat with her head resting on the back of the seat and her eyes tightly closed.

"Suit yourself," he said, shrugging despite the anger simmering in his blood. "But then, princesses always do, don't they?"

With that Trace turned and went back to the men at the cantina. Cindy watched through slitted eyes while another rickety chair appeared out of nowhere. Trace sat down. From inside came a huge, thick-bodied woman carrying a heaped plate of food in one hand and a quart bottle of beer in the other. She set both in front of Trace.

Cindy's salivary glands ached in a sudden onslaught of hunger and thirst. She put them out of her mind. She would rather spit dust and starve to a skeleton than beg Trace for food or water. She would simply rest for a while. In half an hour or so she should have gathered enough strength to gesticulate with the natives until mutual understanding came. And with it, food and water.

"Water..."

She pulled herself into a fully upright position, blinked and looked around with real interest. As did most villages, Popocaxtil had a central well where its citizens drew water and gossiped.

Despite the exhaustion that made her clumsy, Cindy's determination hadn't diminished one bit. She leaned over the seat, fumbled in the toolbox until her hand finally connected with a tin pot from the mess kit, and pulled herself out of the Jeep. When she stood up she felt light-headed. She waited for the feeling to pass, then set off for the local well. No sooner had she filled the pot with cool, luscious water than Trace appeared like an evil jinni and dumped the water into the dirt.

"You little idiot! Have you been drinking the local water all along?" he asked harshly.

Cindy shook her head and looked wistfully at the spilled water. "I was going to boil it."

Trace let out a harsh breath. He took the pot in one hand and Cindy's grubby wrist in the other. "Did it ever occur to you that I might have water in the Rover?" he asked as he hustled her back to the vehicles. "Or did you figure that one peon's water is pretty much like another's, so you'd have to boil it all anyway?'' Without waiting for an answer, Trace threw the pot into the back of the Rover and fished out his own canteen. He shoved it under Cindy's nose. "Drink."

She didn't wait for a second invitation. She fumbled the top off the canteen and began swallowing great mouthfuls of the wonderful water, not caring that some trickled from the corners of her lips. She had never tasted anything half so fine.

Eyes narrowed, Trace watched her. When she stopped for a breath he said, "How long have you been without water?"

Cindy looked at him over the canteen. "Not too—"

"How long?" he interrupted flatly.

"I ran out late yesterday," she said, her tone defiant. "I was going to boil some last night, but couldn't even find a puddle where I parked. Then I was so busy making mud pies today that I didn't get around to cooking any."

"And you would have died of thirst before asking for anything from a peon like me, right?"

"After I saw your smug smile when you pulled up and saw me in the mud, you're damned right!"

Trace remembered the paper bag with its few discarded food wrappers. "When was the last time you ate?"

"No problem. I can always live off the fat of the land," she said, smacking her right hip with her palm.

"How long since—"

"Yesterday," Cindy said, cutting across his words.

"And here I thought you were intelligent!" Trace's hands locked around Cindy's upper arms, hauling her up to within inches of his face. "Listen, princess. This is a wild land with mountains taller than God and meaner than hell. The cloud forest doesn't give one tinker's damn whether you're rich or poor, royalty or peon, dead or alive. And it's dead you're going to be if you don't climb down off your high horse. I'm not a bloody mind reader. If you want something— food or water or any other damn thing—*ask*. And when you're told to do something like leave the Rover's winch cable in place, *do it*.

That particular winch has a tricky release. If you handle it wrong you'll lose a finger.''

"If you had told me about the winch, I—"

"No," Trace said flatly, interrupting Cindy. He looked down into her defiant black eyes. "What happens when something goes wrong and there's no time for me to argue or explain? Should we both get injured or die because you're too spoiled and stuck-up to follow reasonable instructions? There can be only one leader of any expedition, and I'm the leader of this one. If you can't accept that I'll tie you in the Jeep and tow you all the way back to Quito."

Cindy wanted very much to tell Trace to roast his haunches in hell, but she knew that would be stupid—as stupid as some of the things she had already done. She didn't have the experience or reflexes to be on her own in the cloud forest, and she had proven it over and over. Going without food and water at a time when she needed every bit of her strength hadn't been one of her brighter moves.

But then, her IQ seemed to have been on hold since the first instant she had set eyes on Trace and felt dark fire licking beneath her skin.

"All right," Cindy said between her teeth. "You Tarzan, me Jane. Go for it."

"Are you asking me or telling me?"

She closed her eyes and wished she were twice as strong as Trace. Three times. Four.

"Ask me, princess."

But she wasn't strong. She was light-headed and tired and her tongue felt like a dirty mitten in her mouth.

"Have you ever," she said huskily, "had to beg for anything?"

"I'm not talking about begging, I'm—"

"Have you?" she demanded, cutting across Trace's words.

"No," he said curtly.

"I didn't think so." Cindy opened her eyes. They were as black and bleak as a night sky with neither moon nor stars. "I have. It won't happen again. Ever. So if you want the job of finding Susan Parker, I'll pay the way. If you want me to say 'pretty please, help me,' I'll find another way to follow Susan—because no matter how nicely I beg, you'll do what you damned well wanted to do all along, and you'll rub my nose in it every step of the way.''

The bitterness seething beneath Cindy's matter-of-fact tone was almost tangible. Instinctively Trace's grip on her arms gentled until his palms were soothing over her in a slow caress.

"Is that what some man did to you?" Trace asked softly. "Make you beg and then humiliate you?"

There was a swift blaze of defiance, then nothing. Cindy's expression became as empty as her eyes. She had spent several years learning not to think about Jason's treachery. There was no reason to start remembering now.

"That has nothing to do with finding Susan," Cindy said.

For an instant Trace's grip hardened. Then he released her. "Susan was here over a week ago," he said, turning away. "She bought weavings and left for San Juan de Quextil."

Chapter 5

"San Juan de…whatever," Cindy muttered, trying to remember the order of the villages from which Susan's cloth came. "That's not far."

Trace paused but didn't turn around. "It's on the next ridge over to the east."

"Good," Cindy said with relief. "We can be there before midnight."

"Not likely."

Cindy looked at the sky. The sun was already behind the flank of mountain but there was probably an hour of daylight left. As always, there were clouds of one kind or another hanging around, but no real rain threatened. "But the weather is fine."

"You aren't," Trace said bluntly. "You need food, a bath and sleep, in that order."

"But—"

"No."

Cindy clamped her mouth shut against her unspoken protests. *You Tarzan. Me Jane.* It was Trace's cloud forest and his rules. Arguing wouldn't change anything.

Besides, she was too tired to argue.

Without looking back to see how his curt refusal had settled with Cindy, Trace walked into the cantina. Once inside he fought a sharp struggle with himself. He lost. Cursing his lack of willpower when it came to one Cindy Ryan, he tracked down the monumental waitress. He had promised himself that he would make Cindy ask for whatever she needed, but the thought of her being thirsty or hungry defeated him. He would get the expedition on some kind of normal footing once she was fed and rested. Until then he wouldn't be able to look at her dirty, wan face without wanting to turn himself in to the nearest police station and start confessing to crimes he'd never even heard of, much less committed.

Ten minutes later, when Trace emerged from the cantina carrying food, Cindy was curled awkwardly in the front seat of the Jeep, sound asleep.

I'll bet if I'd said she needed sleep, food and a bath, in that order, I'd have found her skinny-dipping in the village well, Trace thought in exasperation, looking down at the tangled cloud of black hair fanned across the seat. *Maybe if I tell her to sleep in the Jeep tonight she won't argue about the two of us sleeping in the only bed in the only room in town.*

Trace reached into the Jeep and shook Cindy awake. The instant she began to mumble protests at being dragged into consciousness he shoved a plate of food under her nose. The effect was immediate and salutary. Black eyes opened, focused on the mounds of tiny potatoes and roast chicken and corn tortillas. Cindy inhaled the fragrance and reached for the food. The sight of her dirty fingers stopped her in midreach.

"Your shower won't be ready for a few minutes," Trace said in a clipped voice. An impatient snap of his wrist unrolled the damp makeshift hand towel he was carrying. He dumped it over her wrists. "I'll be back for the plate. It had better be clean."

With that Trace went to the Rover and began unloading it. Cindy was too busy wiping her face and hands to notice what Trace was doing. Halfway through her cleanup, when the soft white cloth she was using had become irretrievably dirty, she looked closely at it and made a startled sound. She was industriously grinding mud into a formerly clean T-shirt. From its size, it could belong only to one man—Trace Rawlings.

"Well, it's too late now," Cindy muttered. "I might as well make a thorough job of ruining it."

She finished wiping her fingers and face clean before she attacked the plate of food with outright greed. The flavor of the roast potatoes was unexpected, delicate and utterly delicious. The chicken had a chocolate sauce that was equally unexpected and not so delicious. The meat was as tough as the tortillas were savory and tender. She ate everything without a pause, deciding that the odd chocolate sauce improved upon longer acquaintance.

When Trace came back half an hour later, Cindy's eyes were closed and her plate was empty of all but a pile of neatly gnawed bones. He hoped having a full stomach would improve her mood. He reached down to awaken her, then stopped, staring at the luminous, fine-grained skin framed by wings of raven hair. She was breathing deeply, easily, and the tiniest crumb of tortilla was tucked into a corner of her full lips.

Slowly Trace withdrew his hand. If he touched Cindy, he would bend down and lick up the small crumb…and then he would slide his tongue into Cindy's warm mouth and kiss her the way he had wanted to since he had first seen her in the smoky Quito bar.

"Your bath is ready," Trace said, his voice deep.

Cindy stirred. Trace watched hungrily while her rosy tongue roved over soft, very pink lips, tasting the recent food and licking up the tiny crumb. She started to sit upright, groaned softly, and curled into another uncomfortable position in the bucket seat.

"Can you walk or do you want me to carry you?" Trace asked finally, hoping Cindy would opt for walking. If he felt her weight in his arms right now he wouldn't be responsible for the kiss he would surely demand of those deep pink lips.

"Mmph."

"Mmph," Trace agreed, sighing, not knowing whether to smile or swear at the opportunity that had just presented itself.

He plucked Cindy from the Jeep's front seat, carried her through a side door of the cantina and into a tiny room. There were wooden slats on the floor, a rusty pipe poking out of the wall and a bar of improbably blue soap stuck to a high window ledge. Her own shampoo, conditioner and comb had been set out near the door, along with a towel bearing the initials TER.

"You awake?" Trace asked softly.

She murmured a sleepy negative.

"Good."

Slowly Trace let Cindy slide down his body and onto her own feet. He didn't let go of her, simply shifted his arms until she fit his body the way mist fit the mountainside, seamlessly, no gaps and nothing in between. He stared down at her lips and wondered if she tasted half as sweet as she looked. With a final, silent curse at his lack of self-control where this one woman was concerned, he bent and fitted his mouth over hers with exquisite care, leaving no sensitive surfaces untouched.

For a few moments Trace moved his head slowly, parting Cindy's lips by fractions, feeling the subtle changes in her body tension as she went from dazed sleep to sensuous half wakefulness. Suddenly he could wait no longer to taste her. He twisted his head hungrily.

Cindy's mouth opened in surprise and response to Trace's kiss, leaving her vulnerable to the velvet penetration of his tongue. She could neither speak nor move, so tightly was she held in Trace's arms. She had no physical defenses against the slow, hot glide of his tongue. Nor did she have any mental defenses against the consuming kiss, for she had never been kissed with a tenth so much heat, even by the man she had once thought to marry.

With a throttled moan Cindy gave herself to Trace's embrace, moving her tongue over his, tasting him more and more deeply with each racing second until they were locked together in a searching kiss that turned her bones to honey.

The abrupt appearance of the floor beneath Cindy's feet came as a distinct surprise to her. So did the sudden feeling of emptiness when Trace's mouth lifted from hers. Slowly she opened her eyes, aware of a distinct feeling that she had just made a mistake. A bad one. She hadn't been the least bit aroused by any man since Jason, her first lover. And—she had vowed—her last. If she were going to make an exception to that particular personal rule, she knew she should have started with someone a good deal less potent than Trace Rawlings. He was way beyond her level of sensual experience.

But he tempted her almost unbearably. The late golden sunlight slanting into the washroom through the high window made his eyes luminous, nearly emerald in color, twin green fires watching her.

"I do believe I've finally found a way to communicate with a high-nosed little princess," Trace said, smiling, bending down to Cindy's mouth again.

Cindy stiffened and tried to ease from Trace's arms. She didn't have the least bit of success. He was even stronger than he looked, holding her effortlessly, hotly. The caress of his mustache on her sensitive, flushed lips made goose bumps march up and down her arms.

"Now don't get your ruff up," Trace murmured, nibbling along Cindy's lower lip. "All I meant was that since you have such a hard time with words, it only made sense for me to give you another way to thank me for waiting on you hand and foot."

"Generous of you," Cindy managed through clenched teeth.

"I thought so. Care to build up your account against future maid service?" he asked, running the tip of his tongue along her closed lips.

"No thanks," Cindy said coolly, feeling like a fool for having responded so completely to Trace when the kiss had been nothing more than a casual joke to him. "I always take care of maid service with a generous tip."

Trace straightened and released her. "Wide awake now, aren't you, princess?"

"Better late than never."

"Not as far as I'm concerned. The sleepy version is a hell of a lot more woman."

"Woman isn't a synonym for stupid," Cindy retorted.

"I know. I'm surprised you do, though."

With that Trace walked out and closed the door behind him. His voice came back through the badly fitted slats, warning Cindy that she had only fifteen minutes to get clean. She shut her eyes, got a grip on her fluttering nervous system, and turned on the shower.

A thin, erratic stream of cool water came out of the pipe. She looked at her clothes, shrugged, and stepped under the water. Working quickly she wet down and lathered everything from crown to heels with her shampoo, rinsed, and then peeled down to underwear and repeated the process. By the time her hair had been conditioned and rinsed once more, she was feeling deliciously clean.

She turned off the water, which was down to a trickle by now, shed her clothes, wrung them out and her hair as well, and examined her soggy tennis shoes with a rueful smile. They had been white to begin with. Now they were a kind of ruined beige. It was the same for her blouse and slacks. Though clean, they were randomly stained by brown mud and traces of green vegetation.

"Oh, well," Cindy muttered to herself. "Some women pay a fortune for just that kind of tacky tie-dyed look."

She picked up the towel, dried herself quickly, then rolled her clothes up in the big towel, squeezed hard, and squeezed some more.

Trace knocked on the door and called, "Time's up."

"Wait!" Cindy called, unrolling her bikini underpants and pulling them on frantically. "I'm not dressed!"

"Is that an invitation?"

"Don't you dare!" she said, cringing against the clammy cups of the bra as she fastened it in place with flying fingers.

"A dare is better than an invitation any day," he drawled.

"Dammit, Trace…!"

Cindy knew that pulling the damp slacks quickly over her curvy hips was out of the question. She jammed her arms through the short sleeves of her blouse and pulled the clammy sides together over her full breasts.

"Relax," Trace said, opening the door and walking in, unbuttoning his shirt with one hand, carrying clean clothes with the other. "You've got nothing I haven't seen before, and vice versa."

After Trace hung the clothes on a nail and shut the door, he was no more than a foot away from Cindy in the tiny room. For several frozen instants she stood with damp slacks dangling from one hand and towel from the other as she stared at the bare male chest emerging from the shirt. Technically what Trace had said was perfectly correct. She had seen shirtless men before, and had seen Jason wearing nothing more than a triumphant smile.

But seeing Trace was a whole different order of experience. Jason had been good-looking, but not...compelling. Trace exuded a kind of potent, effortless masculinity that went beyond the swirling patterns of dark brown hair and the supple bands of muscle crossing his chest. He was intensely vital, overflowing with heat and life, and he had set her on fire with a single deep kiss, something that Jason hadn't managed to do with the sum total of all his lovemaking.

Cindy didn't realize that she was staring at Trace until his hands went to his waist. Her breath caught with a small sound that was lost beneath the hiss of his descending zipper. She spun and faced the wall. He laughed.

"You are de..." Cindy said angrily, but couldn't force any more syllables past the breath wedged in her throat.

"Desirable?" Trace taunted.

She made a choked sound. He laughed deeply, enjoying himself for the first time since Quito, when he had sensed the dark fire burning within Cindy. Well, he was enjoying himself for the second time, to be precise. He had enjoyed kissing her far too much for his own comfort. Teasing her was a lot safer, as long as he kept his pants mostly on. "And here I thought spoiled, overcivilized women liked being turned on by peons."

"Says who?"

"D. H. Lawrence," Trace said smoothly.

Cindy's mouth snapped shut. By an immense effort of will she managed to ignore Trace long enough to wriggle into her wet slacks.

"Our room is the second door to the left. And don't wander too far in those clothes, princess. They don't conceal nearly as much wet as they did dry."

The door closed behind Cindy with a distinct thump. She looked down at herself, made a stifled sound, and fled to the privacy of the second door on the left. Not until she was inside with the door safely shut did the implication of Trace's words sink in.

"*Our* room?" she asked in a raw voice, looking around.

There wasn't much to look at. The sagging bed was either a generous single or a stingy double mattress lying flat on the floor. There was a blanket but neither sheets nor a pillow. Rugs, curtains, electricity and running water were also among the missing amenities. Not to mention privacy. She couldn't even lock the door for the simple reason that there was no lock in sight, not even a dead bolt or a chair to wedge under the door handle.

And Trace's duffel bag was sitting with her suitcases on the floor, right next to the lone mattress.

Cindy peeled off her wet clothes and pulled on dry ones, moving quickly, not knowing how long she would have before Trace finished his shower. She did know that she wasn't going to be caught in see-through clothing again. Not that it had bothered Trace. For all the response he had shown, she could have been wearing the ratty blanket that was folded haphazardly at the foot of the even rattier mattress.

For his part, Trace spent an unusual amount of time in the shower, trying to forget the picture Cindy had made when he had walked into the washroom. The deep, rich curves of her body had been a shock to him. She must have worked very hard choosing clothes that would minimize the sweet contrast of her small waist with her taut, full breasts and hips. Graceful feet, long legs, a lush triangular shadow balanced at the apex of her thighs...and nipples gathered into deep, pink pouts by the wet cloth of her blouse.

Trace had wanted her just that way, cold cloth and hot flesh and his tongue shaping her nipples into hungry velvet daggers. Just the thought of it brought a grating sound from deep in his throat. He had seen other women wearing much less, but not one of them had brought his body to immediate, full alert. Cindy had. He was still hard, throbbing, so hot he half expected to hear the water sizzle on his skin.

One bed. God. She's so damned soft and that floor is going to be so damned hard. Maybe she'll take pity on me and let me sleep next to her.

Yeah, sure. And maybe all her money will turn to grass and the cow that jumped over the moon will eat it and give green milk.

By the time Trace had finished his shower and dressed in clean clothes, his body had reluctantly accepted the message his mind was sending: *Forget it.*

For Trace to be stuck on an expedition with a spoiled princess who had taken one look down her nose at him and decided he could be bought out of her petty cash account was bad enough. To let her get the upper hand because he wanted her would be the dumbest thing he had ever done in a long life studded with dumb things.

For God's sake, she can't even lower herself to ask me the time of day, and here I am tying myself in knots wanting her?

I'm nuts. That's all there is to it.

Nuts!

Angry with himself, the world, and the thought of a long night on a hard floor, Trace stalked down the unlighted hallway to the bedroom. After a perfunctory knock he walked in.

Cindy had changed from her wet clothes into a pair of slacks that were loose everywhere a pair of pants could be loose—waist, hips and legs. The blouse was big enough to double as a pup tent. Trace knew he should have been grateful that Cindy was no longer wearing sexy, water-slicked, transparent cotton, but he wasn't. It was irritatingly obvious that she was making a special effort to be as unappealing to him as she could manage to be.

"You mug the waitress for that outfit?" Trace asked, balling up and tossing aside his dirty clothes.

Cindy looked down at her slacks and shirt. Handwoven from hand-dyed natural fibers, the clothes were colorful, unstructured and very fashionable, as well as sinfully comfortable.

"This is one of Susan's designs."

"No wonder she's lost. She can't follow the lines of a woman's body, much less a road map."

"She made it to Popocaxtil," Cindy shot back.

Trace grunted and looked around. "That's no recommendation."

Cindy took a better grip on her temper. No one had ever been able to pull her cork quite so quickly, not even Rye at his most maddening.

Trace glared at her. "You know, for someone who's so blazing fond of Susan Parker, you sure aren't very curious. You haven't even asked me if the villagers knew anything else about her but the fact that she left.''

"You know I care about Susan. If you learned anything else—and if you want to tell me what that is—you will. My asking won't make a bit of difference.''

Despite the cool neutrality of Cindy's words, she watched Trace with anxious eyes.

"The villagers sold her some cloth, food and gasoline and went about their own business. They said she was *muy hermosa*, very beautiful,'' Trace added almost grudgingly, "and that she spoke with her hands and her smile.''

Cindy let out a long breath and relaxed, reassured about Susan for the first time since her friend had turned up missing.

"That's Susan,'' she said eagerly, her eyes alive with laughter. "Cinnamon hair and the kind of slender, willowy body that looks good in everything, and she can make anyone understand anything with that stunning smile of hers and a wave of her elegant hands. If she had turned up covered with mud the way I was, she'd have started a new fashion rage.''

"Is this where I'm supposed to gallantly point out that you're hardly a dog yourself?''

The cool sarcasm in Trace's voice took the laughter right out of Cindy's eyes.

"Gallant? You?'' she retorted incredulously, thinking of how Trace had sat and watched her struggle to free the Jeep. "Not very damn likely. For instance, the *gallant* thing to do with one mattress, one man and one woman is for the man to—''

"Put a cork in it, princess,'' Trace said coldly, slicing across Cindy's words. "I'll sleep on the floor tonight but not out of any misplaced sense of gallantry. Sharing a lumpy mattress just isn't worth putting up with your grief.''

Ignoring Cindy, Trace began making the mattress into a bed. First he removed the musty wool blanket and dumped it into a bare corner of the room. With an expert flip of his wrist he spread his tarp over the mattress. When he began untying Cindy's sleeping bag she made an involuntary noise. She was too violently aware of Trace as a man to be comfortable sleeping in the same room with him, no matter who was on the mattress and who was on the floor.

Trace looked up suddenly, pinning Cindy with his icy green glance. "Relax. I'm not going to stick my hand up your blouse while you're asleep. I won't crawl into bed with you, either. And crawling is what you'd make a man do to get close to you, isn't it, princess? Well, I just don't crawl worth a damn. The sooner you figure that out, the easier this trip will be on both of us."

With another impatient movement of his wrist, Trace unrolled Cindy's sleeping bag so quickly that the cloth made a snapping noise as it settled over the mattress. She waited until he let go of the bag before she bent over and retrieved it. Saying nothing, she turned and went to the door, grabbing her own tarp along the way. She barely had the door open when Trace's hand shot over her shoulder and slammed the door shut in front of her face.

"Planning on sleeping in the hall?" he asked in a deceptively soft voice.

Cindy wasn't going to answer, but a single glance over her shoulder at Trace's face told her that he would get his answer one way or another. "No. In the Jeep."

"You'll be more comfortable lying in the bed than sitting up in the Jeep."

"I'm used to it. Besides, after a day of making mud pies, I'm tired enough to sleep standing up. As your day has been considerably less strenuous," she added with a cool smile, "I'm sure you'll appreciate the mattress more than I would. And don't worry, Mr. Rawlings. Where I sleep won't have the least effect on your tip."

Trace hissed a searing word under his breath and turned his back on Cindy. He didn't move until he heard the door open and close behind him. Then he stripped off his clothes, turned off the battery-powered lantern he had brought from the Rover and lay on the contested mattress.

He was still awake when it began to rain.

Chapter 6

The luminous dial of Trace's watch told him that he had been lying on the lumpy mattress for nearly an hour. He had counted sheep, goats, llamas, alpacas, mice and raindrops, all to no avail. He was no closer to sleep than he had been when he went to bed. Even worse, he had run out of new ways to curse himself as a fool and the old ways had lost their zing.

"Hell."

In a single motion Trace shot off the low mattress and stood glaring toward the inoffensive bedroom door. It was quite obvious that Little Ms. Rich Britches wasn't adult enough to admit her mistake and come in out of the rain. That meant that he would have to be adult enough to point her mistake out to her and drag her back inside.

Muttering to himself, Trace yanked on the clean underwear and slacks he had laid out by the mattress. He groped around in the dark until he found the tiny pencil flashlight he had put at the head of the mattress. With a tiny clicking sound the light came on. He found and scuffed into his boots before he stalked out the door, making less noise than the softly falling rain.

Though it was hardly late at night by city standards, the cantina building and the village were absolutely dark. Out in the countryside a rooster was the only clock that kept local time. Trace knew the territory, so he never traveled without a variety of battery-powered lights, one of which was the flashlight that was no bigger than his index finger. The penlight generated a very narrow, very sharp shaft of illumination. Rain fell in gentle silver veils through the cone of light. With another exasperated curse Trace stepped into the rain and stalked to the nearby Jeep. The moldy canvas top was up, but he knew that it must leak somewhere. Canvas always did.

As soon as Trace opened the door he knew where the Jeep leaked. Everywhere. Water ran in cool trickles across the ceiling and down the sides of the canvas top, with occasional diversions down his neck as he stared in disbelief at Cindy. She had the tin mess-kit pot underneath the biggest area of drips, which happened to be left of center in the driver's seat. The other leaks were deflected from the passenger side by a ground tarp Cindy had pulled up to her neck. Beneath the tarp was her sleeping bag, which she had opened and used as blanket. Despite having curled herself almost double, her bare feet stuck out from under the tarp. A trickle of water splashed onto her toes every so often. Water dripped into the tin pan with monotonous regularity.

Cindy was asleep.

Trace stared at her, not knowing whether to swear or to take his stubborn princess into his arms. It was a conflict he was becoming accustomed to the longer he was around her.

In the end Trace gave in, a bittersweet solution to which he was also becoming accustomed. There was really no other choice this time, as there had been none the other times. If Cindy stayed in the Jeep, by morning she would be stiff, sore and doubtless sick into the bargain. And Trace had little doubt that Cindy was more than exhausted enough to sleep despite all the running water. After all, he was the gallant knight who had sat and watched her work until she staggered, all in the name of teaching her how to ask for help when she needed it.

Obviously the lesson hadn't been learned.

"Princess," Trace muttered in a low, gritty voice, "what the hell am I going to do with you?"

There was no answer but the hollow sound of water drops running onto the tarp and from there onto Cindy's soft flesh. Swearing, Trace tucked the penlight behind his ear as a makeshift miner's light. Gently he removed the wet tarp and extricated Cindy from her uncomfortable, leaky bed.

"At least you could have slept in the Rover," Trace continued in a husky, reasonable voice. He arranged Cindy in his arms and tucked in trailing edges of her sleeping bag so that he wouldn't trip. "It doesn't leak and you would fit nicely on the front bench seat. But no, you wouldn't even ask for that much from a peon, would you?"

He sighed a sibilant curse. "One of us is going to have to smarten up a bit, princess, or you're going to keep on being too proud to take a peon's advice and then you'll end up hurting yourself before I can stop you. Then I'll feel lower than a snake's belly and I'll take it out on you and you'll get your ruff up and try to walk on water or something equally stupid and then we'll be back where we were a few minutes ago—me lying awake and you fishing for pneumonia in a leaky Jeep."

Cindy's only answer was a murmured word that Trace didn't catch. Protecting her from the rain as best he could, he carried her to the cantina, then ducked in through the side door and down the dark hallway leading to the small room. He went in and shut the door behind him with his foot, then knelt and put Cindy on the mattress. She stirred again. Her fingers clung to him when he would have withdrawn.

"Rye?" she murmured.

Trace froze in the act of turning off the penlight.

"Rye?" she repeated, her voice growing stronger.

"Yes," Trace lied softly through his gritted teeth. "It's Rye." He turned off the light and tucked it alongside the mattress. "Go to sleep, love. I'm here. Everything is all right."

Cindy murmured something contented that Trace couldn't understand. Her hands linked sleepily behind his head and her cheek sought the warmth of his naked chest once more. He fought a short battle with his conscience, won, and lay down beside her. He pulled her lightweight sleeping bag over both of them.

With a sigh Cindy curled trustingly against Trace's body and sank into a deep sleep again. His hands clenched into fists as he felt the sweet weight of her breasts against his chest and wondered who the hell Rye was. Who was the paragon of humanity Cindy trusted enough to give herself into his keeping without struggle or hesitation? And why in God's name wasn't dear, no doubt *gallant* Rye in Ecuador with Cindy right now, keeping her out of Trace's hair and—more to the point—out of his arms?

Trace breathed in deeply, feeling the warm, spicy fragrance of Cindy radiate throughout his body. What sane man would let a woman like this go off into the wilds alone?

"You're crazy," Trace whispered aloud, his voice a soft rasp.

He had all night to think just who was crazy—Rye, Cindy, or Trace Rawlings.

The woman in Trace's arms breathed softly, her breasts stirring subtly against his chest with each breath, her warmth tangling with his own. Their bodies were equally tangled. His left arm encircled her narrow waist; her torso lay half on his. Her right arm was stretched across his chest and her fingers were tucked into the warm nest of hair beneath his left arm. Her leg lay between his, her thigh so close to his rigid male flesh that he was afraid to breathe. If she accidentally touched him…

And it would be even worse if she didn't.

Trace couldn't stifle the groan that leaked between his clenched teeth. The hunger for Cindy that had nearly brought him to his knees in the shower yesterday had tormented him all night. He had slept little and had awakened so aroused that he ached from his neck to his knees. He had spent all the long hours of darkness that way. The night hadn't been a total loss, however. He had definitely decided who was crazy.

He was.

Very carefully Trace eased away from the smooth, fragrant woman who had shared the mattress with him in a night of unaccustomed chastity. At least it had been unaccustomed for Trace. He had never spent the night with a woman he wanted and not taken her. Nor had he ever spent the night with a woman he hadn't wanted. At the moment he was too aroused to decide if that made two more rules he had broken for Cindy, or only one.

Why not just smooth her legs apart and wake her up from the inside out? If that kiss in the washroom was any sample, she wouldn't mind a bit.

That is the dumbest idea you've had in months! Trace told himself savagely as he rolled off the mattress and stood up.

Wrong. The dumbest idea was doing Invers a favor by getting Big Eddy McCall off his back.

Trace sighed and rubbed his face with his palms, wishing he could get his hands on Invers. But that was impossible. The only thing within reach was a stubborn princess whose eyes and body burned with dark fires she wouldn't let him touch. Cursing Invers and Big Eddy and everything but the softly sleeping woman who was too close and much too far away, Trace rubbed his face harder. Beard stubble rasped back. Without stopping to question why he was bothering to shave when he wasn't even in the lowlands, Trace picked up his shaving kit and silently left the room.

Cindy awakened moments later. Eyes closed, she stretched luxuriously. Suddenly she made a startled noise and sat up, looking around wildly in the semidarkness. She remembered falling asleep in the Jeep and nothing else. Obviously this wasn't the Jeep.

"Trace?"

There was no answer. Slowly Cindy inventoried her surroundings once more. The room was familiar enough. Her suitcases were still there. So was Trace's duffel bag. Ditto for his battery lantern and sandals and a pencil flashlight tucked alongside the mattress. She was covered with her own sleeping bag, which she had opened up to make into blanket last night in the Jeep. She was resting on top of Trace's sleeping bag, which had been similarly unzipped. There was no other bed in sight, not even a makeshift pallet on which Trace could have slept.

The only possible conclusion was that Cindy had spent the night, or at least part of it, sleeping with Trace Rawlings.

Relax, princess. I'm not going to stick my hand up your blouse while you're asleep.

Too sleepy to marshal her usual defenses, Cindy admitted to herself that there was nothing she would have liked better than to awaken with Trace's hand caressing her breasts. Even the thought made her shiver, tightening her nipples until they stood out against the loose cloth of her blouse. The bittersweet irony of her situation made her want to laugh and cry at the same time. She had given up hope of finding a man who would want her instead of her money. She had given up men, period. Then along came Trace Rawlings, a man she found she wanted very much...a man who had kissed her once and apparently had decided that kissing her was more trouble than it was worth.

Crawling is what you'd make a man do to get close to you, isn't it? Well, I don't crawl worth a damn.

A slow, hot flush crawled up Cindy's body as she remembered Trace's icy words. Was that how she seemed to him—a woman whose greatest pleasure was in humiliating men, making them beg for a kiss or a smile?

Teeth scored Cindy's lower lip as she shook her head in silent denial of Trace's indictment. She had once been humiliated in just that manner by a man. She would never make another human being submit to that kind of cruelty any more than she would force herself to crawl for any man again, no matter what the reason. Maybe if she explained that to Trace they could start all over again.

Maybe this time he would want her instead of being angry with her.

"Oh, sure," Cindy muttered, rolling out of bed and standing up. "He's the very soul of understanding and gallant forgiveness. You knew that the instant you looked up from the mud and saw a smug smile plastered on his handsome face."

Gloomily Cindy began packing everything. She had to roll the sleeping bags several times each before she was satisfied that they wouldn't come undone the instant someone picked them up, which was what her own sleeping bag had done the first time she had rolled it. The dirty clothes she had collected without regard for ownership went into the big plastic garbage bag she had packed for just that purpose. Her tennies were still soggy and none too appealing, but a pair of dry socks made it possible to squeeze her feet into the shoes.

With a feeling of foreboding, Cindy pulled her small travel mirror out of her suitcase. A single glance told her more than she wanted to know.

"No wonder Trace couldn't wait to get out of bed this morning," she said, grimacing. "I've seen better looking women riding brooms on Halloween."

A small brush and a lot of patience took the snarls from Cindy's hair. She looked at her makeup kit, shrugged, and put on a minimal amount, not wanting to call attention to herself by wearing something as useless as blusher in a cloud forest. The result of her sketchy pass with the makeup kit was depressingly less than spectacular. And, to be honest, she wouldn't have minded looking spectacular for Trace, if only to prove to him that she could be a desirable woman.

"Hey, princess. You awake?"

At the sound of Trace's voice Cindy guiltily buried her mirror in the dirty clothes bag.

"Yes."

"Good. Get the door, will you?"

Cindy opened the door and tried not to stare. Trace was wearing an old black T-shirt whose soft knit fitted perfectly over his chest, underlining every powerful shift of muscle and tendon. His slacks were khaki, loose, yet they managed to remind her with every movement he made that there were long, muscular legs just beneath the cloth. His dark hair was glistening from the shower, showing a hint of curl in its thick depths. Clean shaven but for a mustache, his face revealed its uncompromising Scandinavian planes. Beneath very dark, steeply arched brows, his eyes were gemlike in the clarity and intensity of their green color.

Cindy had never seen a man who appealed to her senses more. It was all she could do not to reach up and trace the clean masculine lines of Trace's eyebrows, his lips, his jaw, and then to kiss him as she finally had in the shower. Only this time she wouldn't freeze up. She wouldn't stop kissing Trace until he was trembling as much as she had yesterday. If such a thing were possible.

A thoughtful frown settled onto Cindy's face as she wondered if men ever got so aroused that they trembled. If she asked Trace about it, would he answer her or simply make fun of her obvious lack of experience?

"Hello?" Trace said, wondering why Cindy was staring at him as though he were an utter stranger. "Remember me? Your intrepid guide?"

Cindy stepped back hastily from the doorway, feeling a blush heat her cheeks. "Er, yes, Come in."

"Here," said Trace, holding out a plate on which was balanced a cup of coffee, a mound of eggs and a wad of tortillas. "This will take the cobwebs out of your brain."

Wordlessly Cindy accepted the plate, staring at Trace as though he were a magician. She had been so busy drinking in his appearance that she hadn't even realized he was holding two plates in his hands. And very intriguing hands they were—tanned, long fingered, lean, strong, the backs patterned with the same glossy dark brown hair that curled up from the vee neck of his shirt.

"Coffee," Trace explained, giving Cindy a sideways glance when she made no move to eat or drink.

She didn't notice the glance. She was looking up the bare length of his forearms, tracing the exquisitely masculine textures of tanned skin and very dark, shiny hair, and the flex and flow of muscle with each motion of Trace's body. She wanted to run her fingertips and cheek and lips over his arm, outlining each warm ridge of muscle and tendon. Would he like that? Would it shorten his breath just a little? Would it make him look at her as though she were a desirable woman rather than a useless albatross tied around his neck?

"Are you all right?" Trace asked finally, glancing at Cindy's hands, which were clenched so tightly on the plate that her knuckles were pale.

"No." Cindy closed her eyes and wondered at the turmoil of her mind and the curious, slow tendrils of heat uncurling from deep within the pit of her stomach. "I mean, yes. Just a little…scattered."

Trace looked around the room, expecting to find it as disorganized as Cindy's mind obviously was. To his surprise everything was neatly packed and lined up by the door, ready to be taken to the Rover.

Apparently she was eager to be gone from the forced intimacy of the small room and the implications of the single, lumpy mattress.

A thin smile grew beneath Trace's mustache. If Cindy thought the room was intimate, wait until she tried the Rover on for size. But he was no fool. He would say nothing. She could discover the dimensions of the Rover for herself.

Chapter 7

The Rover hit a massive tree root, lurched, wallowed and thumped down the other side. Cindy opened her mouth to ask Trace if he was certain that the miserable track they were on was the road to San Juan de Whatsis. After an instant of deliberation, she closed her mouth again. Trace had been either surly or amused with her since the moment they had left the little room and he had calmly loaded everything into the Rover.

"Everything" had included one Cindy Ryan, who had been hustled into the vehicle with slightly less care than had been given to the bag of dirty clothes. Unlike the laundry, she had protested her treatment in a calm, firm voice. Trace had simply looked at her, called her princess and informed her that he had arranged for the Jeep to be driven back to Quito.

Cindy had been so stunned that she could think of nothing to say. She had remained silent since then. Trace had done the same, except for a few sizzling exceptions. One of them occurred half an hour out of Popocaxtil, when a tire went flat. There were many words then, all of them Trace's and not a single one of them would have graced the approved list of a girl's finishing school. When Trace paused for breath, Cindy spoke.

"Can I help?"

"With the swearing? I doubt it, princess," he said dryly. "I know more languages than you do."

"With the tire," Cindy said, her voice tight.

"You sure can," he said as he slid out of the Rover. "You can stay the hell out of my way."

The Rover's door slammed hard behind Trace. Cindy hung on to her temper and settled in for a long wait.

As had happened many times since she had come to Ecuador, she discovered that she had miscalculated. Despite the uneven, rutted, slippery ground, Trace had the bad tire off and a new one in place within fifteen minutes.

"That was fast," Cindy said as Trace climbed back into the Rover.

He grunted. "Anyone who can't change a tire has no business on these roads."

"I changed a tire on the Jeep," Cindy retorted.

"Yeah. The right front."

"How did you know?" she asked, startled. The Jeep's tires had been so caked with mud that there should have been no way for Trace to tell which tire was new and which was not.

"The lug nuts were so loose the wheel wobbled." Trace turned and gave Cindy a glittering green glance. "You're damned lucky that wheel didn't come off and dump you over the edge of the pass," he said flatly. "It was a long, long way down to the bottom, princess. Or was your nose too high in the air to see the drop-off at your feet?"

Cindy looked at her hands clenched in her lap and said nothing in her own defense, because there really was nothing for her to say. Trace was right: when it came to rough-country skills, she had none. If he thought her stuck-up into the bargain, she could hardly object. She had been abrupt and impatient with him from the first instant she had seen him sprawled like a huge jungle cat in a warm corner of the Quito bar. His lean, relaxed, yet overwhelmingly male presence had done odd things to her nerves. She had taken it badly. Things had started going wrong between the two of them from that moment.

Blindly Cindy turned and stared out the window at the dense greenery that lurched by in time to the Rover's rough forward progress.

Maybe if I try hard enough, things can go right from now on. Maybe I can put my best foot forward and take the other one out of my mouth. Maybe then Trace will stop looking at me as if I'm just one more thing gone wrong with his life.

Gradually the view outside the window resolved itself into separate shades of green reaching up toward a misty, pearl-white sky that was so brilliant it was impossible to look at directly. Leaves of all kinds unfurled to the white sky—leaves short and broad and glossy, leaves long and dark and swordlike, leaves lacy and graceful, blunt and leathery—more shapes and shades of green leaves than the human eye could distinguish or comprehend.

Without realizing it Cindy forgot her unhappy thoughts and became absorbed in the unfolding panorama of the land in a way that had been utterly impossible for her before, when she had been forced to give every bit of her attention to the road and the Jeep. Curious, wondering and finally awed, she began to understand the wild immensity of the country she had blithely taken on with no preparation beyond a dubious hand-drawn map and a rented Jeep of uncertain mechanical soundness.

In places along the narrow track the canopy of leaves closed tightly overhead, putting the road into total shade. In those places Cindy could see into the forest itself. Beneath the dense, leafy canopy, the forest floor was open. Too little sunshine penetrated the layers of leaves for any but the most shade-tolerant plants to survive beneath the tall trees. Where the canopy had been torn by recent tree falls or by the road itself, plants flourished in a solid green mass as they fought a determined, silent, life-and-death struggle for a place in the sun.

Despite the fact that the narrow road pitched up and down as it wound over ridges and through what Cindy suspected was a pass of sorts, the mountains themselves were rarely visible. Part of the problem was the green canopy of vegetation covering everything, muffling all sensory input, all orientation, leaving at best only a vague sense of up and down. Part of the visibility problem was stated in the name of the landscape itself.

Cloud forest.

Moisture was the cloud forest's third dimension. Mist, drizzle, windblown streamers of fog, water drops of all sizes condensed on every green surface to make tiny clear beads that gave off subtle glints of light when wind stirred through the forest. And every bit of the moisture came from the gently seething presence of grounded clouds. The mountains were dark, invisible sky castles more sensed than seen, land swathed in silent, warm billows as though a giant had exhaled against a mirror, blurring all reflections of reality. Clouds were everywhere, permeating everything, even the breaths that Cindy and Trace took.

Stretching from three thousand to eleven thousand feet along the east-facing slopes of the Andes, the cloud forest was bathed in perpetual moisture that came from thick, sultry tropical air rising up mountain slopes, cooling and condensing into clouds, and in the process creating a landscape that was like nothing else on earth. At times impenetrable, at times parklike, always expressed in shades of green on green, infused with the silver rush of water, the cloud forest lived and breathed, complete within its own immensity.

A searing torrent of language snapped Cindy out of her forest-induced reverie. The Rover lurched to a halt. She looked at Trace questioningly.

"Tire," he said in a clipped voice.

Automatically Cindy opened her mouth to ask if she could help, saw Trace's expectant, sardonic glance and closed her mouth once more, limiting her response to a nod. As the door slammed behind him, she looked at her watch. To her surprise, it was nearly noon. Her lips turned down in a rueful line at this latest underlining of her own incompetence relative to Trace's relentless skill. If she had been driving, the hours would have crawled far more slowly than the vehicle, and she would have been exhausted from wrestling with the steering wheel before she had come half so far.

Gloomily Cindy realized there was simply no doubt about it— traveling with Trace was much better in all ways than traveling by herself had been.

Not quite in all ways, she amended rebelliously. *When I was alone I could talk to myself. And better yet, I could get a civil answer!*

The Rover jiggled rhythmically as Trace jacked up the rear. Cindy glanced at her watch again and decided to risk Trace's wrath by rummaging for lunch. She knew there was something back in the cargo area. The smell of roast chicken and fresh corn tortillas was unmistakable.

Outside the Rover Trace pulled off the wheel, unstrapped the second spare he kept on the top of the Rover, and replaced the bad tire. He hesitated, then decided there was no help for it. He had to patch both ruined tubes on the two spares. If he didn't, sure as hell the next flat would come in a pouring rain on the edge of a road that would have given an eagle second thoughts.

Cursing steadily beneath his breath, Trace took the tire iron, levered both tires from the wheel rims, pulled out the tubes and went to work. In both cases the cause of the leak wasn't difficult to discover. Some of the forest trees were very hard. Fallen sticks or branches made very efficient spears, especially when lying concealed beneath a thin layer of mud or moss on top of the road. Usually he was lucky or skillful enough to avoid the hidden traps. Today his skill had been on hold too much of the time because his attention had been divided between the road and his beautiful, silent passenger.

As for his luck...it had been on a holiday since Quito and showed no signs of coming back anytime soon.

Trace heard the Rover's door open and shut. When Cindy didn't approach him, he assumed that she was going to venture into the forest for the obvious reason. He called out to her without looking up from his work on the tubes.

"Don't lose sight of the Rover. And watch out for plants like the one growing near the left front fender. The stems are hollow and are the home of some really vicious ants."

Cindy's answer was muffled but clearly nonrebellious, so Trace gave his attention back to the patches. He heard Cindy return, but she still didn't approach him. He finished checking the new patches on the tubes, put the tires back together and strapped them to their respective places on the top and rear of the Rover. He wiped down the tools and his own hands, topped off the gas tank, checked the water and decided everything would hold together until the next time he was looking at Cindy's profile when he damn well should have been looking at the road.

What the hell has she been thinking about? What's going on behind those beautiful black eyes? She hasn't said ten words since we left Popocaxtil.

Can you blame her? The last time she opened her mouth you landed on her with both feet.

If I had landed on her, it wouldn't have been with my feet. I've never made love to a woman in a car before, but better late than never, right?

Wrong. All wrong. Don't be any dumber than God made you. Get to Raul's place; show Cindy that Susan is okay; go tell Invers his problems with Big Eddy are solved and then start drinking until you forget the dark fire burning just beneath Cindy's lovely skin.

God, did she really shiver in my arms when I kissed her...or was it me shivering and wishing she wanted me?

Trace swore and tried to put Cindy out of his mind as he washed his hands beneath the trickling spout of the big water can attached to the rear bumper of the Rover. When he was finished he wiped his hands on his khakis and stretched. He was just thinking how wonderful a strong, hot cup of coffee would taste when he smelled the stuff of his dreams on the wind.

Inhaling, wondering if he were crazy, he followed the smell to the front of the Rover. The hood had been transformed into a table. Pieces of cold roast chicken and tortillas were laid out on top of a paper bag. Next to that was a mound of roughly hacked chunks of bittersweet chocolate. The food made his stomach growl in sudden demand, but it was the steaming mug that focused his attention. He reached for the mug, already anticipating the familiar, rich bite of coffee on his tongue.

"I didn't know if you took sugar or milk," Cindy said.

She glanced up from the road where she was crouched over a backpacker's stove that consisted of a single burner fueled by a canister of pressurized gas. A small pan of water was just coming to a boil. Next to her was another mug that wore what looked like a tin hat, which was actually the top half of a single-cup drip coffeepot. The mug itself provided the bottom half.

"This is fine. Much more than I expected," Trace added between sips of the scalding brew. He made a sound of satisfaction. "Good and strong, too. The way I like it."

Cindy smiled in relief. "I wasn't sure about how to use your little half pot," she admitted, "but the color of that first cup looked right. Rye taught me to make it strong enough to stand up to a high-country blizzard."

Trace grunted, suddenly less pleased with the coffee. He couldn't help wondering what other ways Rye had taught Cindy to please a man.

"He even taught me to like drinking it," Cindy continued as she poured water into the tiny pot perched over her mug.

She glanced over her shoulder, hoping that Trace had accepted the coffee as it had been meant—as a peace overture. A single look at his hard features told her that coffee hadn't been enough to get the job done. Unconsciously biting her lip, she turned back to her own coffee. By the time her cup was ready, Trace had finished his. When he put his mug aside to reach for tortillas, she substituted her fresh cup for his empty one and set up the coffee maker once more.

In quiet horror Cindy watched while Trace tucked chunks of chocolate and chicken into a tortilla, rolled it up and ate it with every evidence of pleasure. She had meant the chocolate as dessert, not as part of the main course.

"It all ends up in the same place, princess," Trace said sardonically, accurately reading the look on her face.

Cindy's lips turned down at the nickname she had come to hate.

He smiled thinly. He knew that she didn't like being called princess. That was why he did it. That, and to remind himself that she was the spoiled child of wealth, even if she would rather die than admit it to him.

You know, you really should quit riding her with the princess routine, Trace advised himself. *You're not supposed to know who she is, remember? As for you being angry because she doesn't trust you enough to tell you her real name—she'd be a fool if she went around announcing her wealth and you know it. South America is a close second to Italy as the kidnap capital of the world. That's why Invers was sweating bullets at the thought of having Big Eddy's daughter waltzing around the cloud forest looking for another ditzy, ritzy American woman.*

On the other hand, pointed out the devil's advocate that lived within Trace, *if Cindy hates the nickname princess so much, all she has to do is ask me not to use it. Just ask me. That's all. No big deal.*

Except to her.

And to me, Trace admitted silently. *If it's the last thing she does on this green earth, she'll ask me for something. Anything.*

And I'll give it to her, no matter what it is or who it costs.

With his coffee cup Trace drank a silent toast to his vow. Only after he had swallowed did it register on his mind that the formerly empty cup had been magically refilled. He looked at the mug and then at Cindy, who was just pouring a final measure of water through the tiny pot. He realized that she had given him her cup.

Maybe she drank some while I was cleaning up.

"You like this blend?" Trace asked, inhaling the fragrance rising from his mug.

"Tell you after I've had a sip," Cindy said, blowing across the steaming surface of her coffee. "But if this is what I think it is, I love it."

Trace started to say something, then stopped. It gave him an odd feeling in the pit of his stomach to realize that she had given him two cups of coffee before she had taken so much as a taste for herself. That wasn't what he would have expected from a child of wealth, especially from one who was too proud to even ask him for the time of day.

But then, Cindy had been unexpected from the start, and in very uncomfortable ways.

"Wonderful," she murmured, closing her eyes as the taste of coffee spread through her in a fragrant, revitalizing wave. "Just as I remembered from my last birthday. Beans so mellow you could eat them."

"You're sure this is the same coffee?"

"Positive. I almost cried when I used up what Dad had sent me."

"Then your father must know somebody who knows Raul."

"Who?"

"Raul Almeda. This is his private blend, grown from his own coffee plants and given to his friends and business partners. Raul owns a vast *hacienda* up ahead that runs from the lowlands to the cloud forest." Very casually Trace added, "If Susan isn't at the next village, doubtless she'll be with Raul, her feet on an embroidered stool and servants hovering to grant her every wish."

"Sounds boring," Cindy retorted.

"Only to people who have been rich enough, for long enough, to know what it's like. Most never get the chance to find out. But you wouldn't know about that, would you?"

"Would it make any difference if I did?"

Trace's mouth turned up at one corner in a smile that was as cold as his eyes. "I doubt it, princess. Money just doesn't get some jobs done, and they're nearly always the jobs worth doing."

Cindy made no response this time. What Trace had said was a razor truth that she had encountered too many times not to acknowledge it, and each time she confronted it the truth sliced deeper. Money simply couldn't buy the important things. It couldn't buy self-respect or intelligence or talent or real companionship or laughter or...love.

Love was most definitely one thing money could not buy. Nor could begging. Love was a gift freely given.

But nobody gave gifts to Big Eddy's daughter.

Chapter 8

Cindy watched Trace turn away from the natives he had been questioning. He reached the Rover in a few swift steps, slid in behind the wheel and slammed the door just as the overcast condensed into an odd, dense mist.

"Susan left a few days ago, just before the first hard storm," Trace said. "She was hitching a ride with one of Raul's workers."

Biting her lip, Cindy stared out the side window, not wanting to reveal her worry to Trace.

"Don't look so glum. Raul's *hacienda* is just a few hours down the road. When it started pouring, I'll bet they just made a run for one of the hunting cabins Raul has scattered up and down the mountainside. They're fully stocked at all times for just such emergencies."

"Do they have phones?"

"The cabins? Hardly. Despite the greenery, princess, this isn't Central Park."

"Really? What an astonishing revelation," Cindy said before she could stop herself. She really did hate that nickname.

"It might be a revelation if you'd think about what it means instead of making smart remarks. No phones means no way to call and tell people you're all right. That's what the Andean cloud forest is all about. Lack of communication."

"Precisely. If something went wrong for her—"

"Quit borrowing trouble," Trace snarled, letting out the clutch and leaving the village behind. "We've got enough of our own without you hunting for more."

Before Cindy could ask what Trace meant, the swirling mist surrounding the Rover changed into true rain.

In the next hours Cindy came to understand rain and Trace Rawlings in a new way. She passed from nervousness to disbelief to admiration and finally to outright awe as she watched Trace negotiate the narrow, melting, liquefying road. She wouldn't have made it half a kilometer out of San Juan de Whatsis and she knew it. It took experience, strength, coordination and coolness to hold the slewing, sliding, slithering Rover to the course. Time after time Trace guided and bullied the vehicle through situations where Cindy knew she would have ended up sideways or topside down or hopelessly mired. Even if she had managed to extricate herself and the Rover, she knew she would have just ended up in trouble all over again a few yards down the road.

If you could call it a road. She no longer did. It was a pathway to hell; a slippery, sliding, greasy brown string unwinding endlessly downward beneath clinging slate veils and between blackish green walls of vegetation that thrashed like souls in torment. Gray rain hammered down from the heavens without pause or purpose, reminding men of just how the oceans had come to cover three-quarters of the planet.

Cindy lost count of the times Trace dragged a winch cable into the forest, wrapped the cable around a suitable tree and yanked the Rover out of a mud hole. She lost track of the passage of time as well, and of distance, and of all directions except down.

Despite the rain and the wind, the air wasn't cold. It wasn't even cool. That made sense to Cindy in a crazy way. Hell, after all, was reputed to be warm, and she had no doubt that hell must be where they were headed, slithering endlessly downward, a descent that was underlined by the tropical heat of the air, a viscous warmth that deprived her of any temperature sense at all. Everything she touched

seemed to hold the same amount of heat—the window, the uphol-
stery, the rain, her own body.

Numbly Cindy watched as Trace got out in order to investigate a
low spot in the road on foot. Being alone further increased her sense
of unreality, of being suspended within the endless, elemental drum-
roll of water that was battering the Rover. Her body was tense and
her throat ached out of a futile desire to somehow lighten Trace's
burden. Without Trace she would have been helpless, and she knew
it to the marrow of her bones.

The realization neither frightened nor irritated Cindy. It was simply
a fact like rain or mud or a cloud forest that bowed to no man.

Even Trace Rawlings.

"That's it," he said flatly, climbing into the Rover and turning off
the engine.

Cindy blinked as though coming out of a trance. "We're there?"

"If by 'there' you mean Raul's *hacienda*, no. If 'there' means
where we're going to spend the rest of the storm, yes. There's no
point in pushing anymore. At this rate we won't reach the *hacienda*
before midnight. We'd make much better time going on foot."

"Oh." Cindy peered through the windshield, trying to see where
they were. All she saw was rain. Not that it mattered. If Trace said
they couldn't go any farther, then they couldn't, period.

"No argument?" he asked sardonically.

Cindy shook her head. "Frankly I don't see where you got the
strength to go this far."

"That's easy enough. I didn't want to be trapped for the night with
you in the Rover." Trace shrugged. "But here we are anyway."

"Trapped," she repeated, her mouth turning down.

If Cindy had had any doubt about how Trace regarded her, he had
just removed it. He had driven for hours over impossible roads in the
hope of avoiding the opportunity to spend the night with her again.

Trace saw the unhappy line of Cindy's mouth and said coldly,
"Don't worry, I—"

"Yes, I know," she interrupted bitterly. "You won't stick your
hand up my blouse while I'm asleep."

Don't bet anything important on it, princess. I want you like hell on fire. That's why I kept driving long after I knew it was a lost cause. I hoped I'd be too tired to get hard every time I looked at you.

It didn't work.

For the sake of his own pride, however, Trace kept his thoughts to himself. Besides, what woman would put up with a man who was covered with mud and smelled as if he had carried the Rover on his back for the past three hours? In fact, Trace was surprised Cindy hadn't complained about him once through the long afternoon. He could barely stand himself in the confines of the Rover.

"I'm going to take a shower," he said abruptly.

"What? Where?"

Trace's laugh was a bark of disbelief. "You've got to be kidding."

Cindy looked at the warm rain pouring down and understood. She watched while Trace stretched over the seat of the Rover and snagged his shaving kit. It was an easy reach for him because there was no back seat. As had been the case with the Jeep, the Rover's rear seat had been taken out to make more room for carrying equipment and supplies.

After Trace vanished into the rain with a bar of soap in his hand, Cindy rolled down both front windows for ventilation. The rain blowing inside didn't worry her. Trace had been in and out of the Rover so often that everything that could get wet already was. She unclipped the cargo net, crawled over the seat back and began assembling ingredients for dinner.

Given the single burner and the impossibility of cooking outside, Cindy didn't try for anything elaborate. Fresh coffee was first on the list. While the water came to a boil she diced up a small tin of ham and added water to a packet of sliced freeze-dried potatoes. More water went into a mixture that purported to be freeze-dried carrots and peas. Another bar of chocolate turned up. She hid it, afraid that Trace would add it to the stew she was assembling. By the time Trace returned from his makeshift shower, Cindy had made a canteen of coffee, cooked the ham and vegetables together and steamed the remaining tortillas into a renewed flexibility.

"Here," she said, kneeling on the front seat and leaning over into the cargo area until she could grab a mug. Quickly she poured coffee from the canteen and handed the mug to Trace. "The rest of it will be ready in a few minutes."

Wordlessly Trace took the mug. He stared at the darkly reflective surface of the coffee as though he were looking into the future. It was safer than staring at Cindy. In the process of getting the food ready, she had gone close enough to the open windows for rain to dampen odd patches of her clothes. When she leaned over the seat, those wet spots stuck to the curves beneath. When she turned around and sat facing the windshield, her blouse clung to her nipples as though dampened by a lover's mouth.

With an inarticulate curse, Trace forced himself to think about something else. Anything else. Counting raindrops, for instance. Licking them from her body one by one…

"Ready?" Cindy asked.

Trace turned and gave her a smoldering green glance. With a sinking heart Cindy wondered if he would be in a better mood after he had eaten. Silently she handed him a plate of food. She knew it wasn't haute cuisine, but she thought it deserved better than the black scowl he gave it. For several minutes the only sound was that of the rain and the muffled scrape of tin spoons over tin plates.

"More coffee?" she asked finally.

Trace held out his mug. "Yes." Then, softly. "Thank you."

Startled, Cindy looked up from the canteen and smiled. "You're welcome, Trace."

Her smile and the sound of his name on her lips sent streamers of dark fire through Trace's body. Suddenly he knew he couldn't spend another moment in the Rover's enforced intimacy without making a very hard pass at Cindy. That didn't bother him as much as the angry realization that he didn't know what he would do if she turned him down.

And he had every expectation that she would do just that.

"Look," Cindy said, turning toward the window. "It's stopped raining. Well, almost. It's not raining nearly so much."

Trace's head turned. Cindy was right. As suddenly as the hard rain had begun, it had stopped. The end of the downpour was too late to do the road much good, however. Dark would come long before the low places had drained. There seemed to be no help for it—in the next few hours he would get the excruciating opportunity of discovering how long he could hold out before he made a fool of himself, or worse, with Cindy.

A pale flash against the dark green of the forest caught Trace's eye. Slowly he made out a series of blazes on the trunk of one of the bigger trees. Once he had spotted the first blaze he had no trouble at all deciphering the message Raul's workers had hacked with machetes into the tree's trunk. He and Cindy were at the edge of one of Raul's forestry experiments. A few hundred yards down the hill there should be a clear trail used by Raul's men. A few klicks up the trail—straight up—would be the spur road leading to the big house, the main Almeda residence.

And in that residence there would be more than enough rooms to separate two unexpected guests. Trace wouldn't have to see Cindy, much less be forced constantly to brush against her.

Trace finished off his coffee in a gulp. "As soon as you're done eating, we'll walk to Raul's house."

Cindy looked blank. "Walk?"

His eyes narrowed. "That's right, princess. Walk. It's a form of transportation often used by the peons of the world."

It took a considerable effort, but Cindy managed not to say anything more inflammatory than "Is it far?"

"A few klicks as the crow goes. Four or five times that by the road. We'll leave the luggage here. When the road dries out a bit, Raul's men will bring the Rover to the big house."

Without a word Cindy finished her coffee, gathered up the dirty dishes and pushed against the unlatched passenger door. Trace started to protest that she would get wet in the steady drizzle, then realized how foolish that would sound. She was going to get a lot wetter on the way to the big house.

It would make more sense to stay here, Trace told himself.

The hell it would, he snarled in silent, instant response. *I'd be all over her like hot rain.*

Like I said. It would make more sense to stay here.

The door of the Rover slammed behind Trace. Before Cindy could protest he had taken the dishes from her and shoved her purse into her hands. He fired the dishes into the back of the Rover, yanked his machete from the sheath at his waist and stalked toward the blazed tree, hoping that Raul's men had left some encroaching forest for him to hack up.

After a few moments Cindy followed Trace. There was no path, but the walking wasn't too difficult at first. They were in one of the densely shaded, almost parklike areas of the cloud forest. The only thing she had to watch out for were tree roots and moss. By placing her feet carefully, but quickly, she could keep up with Trace. Barely.

Just as Cindy was congratulating herself on her previously unsuspected wilderness skills, her foot slipped on a mossy root and she sat down hard. Hoping that Trace hadn't noticed, she scrambled to her feet and wiped off her palms on her colorful pants, leaving the first of what would be many such smears.

Beyond the blazed tree a trail of sorts appeared. The footing varied between slick and impossible. Cindy found herself grabbing at branches and bark, bushes and drooping vines, anything to help her keep her balance on the narrow path. Most of the time she stayed upright. The rest of the time she gathered new marks for her clothes and body.

Mist closed in again, swathing everything in hushed moisture. Trace was too busy hacking at intrusive greenery to notice that Cindy was barely managing to keep up with him. He moved forward with the steady, rhythmic body motions of a strong man who was accustomed to the cloud forest's demands. From time to time he glanced over his shoulder to check on Cindy, but could see little more of her than a dark shape veiled in the mist of a grounded cloud.

Halfway up the very steep path he paused, looked over his shoulder and saw no one. He called out and was answered by a muffled voice. He started to ask Cindy if the pace was too fast, then stopped himself. If he was going too fast, surely she would have the sense to say something. Wouldn't she?

Sure. Right after she finished teaching stubborn to a Missouri mule.

"Everything all right?" Trace asked, cursing himself even as he spoke.

"Just fine," Cindy said through gritted teeth as she pulled herself upright with the aid of the same tree root that had tripped her in the first place.

Trace hesitated, not liking the breathless quality of Cindy's voice. He checked his watch. If they were going to get to the big house by dark, they had to keep going.

"Let me know if you have to stop," Trace said.

Cindy made a sound that Trace took as a response. With a last look over his shoulder, he turned back to the trail that had only recently been hacked from the cloud forest's solid green body. Unconsciously he resumed the unhurried, unbroken rhythm of chop and walk, chop and walk, chop and walk. Trace made it look effortless, but the skill with which he moved through the dense forest was the result of hard experience and an even harder body.

Only when the new forest trail cut the spur road to the *hacienda* did Trace stop. As he stood quietly, breathing deeply and easily, he realized that he had fallen into a pace that might have been rewarding for him but almost certainly had been too hard on a proud princess.

"Cindy?"

No answer came back from the swirling streamers of cloud.

"Cindy!"

There was no response.

Even before the sound of his call was absorbed into the forest's silence, Trace was back on the narrow path, moving with doubled speed, cursing.

Cindy heard Trace coming toward her long before she saw him condense out of the gray-white mist swathing the steep, rough trail. The last thing she wanted was for Trace to find her sprawled out flat on her face, compliments of a tree root she would have sworn leaped up to grab her foot. Hurriedly she tried to claw her way to her feet, but succeeded only in losing her balance once more. Doggedly she pushed herself to her hands and knees.

Trace stopped and stared at the apparition that was kneeling before him in the narrow trail. Relief and anger warred for possession of his tongue. Anger won.

"What the hell do you think you're doing?" he demanded.

Cindy had no problem with conflicting emotions. Her peace overtures toward Trace had been singularly unsuccessful. That left war.

"Worshipping the ground you walk on," she retorted. "What the hell does it look like?"

Unfortunately for her intentions, Cindy sounded more worn out than sarcastic, and she knew it. She set her teeth and started to pull herself upright again, hating her own weakness, hating Trace for seeing it, hating herself for caring, for wanting to see something besides impatience and anger in Trace's eyes when he looked at her.

Trace hissed a curse through his teeth and reached out to help Cindy to her feet.

"Don't touch me."

Trace was close enough to see the utter fury of defeat in Cindy's black eyes. She was like a cornered animal turning on its tormentor. Pain lanced through him, drawing his face into bleak lines. He hadn't meant to do this to her. Why in the name of God couldn't she even open her mouth and ask him for what she needed?

"I'm not a bloody mind reader! Why didn't you ask me to slow down or stop?" Trace demanded harshly. And then his expression became even more grim as he heard his own question. "Dumb question, right? I keep forgetting. You'd rather die than ask a peon for the time of day. Better watch it, princess. You just might get your wish."

With a single quick motion Trace sheathed his machete. Another even quicker motion brought his hands around Cindy's upper arms. In an instant he had lifted her to her feet.

"Now, if you had *asked* me not to touch you, I wouldn't lay a finger on you," Trace said in a clipped voice. "But you didn't ask. You did what came naturally. You ordered. A princess to the marrow of your elegant bones. Would you like to ask this peon not to touch you? Nicely?"

The surge of rage that had come to Cindy when Trace had once again found her grubbing in the mud faded, leaving nothing behind but defeat. She turned her face away from him and said nothing.

"That's what I thought," Trace said, disgusted with her and with himself for caring that Cindy disliked him so much that she wouldn't ask him for anything, no matter how much she might need it. He pointed her toward the trail. "Walk. I'll be right behind you."

Cindy started up the trail. Three steps later she would have fallen flat had it not been for Trace's left hand closing around her upper arm in the instant after she slipped. He held her upright until her feet found stable footing once more. When she tripped again a few steps later, he grabbed her again. This time he didn't release her. On the steepest parts of the trail he shifted his grip to her bottom, boosting her along as she scrambled forward. When they came to the muddy spur road that led to the Almeda home, Trace moved up alongside Cindy so that his left hand could keep a firm grip on her right arm.

They were still walking that way when Raul and Susan found them.

Chapter 9

"Susan! Is it really you? Are you all right?" Cindy asked in a rush, hardly able to believe her eyes when she saw the stunning, cinnamon-haired woman sitting at ease in a Jeep.

"You just stole my lines," Susan said, looking at Cindy with real concern. "What in God's name happened to you? Did you have an accident?"

Cindy looked at her friend, who was immaculate in an ice-blue silk jumpsuit that perfectly matched her gorgeous eyes. Then Cindy looked at herself. Her unstructured clothes had long since passed beyond the point of fashionable disarray. They were wet, ripped and stained by mud and vegetation to the point that their predominant color was an unappetizing greenish brown.

Cindy started to explain what had happened but the words wedged in her throat. She had just caught a view of Trace from the corner of her eye. He was staring at Susan as though transfixed. It wasn't the first time Cindy had seen a man respond that way to Susan. It was the first time it had hurt, however.

"Ask Tarzan," Cindy said curtly.

"Tarzan?" Unerringly Susan's wide blue eyes turned toward Trace. "It does rather fit, doesn't it?"

Trace's smile was a scimitar curve in his hard face. "I told you

Susan was all right, princess. Raul's very good with women. Aren't you, Raul?''

For the first time Cindy focused on the man sitting in the driver's seat of the Jeep. Her eyes widened fractionally. Raul's hair was silky blond. His skin was a rich, dark gold and his eyes were as black as her own. It was a startling combination, particularly when set against the bold, very masculine bone structure of his face.

Rather cynically Trace watched Cindy's reaction to Raul. She wouldn't be the first woman to fall at Raul's feet after taking one look. Nor would she be the last. That didn't mean that Trace had to enjoy watching it. Somehow he had thought Cindy would have better sense than to be knocked over by a man's looks. God knows she had managed to ignore his own looks without difficulty, and more than one woman had told Trace he was handsome. Not Cindy, though. Not by so much as a sideways glance. The only passion she showed when she looked at him was a desire to commit mayhem on his much stronger body.

"You must be *Señor* Almeda," Cindy said. "I'm Cindy Ryan, Susan's partner."

Raul's jet-black eyes widened as he looked at the rumpled, muddy, thoroughly disheveled creature in front of him. "It is a great pleasure, *Señorita* Ryan," he said. "Susan has told me much about you."

"I left out her enthusiasm for mud baths," Susan said, her eyes still disbelieving. Then she added, "You really are all right, aren't you?"

"Nothing a hot bath and a decent bed won't cure."

"But of course," Raul said instantly. "Please, get in the Jeep."

"Thought you'd never ask," Trace said dryly. Before Cindy could object, he picked her up and dumped her in the back seat of the open Jeep.

"We were just checking on the bridge over Orchid Ravine," Raul explained as he drove down the muddy road.

"And?" Trace asked.

"I would not want to attempt the bridge at the moment," Raul said carefully.

Trace grunted and flashed a jungle-green glance at Susan, who was smiling at Raul. Silently Trace conceded that if Cindy were watching him the way Susan was watching Raul, Trace wouldn't be in any hurry to rush his bridges back into civilization, either.

"Then it looks like you're stuck with us for a day or two," Trace said. "We walked overland on the new trail your men cut up the far side of Thousand Springs Divide."

"We? *Señorita* Ryan was with you?" Raul asked, startled.

"Every step of the way."

"*La pobrecita,*" murmured Raul. "Poor little one. I am a man, yet I would not wish to make that walk with you."

Cindy smiled wanly. "Trace wasn't wild about the idea of having me underfoot, either."

Raul's laugh was low, husky, intimate. "I doubt that very much. My friend has never turned down the company of a charming and beautiful woman."

Just as Cindy found herself warming to the compliment, common sense intervened. At the moment she was about as beautiful as a handful of mud, and as charming, too.

"It is very kind of you to say so," Cindy murmured, "even though it's a gigantic whopper."

"What is this 'gigantic whopper'?" Raul asked.

"A big lie," Trace said succinctly.

Raul blinked, then laughed again. "Now I believe you are truly Cindy Ryan."

"Tongue like a wasp," Trace agreed.

"The hotter the sting, the sweeter the honey," Raul said, smiling with distinct masculine satisfaction.

Cindy bit her tongue and said nothing. Susan winked at her and began fishing for information with all the subtlety of an old, trusted friend.

"What are you doing out here? And how did you end up with Trace?"

"I came to find you. Trace is helping me."

"Why?"

"Because I'm paying him," Cindy retorted.

"Puh-leese," Susan said, calling upon the mist as her witness to

Cindy's recalcitrance. "I meant why did you come after me? Didn't you get my note telling you my change of plans?"

"That was nearly two weeks ago. I was…worried."

Susan made a humming sound that managed to sound skeptical and musical at the same time. "Translated that means you left because Rye and Lisa were busy making another baby and Big Eddy was running around trying to buy studs for you again."

"Susan!" Cindy said, appalled.

"What? You know as well as I do that he offered the last hotshot a ten thousand dollar bonus if he got you pregnant. You see," Susan said kindly to Trace, "her father just recently figured out that a woman only needs a man to get pregnant. Marriage isn't necessary. Even more pertinent, if Cindy doesn't marry, her children will have her last name, which is also Big Eddy's. He was quite pleased by the discovery, because he wants a raft of grandchildren, and he's going to have them if he has to kill his own children trying. Do you blame Cindy for telling the old bulldozer to go to hell and running after me instead?"

"Oh my God," Cindy said faintly, putting her face in her hands without regard for the bits of vegetation still clinging to her fingers.

Trace looked from Susan to Cindy. He picked over the information for the least incriminating parts. "Rye and Lisa, huh? Is she the one who beat you to it?" Trace asked.

"To what? Pregnancy?" Susan asked when it became apparent that Cindy wasn't going to answer Trace. "There was no contest. Lisa and Rye wanted kids."

"And Cindy didn't?" Trace asked.

"She's old-fashioned. She wanted a husband first."

"What was wrong with Rye?"

"Same parents, that's what. He's her brother."

Trace digested that. "Oh."

"She sicced me on Rye once, but it was too late," Susan continued. "He'd already seen Lisa."

Raul smiled. "I can't imagine that would make a difference once he saw you, *corazon*."

"You haven't seen Lisa," Susan and Cindy said as one.

"She's small, delicate, has eyes the color of amethysts and natural platinum hair down to her hips," Susan continued, ticking off Lisa's attributes. "And innocent. God above, she was innocent! She'd been raised with the kind of tribes you only see in National Geographic specials."

"I should have sent Lisa after you," Cindy said softly. "Anyone who can make a wicked knife from an antler and a piece of glass would be right at home in the cloud forest. She would have been a help to Trace, not a burden."

"I am sure you were not a burden," Raul said instantly.

"You're very kind," Cindy said, closing her eyes. She smiled sadly. "I'm sure if it had been you doing the guiding, I wouldn't have felt like a burden. But I would have been a burden just the same."

Susan gave her friend a worried look, then glanced toward Trace. He looked back at her with opaque green eyes.

"You're just tired, Cinderella," Susan said gently, leaning over the seat and stroking Cindy's wet, tangled hair. "The world will look different after you're dry and clean and rested."

Cindy made a noise that could have been agreement, but from the down-turned line of her mouth, Trace doubted that she meant it. Frowning, Susan examined her friend's wan face and closed eyes before she turned around and stared out the windshield again.

A few minutes later the Jeep hit a bump. Cindy didn't open her eyes as a lock of her hair fell forward across her face. With gentle fingers Trace stroked the hair back behind her ear. When she didn't move at all, he realized that she had fallen asleep. Just as the Jeep hit another bump, he reached out and lifted her half across his lap. When she mumbled a question that was also a name, Trace knew what to say.

"Yes, it's Rye. Go to sleep, Cindy. Everything's all right."

Susan's head snapped around. Trace looked back at her with eyes that were as green and as impenetrable as the cloud forest itself. One big hand stroked Cindy's hair slowly, gently, while the other hand held her against his chest. Cindy murmured something and burrowed more deeply into Trace's arms.

After a moment Susan spoke.

"When her mother died, Cindy was just a kid. Rye used to hear her crying in the middle of the night. He'd go and hold her until she fell asleep again."

Trace's eyelids flinched but he said nothing.

"What did you do to her?" Susan asked flatly.

"Nothing major. I'm a lousy mind reader, so I tried to teach Cindy to ask for what she needs. That's all."

"That's all?" Susan's eyes widened into deep, faintly tilted pools of blue. "She never asks anyone for anything. Ever. Not me. Not God. Not even Rye. But she'll give you the heart from her body if she thinks you need it…or if you ask her for it," Susan added.

Trace's mouth curled into a thin, sardonic smile. "The only thing she'd willingly give me is a knife between the ribs."

"That doesn't sound like Cindy."

"Maybe you don't know her as well as you thought."

"And maybe I do," Susan retorted. "If you managed to get under Cindy's skin deep enough to get her angry, congratulations. No man has raised her temperature a quarter of a degree since a walking disaster called Jason came into her life. You would have gotten along fine with Jason."

Trace raised a single eyebrow in skeptical query.

"Like you," Susan said coolly, "Jason believed in making Cindy beg for every little thing from a hamburger to a good-night kiss."

Have you ever had to beg? Well, I have and I'll never do it again.

"There is one hell of a difference between asking and begging," Trace said between his clenched teeth, as though it were Cindy rather than Susan he was trying to convince.

"Try explaining that to Cindy."

"I did."

"Didn't work, did it?"

"No."

"But you didn't give up, did you?" Susan continued icily, looking at Cindy's pale face, her skin drawn by fatigue even in sleep. "You just kept hammering away at her until you beat her down. Like I said. You and dear, sweet Jason have a lot in common."

"*Corazon,*" murmured Raul. "Trace is not like that."

"Not to you, surely," Susan said. "You'd take his head off and make an orchid planter of it."

"You underestimate Trace," Raul said dryly. "And you misunderstand him, as well."

"Said the crocodile's brother to the curious little fish," Susan muttered in disgust. "The only reason a croc has a mouthful of teeth is so he can smile real pretty, right?"

Trace smiled.

Susan threw her hands up and didn't say anything else until the Jeep stopped in front of a stately, multistoried house that grew elegantly in the midst of the cloud forest. Cindy stirred. Reluctantly Trace eased her over onto the seat. Without waiting for anyone else to get out, he vaulted over the side of the vehicle. When a woman's broad, smiling face appeared at the front door, Trace called out in rapid Spanish mixed with hissing, harsh *indio* words. The big woman laughed and returned the bear hug Trace was giving her.

Susan sighed. "I take it that Trace is a friend of the family?"

"He is a member of the family," Raul corrected, smiling. "My cousin."

"Ah, the wonderful taste of raw foot in the mouth."

"I beg your pardon?"

"Never mind," Susan said, pushing a long strand of cinnamon hair aside. "I still think he was too hard on Cindy."

"So does he."

Susan looked startled. Before she could think of anything to say, Trace had returned.

"Tia says we can clean up and eat dinner here, but then I'm to take the Jeep and Cindy to my cabin."

Raul's eyebrows arched upward in an exact echo of Trace's dark ones. "You're not to sleep here?"

"No." Smiling, Trace switched to Spanish. "Tia wants you to have more time to get to know your…guest. Better watch it, cousin. Tia is already making up wedding lists in her mind."

An irritated expression darkened Raul's handsome features. Then he shrugged and answered in Spanish. "As always, with Tia it is easier to be as the forest and bend beneath the wind, yes?"

"You always were more successful at bending than I was, *compadre*," agreed Trace. He leaned into the Jeep, lifted Cindy into his arms and switched to English. "Wake up, princess, or get kissed by a frog."

"That's not how the fairy tale went," Cindy complained sleepily, turning her face into Trace's neck.

He closed his eyes as he felt the accidental brush of her lips against his skin. It was all he could do to control a shudder of violent response.

"That's the thing about life," he said huskily. "It's always so damned unexpected."

For instance, he hadn't expected to be spending another night alone with Cindy. In fact, he'd dragged her up half a mountain just to avoid the prospect...only to find himself booked into the fragrant, hushed silence of the Cloud Cabin. One man. One woman. One bed.

"One hell of a mess," he muttered.

A night on the hard floor had never looked so unappealing.

Cindy looked from the inky wall of forest rising on either side of the Jeep to the black shadows thrown across Trace's face by the dashboard lights. Neither moon nor stars were visible overhead. Mist seethed in silver streamers through the bright shafts of illumination given off by the Jeep's headlights.

"It's not much farther," Trace said.

His tone was like the line of his mouth. Flat, hard, unyielding. Cindy sighed. Apparently he was angry at not being allowed to stay at the big house.

"Don't blame Raul," she said hesitantly. "He couldn't have known we were coming, so he could hardly be expected to prepare rooms for us."

Trace gave Cindy a sardonic, sideways glance. "Rooms are always prepared. Raul just needed time to be alone with Susan. He wants her."

"So does every other man who's ever seen her."

"I don't."

"Yeah. Right. That's why you looked at her like you'd never seen a woman before." Suddenly Cindy laughed, remembering how she herself must have looked a few hours before. "Or not for a few days, anyway," she added.

Cindy looked down at herself and grimaced. She was wearing one of Susan's outfits. The fitted blouse and midcalf cotton-knit skirt looked smashing on Susan. Cindy, however, had more inches around the bust and hips than her willowy friend. The skirt fit in the waist and was the right length. The same could be said of the blouse. After that the only thing that could be said was that the outfit covered everything required by law.

In all, Cindy felt like a sausage stuffed into somebody else's skin. Every time she took a breath she was reminded of Susan's slender, elegant figure—and of her own, less-than-slender self.

"Fishing for compliments again?"

Cindy's bittersweet smile vanished. She didn't say another word, even when Trace stopped the Jeep long enough to put on its canvas top. The silence grew oppressive long before the Jeep's headlights picked out a small cabin tucked away just at the edge of darkness, bathed in mist and the warm silver rain that had just begun to fall. The sound of water running over the Jeep's canvas roof was soothing, almost caressing.

With a corner of her mind, Cindy wondered how Trace had known that it would rain before they reached the cabin. It was just one more of the many ways in which Trace had proven himself to be supremely at home in the cloud forest. And with each of those proofs Cindy herself had become more defensive, more determined to demonstrate to him that she wasn't simply a burden to be hauled through the wilderness like two piglets squealing in a burlap sack.

But she was a burden. It hurt to admit it, yet it was the simple truth.

Trace pulled up close to the cabin, switched to parking lights and turned off the Jeep's engine.

"In order to save a big scene when you walk into the cabin," Trace said in a clipped voice, "I'll tell you three things right now. One: there's only one bed. Two: you're sleeping in it. Three: I'll sleep on the floor or in the Jeep, whichever I decide is more comfortable.''

Cindy tried to think of something to say. Nothing came to her but the intense, unhappy realization that Trace would spend a very uncomfortable night because of her.

''That isn't necessary,'' she said quietly. ''We could share the bed. I know you don't want…that is, you wouldn't…''

''Stick my hand up your blouse?'' Trace offered in a cold voice.

Cindy made a helpless gesture. She knew that she didn't appeal to Trace sexually, but she hadn't wanted to state it quite so baldly.

''Exactly,'' she said, taking a deep breath. ''I know you don't want me so there's no reason not to…'' Her voice died as she looked into Trace's narrowed, bleak eyes and the savage lines of his face. ''I'm doing this badly, aren't I? Trace, I'm not strong enough to carry you off to a comfortable bed after you fall asleep.'' She took a deep breath and said quickly, ''I never even thanked you for that, or for all the other things you've done for me. I should have thanked you. I wanted to. I just…couldn't. Thanking you would have meant admitting that I couldn't have done it by myself, that I needed you. And years ago I swore I would never need anyone again.''

The sad, rueful sound of Cindy's laughter made Trace ache to take her in his arms, but he didn't move toward her. If he touched her he was afraid he wouldn't stop with simple comfort. He wanted her until he could barely breathe.

''But I do need you,'' Cindy continued. ''I'm way out of my depth in the cloud forest. I need you the way I've never needed anyone. It's a terrible burden for you to be needed like that and it's very uncomfortable for me. I didn't handle it well at all. You see, I've been fighting my own battles for years, and losing them when it came to that. Alone.''

Cindy made another futile gesture with her hand and then rolled down the passenger window, wanting to touch the rain. The lights of the dashboard illuminated her face and turned the water drops washing over her outstretched hand into molten gold. She brought her fingertips to her lips and delicately licked up the glittering moisture.

"Sweet," she murmured absently. "Why does that always surprise me?"

Trace clenched his jaw against the raw sound of need that had risen in his throat. Her spontaneous, utterly natural sensuality was killing him and she didn't even know it.

"What I'm trying to say," Cindy continued, holding her hand out in the rain once more, watching warm liquid gather and run down her fingers, "is that I'm sorry I was a burden to you. On the way back to Quito, I promise I'll be better at staying out of your way. As for tonight, there's no good reason that we can't share the bed."

"You are dead wrong."

Trace's dark, gritty voice was so close that Cindy turned toward him in surprise.

"What?"

"This," he said harshly.

Trace's shoulders eclipsed the dashboard lights at the same instant that his powerful hands framed Cindy's face. His mouth came down hard over hers, twisting urgently, and his tongue shot into the warm feminine darkness he had been aching to penetrate. For a long minute that was just what he did, repeatedly, claiming her mouth with a searching intimacy that made her tremble. And then she realized that Trace was trembling, too.

Trace tore his mouth away from Cindy and exited the Jeep in one continuous, savage motion. The driver's door slammed so hard behind him that Cindy flinched. Hardly able to believe that she had been kissed with such intensity, she touched her hot, softly bruised lips with fingertips still wet from the rain. The moisture she licked up with the tip of her tongue tasted of more than raindrops. There was passion and hunger, heat and strength.

She tasted of Trace.

The realization made her eyes close as a tremor of hunger and delight radiated through her, changing her body in the space of a breath, two breaths, dark fire burning.

Rich yellow light flared within the small cabin, then dimmed as Trace put the glass chimney on the lantern. The doorway became a golden rectangle that was all but filled by Trace as he left the cabin.

He stepped off the porch and walked around to the driver's side of the Jeep, heedless of the warmly falling rain that had dampened his hair and shoulders. He opened the door, turned the headlights completely off with an impatient flick of his hand and reached into the back seat. A single suitcase lay there. The suitcase was Raul's. The contents had been donated by Susan. Trace grabbed the suitcase as though he expected it to fight back, yanked it into the rain and slammed the door behind him again.

Eyes wide, Cindy watched every motion Trace made. There was none of the air of lazy, sensual humor about him that he had shown when he had kissed her in the washroom. There had been nothing languid or humorous at all about the way he had just kissed her. He had wanted her.

And he had trembled with that wanting.

The golden light spilling out of the cabin was eclipsed twice more as Trace went in, dumped the suitcase on the floor and went back out to the Jeep. He jerked open Cindy's door.

"Out," Trace said flatly.

Cindy opened her mouth.

"For your information, princess, I'm not any happier about wanting you than you are about needing me," he snarled. "So I'd advise you to get your fanny out of the Jeep and into the cabin and do it *now.*"

Chapter 10

Cindy was too surprised to speak, much less to move. Before she could gather her wits, Trace leaned in, put one arm under her knees and the other behind her back and lifted her out of the Jeep.

"You're a slow learner, aren't you?" he said roughly.

With no more warning than that, Trace caught Cindy's mouth fiercely beneath his own and tasted the soft depths behind her lips once more. This time his passion didn't catch her by surprise. Her arms slid around his hard neck as she returned the deep kiss with a hunger that equaled his. Trace groaned and his arms tightened until Cindy couldn't breathe. She didn't object. She didn't even notice. Trace was filling her senses to the point that there was no room for anything else. She gloried in the feeling, wanting nothing else, only him.

When Trace finally lifted his mouth he was breathing raggedly, trembling, holding Cindy with bruising strength while warm rain fell over both of them. She made an inarticulate sound and turned her face up into the rain, searching blindly for Trace's mouth once more.

"Cindy," he said, then groaned when he saw that light from the doorway had turned the raindrops on her lips into transparent golden gems. "My God, princess, do you know what you're promising me?"

This time Cindy didn't object to being called princess. She knew from the raw need she heard in Trace's voice and saw in his expression that he wasn't baiting her. She whispered his name as she licked raindrops from his chin and the line of his jaw. When the tip of her tongue stroked the corners of his lips, he shivered and made a sound deep in his throat. Her arms tightened around his neck, pulling her closer to his mouth. She was hungry for the heat and taste of his kiss, the sensuous consummation of his tongue mingling with hers while warm rain bathed their bodies.

Cindy didn't know the exact instant when Trace shifted her in his arms, partially releasing her so that her legs and torso flowed down his powerful body. She only knew that suddenly his hands were free to caress the rounded contours of her hips, turning her knees to water, making her as boneless as the falling rain. His long fingers kneaded her buttocks and rocked her against the heated cradle of his thighs, plainly revealing to her the extent of his own arousal.

The honesty of Trace's hunger completely undid Cindy. She had never known anything like it from a man. She gave a husky little cry and moved sinuously against Trace, slowly stroking his body with her own, making the sweet, dark fire within both of them blaze higher. Trace's fingers raked down the back of her thighs, parting them even as he lifted her and held her pressed intimately against the blunt ridge of flesh that was proof of his nearly uncontrollable desire for her. His hips moved once, hard, as though he were plunging into her, and then he moved very deliberately, shaking, listening to her shattered breaths, feeling her tremble wildly as she tried to get even closer to him.

At that instant Trace knew Cindy wanted him as much as he wanted her—and he was so hungry for her that he thought he would die of it. He whispered her name again and again between hard, deep kisses, wanting all of her, wanting to be sheathed within her satin body until she burned out of control, showering both of them with a blazing, incandescent release.

But not yet. Not here. Not this instant.

Now that Trace knew Cindy wanted him too much to refuse him, he was able to control his own violent need. He wanted to share much more with her than a fast tumble in the rain. He needed to know every bit of her skin, to taste her wild hunger, to absorb her into himself. Only then could he begin to ease the raging hunger that had consumed him from the first moment he had sensed the untouched woman smoldering beneath Cindy's aloof exterior.

Reluctantly Trace let Cindy slide down his body until she was standing once more on the soft, moss-covered floor of the cloud forest. She swayed uncertainly, barely able to support herself. Not understanding why he had let go of her, clinging to his hard, bare forearms for balance, she watched him with dazed eyes.

"Trace?" Cindy managed to whisper. "Don't you want—"

The question ended in a husky cry when Trace's hands moved over Cindy's rain-slicked blouse, caressing the nipples that had hardened into crowns beneath wet, clinging cloth.

"Oh, yes, I *want*," Trace said, his voice deep and as dark as Cindy's eyes. "I want you until I'm crazy with it. I want things with you I've only imagined before, and I want things I've never imagined until right now. You make me wild," he said, shuddering as he fought to control the passion that was burning in the very marrow of his bones, burning through the self-discipline he had always taken for granted.

But no more. Through her he had discovered fierce, nearly uncontrollable currents deep within himself, a need to be one with her that was as old as the cloud forest and as new as each breath he took.

Slowly Trace lifted Cindy, bringing her breasts level with his open mouth. With breathtaking care he bit the tip of first one breast and then the other before he returned to the first nipple, drawing it into the hungry, hot depths of his mouth. Wave after wave of sensation burst through Cindy until she felt as though she were dissolving in hot rain, spinning away, burning as invisible streamers of fire seethed through her.

The sound of Cindy's low, broken moan was the sweetest music Trace had ever heard. His fingers caressed her other breast, drawing more of the husky music from Cindy's lips. He lowered her to the ground once more.

Without lifting his mouth from her breast he began unbuttoning her blouse, working up from the taut navel he longed to kiss. When the buttons parted between her full breasts he ran his tongue over her cloth-covered nipple once more before his mouth released her by degrees, biting gently while the whisper of raindrops absorbed her shivering cries.

Finally Trace drew both hands upward from Cindy's waist until they rested in the warm, deep valley between her breasts. Slowly he spread his fingers wide, peeling the wet blouse away from her body until she wore nothing but rain turned golden by the lantern light. Transparent drops fell onto her high, full breasts and gathered on the twin pink crowns.

He had never seen anything to equal her beauty. His hands trembled as he took the warm weight of her onto his palms. With a murmured, reverent word, he sank to his knees and licked the raindrops from her naked breasts.

Cindy saw Trace's lips part, saw the pale flash of his teeth and then felt the piercing sweetness of his mouth cherishing her. Wave after wave of pleasure washed through her, making her sway. Instinctively she braced herself against her lover's powerful body, holding his head to her breasts with a primitive, fierce pleasure.

Trace's hands shaped Cindy's spine, her hips, her thighs, her calves, kneading and caressing repeatedly, sensitizing her flesh with each sweep of skin over skin. The last time his hands stroked down the length of her body, every bit of her clothing came away and pooled around her ankles. The feeling of warm rain gliding over her skin so intimately was indescribable. She started to say something, but her breath and her thoughts scattered when one of Trace's hands slid up between her legs until he could go no higher.

"Open for me, princess," he whispered, biting gently at Cindy's breasts and belly, caressing her with his tongue, his touches as warm and soft as the rain laving her. "I won't hurt you. I just want to touch you. That's all. Just…touch."

With a stifled cry Cindy kicked free of the clothes that were swathing her ankles. Then she stood trembling, open to the rain and to the sensual caresses of the man who knelt at her feet.

Gently, inevitably, Trace's fingertips combed through the thick triangle of midnight hair until he could trace Cindy's layered softness. He cherished her with exquisite care, memorizing her with repeated gliding touches until he knew her better than she knew herself. She said a broken word that could have been his name, but the word was lost in the husky sound of triumph and need Trace made as he slowly penetrated the hot secrets of her body. When he could go no deeper he withdrew as slowly as he had entered, leaving her empty and trembling.

"Trace," she whispered. "Trace, I…"

Cindy's words became a low moan as his caress took her slowly once more. She shivered with each movement of his hand, each tender penetration and gliding withdrawal, tension gathering within her until it burst sweetly, surprising her even as it drenched her in pleasure. Her trembling legs gave way. Slowly she sank down onto the moss-clothed ground until she was kneeling before Trace, bracing herself on his broad shoulders. He smiled darkly and licked the rain from her lips while he stole into her body once more, caressing her, savoring her exquisite softness, absorbing her intimate shivering as her body changed in anticipation of the much deeper sharing to come.

Cindy clung to Trace with her lips and her body while pleasure washed through her to him. He clenched against a tearing shaft of need as he felt her abandoned response to his caresses. He wanted her until it was agony not to take her. He burned to tear off his clothes and sheath himself inside her with a single hot thrust of his body; but despite the repeated, secret rain of her pleasure, she still was so tight to his touch that he was afraid she wasn't ready to accept him.

And he wanted—needed—to be certain of her pleasure. Since they had met she had suffered too much because of his miscalculations. When he finally slid into her clinging heat, there must be no question that whatever cries came from her sweet lips would tell him of ecstasy, not pain.

Trace's hand moved until his thumb could tease the velvet nub hidden within Cindy's softness. Her eyes closed and her head tilted back helplessly as pleasure splintered through her in shivering waves of heat. Her fingers dug into his shoulders and she arched toward him, her body drawn so tightly by need that she couldn't even form the words to tell him that he must take her or she would die.

Trace understood, yet he did not give Cindy what she was crying for. Instead he slid one powerful arm around her waist, supporting her while his caresses took from her the ability to hold herself upright. Eyes half closed, smiling despite his own violent need, he absorbed her sweet cries, wishing he could drink her essence as well, wanting to take her into himself so completely that he would never again feel the emptiness of being separate from her.

After drawing a final, helpless cry from Cindy, Trace caught her mouth beneath his own. Gently he brought her back to herself, stroking her without demand, holding her, kissing her repeatedly, lightly. The heat and taste of him made her sigh with pleasure. Slowly her hands began exploring the broad shoulders and strong arms that had supported her while sweet fire had consumed her. She had never known pleasure such as he had just given to her so unselfishly. She hadn't even known such feelings were possible.

"You're..." Cindy shivered and looked at the golden light and black shadows lying across Trace's face. "There aren't any words," she said huskily. "Masculine. Hot. Powerful. All true, but not the *truth*. I don't know how to describe you except, perhaps, this...."

Slender hands framed Trace's cheeks. Soft lips brushed his mouth again and then again. The moist tip of Cindy's tongue traced the sensitive outline of his lips and dipped hotly into his mouth, withdrawing before he could even react. Her teeth closed lovingly on his lower lip, holding it captive for her caressing tongue. He groaned her name and tightened his arms around her as though to hold her still for the kind of kiss he suddenly, desperately needed. Her fingers spread wide across his chest, but not in an attempt to push him away. She kneaded his flesh with an open appreciation of his hard body that was as exciting as her tongue teasing him.

Hungrily Trace wrapped his fingers around Cindy's head and took all of her mouth, consuming her with deep, hot strokes of his tongue, feeling her instant, utterly honest response. Her hands moved over his chest, tugging at the buttons on his shirt until suddenly it came apart. Her fingers tangled hungrily in the thick, damp mat of hair that she had wanted to touch since the first time she had seen the tempting thatch curling up from his open collar. She could not touch him enough. Biting softly, tugging, tasting, her hands and mouth roamed over the masculine territory she had uncovered.

With Cindy's help Trace shrugged his shirt aside, letting it fall heedlessly to the ground. Her palms slicked across his wet shoulders and down his arms to his fingertips, then back up again until her fingers curled into the fine hair beneath his arms. She made a murmurous sound of pleasure and stroked gently, savoring the unexpected softness concealed on such a hard masculine body.

Trace's breath caught and stayed as a thick wedge in his throat. He hadn't known how sensitive he could be, nor how arousing it could feel to have a woman slowly, tenderly devouring him. The feel of Cindy's lips and hot tongue nuzzling down his neck, her teeth biting in exciting counterpoint, her breath caressing him in soft bursts of heat—everything about her open enjoyment of his body set Trace afire. When her tongue found one of the tight, small nipples hidden beneath his chest hair, he shuddered and dragged at breath, unable to get enough oxygen to feed the searing currents of pleasure and hunger coursing through his body. He tried to stifle a groan when she circled his nipple with her tongue and then caressed him with the changing pressures of her mouth. He couldn't bear any more without crying out for her to stop, yet he would have died if she'd stopped.

"Cindy," Trace said finally, his voice hoarse. "You are killing me so sweetly...."

In answer her hands kneaded down his muscular torso to his waist. Turned back by cloth, Cindy's fingers hesitated, then dipped down inside the waistband. Trace sucked in air with a soft ripping sound that was echoed an instant later as his zipper was drawn down by her warm, wet fingers. Her right hand slid inside his slacks, finding him unerringly, rubbing over his rigid male flesh with her palm, loving his heat and the knowledge that it was she who had made him so swollen and hard.

Trace bit off a curse and a plea as Cindy caressed him, moaning even as he did. Finally he caught her hand with his own, trying to stop her, but he couldn't bring himself to remove the sweet pressure of her palm from his throbbing body. He permitted himself to move his hips once, very slowly, letting her know his full length, feeling a groan wrenched from his throat when her fingernails raked lightly, devastatingly over the cloth that still covered his erect flesh.

"Stop," Trace said hoarsely, moving against Cindy in frank contradiction of his own command. "Oh, baby, stop."

"I can't," Cindy admitted, her voice trembling. "Trace, I've never wanted to touch a man before. I've never wanted…this."

Cindy's hand eased away from captivity and slid inside Trace's briefs. The instant their bare skin met, Trace stiffened and shuddered as though lightning were coursing softly, hotly, wildly through him. He could no more have prevented the slow surge of his hips as he gave himself to her than the warm rain could have prevented itself from falling into the waiting forest.

"Cindy," Trace whispered, holding her hand pressed tightly against him, trying not to move, failing, wanting to die of the pleasure her words and touch had given him. "Cindy, I need you so much I can't even…" His words became a groan as her fingers curled around him, holding him boldly captive, learning his masculine textures in the same way he had learned the secret feminine contours of her desire.

"If you want me, take me," Cindy finally murmured, biting a hard ridge of muscle on Trace's chest.

"Not here. Not now. Not in the rain."

"Yes, here. Now. In the rain." Her lips sucked lightly on Trace's biceps, his shoulder, his neck, his dark, sexy smile. She smiled at him in return. "Did you know that rain tastes like wine when I drink it from your skin?"

Trace's whole body jerked with the lightning stroke of pleasure that raced through him at her words. When she lifted her head he was watching her, his eyes heavy lidded, glittering in the golden light, and she knew that he was going to take her there, right there, with the warm rain bathing their naked bodies.

"Undress me," Trace said almost roughly, biting Cindy's lips, making her moan. He felt her palms on his skin, sliding beneath his briefs, beginning to uncover him. "Wait," he said through clenched teeth, half laughing, half groaning. "If you don't start with my boots, I swear to God I'll still be wearing them when I take you."

Cindy's hands hesitated. She looked up at Trace with hunger and laughter and curiosity in her eyes. "Would you like that?"

Trace smiled down at Cindy as he ran his fingertip over one of her nipples, lifted his hand to his lips and licked up the drops of water he had taken from her tightly drawn crest. "I'd rather be like you, princess, as naked as the rain. But if you want me wearing jungle boots, I sure as hell won't argue the point. I'll take you any way I can get you."

Cindy drew in a deep, ragged breath and brought her hand slowly out of Trace's clothes, caressing him lovingly even in the act of withdrawing her touch. "None of my fantasies involve men wearing jungle boots," she admitted, her voice husky, breathless.

"What do they involve?"

"My fantasies?"

"Yes," he whispered.

"Being wanted for myself. Just me."

"That's all?"

"It's the world, Trace."

"Then I give it you," he said softly against Cindy's lips, kissing her slowly, deeply. "I want you until I can't stand up. You, Cindy. Just you." He bit her lips with tender care, making her shiver and reach hungrily for him. He caught her seeking tongue between his teeth and raked the moist flesh very gently, savoring her tiny whimpers of pleasure. "I want you until it's like dying not to have you. But before I slide into that sweet body of yours, you'll be wanting me in the same way. I swear it."

Slowly Trace released Cindy. He sat and began unlacing his right boot. She went to work on the other one, making little progress because every time she looked up the long length of his legs to his unfastened pants and naked chest her fingers shook so much they were all but useless. After a few moments she simply gave up and stared at him, lost in wondering enjoyment of his powerful body.

When Cindy's hands went completely still, Trace glanced at her, saw her looking at him with frankly sensual approval, and asked himself almost wildly how he was going to keep his hands off her long enough to get undressed.

"Close your eyes, princess," Trace said huskily, kicking off one boot and reaching for the other.

"Why?" she said, startled out of her reverie. "Are you shy?"

"Not likely," he said, his voice caught between laughter and raw passion. "But I'll never get this boot off if you keep looking at me like you can't decide whether I'd taste better with ketchup or mustard. The way you lick your lips is distracting and sexy as hell."

There was an instant of silence before Cindy's laughter rippled in musical counterpart to the rain. Still smiling she closed her eyes and began patting air and raindrops until she found Trace's single booted foot. Getting in the way more than she helped, tangling her fingers with his, she loosened laces until together the two of them managed to tug off Trace's remaining boot. Going only by touch from his naked feet to his clothed knees, her hands worked their warm way up his legs.

"I've never done this with my eyes closed," Cindy said, searching blindly, caressingly, slowly, heading in the general direction of the waistband of Trace's pants. "Or open, either," she added absently, kneading the clenched power of his calves, his thighs, testing the strength and resilience of his muscles. "You're very strong." She heard her own words and laughed softly. "That's like saying rain is wet. Of course rain is wet and Trace Rawlings is strong. It's just that I've never felt…and you're so…"

Cindy's voice trailed off into the sound of raindrops falling as her hands caressed slowly higher. Somehow Trace had managed to peel his remaining clothes down over his hips while Cindy explored her way up his legs. Now he watched, frozen, while her slender fingers progressed upward toward his naked, rain-slicked flesh. He felt as though he were being drawn on a rack. When he could bear it no longer, he twisted suddenly, kicking free of the last of his clothing.

"Trace?" Cindy asked.

He watched the widening of her eyes, the parting of her lips, and her fingers reaching toward him, trembling. Suddenly she became motionless and looked only at his eyes.

"Trace?" she whispered.

"Whatever you want, princess," he said huskily.

She smiled almost wistfully. "And here I am without a lick of mustard or ketchup," she murmured.

Trace laughed until Cindy's palms stroked all the way up his thighs and her thumbs traced the deep creases where his legs joined his powerful torso. Then his laughter became a hoarse groan. She jerked her hands away.

"Oh, Trace, I'm sorry! I didn't mean to hurt you!"

At first Trace couldn't believe he had heard Cindy correctly. A single look at her downcast face told him that she had meant every word. The memory of her tight satin depths returned to him. Although there had been no virginal barrier to his searching caresses, it was clear to him now that whatever Cindy's past experience with men might have been, it had been long ago and not terribly illuminating.

"You didn't hurt me," Trace said, his voice gentle and rough at the same time. He took Cindy's hands in his own and pulled them back up his thighs. "It just felt so good that I…ahhh," he groaned, "*yes*, like that, just like that…again, princess. Just once more," he groaned, "then…no more, please, no…"

"You're so hot," Cindy whispered, feeling Trace's vitality radiate through her encircling hands as she caressed him wonderingly, savoring his unexpected response, sensing more than the slick heat of rain on her fingers.

Shuddering with pleasure, Trace gently, inexorably freed himself from the sensual captivity of Cindy's hands. Slowly he lifted her until she was astride his thighs. Raindrops and the lantern light falling through the cabin's open door gilded her breasts and the subtle curve of her stomach and made a shimmering mystery of the lush black cloud nestled between her thighs. He tangled his fingers in that cloud slowly, searchingly, rediscovering the depth of her softness and the hot pleasures of her secret, sensual rain. When he finally withdrew she whimpered deep in her throat.

"Did that hurt?" Trace asked, already knowing the answer, wanting Cindy to know it, too.

"Only when you stopped." Cindy's eyes opened and focused on the harshly drawn lines of her lover's face. "Don't stop, Trace," she breathed. Then she saw the rain glistening on his lips and added huskily, "And a kiss…your taste…I love the taste of you."

Trace's hands were trembling when he pulled Cindy down to him. Even as his tongue thrust between her lips, the taut peaks of her breasts rubbed against the mat of hair covering his chest, sending sensations twisting wildly through her. She moaned into his mouth, tasting him, wanting him, shaking with her wanting. When his hand slid between their bodies and captured one nipple, rolling it, tugging on it, she felt fire radiate out from the pit of her stomach. Instinctively her hips moved, caressing him even as she searched for a way to ease the hungry aching between her legs.

Trace knew what Cindy wanted. He wanted it too, wanted it the same way she did, shaking with the wanting. Suddenly his palms slicked over her hips and down the back of her legs. Long, powerful fingers bit sensually into the soft flesh high on the inside of her thighs, easing them farther and farther apart while his mouth mated rhythmically with hers and his tongue promised her pleasures she had never imagined. With his teasing fingertips he encouraged her to abandon all hesitation, arousing her until she wept and opened herself to him and to the hot rain washing over her violently sensitive skin.

When Cindy felt the first blunt probing of his flesh she gasped. Trace caressed her slowly, outlining her, learning her once more, letting her know his own textures, teaching her that for all his hard strength he could be deliciously smooth, like satin stretched over throbbing heat. For long moments he teased her, preparing her with tiny penetrations and withdrawals until she moaned brokenly and moved her hips, instinctively trying to capture more of him.

"Easy, princess," Trace said, his voice soft despite the cruel need that made his body clench as though he were being tortured. Once again he eased into the outer edges of her feminine warmth, parting her delicately, withdrawing, returning. "We're going to take it slowly…sweetly…slowly…."

"Trace," Cindy said raggedly, shivering, wild for more of him yet not experienced enough to know how to manage it. "Now? Like this?"

"Oh, yes. Just like…*this*. You're so tight, so sleek. Slowly, baby, slow..." Trace groaned against her lips. "You're beautiful, Cindy...hot...perfect. Don't let me hurt you," he said raggedly, pressing deeper, feeling her trembling response as though it were his own. "Am I...hurting you?"

Cindy tried to answer but she could not. The slow consummation was taking her breath, her voice, her mind, her soul. She tried to tell Trace how exquisite it felt to be filled so tenderly, so carefully, so completely, but speech was impossible for her. She shivered repeatedly as rings of pleasure expanded up from their joined bodies and burst, drenching her in sweetness and heat.

Trace felt each hidden quivering of her satin flesh, each secret rain of pleasure easing his way. The unexpected, deep intimacy of the sharing took him right up to the edge of his self-control, wrenching a groan from him, unraveling his voice and his breath, unraveling him.

"Dark...fire," Trace groaned, kissing Cindy between each word, biting her tenderly, pressing farther into her with each caress, each word. "So hot...so...deep. Ahh, love, I..."

And then Trace could say no more. He was fully sheathed within Cindy, held tightly, completely, and they were sharing every fragmented breath, every soft groan, hot rain sliding over them, joining their bodies in an incandescent intimacy that was so intense he didn't know if he would survive it.

Cindy felt the shudder that took Trace even as he moved within her. In the wake of his movement, exquisite sensations radiated through her, overwhelming her. She moaned and moved in instinctive counterpoint to Trace, redoubling the advance and retreat of his hard flesh within her, crying softly as ecstasy stole through her again and again, dark fire blooming, lush flames climbing higher, consuming her until she called out with something close to fear.

Despite his own violent need, Trace heard Cindy and went utterly still. His hands shook as he threaded his fingers through her wet hair, lifting her head from his chest until he could look into her eyes. Her face was streaked with tears and rain, her eyes were wide, nearly wild, and her mouth was swollen by the passionate kisses she had given and taken.

"Am I hurting you?" Trace asked, his voice ragged.

Cindy's head moved in a slow negative that made her breasts stir over Trace's hot, wet skin. "It felt so good...incredible...and then almost...frightening."

"Frightening? How?"

"I don't...I can't..." Her voice frayed. "When you move...when I feel you inside me..." She shivered and cried out softly as echoes of ecstasy stirred within her, urging her to give herself to her lover once more. "It's the sweetest kind of burning," she whispered, "and I'm being consumed by it, each breath I take, each time you..."

"Do this?" Trace asked, measuring himself slowly within Cindy, smiling darkly when she moaned her pleasure.

"Yes," she said shakily, closing her eyes. "Oh, yes, Trace."

"That's how I want you to feel," he whispered, easing his hands from Cindy's hair, finding and caressing her breasts, rubbing her nipples until she moaned and he felt again the melting heat of her pleasure as she tightened around him. "I feel the same way when you move. Look at me, Cindy."

Her eyes opened slowly, heavy lidded and almost wild with a combination of passion and hesitation. "Do you really feel like I do?" she asked.

Trace moved again inside her; retreating and returning with excruciating care, pleasuring both of them until they trembled.

"Yes, I feel it. I'm in you so deep and you take me so perfectly...you're in me, too," he said in a gritty voice, sliding into Cindy slowly, feeling her move with him again, wanting to drown in the wild, honeyed rain of her passion. "That's where the sweetness comes, and the fear," he said.

He watched her expression change as ecstasy consumed her softly with each of his motions within her. Seeing his body transforming her excited him almost beyond bearing.

"I've never been this close to anyone before," he said almost roughly, shaking with the restraint he was imposing on himself. "You're burning me so softly, so hotly, it's like dying. Move with me princess. Please. Tell me that it's good for you...." Words died as a low groan was dragged from Trace by the gliding motion of

Cindy's hips. "Yes," he said deeply. "Yes, like that. Come with me, love. I need you…with me."

Trace's words and his hands and his heat dissolved all of Cindy's fears. When his fingers closed lovingly around her nipples, tugging at them, hot streamers of sensation overwhelmed her. She arched helplessly into the caress, sliding over him, making both of them cry out with the pleasure they were sharing. Heat welled up within her once more, a shimmering need that could no longer be denied. He thrust deeply into her, taking everything she had to give, giving everything he had in return.

Wonder shivered in Cindy's voice as rapture gently convulsed her, stealing through her body again and again, consuming her. Trace heard the rippling cries of her completion even as he felt the sweet contractions sweeping through her. His own release burst from him, more piercing with each deep pulse, ecstasy pouring through him until he thought there could be no more…yet still the pulses continued through him until he arched like a drawn bow and cried out hoarsely, giving himself to her as he had never given himself to anything, even the hushed mystery of cloud forest and rain.

Chapter 11

Cindy slept long after dawn filled the cabin with a diffuse silver-gold light. She awoke for only an instant when Trace eased from the bed. As soon as he brushed her lips with love words and soft reassurances she slept again. He smiled down at her while he drew the sheet up over her breasts. The temptation to lie down next to her and make love to her in the full light of day was almost overwhelming. All that kept him from giving in were the pale lavender shadows that lay beneath Cindy's eyes, shadows that silently announced her need for more sleep.

Trace lifted his hands carefully from the sheet and turned away from Cindy. He knew if he kept on looking at her, he would touch her. If he touched her, he would make love to her. If he made love to her, he would take her again and again until he lacked the strength even to raise his head, for she was both a wild sweetness in his soul and a dark fire burning in his blood.

Just the thought of joining his body to hers once more made breath hiss between Trace's teeth. Blood pumped through him suddenly, hotly, filling him until he ached. He had never known a lover who suited him half so well. There were so many things he wanted to share with her, so many ways two people could enjoy one another. He wanted them all with her, every one of them, but most of all he wanted to watch her while he pleasured her, to see her skin flush with passion, to taste her, to feel her give herself to him over and over again, sensual fire burning through all inhibitions, all differences, fire burning until nothing remained but two lovers joined all the way to their souls.

If I don't get the hell out of this cabin, I'm going to pull down that sheet and slide into her before she's even awake, before she even knows if she wants me.

And then Trace caught a glimpse of himself in the mirror—stained khaki shirt and pants, beaten-up jungle boots, heavy stubble making his jaw even more square, his dark hair and mustache combed by nothing but sleep and Cindy's fingers. He looked rough, primitive, fully suited to the untamed land surrounding him.

Will my princess want me now, in daylight, when she can see so clearly what a peon her lover is?

Frowning, Trace turned away from the mirror and tried to shake off the feelings of rootlessness and worthlessness that had once defined his life. He and Raul were related, but only because Raul's uncle had felt a sense of responsibility toward a wild American rose whose child probably had not been his. Megan Rawlings had died weeks after giving birth to Trace. Though her passport proclaimed that she had been American, no family could be found in the United States. There was no one to take in the motherless baby.

Finally a priest had picked up Trace and carried him to the Almeda *hacienda*. Once there he had calmly announced that God had answered Esteban Almeda's prayers. A son had been born. Esteban's barren wife had wept, crossed herself and accepted her husband's purported child into her arms and her life with the sweetness of a true angel. Yet despite Maria's love and Esteban's pride in having finally attained a son, Trace had grown up knowing in his soul that he didn't belong. He wasn't a true Almeda. The Almedas were the aristocracy of Ecuador, and he was the bastard child of an American woman who had had neither family nor husband to call her own.

Trace had grown up half in the United States and half in the Andes he loved so well. It had taken him decades of hard, dangerous living before he had accepted his own worth as a human being. It had been many years since he had felt himself less than the equal of any man solely on the basis of family background or personal wealth.

Yet he felt inadequate today. Cindy had given him so much, surrendering her fears and herself to him, trusting him with her lovely, responsive body...and there was nothing he could give to her in return that wasn't already hers by birth.

Cynthia Edwinna Ryan McCall and a man whose only birthright is a hard body and a skull to match. What a pair to draw to. It's so funny it hurts.

Shutting the cabin door softly behind himself, Trace stepped out into the brilliant mist that permeated and defined the cloud forest. The rain had stopped sometime during the night, leaving behind little evidence of the storm. Only the places where man had carved out roads or fields showed the results of last night's rain in swaths of mud and puddles. The untouched forest took in moisture like an immense, living sponge. Later when the true monsoon rains came, even the forest's capacity to absorb water would be exceeded and the rivers would run brown, but for now the streams were still clear and sweet, gleaming like polished crystal in the diffuse light.

Trace found a nearly invisible trail leading down into the huge, steep ravine that lay just beyond the cabin. He had discovered the twisting, rugged trail years before. It led to a series of waterfalls and pools that were visited only by mist and wild animals. There orchid plants thrived in lush profusion, their extraordinary flowers swaying gracefully in the silence. The orchid garden was a secret place, a hushed landscape where time didn't exist. Trace had gone there often during his wildest years, when he had fought against everything—and himself most of all.

The trail hadn't changed. It was still narrow, easily lost, overgrown, infused with mist. Even so Trace rarely wielded the machete that hung at his belt. He didn't want to make a clear path for any man to use. He wanted the place of orchids and silence to remain as he had found it. Unknown.

He had never taken a single orchid from there, though he knew that even a thousand flowers would not have been missed from the massed magnificence of the ravine's garden. It was simply that there had never been a good enough reason for Trace to make the difficult descent to the hidden river and the arduous ascent out of the ravine simply for a handful of flowers, no matter how rare or beautiful they might be.

But there was a reason now. Down in the ravine's misty silence grew an orchid that had no name, an orchid that had never graced civilized greenhouses or the jeweled breasts of royalty. Of all the orchids Trace had ever seen, that wild orchid was the most superb, as perfectly sensuous and elegant as a pearl. That orchid was something no amount of money could buy, because only Trace knew where the orchid grew and no amount of money had tempted him to tell of the hidden ravine.

It wasn't money that tempted him now. It was the fact that he had finally found a woman worthy of the orchid's beauty.

The morning was half gone when Cindy woke again. The sound of the cabin door opening and closing curled through her dreams, followed by less definable sounds as Trace took off his boots and clothes and walked to the bedside. Cindy murmured and stirred languidly, reaching for Trace before her eyes were even open, wanting to curl up against him and hear his heart beating beneath her cheek as she had before she slept. When her hands met only tangled sheets, she opened her eyes.

"Trace?"

His name spoken in Cindy's husky voice sent a primitive shiver of sensation down Trace's spine.

"I'm right here, princess."

She turned toward the sound and thought she was still dreaming. Trace's nude body glowed with a sheen of moisture as though oiled. Various textures of hair had been slicked by water until curling patterns were created across his thighs and torso. The muscles she had kneaded with her hands and tested with her teeth were no longer concealed by darkness. He was even more powerful than she had guessed, and so compelling in his masculine beauty that she forgot to breathe.

Trace wanted Cindy with a force that he couldn't conceal, a hunger that made an answering heat uncurl deep in the pit of Cindy's stomach. As she looked at his strength and his arousal, she could scarcely believe how gentle he had been with her last night. He could have overwhelmed her, taken what he wanted and given nothing in return…yet he had loved her so tenderly, making her feel as fragile as a virgin, as cherished as a fairy-tale princess.

"But I'm not a princess," Cindy said, her voice soft, her eyes openly approving of everything she saw in the man who stood naked before her.

"You are to me," Trace said simply. Green eyes searched Cindy's face, hardly able to believe the sensuous elegance of silky black hair, porcelain skin, eyes as brilliant as black diamonds and a mouth whose intense pink exactly matched the flushed heart of the orchid cupped in his hands. As Trace bent down to brush his lips over Cindy's soft mouth, he whispered, "You're too beautiful for a peon, but I want you so much my hands are shaking. Will you make love with me, even though I'm not a prince?"

Cindy's heart turned over at the combination of hunger and hesitation she saw in Trace's haunted green eyes. She reached for him, ignoring the sheet that slipped down to her waist. Slowly she rubbed her fingers over his skin, savoring its satin dampness. He smelled of mist and forest and passion. The combination made her dizzy.

"You're a man," she said huskily, "more man than I've ever known. That's all I care about." A delicate shiver took her as her lips pressed against the taut heat of Trace's navel. "And if I can't hold you inside my body soon, I'll die."

Trace's eyes closed but for a shimmering flash of green as a knife of pleasure and desire turned in his loins. The merest thread of a groan escaped his lips while the tip of Cindy's tongue probed the taut hollow of his navel. When her hands smoothed down his torso, a torrent of desire poured through him, bringing him to his knees beside the bed.

"Cindy, I…" he whispered, but no other words could push past the aching closure of his throat when he looked into the midnight clarity of her eyes. He bent his head until he could cherish her lips with his own. When he lifted his head once more, he could speak.

Slowly he opened his hands so that she could see what had been cupped protectively within. "I brought this for you."

For an instant Cindy thought that it was a butterfly poised so delicately on Trace's hard palm. Then she inhaled an elusive, fragile fragrance and realized that the graceful curves belonged to the most extraordinary orchid she had ever seen. The satin petals were long and creamy, with the faintest flush of living pink in the veins. In sensuous contrast was the flower's lush fuchsia lip with its elegant frill. At the edge of the frill the pink color darkened until it was nearly black. The balance of color and shape in the orchid was flawless, drawing the eye unerringly toward the throat of the flower, where vibrant fuchsia again slid down the scale of color into a velvety darkness that was just a few shades removed from midnight.

"When I undressed you, I thought of this orchid," Trace said huskily, bending over Cindy, softly pressing her back into the bed until she was half sitting, half reclining against the heaped pillows. "Your breasts are like the orchid's petals, fine textured, creamy, flawless." He bent his head and kissed one of her breasts, catching its tip in his mouth, drawing the sensitive flesh into a tight peak before he released it. "When you're aroused, your lips and nipples are the same color as the orchid's mouth."

The hand holding the orchid came to a rest between Cindy's breasts. "Yes," Trace murmured, comparing the colors. "Like that. Vivid and alive. It's the same here," he said, easing the sheet down until his hand nestled between her legs. "So perfect. Too perfect for a peon. *Princess.*"

"Trace," Cindy whispered, sensing sadness beneath his words, as though he were retreating from her even while his words turned her into honey and sweetly devoured her. "I'm not a princess and I'm far from perfect. My nose is too long and my eyes are too far apart and my figure went out of style a hundred years ago and I've got broken fingernails and scrapes and bruises all over and my hair—" The tumble of words stopped as though cut by a knife. "Trace?" she asked in an aching whisper. "What is it? What's wrong?"

He released the orchid, letting it settle over Cindy's navel as gently as a breath. For the first time he saw the signs left by the cloud forest on her soft body. With gentle fingertips he touched each small shadow bruise, each tiny abrasion, and he cursed himself in searing silence for what he had done to Cindy when he had forced her to march through the cloud forest simply because he hadn't been able to bear the thought of spending another night alone with her and not having her.

And then the night had come, and they had been alone and he had taken her waiting softness and known the beauty of her dark, shimmering fire.

"Does this hurt?" Trace asked, gently picking up Cindy's hand and kissing a slender finger that had a scraped knuckle and a broken fingernail.

"No, it's—"

"Does this?" he interrupted, brushing his lips across a pale bruise on the inside of Cindy's arm.

"No, I—"

"This?" Trace interrupted again, touching his mouth to a small abrasion on her shoulder.

"No, really, I—" Suddenly Cindy's breath sucked in and her thoughts scattered as Trace's tongue gently laved a nearly invisible scrape. Her pent-up breath came out as a sigh when his mouth moved on, leaving her hungry for more.

The tender catechism continued as Trace brushed caresses across Cindy's face and down her other arm, asking at each tiny wound if it hurt, being reassured that it didn't by her half breaths and shivering murmurs of pleasure before he went on to explore other satin territory. Then he came to a faint, rosy mark at the base of her neck and another matching mark between her full breasts.

"Oh, princess, I'm sorry," Trace whispered. "I didn't mean to hurt you."

"You didn't," Cindy said in a husky voice, trembling as his tongue and lips caressed the narrow valley between her breasts.

"Like hell I didn't."

The mattress shifted as Trace flowed onto the bed and knelt over Cindy, looking for other telltale marks of his passion on her creamy skin. She started to object once more that he hadn't hurt her at all, that he had been so gentle despite his own violent need that it still made her heart turn over just to think about it. The words never got past the breath closing her throat when she saw the contrast of Trace's dark stubble and her pale breasts and the sensuous stroking of his tongue over imagined hurts.

"You're so smooth, so gentle," Trace said, caressing her with each word, "and I'm neither. Cindy…Cindy…" His voice caught as he kissed the taut inward curves of her waist. With each caress he looked for and sometimes thought he had found the barest shadows of the previous night, when his mouth and hands had not been smooth enough, gentle enough for the princess who had trusted him. "So perfect," he whispered, caressing the fine-grained skin below her navel with his lips. "I never should have touched you, princess. God knows I tried not to. And God knows I failed."

Cindy tried to reassure Trace, but all she could force past the aching in her throat was an unraveling sigh that was his name. The sight and feel of his face pressed against her abdomen while the tip of his tongue just brushed her skin, caused heat to uncurl in the pit of her stomach, dark fire rippling out through her body, transforming her.

One large hand closed gently around the orchid, caging the flower without moving it. While the tip of his tongue skimmed the orchid's outlines, his other hand gently stroked the silk of Cindy's inner thighs. With tender thoroughness his tongue traced every curve and fold and indentation of the warm orchid held within his circling fingers. He breathed in the flower's exotic essence even as he ravished it so softly that not a mark was left on its lush surface.

"So delicate," Trace said, his voice deep as he sipped at the orchid's exquisite fringe and at the same time stroked his warm palm along Cindy's inner thighs, coming closer to her most sensitive flesh without ever quite caressing it.

When only the center of the orchid remained untouched, his tongue dipped into the soft fuchsia throat until he could taste the fragrant, velvet darkness hidden within the yielding petals. "So lush," he breathed, skimming just once over Cindy's flushed, aching softness.

Cindy tried to stifle a small sound of pleasure and need, but Trace heard it. Slowly he looked up into her midnight eyes. The hand that had caged the orchid during its tender ravishment opened, leaving the flower nestled in her navel. Languidly he rubbed the back of both hands against her inner thighs, caressing and teasing her legs farther apart, giving her light touches and skimming promises that made her breath catch. When at last she lay before him with nothing between them but the memory of the orchid, he bent down to her. As his breath flowed across her flushed softness she gasped.

"Trace?"

"It's all right," Trace said tenderly, his deep voice as caressing as his breath. "You're like the orchid. Perfect. And like the orchid, you were made for this. This is what I should have done last night, enjoying you without hurting you, leaving you…unmarked."

"You didn't hurt me last night. You…" Cindy's breath tore softly. "What are…ahhh, Trace, you're making me…"

The ragged whimper of pleasure that came from her trembling lips was all that she could say, the only sound left to her, and she made it repeatedly while Trace caressed her as completely as he had the orchid. The knowledge that he was taking as much pleasure from the intimacy as she was made the gentle ravishing all the more overwhelming. She tried to speak, to tell Trace what sweet wildness he was unlocking within her, but all that came from her lips were rippling cries of passion.

When Cindy moaned and arched against Trace, he fought against thrusting into her, losing himself in her sultry satin depths as she was silently, unmistakably demanding that he do. He wanted that. He wanted it until he felt as though he were being slowly torn inside out, every nerve on fire, his blood burning in savage rhythms that matched the violent hammering of his heart. All that kept him from losing control was an even greater desire; he wanted to bring his trusting princess to shivering completion in his hands. He wanted to know every aspect of her sensual release with all five of his senses unclouded by his own pleasure. He couldn't manage that if he were inside her, for then her sweet fire would burn through his self-control.

When Cindy arched into Trace again, requiring more from him than his relentless delicacy, he shuddered and caged her very carefully in his hands. The words he spoke to her then were unrestrained and elemental in their demands, yet the tenderness of his caresses didn't vary, each touch unraveling her, each word a hushed burning in her responsive flesh, extraordinary sensations radiating up through her body, softly devouring her flesh until only fire remained and she was its center, burning.

Trace shuddered and absorbed Cindy's release with all of his senses, savoring the knowledge that he had given her such intense pleasure. With redoubled tenderness he caressed her, feeling oddly satisfied even as he clenched against his own violent need.

Slowly Cindy opened her eyes, breathing raggedly as echoes of ecstasy rippled through her. She started to speak, but the sight of Trace caressing her so intimately made her tremble. Pleasure burst softly within her once more. In its trembling wake came the knowledge that for all the sweet fire rekindling in her, consuming her, she wanted more. She could hardly believe it, yet she still...*needed.*

"Trace."

The husky timbre of Cindy's voice sent a shaft of raw hunger through Trace. He looked up and saw the orchid she was extending to him on the palm of her slender hand. The flower's scent mingled with the heady fragrance of the woman held between his hands. She shivered within his grasp as he caressed the velvet bud of her passion.

"Trace, I..."

Breath and words came apart in a shower of heat. When Cindy knew the sultry pleasure of his touch again, she moaned softly and pressed against him, twisting slowly. She felt the shudder that ripped through his powerful body, tightening his hands on her for just an instant.

"Trace," she breathed, reaching for him.

The orchid tumbled softly from her hand to his cheek and then to her thigh. He turned and brushed his lips over the flower before he picked it up and gently set it aside.

"You're more beautiful than any orchid," Trace said, bending to Cindy again.

"So are you," she said, her voice husky with the shivering pleasure that was rising in her once more, seduced from the secret places of her body by Trace's elemental masculine sensuality.

Smiling, Trace turned and kissed the slender fingers that were caressing his cheek. "I'm about as beautiful as that mud hole I finally winched you out of, princess."

"You're wrong," Cindy said, her voice breaking with pleasure at Trace's touch. Looking at him was another kind of pleasure, equally intense. He was utterly male, hard with muscle and brushed with tempting swirls of hair, and the sultry heat of his mouth held her in thrall.

"Trace?"

He made a gently inquiring sound as he caressed her with slow pleasure. Cindy started to speak, then stopped as pleasure shimmered and burst within her. She wanted to tell him what she needed, but the only words she could think of made her blush.

"Trace," she breathed, rubbing her fingers through his hair and being rewarded by a caress that scattered her thoughts. "Come here. I want to whisper..." The words became a moan as he touched her with ravishing delicacy.

Trace closed his eyes and fought a sudden, savage thrust of need at the thought of Cindy's husky voice whispering sensual demands in his ear while he buried his hungry flesh in her softness.

"I'd better stay where I am," he said finally. "If you whisper in my ear, I'll take you slow and deep and hard."

"Yes," Cindy said, sliding down the bed, insinuating herself beneath Trace, discovering that his skin was as steamy as hers and that he shook when her hands found the fascinating combination of satin and pulsing strength that was quintessentially male. "That's what I want," she said huskily. "You inside me. Slow and deep and hard. And then fast, Trace. And hard, very hard."

Cindy's fingertips raked softly, urgently, over Trace's aroused body, measuring with wonder how much he wanted her. Even as his breath fragmented into a groan, her fingertips discovered the single sultry drop she had called from his violent restraint.

"Trace," she said shakily, "take me now." As she spoke she moved her hips slowly beneath him.

"I'll hurt you, princess," Trace said harshly. "I'm too big, too rough for you."

"No," Cindy said, kissing his hot skin as she drew him closer and then closer to her hungry softness. When the blunt heat of him touched her, she shivered eagerly. "You're perfect for me. I need you, Trace. Inside me. Filling me."

He felt the truth of her words in the satin flesh that eagerly parted for him. The hot rain of her passion bathed him, silently begging for a deeper joining. The tangible evidence of her need dissolved his control. His arms swept up beneath her knees as he pressed slowly against her, into her, giving her what both of them so desperately wanted, joining them with a slow thoroughness that was a consummation in itself. She made a broken sound as she felt him taking her, filling her until she overflowed, filling her until she could take no more.

And then Trace gently lifted Cindy's hips as he slid deeper and then deeper still, joining himself completely to her, sealing them one to the other, stopping only when his thighs were cradled against hers and he was fully sheathed within her welcoming fire. Only then did he begin to move, his hips describing slow, sensuous circles against her heated body. She had never felt anything half so intimate, so utterly exquisite. Each time he moved, streamers of glittering pleasure swirled up through her body.

Without realizing it Cindy began to murmur breathlessly, moving in deliberate, sensuous counterpoint to Trace, doubling and redoubling their shared pleasure, until gentle convulsions began to undo her, feeding upon her languidly, sweetly, and she wept with each unraveling ripple of ecstasy. He smiled and rocked slowly in the tight satin cradle of her body as he bent down to sip the tears of ecstasy from her...and still it continued, rocking, shimmering, building and she knew she was going to die of it and she didn't care as long as he was with her, deep inside her, moving, rocking, and flames of pleasure quivering through her, growing, burning.

Cindy called Trace's name as he retreated slowly, unbearably, leaving her empty when she knew she could not live without him. Instinctively her hands slid down to his hips, nails scoring his skin in passionate demand. His breath caught in a deep groan as his whole body clenched. This time he took her in a hard thrust, moving powerfully, restraint slipping away as her nails sank into the flexed muscles of his buttocks at each stroke, nails stinging him sweetly, telling him to withhold nothing of his power.

The urgent caresses inflamed Trace, but not as much as Cindy's husky words shivering against his ear, her body luring him deeper and yet deeper, faster, harder. Her nails scored him with ecstasy, stripping the world away, taking inhibition with it, leaving only the hot pricking of her nails and her passionate words and her fiery softness sheathing him, taking everything he had to give and giving him shattering ecstasy in return.

She caressed him with her hands, her words, her abandoned response, infusing his driving body with more strength, more heat, rapture pulsing from him to her and back again with each breath, each shimmering convulsion deep within her body, and still it was not complete, not enough. He was dying and he couldn't plunge far enough, deep enough, hard enough.

With ancient instinct her hands swept down to cradle and caress the twin sources of his primal need. At the first enfolding touch he thrust into her with a hoarse cry that was her name, abandoning himself to her as completion burst repeatedly from him in an ecstasy that had neither beginning nor end, simply an incandescent pulsing center that was both himself and the woman whose softness called forth and drank the searing pulses of his release.

Racked by ecstasy, Trace held Cindy, knowing that he had touched her soul and she had touched his and nothing would ever be the same again.

Chapter 12

"Well, you don't need to look so happy to see me," Susan said in exasperation, put out by Cindy's frankly dismayed expression when she opened the cabin door and saw guests on the doorstep.

Unsuccessfully, Cindy tried not to look guilty. "Of course I'm glad to see you," she said quickly.

"Uh huh. Pull my other leg. It has bells on it."

Raul laughed even as he gave Trace an intent, probing look over Cindy's shoulder. "I would have called, cousin, but you know the difficulty."

"Yeah. The phones are still out, right? Or is it the bridge that's keeping the world at bay?"

Trace's sardonic inflection and smile weren't lost on Raul. Nor was the frank irritation that had come to Trace's expression when he had looked over Cindy's head and seen the other couple standing at the cabin door. Trace had known that his time with his captive princess would inevitably end, but he hadn't known how fiercely he would resent that end when it came.

"Tia would like you to come to dinner," Raul said smoothly. "There might be other guests as well, if the roads are dry enough. If that is the case, there might be unhappiness if you were unable to attend."

Though Raul said no more, Trace got to the bottom line very

quickly. The outside world was no longer accepting Raul's radio silence at face value. If communications weren't reestablished at the Almeda *hacienda*, someone from Quito would drive up and "fix" the equipment for them.

That someone would probably be Invers, spurred on by Big Eddy McCall.

Cindy didn't notice Trace's grim expression. She was too busy looking at Susan's daunting physical perfection and remembering how, when Trace had first met Susan, he had looked from Susan to Cindy and then away. Cindy sighed. She didn't measure up to Susan's standard of beauty and she knew it. And even if she tried to forget that unhappy fact, standing around in Susan's clothes—which were a bit loose in the middle and much too tight on top and bottom—was a constant reminder.

Sighing again, Cindy resigned herself to accepting an evening of inevitable comparisons with as much good grace as she could muster.

Trace saw the shuttered look that came to Cindy's face and remembered he had seen that same look once before, when they had first encountered Susan and Raul.

"Cindy?" Trace asked, looking into the enigmatic, crystalline midnight of his lover's eyes. "We don't have to go anywhere if you don't want to."

"It would be best if you did, if only for a few minutes," Raul countered smoothly before Cindy could answer. "While radio reception has been erratic, I suspect that someone is worried about *Señorita* Mc—ah, *Señorita* Ryan."

"You suspect?" Trace asked in a clipped voice.

"Um," Raul agreed. "It is only common sense, is it not? *Señorita* Ryan is a woman alone in a foreign land. Surely her family would be concerned by the fact that she has not been in contact with them for nine days."

"Nine?" Cindy blinked. "Oh, that's impossible. It can't have been that long."

"Forgive me for insisting," Raul said, smiling slightly and giving Trace an amused look, "but it has been closer to ten days than to nine."

Mentally Cindy counted forward from the instant she had left the plane in Quito. First the argument with Trace, then two days on the road, then he had found her and they had slept in the village and then the storm and they had come to the Almeda *hacienda* and then...

Images of Trace splintered suddenly through Cindy's mind. Trace undressing her, loving her with his words, his hands, his mouth, every part of him, and all around them the cloud forest's sensuous rain bathing their interlocked bodies. Trace standing naked before her with an incredible orchid in his hand and sad shadows in his eyes. Trace joining himself with her slowly, deeply, repeatedly, teaching her so many exquisite ways to touch the shimmering ecstasy that waited within.

"We can't have been here six days," she said weakly. "It seems more like two, or maybe three."

Raul just managed not to smile. "I am delighted that you have found your stay with us so pleasant. Especially with Trace as your, ah, host. My cousin tends to regard the cloud forest much more highly than he regards mere men."

"Cindy isn't a man," Susan pointed out reasonably.

"But of course," Raul said, bowing slightly, failing to conceal his smile. "That explains it."

Trace grunted. All that kept him from being outright hostile to Raul was the fact that Cindy had barely looked at the other man—that, plus the clear dismay in her expression when she had opened the cabin door and had seen the end of their timeless days of mutual exploration and passion. The knowledge that Cindy was no more ready to rejoin the world than he was satisfied something deep within Trace, something that he had not even known was there.

"Tell Tia we'll come to the big house for dinner," Trace said in a clipped voice. "It might be nice if you worked very hard on the radio connections between now and then. Even if you can't *receive* messages, you might be able to send them. Try the American embassy, for instance. They have more powerful equipment than most. Tell them Cindy is doing very well, so no one needs to worry about the fact that she's going to stick around the cloud forest until the roads dry out."

Raul's eyebrows climbed. He turned to Cindy. "Is that the message you wish passed on to your family?"

Cindy turned to Trace, whose vital warmth was even now radiating out to her, touching her, enfolding her. His hard hands reached out and gently cradled her face. He bent and brushed his lips over hers once, twice, three times, tasting the warmth of her breath as it rushed out to him in an invisible caress.

"Is that what you want?" Trace whispered too softly to be overheard, touching Cindy's lips with his own between words. "Just ask me and if it's mine to give, it's yours. I promise you, princess. All you have to do is ask. I'll let you go if that's what you want, or I'll keep you here and make love to you in the midst of orchids and rain."

Sudden tears gleamed between Cindy's thick black eyelashes. She stood on tiptoe and pressed her lips against Trace's hungry, sensual, familiar mouth. His arms closed around her with fierce strength. She didn't object to the possession. She simply closed her eyes and hugged him as hard as she could in return.

"I told you that *Señorita* Ryan wasn't being held against her will," Raul said dryly, turning to Susan in the manner of someone continuing an argument. "Trace may lack a certain superficial charm at times, but he has more decency in him than a regiment of polished aristocrats."

Susan's skeptical blue eyes went from Raul to Trace. As she looked at her friend nestled within Trace's powerful arms, she sighed. There was no doubt about it. If Cindy was a captive, she was definitely a willing one.

Susan met Trace's blazing green eyes and said distinctly, "She doesn't need another Jason."

"You don't know me," Trace said in a cold, flat voice.

"Does Cindy?" Susan retorted.

"Susan, don't," Cindy said quickly. "It's all right. Trace isn't like Jason. Believe me. You won't have to put me back together after we... I promise. This is different."

"I hope so," Susan said, touching Cindy's arm. "You deserve to be loved more than anyone I know." Susan's smile was both beautiful and very sad as she turned to Raul. "What is it that you Spanish say? *Que sera, sera.*"

"What will be, will be," murmured Raul. "Yes."

"A primitive point of view," Susan said, looking directly at Trace.

"Don't knock primitive until you've tried it," Cindy said quietly, looking at Susan. "I've discovered I'm rather primitive myself. Like my brother. He spent his life looking for a woman who would want him just for himself. Just a man called Rye. And then he found Lisa and now he spends his days looking like a man who has just swallowed the sun."

Trace heard the complex resonances in Cindy's voice—joy for her brother, wistfulness, hunger—and knew in that instant why Cindy traveled and lived under a different name. It wasn't kidnapping she had feared, it was being wanted for all the wrong reasons. She had hoped to be as lucky as her brother, desired for what he was, not who he was.

"I had given up hoping to find a man who would want me, just me, Cindy Ryan," she continued, pressing her hands over Trace's. "Not my family ties, not any future expectations of wealth or power, nothing but me." Smiling, she brought one of Trace's hard hands up to her mouth. Eyes closed, she kissed his palm and cradled it against her cheek before she said softly, "Now I know how it feels to swallow the sun."

Trace met Raul's enigmatic black glance without flinching while Cindy's words echoed between them. *A man who would want me, just me, Cindy Ryan. Not my family ties…nothing but me.*

Even as Trace's arms tightened around Cindy, he knew he would have to let go of her very soon. There was no hope that she wouldn't find out he had known her real name even before he met her. That kind of secret could never be kept. His only hope was to let her go before she knew the secret. Then, when she learned the truth, she would look back and know that he must have wanted her, just her, for if he had wanted her money he never would have let her go.

When she realized that, she would come to him again in the cloud forest. And he would be there, waiting for her, wanting her with a complex, elemental hunger he had never known before.

"But I'm not going to make Rye's mistake," Cindy continued, turning in Trace's arms, looking at him. "My brother didn't want Lisa to know about his family because he was afraid it would change the way she looked at him. He was afraid she would see money instead of just a man. He didn't trust her, not really, and he almost lost her because of it." Cindy took a deep breath and looked into Trace's shadowed green eyes. "I want you to know that I trust you."

She paused, closed her eyes for an instant and then opened them. When she spoke her voice carried clearly, as though she wanted to be sure that Trace understood every word. "My full name is Cynthia Edwinna Ryan McCall. My father is very...well off."

"Well off," Susan echoed in an amused aside to Raul. "You have heard, perhaps, of 'filthy rich'? That's Big Eddy McCall. Filthy. Rich. Cindy is his one and only daughter."

Cindy searched Trace's eyes, trying to chart any changes the knowledge of her wealth might make between them. Nothing changed, unless it was the bleak twist of pain that showed in Trace's expression the instant before his mouth kicked up at the corner in his familiar, bittersweet smile.

"I always knew you were a princess," Trace said, brushing a kiss across Cindy's upturned face.

"It doesn't matter," she said almost fiercely.

"No. It doesn't matter," Trace said simply. "Not to me. Believe me. *It doesn't matter.*"

Cindy let out a breath she hadn't even been aware of holding. She smiled at Trace, her eyes radiant. She kissed him softly, hardly able to believe her luck. Trace knew who she was and it had changed nothing. The relief was so great she felt almost giddy. She laughed up at him.

"Now that that's taken care of," Cindy said, smiling, "I'm ready to face dinner in Susan's shade."

"Her what?" Trace asked.

"Her shade. You know."

"No, I'm afraid I don't have the faintest idea," Trace admitted, looking perplexed.

"Remember when we first saw Raul and Susan in the Jeep?"

Trace nodded slowly.

"You looked from Susan to me and then you didn't look at me any more." Cindy shrugged. "That's a man's usual reaction. Susan just puts every other woman in the shade."

Hardly able to believe what he was hearing, Trace looked from Cindy to Susan. "Has she always been this blind?" he asked bluntly.

Susan smiled, but there was no laughter in her eyes. "Big Eddy has been buying men to seduce his daughter into founding a dynasty since she turned eighteen. Little wonder she thinks she's not attractive. The men never saw her for the dollar signs in their eyes. That's why she fell like a ripe peach into the hands of the first man who wanted her body rather than her daddy's bank account."

"It's a damned fine body," Trace agreed matter-of-factly, giving Cindy the kind of loving once-over that made her bones melt, "but it's not why I wanted you."

Her eyes widened in dismay.

"There's a dark fire in you that has nothing to do with your body," Trace said, watching Cindy with eyes that reflected that fire. "That's what drew me, what drove me crazy. I would have wanted you if you'd been short, fat and blond. You…burn," he said, running his fingertip over Cindy's full lower lip. "And while Susan isn't bad-looking if you like skinny women…"

"My, how the man gushes," Susan said dryly.

"The reason I looked away after seeing you next to your wise-mouthed friend," Trace continued, ignoring Susan, "was that I felt guilty as hell for what I'd put you through. You were exhausted, wringing wet, muddy, scraped and your clothes were in shreds, and every time I looked at you I wanted to hire three men to beat me for being such an unfeeling bastard as to force-march you through the cloud forest in the first place. So I tried not to look at you. But I failed. Even looking as if you'd been dragged backward through a muddy knothole, you were still more beautiful to me than any other woman ever will be."

Cindy's eyes widened. "Oh," she breathed.

Trace smiled almost sadly, his lips curving so little that his mustache was barely disturbed. He touched Cindy's lower lip again, a caress that was both intimate and oddly withdrawn, as though he were afraid to come closer.

"I hate like hell giving you back to the world, princess," Trace whispered. Then he looked up at Raul. "I'll bring Cindy to the big house before dark."

"Ride over with us. One of the men can drive the Jeep back after—"

"No," Trace interrupted, looking back at Cindy. "I have a few hours left with my princess. I don't want to share them, or her, with anyone."

Without waiting for Raul's response, Trace drew Cindy back into the cabin and shut the door. She looked into his eyes and felt tears burn in her own. Before she could ask a question, the silken brush of Trace's mustache stroked over her lips until they parted on a gasp, permitting the hot glide of his tongue into her soft mouth. He tasted her with aching hunger while he pressed her against himself with slow, powerful sweeps of his hands.

In the space of a kiss Cindy became both pliant and fierce, for she knew that ecstasy waited within the shimmering heat of their joined bodies. And suddenly she couldn't wait for it.

It was the same for Trace, a primal urgency that could not be denied, a stunning foretaste of what it would be to go without the sense of completion that only Cindy had ever brought to him. He groaned and tore open his shirt as her hot mouth slid down his chest. By the time her lips reached his navel he had kicked aside his clothing to stand before her trembling and naked and gleaming with passionate need.

"Love me, Cindy," Trace said hoarsely, reaching for her even as the sultry heat of her mouth bathed him. "Love me as though it were the last time."

Chapter 13

Just as Trace drove the Jeep up to the big house, wind blew over the land, making trees bend and ripple like grass. Mist swirled and disappeared, shredded by flashing knives of metallic gold light. Shadows suddenly appeared as sunlight streamed through the cloud forest, making drops of moisture glitter with alien brilliance.

Trace parked next to the Land Rover, turned off the engine and looked over at Cindy with eyes that reflected both the jeweled greens and the deep shadows that surrounded the Jeep. Cindy didn't notice Trace's silent regard; she was lost in the forest's unexpected transformation. He watched her in aching silence. The unveiled light heightened rather than washed out Cindy's colors. Her beauty squeezed Trace's heart in a foretaste of the bitter loneliness that would come when he let his princess go. He reached out to touch her cheek, needing to feel her warmth.

The front door of the big house slammed open and Susan rushed across the screened porch toward the Jeep. Trace's hand fell back to his side before touching Cindy.

"I thought you'd never get here!" Susan said hurriedly, opening the passenger door for Cindy. "Rye has been calling every half hour since Raul patched up enough equipment to get through to the embassy."

"Rye? What does he want? Is something wrong?" Cindy asked as she got out.

"He said it was a 'family matter' and that everyone's fine but that he had to talk with you as soon as possible to make sure things stayed that way. Does that make sense to you?"

"Not—"

"That's a relief," Susan continued, interrupting. "I thought I was the only crazy one around here. Hello, Trace. You look like your usual cheerful self."

Trace gave Susan a sideways glance as he shut the passenger door behind Cindy.

"Brrr. A look like that would freeze sunlight," Susan said in a stage whisper to Cindy. "Do you suppose he'll ever forgive me for thinking that the only way he could keep you at his cabin was if he tied you to a chair? After all, men with dark beard stubble who look and move like jungle predators are hardly likely to inspire confidence in a civilized woman."

Cindy laughed softly. "I've discovered I'm not very civilized, so don't worry about me."

"I'll try, but after Jason…" The sophisticated mask dropped from Susan's face, allowing her worry and love for Cindy to show through. "I didn't think you were going to make it," Susan said frankly.

Before Cindy could say anything, Raul called from the house. "*Señorita* Ryan, your brother wishes to talk to you!"

Cindy looked at the blue sky, sighed, and said, "Guess I'd better find out what Dad's up to now."

"Your father?" Trace asked sharply. "What do you mean?"

"'Family matter' is our code for problems with Dad or our third sibling, who takes after Dad," Cindy called over her shoulder as she ran up the steps to the porch. "Since Mom died, Rye and I sometimes think we're the only reasonably sane people left in the family."

Cindy followed Raul to the radiophone. With impeccable manners he waited until he was sure that she needed nothing more, then shut the door behind her, allowing her all the privacy she might require.

"Hello," Cindy said, picking up the phone. "What is he up to now, and which he is it?"

"Hello, Cinderella. Where the hell have you been?"

Rye's familiar voice made Cindy smile. "I've been enjoying a guided tour of paradise," she said.

"Impossible. Lisa and I own it, remember? It's called McCall's Meadow."

"To each his own paradise. Mine happens to be a cloud forest where mountains and orchids hide."

"Is that where Susan was hiding, too?"

"She wasn't hiding, but she was here. She's fine."

"How about you? Are you fine, too?"

"Never better."

"Thank God. I was afraid that Dad had outmaneuvered you for the second time."

"What do you mean?"

"He's been flying in and out of here like Peter Pan, rubbing his hands and smiling and talking about the grandkids he's going to have from you at last. Seems he's paying some stud called Trace Rawlings a thousand dollars a day to keep an eye on you in Ecuador, and double that if you come home pregnant. Now I know you're a big girl and can take care of…"

Rye's voice began fading in and out oddly, like the light in the room itself. Shakily Cindy groped for the chair that was positioned close to the phone. She sank into the leather cushions and waited to find out if she was going to survive.

"Anyway," Rye's voice continued in Cindy's ear, "I got to thinking about it and was afraid you might be more vulnerable in a foreign country than you would be at home. I didn't want you getting cut up again like you were over that miserable son of…"

Sound faded as Cindy dragged air into her lungs despite the knives of pain twisting inside her body. She barely had the presence of mind to press her palm over the receiver so that Rye wouldn't hear her tearing breath. By the time she had herself under some kind of control again, Rye was beginning to wonder about the lack of input from her end of the conversation.

"Cindy? Yo, sis. You still there?"

Cindy stared at the radiophone. Slowly she reached for the volume control. As she spoke she ran the volume up and down erratically.

"I'm still here, Rye, but the connection is lousy. Can you hear me?"

"I can hear someone fading in and out. Sure as hell doesn't sound like you, though."

"Yes. Well, things are breaking up pretty badly on this end, too. What was that name again?"

"Trace Rawlings. He's some sort of jungle expert according to Dad."

"I can barely hear you." Cindy closed her eyes. "I'm flying out of Ecuador tomorrow. Can I—can I come see you and Lisa for a while?"

"Hell, yes. You're always welcome, sis. You know that. Why do you think I built on the extra suite of rooms after I was married? Lisa loves you as much as I do. She was so excited about having you for a sister that I thought for a while there she would move in with you rather than me."

Cindy gripped the phone so hard that her hand ached as much as her throat. "I love both of you, too," she said as she ran the volume all the way to zero.

Slowly Cindy hung up. She sat in the chair for a long time without moving, not trusting herself to be able to stand, hardly able to think. And then, when she could think, she wished that she hadn't.

How could I have been so wrong about Trace?

The question was painful, but not nearly as agonizing as the knowledge that she had given herself to a man whose body—all of it— was for hire.

Even as Cindy silently screamed that Rye must be wrong, Trace couldn't have made love to her so beautifully if all he had been thinking about was money, she felt herself dying inside. It was Jason all over again, except that Jason had been cruel every inch of the way, making her pay for the fact that his own greed had forced him to pursue a woman he didn't really want.

Trace hadn't been cruel in that way, but the ultimate result was the same. She had trusted herself to a man whose only interest in her was her money. And she had done it twice.

Cindy made a low, choked sound, but no tears came to ease her grief. It was as though Trace had killed even the ability to cry. Yet after Jason had left, she had wept until Susan had been afraid to leave her alone. It would be different with Trace. She couldn't cry for him any more than she had been able to cry at her mother's funeral. She had been a child when her mother had died, and she had felt a child's raw, incoherent sense of betrayal at her mother's absence.

That was how it was with Trace. Cindy loved him as she had never loved anyone. And when that kind of love was betrayed, there weren't enough tears to wash the wound clean, much less to heal it.

"What's wrong, princess?"

Trace's voice came to Cindy as though from an immense distance. Slowly she opened her eyes and looked at the man she had thought was beyond price, only to discover that he was just one more of Big Eddy's greedy recruits after all. Distantly she wished that she could be angry. She wished that she could rage at Trace, releasing the numbing grip of pain on her mind and body. But she could not.

Raging at Trace would be even more stupid than she had already been in trusting him. She needed him for just a bit longer. There were too many miles of rain forest between herself and freedom.

You Tarzan. Me Jane.

But Trace wanted to stay in the cloud forest for a while longer. No big surprise there. He was being paid a thousand dollars a day for his time. Plus the pregnancy bonus, of course.

Cindy closed her eyes and prayed that the numbness would last until she was on the plane out of Quito.

"Cindy?"

She took a deep breath, ignoring the knives sticking into her body, forcing herself to think rationally. If she said she had to leave, Trace would want to know why. There was no way she could tell him. Not yet. Not until she was certain that she could smile and congratulate him on his sexual prowess and then casually walk away from him. She didn't know how long it would be before she attained that level of serenity.

Probably never.

In the meantime she had to get to Quito. She could ask Raul for a driver, but she had seen enough of Raul to know that he wouldn't go against Trace's wishes without a good reason. She doubted that a woman's hurt feelings would even show up on Raul's scale of measuring good reasons.

"Love?" Trace came up to the chair and sat on his heels. Gently he cupped his hand beneath Cindy's chin and lifted her head until she opened her eyes. "Tell me about it. Let me help you."

Cindy looked into Trace's gentle green eyes and found herself believing that he truly cared for her rather than for her father's money. Despite what she knew, despite her past experiences, *she wanted to believe in Trace.* She had no defenses against him even now that she knew what he was.

She was hopelessly in love with him.

The realization panicked Cindy. Ten days ago she would have grabbed the keys to the Land Rover and rushed out of the house and gotten herself stuck in the first bog, where she would have stayed until Trace came along and pulled her out—but not until she first asked for his help. Nicely. And told him why she had been in such a big hurry in the first place.

For a moment Cindy considered trying to buy Trace's cooperation outright, but she knew beyond doubt that he would turn her down flat just the way he had in Quito. Trace did things his way or he didn't do them at all.

She took a deep, careful breath. There was no point in wasting time being more stupid than she already had been. She didn't have the skill or the strength to get herself back to Quito. Trace did. But she couldn't buy his skill. She could only ask for it a few miles down the road when she got stuck on her own—or she could be smart and ask for it right now.

Slowly Cindy's eyes focused on the man she had learned too much about, too late.

"This morning…" Cindy's throat closed.

She cleared it with a sound so tight, so painful, that Trace's eyes narrowed in unconscious empathy.

"You told me…if I wanted something, all I had to do was ask," Cindy continued in a dry voice. "If you could, you would give it to me. That's what you told me, isn't it?"

Trace nodded as he touched her cheek. She flinched subtly at the caress.

"I have to go home," Cindy said starkly. "Will you take me to Quito?"

Trace lifted his hand and looked at her in silence for a few moments. She was far too pale and her eyes were almost wild. Her fingers were clasped together so tightly that her nails were digging into her hands.

"Why?" Trace asked.

"Is that yes or no?"

"Cindy…" His voice died as he looked at her desperately calm face. "Do you really want to leave?"

"Yes."

"When?"

"Now. Right now. This instant. Please, Trace. I'm beg—"

"Don't," Trace said roughly, unable to bear hearing Cindy's pleas. "It's all right, princess," he said, holding her, feeling her lack of response, wondering what had happened, why she was retreating from the cloud forest. From him. "We'll leave right away." His green eyes searched hers. "Can't you tell me what's wrong?"

Cindy closed her eyes and whispered, "Is that the price of a ride to Quito?"

Trace came to his feet in a single savage motion. "We'll be in Quito before noon."

Trace was as good as his word. He took a direct route from the Almeda *hacienda* to the nearest paved road, and from there he drove like a bat fleeing hell. Cindy slept when she could, pretended to be sleeping when she couldn't and said nothing that didn't relate to the necessities of the trip. Trace had little attention to spare from the road in any case. He drove hard and fast, pushing the Rover right to the edge of its mechanical capabilities and holding it there ruthlessly. Driving like that not only made good time, it kept Trace from grabbing Cindy and demanding to know what was wrong. It kept the rage he felt at being cut off from her under control.

And it kept him from asking himself why he felt such turmoil over the end of an affair that was less than ten days old—an affair that he had known must end.

Driving like a bat out of hell didn't, however, keep Trace from sensing at a visceral level that he was somehow the cause of Cindy's pain. There was no other explanation for her distance from him. Assuming he was at the center of her pain, there could be only one reason. Somehow she had found out that he had always known she was Cynthia McCall, not Cindy Ryan.

By the time Trace pulled up in front of Cindy's hotel, he had decided that he was going to put an end to her distance and silence, beginning right then. He shut off the engine and turned toward her. Cindy took one look at his bleak, jungle-green eyes and reached for the door handle. She was too slow. Before her fingers closed around the handle, Trace was holding her in his arms, pinning her back against the seat with his powerful body.

"Since you won't talk to me," Trace said, lowering his mouth to Cindy's, "I'll try another way of communicating with you."

For a few instants Cindy fought against both Trace's superior strength and her own wild desires, but resisting was futile. Her body knew him too well, responded to him too quickly, hungrily reaching for his sensual fire, wanting to burn away the icy grief that was numbing her. With a small, choked cry she stopped fighting against herself, against him, against the need that only Trace had ever been able to arouse and satisfy within her.

When Cindy's lips finally parted for Trace, he sensed the sweetness waiting for him, a sweetness that he needed as much as breath itself. He groaned and took her mouth almost violently, tasting her deeply, wanting something from her that he could not name. When he realized she wasn't fighting him any longer, he tore his mouth away and began sipping tenderly at her eyelids, her cheeks, the corners of her mouth, her lower lip, kissing her so gently that she shivered between his hands, against his body, telling him everything he wanted to know.

"You see, princess?" Trace murmured, nuzzling Cindy's ear, feeling her shiver again, tasting her, biting her with exquisite care. "It doesn't matter that I knew who you were before you came to Quito. After I saw you I would have wanted you if your father was broke and you were wearing rags. Just like it doesn't matter that I'm a peon, a bastard with no real family. You burn when I touch you. I burn when you touch me. That's all that matters. Everything else is just words without meaning."

Cindy's eyes closed as the last flicker of hope that Rye had been wrong was destroyed by Trace's own admission. *I knew who you were the first time I saw you.*

"Cindy?" Trace said huskily, feeling the change in her body, tension draining away, leaving nothing behind. He was holding her but she wasn't there. Not anymore. Not the way she had been, shivering with pleasure at his touch. "Talk to me, princess."

"Thank you for driving me to Quito," Cindy said politely.

"Don't you believe me?" Trace asked, his hands tightening on Cindy's shoulders.

Everything else is just words without meaning.

"Oh, yes," she said softly, opening her eyes. "'Words without meaning.' I believe you. Now, if you'll excuse me…?"

Trace looked at Cindy's fathomless black eyes and felt a chill ripple over his skin.

"Please," she added carefully.

Trace felt a stroke of anguish as he lifted his hands from Cindy's shoulders. He had vowed that he would make Cindy ask him for something, and he had. Twice.

And each time the request had been that he separate himself from her.

"You don't believe me!" Trace said savagely, anger clear in his voice. "You just can't bring yourself to trust a peon, can you?"

Words without meaning.

The only words that mattered were still tolling in Cindy's mind. Trace had known who she was. He had let her make her little speech about trust and had said nothing. Sudden humiliation galvanized her, giving her the strength to leave him.

"I don't know any peons," Cindy said, opening the door.

"You know me," he shot back.

"You're a stud for hire. Studs and peons are two entirely different things."

"What?"

"Big Eddy hired you."

"Your brother was a regular mine of information, wasn't he?" Trace said viciously.

"Did my father hire you?"

"Technically, yes; but what does that—"

The door closed, cutting off Trace's words, leaving him alone in the Rover. He started to get out, then thought better of it. Cindy was angry now. So was he. Much too angry to accomplish anything. It would be better to wait for her to cool down. When she did, she would realize that what they had was too good to throw away just because Big Eddy had been the one to bring them together.

Trace shifted gears angrily and drove away from the hotel, telling himself that he could be patient and understanding about how Cindy felt. From what Susan had said, Cindy had had a rough time with men because of her father. Naturally Cindy would be upset to find out that Trace had always known who she was. But surely it wouldn't take long before she realized that he wasn't some kind of low-life gigolo. He had been hired by Big Eddy to keep an eye on his daughter, period.

When Cindy got past her anger, she would understand that making love to her hadn't been any part of Trace's deal with Invers and Big Eddy. If she just slowed down and thought about it, she would know that the kind of passion they had shared was one of those things that money simply couldn't buy.

Let's face it, Trace told himself. *A man can't fake it in bed. What he wants—or doesn't want—is right out front for anyone to see. Cindy must know that. All she has to do is slow down and think.*

He was still comforting himself with those thoughts when Invers knocked on the front door of Trace's apartment that night.

"What the hell are you doing here?" Trace asked.

"Delivering mail," Invers said in a resigned voice.

"What?"

"Got some more of that for me?" Invers asked, gesturing toward the glass in Trace's hand.

Trace stepped back into the room. Invers followed. A few moments later he took an eye-watering swallow from the glass Trace handed over.

"Thanks," Invers said after a moment. "At least I'll die with the taste of good Scotch in my mouth."

Trace's mouth lifted slightly at the corner, which was as close as he'd come to a smile since he had walked into Raul's radio room and seen Cindy looking like the world had been jerked out from under her feet.

"Is it that hard to be a mailman in Ecuador?" Trace asked.

"You know what they used to do with the bearer of bad news," Invers retorted. He pulled an envelope out of his breast pocket. "This came to my office by special messenger. I'm afraid it's meant for you."

Trace looked down. The envelope bore the name of Cindy's hotel. Written on the outside of the sealed envelope was: "For Stud Rawlings, the best man money can buy."

Trace said several vicious words as he ripped into the envelope.

Invers finished his Scotch in a single swig and muttered, "I was hoping it was a case of mistaken identity. Guess not."

A shower of money spilled from the envelope onto the floor. American bills. Big denominations. Big enough to make Invers suck in his breath hard and fast. Trace didn't even glance at the money, much less try to pick it up. He had eyes only for the message inside.

Big Eddy taught me that a workman is worthy of his hire. The enclosed covers both our original agreement and the days we didn't spend in the cloud forest waiting "for the roads to dry." I've included the pregnancy bonus because if I'm not, it certainly won't be for lack of effort on your part. I doubt that Big Eddy will be so generous but, as you taught me, you never know until you ask.

Too bad I didn't ask the right questions sooner.

The note swiftly became pulp in Trace's powerful hand. He pinned Invers with a savage look.

"*Pregnancy* bonus?" Trace asked with dangerous softness.

A single glance at Trace's grim face made Invers wish himself elsewhere. Immediately. He looked toward the door, wondering if he could make it before he was stopped.

"Not a chance in hell," Trace said succinctly, following Invers's glance. "You're not going anywhere until you tell what you left out when you conned me into getting Big Eddy off your back."

"It's a long story," Invers said.

"So was Scheherazade's. If you're as lucky as she was, you'll survive to finish it."

A long time later Trace sat alone in his apartment, a drink in one hand and thousands of dollars scattered across the floor at his feet. He no longer expected the phone to ring, no longer waited to hear Cindy say that she believed him and wanted to be back in his arms, no longer expected her warmth to fill the aching hollows of his life. She had flown out of Quito hours before, leaving nothing behind but the envelope explaining why she didn't believe in him.

Trace didn't blame her. If he had been Cindy, he would have felt as angry and betrayed as she did.

Wearily Trace leaned his head back against the cushion and thought of all the things that might have been: the woman of his dreams burning in his arms, loving him, and the cloud forest enfolding them....

A draft stirred through the room, whispering over the green bills, herding them across the floor until they gathered around Trace's feet. He didn't notice the money. He never had.

But he didn't expect her to believe that, either.

Chapter 14

Autumn had turned the aspen trees into thousands of yellow torches burning against the coming night of winter. Granite peaks thrust against the cloudless blue sky in saw-toothed magnificence. Dark green pines, silver sage and blazing aspens covered the rugged mountain slopes with a living patchwork quilt that stirred beneath a chill, pure wind.

Cindy noticed none of the grandeur of her surroundings as she stood with Lisa and Rye on the porch of their ranch home. In Cindy's soul she was in the center of a cloud forest swathed in mist and orchids and warmth, and Trace's heart was beating slowly beneath her cheek while she slept in his arms.

"Beautiful, isn't it?" Lisa asked, watching the horizon with amethyst eyes.

Rye stood beside her, looking at the woman, not at the land. He smiled with a gentleness that was at odds with his muscular appearance. It was the same for his hand touching his wife. There was a tenderness that was unexpected in a man who looked as rugged as he did. Slowly his fingers twined in Lisa's long, almost transparently blond hair, which fell in a shimmering cascade to her slender hips. The silken veil was a continuing source of delight to the violet-eyed, black-haired daughter who was gurgling serenely in Lisa's arms. Lisa's hair delighted Rye, as well. With open pleasure he stroked a shining tendril between his fingers while he smiled at his wife and child.

"The view isn't nearly as gorgeous as you are," he murmured, bending down to kiss Lisa. "And you, too," he added, laughing, when his daughter patted his mouth with her tiny hand.

As Cindy watched the others, she felt a combination of sadness and joy. Lisa and Rye's love for one another welled up invisibly between them, spilling out to enrich everything they touched...and telling Cindy wordlessly just how much she was missing in her own life.

Trace.

Cindy pushed the silent cry into a dark corner of her mind, the same place where she kept the irrational sadness that came every time she realized that she wasn't pregnant. She should have been relieved that there was no legacy of her bittersweet brush with love. But she wasn't relieved. With her period had come a melancholy that could only be lightened by her niece's artless smiles.

The fact that Cindy wasn't pregnant had so depressed her that she had told no one. She was afraid that talking about it would shatter her brittle calm. Besides, as long as her father believed he had been successful, he wouldn't lay any more traps for her.

"Who was that on the phone?" Lisa asked.

"Dad," Rye said, turning reluctantly toward his sister. "Will you call him back?"

Tension tightened every muscle in Cindy's body. "No," she said without looking away from the horizon.

Rye ran a hand through his thick, unruly hair and said, "I don't blame you, sis. If it helps any, when I found out what he'd done, I tore a strip off him wide enough to cover the barn."

"Nothing will change. You know it as well as I do. Nothing either one of us says matters to him. He'll do what he has since mother died—whatever he damned well wants to do."

"What he wants is to talk to you," Rye said bluntly.

"Not really. All he wants to know is if I'm pregnant."

"So tell him."

Cindy fought against the tears welling up inside her, closing her throat. She shook her head in a silent negative and said nothing more. She had refused all calls from her father since she had returned from Ecuador. She had every intention of refusing Big Eddy's calls until she was too old and feeble to pick up a phone.

"He said that Trace Rawlings is on his way to the States," Rye continued. "Dad wants to know if he should pay the pregnancy bonus. If you don't call him, I'll bet he'll be on the first flight out of Texas to here."

For an instant Cindy felt off balance, as though the earth had hesitated in its turning. Then came a slashing disappointment at this further confirmation that Trace was her father's hired stud.

"He can do what he always does," Cindy said after a long moment, her voice as expressionless as her face. "Whatever he pleases."

Lisa looked at Cindy, hesitated, then said quietly, "If you're pregnant, will you stay with us? Please? We want very much to share that time with you. Babies were meant to be shared."

Cindy searched her sister-in-law's unusual eyes and found the same unselfish love there that Rye had discovered during a timeless summer in McCall's Meadow.

"You may have been raised among Stone Age tribes, but you could teach angels how to be kind," Cindy said huskily.

"Kind?" Lisa laughed and kissed her daughter's tiny, waving fist. "More like selfish. I love seeing new life grow, feeling it kick beneath my hands, knowing that someday the miracle will be complete and another person will be standing close to me, talking to me, seeing a world that is both different from and the same as mine. A new mind, a new laugh, a new smile—even new anger and tears. A whole new person to love and be loved."

"Or hurt and be hurt?" Cindy asked painfully.

"Sometimes that's the only path to love," Lisa said, turning to brush her lips over Rye's lean hand. "It was for us."

"And sometimes there's no path to love at all." Cindy's mouth turned down in a sad curve. "We're told that the road to hell is paved with good intentions. I don't think so. I think it's paved with Big Eddy McCall's money."

Cindy stepped off the porch and walked to the beginning of a trail that led to a small creek. She had spent a lot of time by the creek since she had come back to the States. The crystal dance of water reminded her of the many liquid voices of the distant cloud forest where she had loved...and lost.

Rye started after his sister, only to be stopped by a light pressure from Lisa's hand.

"Let the sound of running water and the turning of the seasons heal her if they can," Lisa said. "We can't. We can only love her."

"I would like," Rye said too softly, "to get my hands on this s.o.b. called Trace Rawlings."

"And I would like to help you."

Lisa's smile was as chill as the wind blowing down from the mountain peaks. Rye lifted his wife's small hand to his lips and pressed a kiss into her palm. Other people judged Lisa by her fragile appearance and spontaneous, radiant smile, forgetting that she had been raised among tribes for whom life was very simple, very direct. Rye never forgot the primitive fires that had forged Lisa's character. She not only loved, but she defended the things she loved with every bit of strength and intelligence she had.

And one of the things Lisa loved was Cindy.

"Too bad we'll never get to meet him," Rye said.

"Yes," Lisa said softly.

She rubbed her cheek against Rye's hand, sending a veil of hair shimmering over her deceptively delicate features.

Trace pulled up in front of the sprawling, recently remodeled ranch house and shut off the engine of his rented car. There were five vehicles parked in the ranch yard. He wondered which one of them belonged to Big Eddy. The Mercedes, probably. It sure as hell didn't belong on the lumpy dirt road that wound from the state highway to the ranch house.

No one came out to see who had just driven up. Trace lifted a small, hand-size box from the seat before he got out. He mounted the three front steps in a single flowing stride and knocked on the door with more force than finesse. It had been a long flight from Ecuador to Texas, where he had been told that Big Eddy had gone to see his son in Utah. Another airplane had brought Trace to a small airstrip, a rented car and a washboard road leading—he hoped—to Big Eddy.

Trace had dreamed of getting his hands on the man who had cost him the woman of his dreams.

The instant the door opened, Trace knew that the person facing him wasn't his quarry. The man was about Trace's age, slightly smaller in height and build, with the kind of eyes that Trace liked in a man—direct, confident, self-contained.

"Rye McCall?" Trace asked.

Rye nodded.

"I'm looking for Big Eddy."

"You've found him. He expecting you?"

"Yes. But not here."

Rye smiled slightly and moved inside. "Come in out of the wind."

Trace stepped into the house and waited while Rye closed the door behind him.

"Been on the road long?" Rye asked.

"Two days."

Rye's dark eyebrows climbed. "Long drive."

"Only for the pilots. I slept from takeoff to landing both times."

Within Rye, suspicion crystallized into certainty. His gray glance raked up and down the tall, powerfully built man who stood just a few feet away, looking both out of place and quietly dangerous in his worn khakis and jungle boots.

"You're Trace Rawlings."

The shift in Rye's tone didn't escape Trace. He wasn't welcome here. At all.

"Don't worry," Trace said coolly. "My business won't take long."

"You have five minutes."

Rye said nothing more. He didn't have to. Trace knew that he had five minutes to get out of Rye's sight or take the consequences. For an instant Trace wanted nothing more than the violent physical outlet of the fight Rye was offering. Then Trace realized it would solve nothing. It would simply make things worse.

"If you weren't her brother, I'd take you up on it," Trace said calmly. "But she loves you, so hurting you would only hurt her."

Rye met Trace's savage green eyes and knew that Trace meant every word. Curiosity began to compete with anger in Rye. Why should a man like Trace Rawlings care what hurt Cindy? And there was no doubt in Rye's mind that Cindy was the only thing keeping Trace in check. The subtle change in the way Trace held himself while he waited for Rye's reaction told Rye that the other man was both unafraid of and trained in physical combat.

A motion in the doorway at the far end of the living room made both men turn. Lisa stood there, watching and listening to Trace with the intensity of a wild animal searching for danger. Just beyond her was a half-open door and a partial view of a man sitting behind a desk.

"Are you the man who took Cindy's laughter?" Lisa asked.

Trace's flinch was so subtle that only someone who was watching for just such a reaction would have seen it.

"Yes, I guess I am," he said softly. He looked at the shimmering fall of platinum hair and remembered Cindy's description of her sister-in-law. "You must be Lisa, the woman who makes knives out of glass."

As Lisa nodded, her hair shifted and glistened with ghostly radiance. "Are you here to see—"

"Big Eddy," Rye said quickly, not wanting Trace to know that Cindy was at the ranch.

"About the pregnancy bonus?" Lisa asked.

"I don't know," Rye said before Trace could answer. "He didn't tell me."

"Of course," Lisa said. "It's none of our business, is it? It belongs to Big Eddy and this man and whatever passes for a conscience between them."

"You use those glass knives to cut out men's hearts, don't you?" Trace asked softly as he walked past Lisa to the half-open office door.

"That shouldn't worry you."

Trace hesitated, then gave Lisa a green-eyed glance that concealed none of the shadows within his soul. "You're right. I don't have a heart. I gave mine away. But she didn't want it. I don't blame her. Hearts cause more pain than pleasure."

Before Lisa could speak, Trace walked into the office and stared at the man sitting behind the desk. He was the right size, the right age, and his eyes were a faded gray match for his son's. Big Eddy ignored the interruption. He sat looking off into the distance with an air of melancholy that was almost tangible. His daughter had refused to speak to him.

Trace walked up to the desk, pulled a wad of bills from his hip pocket and dropped the money in front of Cindy's father. The bills slithered across the desk in green disarray.

"What's this?" Big Eddy asked, focusing his shrewd gray eyes on the money.

"A refund. Your money and hers. You can sort it out between you. You're real good with money, I hear. You're hell on people, though. If I'd known you were crazy I'd never have taken the job."

"What job?"

"Guarding your daughter in Ecuador."

"Guarding?" Big Eddy smiled. "Is that what Invers told you? Well, it was true as far as it went."

"It didn't go nearly far enough, did it?"

"But apparently you did," Big Eddy said with real satisfaction. "Is she pregnant?"

Very carefully Trace set down the small box he had been carrying. With a good deal less finesse, he spread his fingers and planted his palms flat on the scarred surface of the wooden desk with enough force to scatter money in all directions. He leaned hard on his hands, hoping that would lessen the temptation to throttle Cindy's father. It didn't.

"Old man," Trace said in a low, rough voice, "you cost me the love of a good woman. If you weren't her father, I'd make you hurt as much as you've hurt me."

There was a sudden movement behind Trace, but he didn't turn away from Big Eddy.

"Love?" the older man asked softly, tasting the word as though it were unfamiliar on his tongue.

Trace's only answer was the predatory violence in his eyes as he watched the older man.

"A good woman loved me once," Big Eddy said quietly. "She died and nothing was ever the same...." He sighed deeply. "We all die, boy. The only thing that goes on is the children of our love, and their children, and their children, world without end. With enough children, she isn't really dead. She's alive. And someday she'll look out at me through the black eyes of my grandchildren or great-grandchildren and she'll smile." He nodded to himself. "Enough children, that's the key. Everyone thinks I want my own name and image out there—Edward McCalls down to the end of time." His mouth curved in a sad smile. "I did, once. No more. I'd rather see her face, young and alive, laughing and loving. Love is all there is that matters in life. The rest is just flash and fertilizer."

For a long moment Trace and Big Eddy looked at one another. Then Trace slowly closed his eyes. When they opened once more, the predatory gleam was gone, leaving behind only emptiness.

"Is there nothing of your dead wife in Cindy?" Trace asked quietly.

Bittersweet pleasure lighted Big Eddy's face. "Cindy is the image of her mother."

"Is that why you don't want her to trust any man enough to marry him?"

"What the hell are you talking about! I've moved heaven and hell to get my daughter married. When that didn't work I settled for pregnant."

"Is that what she wanted?"

"Who?"

"Cindy. Your daughter. Remember her? Or are you so busy thinking about your own dreams and needs that you don't know what you're doing to her?"

"Just who the hell do you think you are to—"

"I'm Trace Rawlings," he said coldly, cutting across Big Eddy's protests. "I'm the man who can take Cindy so far into the cloud forest that the twentieth century isn't even a rumor. And that's just what I'll do if you don't leave her alone. I'll take her away. I swear it. You've ridden long and hard on your solid gold horse, but it's over.''

''Do you know how wealthy I am?'' asked Big Eddy, more curious than overbearing.

''Do you know what I'd do with your money if I had it?'' Trace said coolly. ''I'd use it for toilet paper.''

Reluctantly Big Eddy smiled. ''She said the same thing.''

''Your wife?''

''My daughter.'' He eyed Trace shrewdly. ''You really think she'd go with you to that cloud forest?''

''Willingly?'' Trace's mouth flattened. ''Not a chance, old man. You ruined that for us. But I'd take her just the same. She belongs there. Most people hate the mist, hate the dense forest, hate the wildness. She didn't. So think about it and think hard. Leave her alone or lose her to a cloud forest where all your money doesn't mean one damn thing. Take your pick.''

''I should have listened to Invers,'' Big Eddy said, sighing again. ''He told me if you didn't want Cindy, no amount of money would change your mind. And if you did want her, nothing but killing you would stop you from having her.''

''One thing would. It has. She doesn't want me.''

''Thanks to me?''

''And to me,'' Trace admitted softly. ''We could have survived your meddling. My bungling was different. I didn't believe a princess could love a peon until it was too damn late.'' Trace watched Big Eddy with opaque green eyes. ''Have you decided?''

The older man smiled. ''She's all yours, son. I decided that when your friend called and told me that you had shown up at the *hacienda*, that you wanted Cindy and that she wanted you. I was as excited as a kid at a birthday party. She hasn't looked at a man since I bought Jason for her, and that was years ago. I'd given up hope of getting her interested in any man. That's why I picked you. I figured if you wanted her, a determined man like you would find a way past her defenses. And you did, didn't you?''

"Once." Trace looked at his big hands and wondered if he would feel any better after he had had another talk with Invers, who had once again withheld more than he had told. "Are you particularly attached to Invers?"

"Who?"

"My 'friend.' The one who helped you set up Cindy."

"Raul Almeda was the one who helped me. Invers damn near scotched the whole deal. Said if it turned out badly you'd use our butts for a boot rack. Raul had to lean on Invers pretty hard before he'd agree. I still don't know how it went wrong," Big Eddy said, shaking his head. "You know, at first I thought Raul would be the ideal man for my daughter. I suggested it and described Cindy to him. He described you to me. I liked what I heard a whole lot. So I told Raul about Cindy's friend buying cloth in South America, and the rest was so easy, I thought it was meant to be."

Trace hissed a harsh word.

"Well, the logistics of getting you two together and keeping you together were easy enough," Big Eddy amended hastily.

"Was Susan in on it?"

"Hell, no, boy. She'd as soon cut my throat as look at me. But Raul kept his men on her all the way from Quito to the *hacienda*. It went so damned slick." Big Eddy sighed. "Then I had to go and brag to little Eddy and he squeezed Raul's number out of Invers and everything blew to hell and gone."

"Little Eddy?"

"My boy, Rye."

"Cindy would have found out sooner or later. Only dead men keep secrets. Be grateful I wasn't in on the secret sooner, old man. It would have been worth killing to keep."

Trace straightened, retrieved his package and turned to leave in a smooth, continuous motion. As he had expected, Lisa and Rye were standing behind him.

"Relax," Trace said coolly. "I haven't touched a single gray hair on that slippery renegade's head." He hesitated. "Do you know if she's pregnant?"

"Would it matter?"

"She was my woman. If she's pregnant, I want to take care of her. I want the child to be born into my hands...." Trace looked from Rye to Lisa. "But you don't believe me and Cindy doesn't need me, anyway. She has you two." Trace held out the box to Rye. "She left this behind. Will you give it to her after I leave?"

"What makes you think she's here?" Rye asked, taking the box.

"She loves you and you love her," Trace said simply. "If I had been hurt the way Cindy was, I'd go to a place where I was loved."

Trace started to walk around the other two, only to be stopped by a light touch from Lisa's hand.

"Is that where you're going now?" she asked. "To a place where you're loved?"

Trace looked into Lisa's compassionate eyes for a long moment before he said, "I don't have a place like that. I never cared about love until it was too late." He looked at the box in Rye's hand. "When you give that to Cindy, tell her..." Trace's voice faded into silence as he fought for self-control. It was too long in coming. When he spoke, his voice was too husky, almost rough. "I'll always look for her in the mist, even though I know she'll never be there."

Suddenly Trace was moving quickly, brushing past Lisa and Rye, leaving everything behind.

"Wait!" Lisa said.

Trace didn't even hesitate. Lisa ran after him into the living room and caught his arm with surprising strength.

"I want to talk with you. Privately. Please?" Lisa asked, her hand tightening on Trace's arm. "It won't take long. There's a room in the new wing where we won't be bothered. Please, Trace. It's very important."

Trace wanted to refuse but it was impossible. Her soft pleas had sounded too much like Cindy's. Reading his acceptance before he could speak, Lisa smiled gently and took Trace's hand.

Rye waited only long enough to be sure that Trace was listening to Lisa before he turned and walked swiftly through the kitchen and out the back door. He saw Cindy coming from the barn and waved her over.

"Did Dad finally give up and leave?" she asked.

"Not yet, but this came for you." Rye held out the box to Cindy. She took it with a puzzled look.

"Open it," Rye urged.

Cindy peeled the tape off the top, lifted the lid and gave a broken cry as she saw an incredible orchid that had grown wild in a cloud forest thousands of miles away. A haunting fragrance drifted up from the flower, enveloping her, wrapping her in memories as she had once been wrapped in mist.

There was no note. Nor was there any doubt as to who had sent her the orchid. Gently she lifted the flower from its mossy nest and let the box fall away. Feeling as though she were being torn apart, she bent her head over the orchid while hope and fear warred within her.

"He just wants to know if I'm p-pregnant," Cindy said, fighting against hope, knowing she wouldn't survive if hope won only to prove false once more.

"He said, 'I'll always look for her in the mist, even though I know she'll never be there.'" Rye looked at the orchid Cindy was holding and added softly, "His hands were trembling like yours. You can't buy that with money, sis. Not from a man as hard as Trace Rawlings."

Slowly Cindy lifted her head. Tears shimmered like raindrops on her cheeks and on the orchid's creamy petals.

"Is he—here?" she asked huskily.

"If I know Lisa, right now Trace is alone in the new den, watching the fire and wondering how in hell she sweet-talked him into staying when every instinct he has is screaming at him to run back to the cloud forest and lick his wounds in peace."

Before Rye finished speaking, Cindy was running into the house.

At the sound of the door opening behind him, Trace turned away with the primitive masculine grace that had haunted Cindy's dreams. As she walked toward him she saw that he looked older, harder, more alone, and his green eyes devoured her with a complex yearning that said more than words.

"Princess…?" he whispered, afraid to hope.

"I love you," Cindy said, holding out her cupped hands to Trace, within them the orchid trembling as though it were alive. "I love you."

Slowly Trace cupped his hands beneath Cindy's and bent until he could breathe in the fragrance of both flower and woman. When he straightened, more clear drops gleamed on the orchid's flawless petals. Very gently he took Cindy in his arms, kissing the tears from her eyelashes, whispering his love for her again and again. Then he held her close and hard, trying to absorb her through his skin into his bones, feeling tears like warm rain on his cheeks, on hers.

And he knew all the way to his soul that the next time he looked for her in the cloud forest's swirling mist she would be there, holding her hands out to him, running to him, bringing to him the sweet, dark fire of love.

WILDCAT
Rebecca Brandewyne

For my editor,
Tara Gavin,
with heartfelt appreciation
for her faith, her friendship and her kindness.

Wildcat

Now, he was just a good ole country boy,
An outlaw, pure and wild,
While she was a redheaded city girl,
Not easily beguiled.
But opposites attract, it's often said—
And that proved true for them.
One glance, and he felt a longing for her,
And she the same for him.

Wildcat...it's a fire burning out of control.
Wildcat...it's two halves that are finally whole.

East met west on a dusty country road,
And sparks flew from the start,
Igniting a blaze untamped, untamed,
Deep in each other's heart.
The fought, they wrangled, they made up, but just
Could not break up the team,
Begun with a pair of bold, one-eyed jacks,
Then a dance to a dream.

Wildcat...it's a fire burning out of control.
Wildcat...it's the hand, the heart and the soul.

Chapter 1

Country Boy
Wichita, Kansas

Morgan McCain was an outlaw.

He had always been an outlaw, and he suspected he always would be an outlaw, cut from the same rough cloth as Waylon Jennings and Willie Nelson and all the rest whose heroes had always been cowboys and who had been born a century too late for Deadwood, Dodge City and Tombstone. Hell. Morgan had even arrived too late for the Cimarron Strip, when men had gambled at oil instead of cards, and the outlaws had all been wildcatters, betting that black gold would come gushing out of the rich, rolling prairie earth. Yes, those had been the days—and Morgan, much to his regret, had missed them. The only bronco he rode was a Ford; the closest he had ever come to a showdown at high noon was a Saturday-night brawl in some rowdy bar; and at the moment the oil business was not booming, but bust. Still, the fact remained that in his heart he was an outlaw, pure and simple.

That he was a throwback to the nineteenth century had not proved detrimental to Morgan's well-being, however. Rather, this characteristic had held him in good stead. For, from their winnings one night at a boisterous, back-room poker game straight out of a Western movie, he and his partner, Frank Devlin, had together started their business, the One-Eyed Jacks Oil & Gas Company, afterward somehow managing to hang on through the tough, lean years, when a lot of other oilmen had gone under. But although Morgan's initial gamble had paid off, it now appeared that his lucky streak had finally played out. Frank was unexpectedly dead of a heart attack, and the future of the corporation they had owned fifty-fifty was currently up in the air due to his last will and testament.

Frank's attorney, Richard Hollis, had refused even to hint at the document's contents until Frank's only living relative, his daughter, was informed of her father's death, and Morgan had not pressed the issue. Still, he felt certain Frank had willed his shares in the company to that only child, that snooty, ungrateful daughter who had not only left all her father's funeral arrangements up to Morgan, but who had not even bothered to show up at Frank's grave-side service. Instead, upon being notified of her father's death, she had cabled instructions to both Frank's attorney and Morgan, informing them that she was out of the country and would be in touch with them when she returned.

Of course, it was not her fault that she had been abroad when Frank had died. Still, Morgan could not rid himself of the suspicion that Ms. Catherine Devlin had not cared two hoots in hell about her father—one of the finest men Morgan had ever known. Nor, as a result, did he think she was going to have the slightest bit of interest in the oil company he and Frank had worked so hard to build over the years. It was more than likely, Morgan thought as he stared morosely out his wide office window, that she would want to sell her father's shares as soon as possible, and Morgan was not sure that at the moment he could put together the necessary financing to buy her out. That left him with some pretty unappealing alternatives: he could attempt to sell his own shares in the company; he could waste his own time and money looking for another partner; he could resign himself to getting stuck with whatever investor Ms. Catherine Devlin wound up selling her shares to; or he could try to talk her into dissolving the corporation and liquidating its assets.

Morgan's mouth turned down sourly at the corners as he considered those options. Damn it! He was not about to throw away without a fight everything he and Frank had striven so hard to achieve. They had not scratched and clawed their way through the muck to strike oil, only to lose it all because of some big-city, Seven-Sisters woman from back East. Why Frank had always, in his generous heart, had a tender spot for that daughter of his, Morgan could not fathom. Not once had she ever deigned to come visit her father in Wichita, although Frank had on several occasions traveled to New York to see her, returning to sing her praises until Morgan, scowling, had made his apathy and annoyance plain, cutting Frank off in midsentence.

Frank had always shaken his head ruefully at that, claiming that Morgan, never having been a father himself, just would not and could not understand. That he, Frank, had been estranged from his daughter for so many years was regrettable, but their lack of contact could not be laid at Catherine's door. It was not her fault. Her mother, Julia Talbot, Frank's ex-wife, had filled the girl's head with bitter, spiteful tales against him and had coldly made it clear to both Cat and Frank that his presence was entirely unwelcome in the Talbot family mansion, to which Julia had returned following the divorce.

"I should have fought harder to stay in touch with Cat from the beginning," Frank had always insisted. "But back then, I was just a nobody struggling to make ends meet, while the Talbots had social standing and money. Naturally, they hired all the best lawyers to ensure that I had no rights whatsoever when it came to Cat. What could I do—me, Julia Talbot's one moment of youthful rebellion and indiscretion? I'd worked on the grounds of her daddy's estate before she and I eloped, and her old man subsequently fired me for seducing his innocent little girl. It didn't matter that she was neither innocent nor little, nor that she had shamelessly flung herself at me, claiming she didn't care about the consequences—a lie she soon came to regret, once she learned what it meant to be poor. No, I didn't stand a chance against her daddy and his attorneys, and I knew it, so I just walked away and never looked back, until Cat was old enough to make her own decisions. Cat's not to blame for that."

In his heart, Morgan had sensed the truth of that declaration. Still, he had never found it within himself to forgive Ms. Catherine Devlin for her indifference toward her father. It galled Morgan no end that now, because of Frank's soft heart, Catherine was in a position to destroy the One-Eyed Jacks Oil & Gas Company.

Muttering angrily to himself, he abruptly swung his booted feet down from his oak credenza, swiveled in his big, burgundy leather chair and stood. It was plain to him that in his ill mood he was not going to accomplish anything in the office today. Despite the fact that he had arrived at the crack of dawn that morning, his massive oak, antique rolltop desk was still piled high with unsigned contracts, unread letters and unreturned messages. Trailing from his leather-bound wastebasket was a long, crumpled paper chain of oil derricks, which he did not even remember cutting out earlier. Glancing at the heirloom grandfather clock towering against one parchment-colored wall, he saw that he had been staring out the office window now for more than an hour, oblivious of the swans and ducks that floated lazily on the winding waterway beyond—normally a tranquilizing sight—and of the resonate chiming of the clock itself, marking the passage of time. Grabbing his black Stetson hat from the brass coat-rack that stood in one corner, he jammed it on his head, then ripped open his office door with such force that his secretary, Mrs. Whittingdale, seated at her desk just outside, jumped.

"Whitty, cancel any appointments I have this afternoon. I'm taking the rest of the day off," Morgan growled, uncomfortably aware of how surly he sounded, but unable to summon a politer tone.

Fortunately, Whitty, as he had nicknamed her within days of having hired her, was an older, motherly sort who had been with him for many years, so she was long accustomed to his bad temper.

"Yes, Morgan," she replied smoothly to his broad back as he stamped past her, for she saw no reason to agitate him further by announcing that upon determining his mood earlier that morning, she'd already taken the liberty of clearing his calendar for the day. As his and the late Frank Devlin's personal secretary, Whitty was privy to every business detail at the One-Eyed Jacks Oil & Gas Company, so she knew that with the company's future now wholly uncertain, Morgan had good cause for his current disposition—besides which, he had taken Frank's death pretty hard. "It's too beautiful a day to be cooped up inside, anyway," she declared sympathetically. "It'll do you good to get away for a while. You work too hard, Morgan. You always have."

His only response was a scornful snort that left Whitty shaking her head sadly and clucking with distress as he vanished into the hallway. *He ought to be married and raising a family,* she thought, not for the first time. But once bitten, twice shy, and Veronica Havers, the one woman Morgan had ever been serious about, had dumped him in the end for a cool, sophisticated financial investor with old money.

Once outside in the parking lot, Morgan climbed furiously into his Bronco. After slamming the door and tossing his Stetson onto the seat beside him, he punched the key into the ignition and started up the engine with a roar, gunning it once or twice before, spinning the steering wheel and burning rubber, he lurched out onto Woodlawn, unconsciously heading north toward the country, as he always did when he needed to be alone for a while.

His one clear thought as he did so was how much he would like to have just ten minutes of Ms. Catherine Devlin's precious time, so he could give her a piece of his mind, tell her exactly what he thought of her—the stuck-up, hard-hearted witch!

Chapter 2

City Girl

When Catherine Devlin jerked awake from the fitful doze into which she had fallen, she was dazed from jet lag and lack of sleep and disoriented by her unfamiliar surroundings. Her first thought as she stared through the sun-warmed window her cheek was pressed against was that she must still be asleep and dreaming—a bizarre, disjointed dream in which she had become a pioneer woman, braving the frontier. Upon gradually realizing she was awake and aware, however, her second thought was that, like the bewildered heroine of some time-travel novel, she had somehow while she napped been zapped and transported back in time. For what met her startled gaze was a small cluster of old buildings that belonged not to the twentieth century and a modern city, but to the nineteenth century and a Wild West town in which Wyatt Earp and John Henry "Doc" Holliday would have been perfectly at home.

Good heavens. It's finally happened. I've snapped at last, Cat reflected with a strange sense of calm detachment. *I've gone clean off my rocker, over the edge, off the deep end, out of my head....* Funny, until now she had never thought about how many ways there were to say you had lost your hold on reality, on sanity, and now dwelled in the chaotic realm of the lunatic, the deranged. But that was surely what had befallen her, she mused as she stared at the grill in front of her face, the rusty iron fretwork that separated her from the man in white who must certainly even now be driving her to some sanatorium.

Slowly straightening from her slumped position, Cat ground the heels of her palms into her bleary eyes, red rimmed from fatigue and weeping. At least she had the use of her hands, was not confined by a straitjacket.

"You all right, ma'am? You seem awful tired, if you don't mind my saying so. You must have had a long flight. Funny thing, how we can fly all over the world and even put a man on the moon, but nobody appears to be able to find a cure for jet lag. You ought to be in bed, ma'am. But you *did* tell me to take the scenic route." The kindly tone of the driver, a young college student dressed in a white T-shirt and blue jeans, turned slightly defensive at the end.

All at once, Cat remembered where she was—and why—and the sorrow that had threatened to overwhelm her the past few days rose anew to haunt her.

"Yes, that's right, I did," she replied quietly to the driver, who was glancing at her with concern in his rearview mirror. "I've never been to Wichita before, and I wanted to see something of the city." The minute this confession left her mouth, she silently cursed herself for a fool.

She might not have lost her mind, but she clearly was not thinking straight all the same. She had been under such a terrible strain lately, and her father's death had been the crowning blow. One of her cardinal rules for survival was never to tell a taxi driver she was new in town. Now he undoubtedly saw her as an easy mark and would meander all over the city in order to rack up charges on the meter. Still, Cat was too weary to protest, as she normally would have done, her long experience with New York City cabbies making other cities' taxi drivers appear wholly unintimidating.

"Are they shooting a film here...a Western?" she asked curiously, indicating the buildings that had so startled and confused her moments before.

"What? Oh, no, ma'am. That's Cowtown...old Wichita. Among other things, Munger House, the city's first story-and-a-half house, is there, and the original jail. Wyatt Earp was a policeman here back in those days, you know," the driver announced, eliciting an unexpected smile from Cat as she remembered her thought just moments ago about the famous lawman.

Encouraged by her smile, the driver continued to point out sights along the way as he wound through the city and its riverside parks, indeed obviously taking the scenic route. They passed the Mid-America All-Indian Center, a museum. Botanica, a botanical garden. Like a tour guide, he was a veritable font of information and kept up a stream of congenial chatter Cat only half heard. Although she made appropriate polite responses, her mind was now focused on collecting her thoughts as she prepared herself to step into her father's life here in Wichita, feeling both guilt and grief that she should do so only at his death. How horribly ironic that she had planned on visiting him here this summer, only to learn a few days ago that she had left it too late.

Informed of her father's death, being unable to get to Wichita in time for his funeral, Cat need not have come here at all. Frank Devlin's attorney, Richard Hollis, had told her that her actual physical presence was not necessary for the legalities to be handled. Arrangements could be made for a realtor to sell her father's house, for its furnishings to be auctioned off beforehand at an estate sale and for his vehicles to be sold. If she wished, Morgan McCain, her father's partner, would even pack up her father's personal belongings and send them to her. Still, once back from Europe, Cat had, from New York's La Guardia Airport, caught the first flight bound for Wichita, damning the expense and not caring that time-consuming connections and exhausting layovers had been required. Why she had come, she still did not know—except that she had felt she somehow owed it to her father.

By now they had left downtown Wichita behind, and the driver was explaining that the neighborhood in which her father had lived, Vickridge, had been named after the estate of a local oilman, Jack A. Vickers, who, back in the early, booming days of oil, had founded the Vickers Petroleum Company. There were a lot of oil companies in Wichita, it appeared. Even Koch—as famous for its bitter family feuds and Bill Koch's 1992 win of the America's Cup as for its industries—had headquarters here. Then all too soon, it seemed, the taxi was pulling into the half-circle driveway before her father's house.

For a long moment Cat just sat in the cab, staring at the huge Tudor home and wishing her mother were here to see how high "that penniless, worthless bum Frank Devlin, your father," had climbed. A lump rose in Cat's throat and tears stung her eyes. Her heart filled to overflowing with love for and pride in her father.

You done good, Dad, she thought, hoping that some way, somewhere, her silent words reached him. *You done real good.*

She had her father's keys, express mailed to her by his attorney in case she decided to make the trip to Wichita, as well as various items of information that included how to deactivate the alarm system. So once the taxi had driven away, she turned the house key in the lock and pushed open the heavy, solid oak front door. After entering the proper code sequence to shut off the alarm, Cat carried her luggage inside.

She knew at once, as, from the marble-floored foyer, she surveyed her beautiful, tasteful surroundings, that the house's interior had been decorated by a professional. Frank Devlin had been a plain, honest, hardworking man of humble beginnings. Unlike her mother, he had never known a Rembrandt from a reproduction, Baccarat from cut glass or Porthault from percale. Once she had got to know him, Cat had always found that oddly endearing. Every time they had ever passed a street vendor in New York, she had had to haul her father away, scolding him good-naturedly and explaining that the hucksters weren't *really* selling Rolex watches for twenty bucks apiece, but cheap counterfeits or knockoffs.

"But, Cat, the last time I was here I bought a damned good umbrella from one of these guys!" her father had always protested, his eyes twinkling with mischief.

"Umbrellas are different, Dad," she had invariably answered, shaking her head ruefully. "It's a public service to sell decent um-

brellas in New York—because you can never get a cab here when
it's raining!''

Now, as these memories of her father assailed her, Cat could not
help but smile through her tears. She almost expected to see his tall,
handsome, silver-haired figure striding toward her, a big bear of a
man, larger than life—and with a heart even larger still. But the house
was empty, bereft of her father himself, if not his presence. The smell
of the cigars he had smoked, of the cologne he had worn, lingered
in the rooms she gradually explored one by one, until she came to
the last room. *Her* room. She knew it instinctively when she saw it,
for all her favorite things were here: an old canopy bed she had once
admired in an antique store in New York during a shopping spree
with her father; a nightstand stacked high with books Frank Devlin
would never have read and compact discs he would never have listened to; a dresser filled with Victorian perfume flacons, which she
collected.

''Oh, Dad,'' she whispered aloud in the thoughtfully, so obviously
caringly prepared room, her heart breaking, her voice catching on a
ragged sob. ''I'm sorry...so sorry for all the lost, wasted years...so
sorry I didn't get here in time! I should never have listened to all of
Mother's tales about you! But I never realized until I was older how
selfish, self-centered and bitter she was. I should never have worked
so hard at my job, either, been so damned busy climbing the corporate
ladder that I had too little time for my family and friends. I should
have *made* time! I should have come here while you were still
alive....''

Worst of all was the letter Cat found later that evening in her
father's study, once she had begun the task of sorting through some
of the papers in his desk. It was a loving, enthusiastic missive written
to her, detailing all the things he planned for them to do together this
summer, when she would at last make the long-awaited visit to Wichita. She had never received the letter, of course; her father's sudden
heart attack had killed him before he had had a chance to mail it to
her or even address an envelope.

Earlier, during her foray into the kitchen, Cat had discovered nothing edible in her father's big, built-in Sub-Zero refrigerator. For sup-

per, therefore, she had made do with ordering a pizza, which she had learned, much to her frustration, was the only food anybody delivered in Wichita—and that probably only because the Carney brothers, Dan and Frank, had, in a little hole-in-the-wall building here, started what had eventually grown into the worldwide corporation of Pizza Hut. Now, as she read her father's words, the bite of sausage and pepperoni on a thin crust that she had just eaten stuck in her throat, tight with emotion, and the taste of the hot, fresh pizza was suddenly like cardboard on her tongue. After slowly folding up the letter, she laid her head on her father's desk and wept for a very long time.

When she was all cried out, Cat finally understood what had compelled her to come to Wichita: she wanted to do all those things her father had planned for them and about which he had written to her. She wanted to be a part of his life, just as he had been a part of hers. In that moment her decision about her immediate future was made.

"I'm going to stay here…at least for a while, Dad," she said aloud, as though her father sat with her in his study. And in a way, perhaps he did, she thought as she played idly with the things on his desk: his wooden box of cigars, his gold letter opener, his gold pen-and-pencil set, a small brass oil derrick he had evidently used as a paperweight. "I don't know how I'll do here, a big-city girl like me in this 'Cowtown' of yours. I suppose they don't deliver groceries here, either! But I'm going to give Wichita the chance you wanted me to, even so." Cat paused for a moment, considering that declaration. Then she continued.

"The truth is it'll do me good to be away from New York for a while, seeing as how my life's in such a shambles at the moment. You see, I've fallen off the corporate ladder, Dad, fallen long and hard. Right before you—before you…died, Spence and I had a dreadful argument in Europe during our buying trip for the firm, and well, the upshot of it was that I not only broke off our engagement, but in retaliation, he fired me."

Spencer Kingsley, her fiancé, had been her boss at the import-export firm where she had worked. He had been attracted to her from the very first day she had walked into his office, but in the beginning Cat had been wary of mixing business with pleasure, of having an affair with her employer. Spence, however, had pursued her with all the relentless determination he had used to pursue a prized order for the firm, and in the end she had allowed her reservations to be overcome, herself to be persuaded that his intentions toward her were both honorable and serious. And they had been. He had wanted to marry her.

But from the minute he had got his three-carat-diamond engagement ring on her finger, Spence had behaved as though he had owned her; and gradually, Cat had come to recognize that he was as dictatorial and disapproving as her mother, forever preaching about "knowing the right people, moving in the right circles and being seen at the right places." Her mother had adored him, exclaiming effusively—*gushing* was actually the word that had applied to her mother's behavior, Cat thought now—about Spence's impeccable background, breeding and money, how well he "fit in" with the Talbot family, how "wise" Cat was not to make a terrible mistake by running off with someone like her father, someone "not of their class."

"I was so young and foolish when I married that penniless, worthless bum Frank Devlin, your father," Julia Talbot had insisted, her carefully lipsticked mouth twisting in a wry grimace. "I thought the things with which I'd been reared and which I'd come to expect didn't matter. I thought Frank and I could live on love alone. What a stupid notion that was, I soon learned! After marriage, love goes right out the window, dear…you'll see. You'll be glad then of the rewards and comforts that Spence's position and money will bring."

"That's when I first realized that if I married Spence, I was going to turn into Mother, Dad," Cat added, continuing her one-sided conversation in the shadowy study. "You were right about Spence—he *was* as dull as ditch water! And there *was* some vital spark missing in our relationship. But if I ever *do* find that certain something with some certain someone, I think I'll know it now, Dad."

As she stood and reached to turn off the banker's lamp on her father's desk, Cat spied his letter, lying where she had laid it earlier on the black leather blotter. The missive had come unfolded, and now his last words to her leapt up at her again from the page: *P.S. I can hardly wait for you to meet Morgan! My two "wildcats"—together at last!*

"You trying to tell me something, Dad?" she inquired, her eyebrows arching faintly at what she now perceived as his sheer impudence, even from the grave.

It was surely only her imagination, but as Cat left the study, she could have sworn she heard her father's laughter echo softly behind her in the dark, empty room.

Chapter 3

East Meets West

Morgan had left the city limits behind. Now he barreled north down a dirt road along which farmers' fields seemed to stretch endlessly for miles—acres and acres of wheat, corn and milo, mostly. The green-and-gold fields of grain were a beautiful sight. The wheat, especially, was like an amber sea in the sunlight, its feathery heads rippling gently like waves in the wind that stirred the prairie. Morgan's gaze, however, took in only the ugly beam pumps that sparsely dotted the earth, the pumping units of some standing still, motionless, while others churned steadily, sucking up the oil, the black gold, that lay deep beneath the surface.

He did not own the fields themselves, but he *did* hold the oil and gas leases on some of them—or, rather, the One-Eyed Jacks Oil & Gas Company did. So periodically, even though the corporation had maintenance men for the task, he drove out to various sites to assure himself that all the machinery was working properly, that those beam pumps currently in operation were functioning as they ought. No matter how they scarred the earth, rising like an army of titanic, alien robots, Morgan found that the sight of the beam pumps always soothed his temper and filled him with pride. From nothing but a pair of jacks and a one-eyed axman, which had provided a winning hand at poker for each of them, he and Frank had built all of this, starting out as wildcatters—those who took chances on fields not previously known to harbor oil.

But Morgan possessed, as had Frank, an uncanny gut instinct about oil. It was as though he could smell it a mile away. Sometimes he had only to walk onto a field and he would know oil was there, lying deep beneath his booted feet, waiting to be freed, to come spewing out of the rich earth that yielded it.

"Drill here," he would say suddenly, quivering with excitement and anticipation, certain that were he a dowser, his divining rod would be shaking uncontrollably as it pointed toward the ground upon which he stood.

He proved right so much more often than wrong that even the geologists, baffled by his finding what had not appeared to them to be present, eventually ceased arguing with him, stopped holding up their education and training against Morgan McCain's "nose." The first time the crude had come gushing from the earth, he and Frank, shouting and laughing, had thrown their Stetsons high into the sky and had danced about like crazy men while the black gold rained upon them. Even now, the memory of that day was as clear in Morgan's mind as though it had happened only yesterday, and as always, the thought brought an irrepressible grin to his handsome, tanned face.

Adding to the gradual lightening of his dark mood was the fact that he had the windows of the Bronco rolled down, so the wind streamed exhilaratingly through the vehicle, and the radio, tuned to a country-and-western station, was playing his favorite good-time music. As he drove he banged one hand against the steering wheel in time to the beat, and now and then he sang along, too. His mama, before she had died, had surely never listened to this particular song, he thought, still grinning, or else she would never have let him grow up to be a cowboy, but would have made him become a doctor or a lawyer.

By now, despite all his troubles, Morgan's spirits had lifted so considerably that when he spied a striking young redheaded woman standing in the wheat field he was currently passing, he did not pause to wonder what she was doing out there, all by her lonesome self, or how his actions might affect her. Instead, he did the only thing any other red-blooded American cowboy would have done: he hollered out the window at her and laid on the horn—full blast.

Cat had not informed either her father's attorney, Richard Hollis, or her father's partner, Morgan McCain, that she was coming to Wichita; nor had she yet notified them of her presence in their city. She had wanted a day or so to rest, to come to grips with the loss of her father and to get her bearings, especially since she had decided to stay awhile. So the following morning, when she awoke, she determined that the first thing she needed to do was shop for groceries so she wouldn't turn into a Ninja Turtle from a steady diet of pizza. Also, she needed to locate a bank, where, with her traveler's checks, she planned to open a checking account.

Finding the two closets in her bedroom empty save for several padded satin hangers her father had thoughtfully provided, she finished unpacking her luggage, having removed only the bare essentials last night. She was glad the dresser and armoire were also empty, because such had been her haste in getting to Wichita that she had come straight here, carrying with her every piece of luggage she had taken to Europe, never having bothered to unpack between the two trips. Since the European business venture had lasted three weeks, Cat had plenty of clothes with her, and she was confident she could buy anything she might lack.

An invigorating shower washed away the remaining vestiges of her jet lag and weariness, after which she donned a matching set of silky, lacy underwear, a pair of Calvin Klein jeans and a simple green knit shell. Then she slipped a pair of heeled sandals onto her bare feet. She wore minimal makeup: black mascara to darken her long, thick lashes; fawn-colored eyeshadow to emphasize her slightly slanted green eyes; pink blush to highlight her fine cheekbones and porcelain skin; wine red lipstick to accentuate her generous, sultry mouth. After a quick brushing, her dark red hair hung shining and free, falling to just below her shoulders.

Grabbing her purse and her father's keys, Cat made her way to the garage. There she discovered a brand-new Jeep Cherokee Limited, a classic Cadillac convertible and a sleek speedboat. Living in New York, she had not needed a car, so it had been a long while since she had driven. The Jeep looked sturdy and practical, so she attempted to open the garage door behind it, tugging with increasing frustration when the door refused to budge. Finally, feeling like the world's biggest fool, she discovered in the Jeep itself a remote control for the automatic garage-door opener, which she had not previously noticed.

"Presto, chango," she commented dryly as she pressed the button and the garage door rose easily.

After backing out the driveway, she wound slowly through Vickridge, taking time to familiarize herself with the Jeep and with the neighborhood, noting street signs so she could find her way home again. Reaching a four-lane main street that she observed was named Rock Road, she turned right, not trusting her driving ability enough to turn left instead, across two lanes of oncoming traffic. A few blocks later she pulled into a gas station, bought a map of Wichita and inquired of the attendant about the area's grocery stores and banks. To her amazement and delight, the grocery store he recommended, Dillons, proved to be a "superstore" that boasted not only groceries, but also meat and fish markets, Chinese takeout, discount items, a pharmacy, a post office, a dry cleaner, a shoe-repair drop, a branch library and a branch bank.

Cat transacted her business at the bank first, then did her shopping. By the time she was finished, her grocery cart looked to her as though she were preparing for a siege. She was not used to being able to buy so much all in one place at one time. In an hour she was back home again, ruing her impulsiveness when she had to unload the Jeep, carry all the sacks inside and put everything away by herself. But then she realized she would not have to do this every other day, making several small trips a week to the market as she had often had to do in New York to supplement her usual delivery of groceries.

"So, okay, Dad," Cat conceded aloud with a wry smile, as she deposited milk, eggs and cheese in the refrigerator. "I'll admit I wouldn't have supposed it, but you were right—apparently there *are* some advantages to living in this Cowtown of yours. And as you kept badgering me to do, I've taken a step in broadening my horizons. For the first time in a long while, I drove a car today—not very well, I confess, but still, I drove it. And I managed to find my way around town a little, too. And guess what? In just a minute I'm going to go back out again. I want to see some of these oil wells and wheat fields you talked about, Dad, some of this prairie you loved so much that you called it God's country.''

There had been a map in her father's desk, with marks on it to indicate the locations of various oil wells belonging to the One-Eyed Jacks Oil & Gas Company. So, armed with that and her city map, Cat, true to her word, resolutely headed back out in the Jeep once she had emptied all the grocery sacks.

And that was how she came to be standing alone in a wheat field when Morgan McCain passed her in his Bronco, grinning and yelling out the window at her and blaring the horn for all he was worth.

Lost in reverie, Cat jumped a mile, catching her heel on a clod of dirt, so her ankle twisted beneath her and she fell smack upon the curvaceous posterior that, among other attributes, had prompted Morgan's hollering and horn blaring in the first place. But not for nothing had Cat survived and even thrived in New York.

"You damned rude, insolent, crazy man!" she shouted heatedly, shaking her fist at the Bronco, which sped on by, trailing a cloud of dust in its wake. Whether its arrogant driver had heard or seen her, she did not know. But she fiercely hoped he had; she hoped he knew she had not appreciated his damned fool antics one bit! "Oh, Jeez Louise, why didn't you wear more-sensible shoes, Cat—some hiking boots or something if you were going to be traipsing around out here in the boondocks?" she chided herself after a moment as, gingerly reaching beneath her, she drew forth a small clump of sharp cockleburs that had been stabbing her in the behind and that now pricked her fingers, as well.

With anger and disgust she tossed the cockleburs away, realizing as she did so that some large black bug had taken advantage of her current position to begin crawling up her jeans. Screeching and swiping wildly at the insect, Cat scrambled to her feet, wincing at the pain as her weight bore down upon her injured ankle. Cursing and muttering to herself every step of the way, she limped toward the Jeep, which she had parked on the grassy verge of the road.

"Damned grinning lunatic!" she groused. "Probably escaped from some asylum." What was it he had yelled at her? *Looking good, baaaby!* No doubt he had meant both it and his horn blasting as a compliment, and she should feel flattered. Instead, Cat equated him with the construction workers on the sidewalks of New York, whistling and hollering down from steel beams at unsuspecting women— or looking up their skirts from vantage points below ground level, where bulldozers had gouged deep pits in the earth. "I'll tell you this, Dad—I don't care if they *are* California *boys,* east, west, north or south, men are all alike!"

Still fuming, Cat got into the Jeep and started the engine. Her ankle was swelling up and hurting like the dickens, and at this point all she wanted to do was go home, where she could soak it in some warm salt water. But she did not yet feel confident enough of her driving ability to attempt to turn the vehicle around on the narrow dirt road and so was forced to continue north, searching for someplace where she could maneuver the Jeep about more easily.

It was not long, however, before she spied the Bronco and its infuriating driver ahead of her, no longer going like a bat out of hell, but poking along at a snail's pace. Through the Bronco's rear window, she could see that the driver was now yakking on a cellular telephone. At the sight, some devil seized Cat, and she hit the button that rolled down the window of the front passenger seat of the Jeep. Then, disregarding her injured ankle, she stamped on the accelerator and jammed her hand down on the horn as she whipped into the empty, oncoming lane to pull up alongside the Bronco.

"Hey, you! Eat dirt, you—you...*sodbuster!*" she shouted, to her satisfaction wiping the smug grin off the driver's face before she put the pedal to the metal and raced on by.

Unfortunately for Cat, however, she knew nothing about handling a vehicle while speeding down a dusty country road, and within moments she was fishtailing all over the place, wheels sliding on the sandy dirt. To her horror, the next thing she knew the Jeep was plunging wildly off the road into the shallow ditch and slamming into the trunk of a lone tree that, at the impact, rained chartreuse, grapefruit-size fruit on the vehicle's hood, denting it.

For a moment Cat just sat there dumbly, stunned, shaking, her heart pounding, her one clear thought a silent thanks to God that she had had her seat belt fastened and hadn't gone through the windshield. She was not hurt, she realized at last as she slowly gathered her wits and composure. Just badly rattled, a condition that increased alarmingly when in her rearview mirror she observed the Bronco rolling somehow ominously to a stop behind her. Its engine had barely died before the driver's door was shoved open, and what got out was six feet, two inches of lean, powerful muscle topped by the most ruggedly handsome face she had ever seen and that at the moment had murderous rage written all over it.

Cat was not normally a coward. But as her stricken glance took in not only the figure now stalking her determinedly, but also her isolated surroundings, she thought she would rather be facing a mugger on New York's 42nd Street than the fast-approaching man who looked like some lethal gunslinger stepped from the pages of a Western novel. As they clenched the steering wheel, her hands trembled from both apprehension and guilt. No matter if the brazen man *had* hooted and honked at her, she knew she had no one but herself and her fiery redhead's temper to blame for her current predicament. It was a wonder she had not accidentally run the Bronco off the road, too—a thought she felt certain was uppermost in the man's mind as, in a few long strides, he reached her and wrenched open her door.

''What in the Sam Hill blazes kind of a fool stunt did you think you were pulling, lady?'' Morgan bellowed as he stared down furiously at the woman inside the Jeep, his adrenaline pumping, his emotions in such a turmoil that he abruptly did not know which he wanted to do worse: thrash her or kiss her! For the sight of her up close and personal unexpectedly hit him as hard as the chair he had had smashed over his head the last time he had got into a Saturday-night brawl at one of the rowdy local bars, and he felt no less staggered.

God, what a knockout! The woman's long red hair was tumbled in wild disarray about her pale, piquant face, and her flashing eyes, slanting up at him from beneath her thick, sooty lashes, were so green and brilliant that they momentarily took Morgan's breath away. *Cat eyes...bedroom eyes* were the phrases that came unbidden to his mind, made somehow even angrier by his primal-male reaction to her, as he glared down at her. But then a man would have had to be pushing up daisies not to be aroused by those eyes, that mouth—and Morgan was not only alive and kicking, but also in his prime. Sweet heaven, he thought as his gaze was irresistibly drawn to that tempting mouth: moist, wine red, slightly parted, sinfully kissable; the upper lip short, cupid's bow-shaped; the lower lip full, sensuous, sultry. Nor was he oblivious of the tantalizing glimpse of the swell of the woman's ripe, generous breasts, of their shallow rise and fall beneath the wide, scooped neckline of the green knit shell she wore.

"Look, I'm—I'm terribly sorry.... All right?" Instead of appeasing Morgan, however, Cat's low, smoky, faintly breathless voice was like a teasing caress running down his spine. "I—I know you've got every right to be mad—"

"Mad!" Morgan laughed shortly, jeeringly. "Lady, that doesn't even *begin* to describe what I'm feeling right now! Why, I could—" *Snatch you up, fling you down, tear your clothes off and make you beg and moan for mercy* were the words that sprang without warning to his tongue and that, stunned by the wild, primitive notion, he bit back with difficulty. "Horsewhip you," he finished lamely, swallowing hard. "Of all the reckless, foolhardy—"

"I'm—I'm not used to driving, you see," Cat managed to say, still breathless, as though the Jeep's impact had knocked the wind from her—although honesty forced her to admit the sensation was due to the man towering over her.

Although not so heavy, he was as big and tall as her father had been and appeared to be cut from the same rough cloth. His wind-tousled, mahogany brown hair was thick and had a tendency to curl at the collar, and she had a crazy impulse to run her fingers through it, to see if it was as soft and silky as it looked. Framed by equally thick, unruly brows, his eyes gleamed a startling shade of sky blue against his face, which was tanned and weathered from years of exposure to the sun. Beneath his chiseled Roman nose, his sensual mouth was half-hidden by a mustache, against which the whiteness of his even teeth contrasted sharply and which made Cat wonder wildly, inexplicably, if his kisses would tickle her lips.

The short sleeves of his blue chambray work shirt revealed sun-darkened arms corded with muscle, and its open collar exposed a hint of the fine hair that matted his broad chest, which looked somehow as though it ought to have a marshal's badge pinned on it. Encircling his waist was a leather belt with a decorative gold-and-silver buckle engraved with a bronco rider. A pair of jeans clung to his narrow hips and strong thighs. But the gold-nugget-banded Rolex watch he sported on his left wrist, the heavy gold, diamond ring that flashed on his right hand and the ostrich-leather Tony Lama boots he wore informed Cat that while he might look like he'd just ridden in off some high, lonesome trail, he was no ordinary cowboy.

Robert Redford had nothing but a few decades on Morgan McCain.

Breaking the taut, electric silence that had fallen between them, Morgan at last asked gruffly, "Are you hurt?" He felt suddenly ashamed he had not inquired before now, that his temper, as well as his unexpected reaction to the woman, had caused him to rail at her instead—even if she *had* deserved it!

"No," Cat answered, although her hands still shook as, finally recognizing that she ought to get out to investigate the damage to the Jeep, she began to fumble at the clasp on the unfamiliar seat belt, trying to release it.

After a moment, cursing under his breath at her difficulty, Morgan bent, reached inside the Jeep and snapped the clasp open, freeing her. It was an act he had initially hesitated to perform, all too aware of Cat's potent effect upon him. The accidental contact of his strong hand against her slender hip jolted him. He swore softly once more. What in the hell was the matter with him? He felt as though he were a teenager again, his hormones raging clean out of control. The fragrance of Cat's perfume permeated the vehicle, wafted delicately from her skin...White Shoulders, one of Morgan's favorites. His nostrils flared slightly as he inhaled it, thought suddenly of pressing his mouth to the tiny pulse beating rapidly at the hollow of her graceful white throat. As though she were cognizant of his thought, her eyes widened, her lips parted, her breath came in quick little gasps that unintentionally excited him.

Somehow, the interior of the vehicle seemed to Cat both to shrink in size and to rise twenty degrees in temperature in that moment. With Morgan stretched across her, she was vividly conscious of the warmth of his body, of the strength of his arms, of the masculine scents of soap and cologne and sweat that clung to him, of his mouth so tantalizingly close to her own. The inadvertent touch of his hand against her hip was like a shock from a cattle prod, sending a tremor coursing through her and setting her pulse racing. When his narrowed blue eyes pierced her wide-open green ones, she saw in their depths a smoldering desire he did not bother to conceal. At the sight, her gaze fell in embarrassment and confusion and a blush rose to her cheeks. God, she had not felt like this since high school. It really was terribly unnerving, Cat thought, as though a decade of her life had suddenly vanished, taking with it all the confidence and competency she had worked so hard to acquire in the cutthroat, corporate world of New York.

The man was only a rough-diamond cowboy, for heaven's sake! And she was not only on unfamiliar territory, but also grieving, and so in a particularly vulnerable state—and not just mentally, either. She had not seen a house or even another car, except for the Bronco, for miles. She was totally alone with a strange man much bigger and stronger than she, whose eyes said he wanted her. What woman *wouldn't* be unnerved under the circumstances?

As though reading her mind, Morgan declared, "Lucky for you, lady, that I'm not the kind of man to take advantage of a situation like this," as he released her, then assisted her from the Jeep. Cat's knees trembled, and she would have fallen had he not caught her as her injured ankle abruptly gave way beneath her, causing her to stumble against him. "You *are* hurt!" Morgan exclaimed, his concern overriding the sudden tightening in his groin at the feel of the unknown woman in his arms.

"No...yes...well, what I mean is...earlier, when you honked at me, I was startled, and I fell and twisted my ankle," Cat explained, scowling now at the memory and attempting to disengage herself from his grasp, still not trusting him—or herself, either, given how her heart was thudding at his proximity. But Morgan held her fast.

"So that's what got you all riled up, was it?" His eyes now danced unmistakably with mischief, and the lopsided grin he gave her was tinged with wicked insolence. "I tell you what…man compliments a pretty woman these days, and instead of thanking him, she labels him a pervert and reaches for her pepper spray! But then I guess I should have known that you'd have a temper to match that fiery red hair of yours! What was it you called me right before you damned near ran me off the road? Sodbuster, wasn't it? Hell. I thought that term went out long before designer jeans, but then I reckon I must have been mistaken on both counts."

His eyes roamed not only with heat, but also with amusement over her Calvin Klein jeans. *Why, he was laughing at her!* No doubt at any moment he would be asking her what was between her and her Calvins. After his previous antics, she wouldn't put it past him!

"Yes, well, I saw that particular epithet used in a Western novel, and it seemed apropos at the time." Cat's tone was tart, intended to put him in his place. "However, I don't believe my temper could possibly be any worse than yours. So why don't we just agree there was provocation on both sides that led to this incident, and let it go at that? Now if you don't mind, I really do need to inspect the damage to the Jeep. It's getting late, and I don't know how long it will take to get a tow truck out here if I have to call one."

Although Morgan released her, he kept a supportive hand beneath her elbow to hold her steady as Cat limped to the front of the vehicle. To her relief, she saw that except for a couple of dents in the hood from the chartreuse, grapefruit-size fruit that now lay scattered on the ground, a mangled bumper and a smashed fog light appeared to be the only real injuries. She had probably done more harm to the old, hard, thorny tree than it had to her.

"Well, the damage isn't too bad. Your Jeep's drivable, at any rate," Morgan announced, confirming her thoughts. "It just needs to be hauled out of the ditch, and I can do that with my Bronco. I'll get my tow chain." Leaving her leaning against the side of the Jeep, he turned away, heading toward his own vehicle.

"Thanks, but I don't want to impose—" Cat began.

"I owe you one. So consider it my way of making up for your sprained ankle," he called back over his shoulder, his mouth curving once more in that impudent, crooked grin of his. It did something strange to her insides.

Once Morgan had maneuvered the Bronco into place and had got out a heavy chain to hitch the two vehicles together, Cat inquired, "What kind of a tree is that?" Its green leaves shone glossily, almost as though they had been waxed. Its trunk, where the bark had been scraped during the accident, revealed an orange core, and its fallen fruit—some of which had broken open to display pulpy, pale yellow insides—had a pungent, distinctive aroma.

"You're not from around these parts, are you?" Morgan glanced up from where he now knelt behind the Jeep, fastening the chain around the axle beneath the cargo space.

"No, I'm—I'm...here on vacation," Cat lied, not wanting to talk about her father's death.

"It's an osage orange...a hedge apple, most people hereabouts call it. Farmers plant 'em for windbreaks usually, although they grow wild, too. Horses generally like the fruit—although I wouldn't recommend your eating it, if that's what you're contemplating."

"No, I was just curious, that's all. I've never had a run-in with a tree before, so I just wanted to know what kind of a tree it was. My mother always used to say that if you *had* to be run over by a car, you should at least pick a Rolls-Royce."

"Well, I'm afraid your choice of tree wasn't quite in that league. A lot of farmers will let you have dead hedge free for firewood if you just come clear it off their land. Hedge burns real hot and shoots sparks all over the place." Morgan's eyes glinted as he looked up at her intently.

If there were, as it seemed, a double entendre to his words, Cat chose to ignore it—just as she determinedly attempted to ignore the heat and sparks that continued to flare between her and Morgan, as though electricity crackled and arced tangibly between them. She averted her gaze, flushing again, and with a sigh and a shrug, Morgan returned to his task.

"Do you need me to get back into the Jeep, to put the gearshift into Neutral or something?" Cat asked once he had finished coupling the two vehicles together.

"Yes, I do." Minutes later Morgan had the Jeep hauled from the ditch and unhooked from the Bronco. Coiling up the heavy chain he had used, he approached the driver's side of the Jeep, where Cat now sat inside the vehicle, its engine running. He hesitated for a moment over the words that sprang to his mind. Then he thought, *What the hell...no drill, no well,* and he spoke. "Look, I know we've only just met and all, and that we sort of got off on the wrong foot, besides. But, well, how 'bout if I buy you supper tonight to make up for today?"

To say she was not tempted by his offer would have been a lie, Cat knew. But she had never in her life succumbed to a one-night stand, even with a man who was *not* a stranger to her, and she was not about to start now. Although she suspected Morgan was truly nothing more than what she had in the past heard her father refer to as a "good ole boy," her life in New York had made her naturally wary and distrustful. Still, she smiled to take the sting from her response.

"Thank you," she said pointedly, remembering his earlier remark about compliments, perverts and pepper spray. "I'm flattered... really, I am. And I *do* appreciate your time and trouble in helping me get the Jeep back on the road. But—"

"But your mother warned you never to speak to strangers and never, ever to go off someplace alone with a strange man," Morgan finished wryly.

"Yes, something like that." Cat nodded.

"Well, you can't blame a guy for trying." A *tsk* of regret issuing from one corner of his mouth, Morgan shook his head ruefully, making light of his disappointment. "Still, for all its city status, Wichita's basically a small town at heart, so maybe I'll see you around, huh?"

"Maybe," Cat agreed, glad and relieved he had not turned ugly and made some cocky, insulting remark about her not knowing what she was missing, as though he were the biggest stud around and she were a frigid fool. "You just never know. If there's one thing I've learned in life, it's to expect the unexpected."

"More words of wisdom from your mother?" Morgan lifted one brow teasingly.

"No...from my—from my father." Cat's voice caught at the memory, and as she felt tears fill her eyes afresh, she said quickly, "Well, thanks again for all your help." Then she put the automatic gearshift into Drive and hurriedly pulled away, leaving Morgan standing there gazing after her thoughtfully, feeling a peculiar, inexplicable sense of loss and cursing himself soundly when he realized abruptly that he had not even learned her name.

Chapter 4

A Case of Mistaken Identities

Although it certainly was not out of the ordinary for Morgan to dine alone, he seemed somehow tonight to feel the solitude worse than usual. The prime rib he ordered at the upscale Chelsea Bar & Grill was excellent, as always, yet despite his hunger, he found he could not concentrate on his meal. As he gazed at the talking, laughing couples gathered around the piano bar, his mind kept dwelling on how different the evening would have been had the unknown redhead with the fiery temper agreed to join him. She had possessed a sass and spunk that had intrigued him—not to mention a gorgeous face and body that had cried out to him like a sweetly deceptive siren's. She had been…special, somehow. And he had not had sense enough to find out her name or even to write down her license-tag number so he could track her down later by means of his considerable computer resources.

Damn! Was he slipping or what? A few months ago he would have charmed that redhead not only into having supper with him, but also into his bed afterward. Why had he not pressed her harder? Was it because he had finally and truly tired of that game? Was it because now, at Frank's death, he, Morgan, had begun to feel his own mortality more keenly, to recognize and to admit to himself at long last that he *did* want more out of life than just the footloose and fancy-free bachelor's existence he led? A home instead of a town house. A wife instead of a string of affairs and one-night stands. A couple of kids instead of an aquarium full of fish. Was it because he had begun to question what all he had worked so hard to achieve was for, if not for that? Damn it! He did not want to wind up like Frank— alone and dead of a heart attack before he was even sixty. What was it his partner had always said? *Life's a bitch, and then you die, Son.* No, there had to be more to life than that—or what was the point?

Following supper, Morgan returned home to his town house in The Mews, waving perfunctorily at the guard, who admitted him through the gate of the enclave clustered on the western edge of Vickridge. Once inside, Morgan tossed his key ring on the kitchen counter and grabbed a beer from the refrigerator. From the freezer he withdrew a package of frozen brine shrimp, a portion of which he cut into chunks and fed to the fish in his aquarium. Then he checked his answering machine. The red light was blinking, indicating a message had been received in his absence. He punched the Rewind button and, while the tape was running back to its starting position, twisted the cap off the bottled beer and took a long swallow. When the tape had come to a stop, he pressed the Play button.

"Morgan, this is Virginia Lorimer," a woman's plaintive voice announced from the machine. "I hesitated calling you, because I really do hate to bother you, especially at such a sorrowful time as this and so soon after poor Frank's funeral—such a nice service you had for him, by the way! I'm sure he would have been so proud of it! And I guess I probably ought to have called the police instead.... But, well, I just didn't want to cause any unnecessary trouble for you, you understand, if it was only you going through Frank's business papers and personal belongings, sorting them out and all...."

"Yeah, so get to the point already, why don't you, Virginia?" Morgan muttered as he took another sip of beer and listened impatiently to Frank's nosy, half-crocked neighbor.

"But if it wasn't you over at Frank's yesterday evening," Virginia's voice droned on, "then I really think someone's broken into his house, and that you should go over right away and investigate, because I saw lights on there last night. I know I did! And I've heard there are some robbers, you know—as unconscionable as it certainly is—who actually read the obituary columns in the newspapers, looking for easy marks...houses that are standing empty due to their owners' deaths. And of course, Frank's address being what it is, that house of his must surely be a temptation to thieves.... Oh, I'm probably just a nervous old Nellie, and it was only you at Frank's house. But, well, you can't be too careful these days, and so I thought you should know, that's all. Again, I'm sorry to have disturbed you, Morgan.'' There was a short click as Virginia rang off. Then, with a brief hiss, the tape wound to a stop.

"Wonder if you saw the lights at Frank's house before or *after* you'd started hitting the sauce for the evening, Virginia?'' Morgan mused dryly, shaking his head and rolling his eyes, knowing it was a wonder the woman had *not* called the police—and reported that lights were streaming from a UFO that had landed in Frank's backyard!

Poor Virginia! Well, that was what came of having too much money to spend, too much time on your hands and too little excitement in your life. You wound up as the neighborhood's resident moralist, snoop and crackpot—taking pictures of your neighbors' houses to prove to your homeowners' association that the Smiths lacked the requisite number of trees in their yard or that the Joneses were concealing a forbidden satellite dish in their bushes!

God, Morgan thought as he groaned inwardly, *spare me from the Virginia Lorimers of this world!* Still, no matter what he thought of her, he supposed he would have to go by Frank's house later to check it out and make certain it really *hadn't* been broken into—simply because there was always the slim possibility that this time Virginia was not just crying wolf. Nevertheless, Morgan intended to finish his beer first—and maybe even have a second one—and read his mail and watch the 10:00 p.m. news, as well. Then, even though he felt sure Virginia's suspicion was entirely ungrounded, he would, on his nightly jog through the neighborhood, cruise by Frank's house.

Now that she was no longer jet lagged and exhausted, Cat realized for the first time how big and empty and lonely her father's house was. It might as well have been standing all by itself out in the country, such was the silence that enveloped it. Accustomed to the hustle and bustle of New York, to the sounds of the neighbors in her apartment building, of the incessant traffic and subway trains, of the night life in a city that never slept, she found the lack of noise disturbing. It was as though, somehow, she were all alone in the world— an eerie, unsettling sensation.

To dispel it and fill up the silence, Cat turned on the small television that sat on the kitchen counter as she limped around her father's country kitchen, fixing herself a simple dinner consisting of a tossed salad and a chicken potpie. While the potpie was baking, she soaked her ankle in a stainless-steel mixing bowl filled with warm salt water, which so helped the swelling and eased the pain that she knew her sprain was not serious, just a nuisance. Afterward she ate at the kitchen table, in front of the television.

Other than the news, Cat didn't watch much television usually. But her father's house was hooked up to cable, and so, a little to her surprise, she discovered myriad channels from which to choose. With the remote control she flicked through them one by one until her eye was caught by an old movie, *Butch Cassidy and the Sundance Kid,* starring Paul Newman and Robert Redford. All at once Cat was struck by the resemblance between Redford and the cowboy who had so infuriated and attracted her earlier that day. The unknown man had been a younger, darker version of the actor, she realized now. Thousands of women would, given the opportunity, run off with Redford, she knew. Was it any wonder she should have felt her pulse quicken in the presence of the actor's look-alike?

Now, however, Cat felt horribly guilty that the cowboy had managed, even for so short a while, to force her thoughts away from her father's death. It was not unusual to be drawn to another human being sexually in the face of death, to be driven by a primal urge to create life; and her father would not have condemned her for that. Still, she chastised herself for having a hard time putting the unknown man from her mind.

Cat watched the entire movie, sobbing more than she normally would have at its end, grieving for her father and wondering for the first time if she had perhaps been too hasty in breaking off her engagement to Spence. It was not a crime to be single, and it was certainly possible to live a full, happy life without ever having married. But despite her professional career and independence, her heart cried out for companionship and children. As greedy as it might seem, she wanted all life had to offer.

Having finished her meal, Cat rinsed her few dishes and stacked them in the dishwasher. Then, feeling terribly depressed, she went upstairs to get ready for bed. A long hot bath was in order, she decided, followed by immersion in the pages of some favorite novel, or she would not sleep well tonight. She flicked on the lights and the television in her bedroom, setting the channel to CNN. For a moment she yearned desperately to telephone Spence. But the memory of their argument and breakup, of his firing her so callously, followed so hard on the heels by her father's death, dissuaded her from weakening and giving in to the temptation. She was made of sterner and more prideful stuff than to go crawling back to Spence, who had wanted just another showy possession instead of a wife.

Once more, thoughts of the cowboy intruded in Cat's mind. He had been vibrant and earthy, the kind of man, she had sensed, to fling a woman down upon the ground, taking her in the tumultuous heat of passion—a notion from which fastidious Spence would have shrunk, labeling it common and uncivilized. But somehow Cat could not put from her head the idea that a woman lying beneath that unknown man would feel not only the earth, but also the heavens move for her, that he would make damned sure she felt it!

Smiling despite herself at the thought, she settled into the warm water of the sunken, marble bathtub, leaning back, closing her eyes and letting the scented bubbles engulf her.

Hell's bells! For once in her life, Virginia Lorimer had *not* been pulling a Chicken Little, Morgan thought, stunned, as he stared at the lights glowing softly from behind the closed plantation shutters that screened the casement windows of Frank's house. Somebody had indeed broken into the place, might even at this moment still be ransacking it! At the thought, Morgan felt hot rage boil up inside him, as though it were his town house that had been violated. His parents had been killed in a car accident when he was a youth. An elderly, widowed great-aunt had taken him in and reared him until he was old enough to be out on his own. So, for all practical purposes, Frank Devlin had been the only father he had known for most his life. Morgan's eyes narrowed murderously. Come hell or high water, he was going to get the bastard who had dared to break into Frank's house!

As Morgan advanced stealthily up the driveway, he realized there was no unfamiliar vehicle parked out front, half loaded with the burglar's loot. But then it was not uncommon, he knew, for a thief to steal a victim's own car during a robbery, using it to carry away the illicit haul. Frank had owned both a Jeep and a classic Cadillac convertible. Jeeps were popular at chop shops, and the Cadillac was worth a mint; either one would bring a tidy, however illegal, profit.

The front door appeared secure, as did the front windows. So Morgan crept around the side of the house and vaulted over the high wooden fence into the backyard. As he did, from Virginia Lorimer's house next door, the furious, high-pitched yapping of her two cockapoos reached his ears. Minutes later her exterior security lights blazed on, her back door opened, she herself poked her head out and the two little dogs came barking and bounding out into her backyard, to race alongside the fence between her property and Frank's.

"Damn it, Virginia!" Morgan yelled to her above the ruckus. "It's me, Morgan. Call those mutts of yours back inside!"

"Oh, my goodness gracious!" Virginia laid one hand against her breast, visibly agitated. "What a fright you gave me, Morgan! My heart's just pounding! Why, I'll be lucky if I don't follow poor Frank to the grave! Muffin! Crumpet! Come here, darlings. It's only Morgan McCain. You know Morgan, babies...poor Frank's partner. What're you doing out there in the dark, Morgan, prowling around like some Peeping Tom? Is everything all right?"

"Yes," he lied, wanting to be rid of her as quickly as possible. "Everything's fine. I've been out jogging, and I just dropped by to check on Frank's house, that's all. Now, for heaven's sake, go back inside before those mutts of yours wake up the entire neighborhood!'' he hissed angrily, glancing anxiously at Frank's place, wondering if all the noise had alerted whoever was inside. "Good *night,* Virginia!'' he said firmly when she continued to peer at him curiously from her doorway.

"Well, if you're sure nothing's wrong... Good night, Morgan.''

Finally, to his relief, she withdrew, taking the two cockapoos with her. Her security lights winked out shortly afterward—although he spied her at a window, furtively drawing back her drapes to peek out at him. He cursed and groaned inwardly, wondering how Frank had not only endured her, but had actually taken her out more than once. Then Morgan chided himself for his irritability. Virginia was a widow, and lonely. She was probably feeling Frank's loss as keenly as Morgan himself was. Still, right now he would gladly have pitched those two mutts of hers into the Big Arkansas river!

Forcing himself to tamp down his anger, he carefully skirted the swimming pool and hot tub, then sneaked across the multilevel wooden deck to the French doors at the back of Frank's house, which were also secure. To gain entry, the thief must have broken a side window somewhere or somehow gained access through the garage, Morgan thought. Withdrawing from the inside pocket of his sweatpants his set of keys to Frank's house, Morgan inserted the proper one into the lock of the French doors and turned it. Moments later he stood inside the house, warily surveying his surroundings and certain now from the noises he heard coming from upstairs that he was not alone.

It was the dogs' feverish yapping that attracted Cat's attention as she stepped from the bathtub and began to towel herself dry. Since, earlier, the neighborhood had been so quiet, she was intelligent enough to realize something must have stirred the dogs up, and because she was alone, she was prudent enough to investigate the cause. Slipping into her panties and a vibrant, lime green caftan, she limped to her father's dark bedroom at the back of the house, where she peered through the open wooden slats of the plantation shutters that screened the casement windows. The barking of the dogs, which had seemed to be coming from beyond the backyard, had now ceased.

But as she peeked out, Cat observed in the moonlight the shadowy figure of a man on the lawn, moving furtively toward the French doors.

Her mouth went dry and her heart pounded with fear as she tried to remember whether she had set the alarm before coming upstairs. She was almost positive she had not, so there was no use in counting on its going off to summon assistance. She was on her own. Even as she watched, the man disappeared from her view. Moments later, before she could even think what to do, Cat heard one of the French doors open and realized he must have jimmied the lock, was even now inside the house with her! God, the irony of it! In all the years she had lived in New York, she had never even been mugged. The idea that she was now perhaps about to be robbed, raped and murdered in Wichita, Kansas, in the very center of America's Heartland, was so ludicrous that she nearly laughed aloud with hysteria.

Torn, panicked, Cat glanced longingly at the telephone on her father's nightstand. Aid was surely only a phone call away. But then she thought that even if the 911 emergency number was not busy, there was no telling how long it would take for the police to arrive; and every passing minute of delay might prove fatal. No, she had to get out, to get away! Even if none of the neighbors would help her, there had been a guard posted at The Mews, the enclave of town houses clustered at the western edge of Vickridge. Physically, Cat was in excellent shape from her three-times-weekly workouts at a gym. Even barefoot and with a sprained ankle, she could run as far as the guard tower if she had to, she decided resolutely. Slowly, she crept from her father's bedroom and started down the back staircase that led to the kitchen, praying that whoever was in the house would hear the noise of her television upstairs and would move in that direction, toward the front staircase, hoping to take her by surprise.

As she reached the foot of the stairs, Cat paused for a surreptitious look around the corner of the wall. To her terror, she spied the intruder standing in the family room beyond the big, open country kitchen. She clapped one hand to her mouth to stifle the gasp of shock and fright that rose in her throat. It was *him!* The cowboy who had hollered and honked at her earlier, who had towed the Jeep from the ditch and then asked her to dinner. Oh, God, her initial assumption about him must have been correct! He was some kind of a lunatic, a pervert—a *stalker!* Doubtless enraged by her refusal of his invitation, he had followed her home and had broken into the house, intending heaven only knew what. Oh, God, he was leaving the family room and coming into the kitchen, moving toward *her!* Some sound must have passed her lips after all, alerting him to her presence....

If she ran back upstairs, she might be trapped up there, unable to escape from the house, Cat realized, the wheels of her brain churning furiously. Quickly, she dropped down to her hands and knees so the kitchen counters and cabinets would, she prayed, hide her from the man's view as she skittered across the kitchen floor into the dining room. Just inside the doorway a huge vase sat upon the massive sideboard against the wall. With trembling hands Cat snatched up the vase, her heart in her throat as she heard the man's footsteps drawing ominously nearer. Evidently, he must have seen or heard her and was now coming toward the dining room. When he entered, she did not hesitate, but smashed the vase down as hard as she could upon his head.

She heard the man groan and then, with a loud thud, hit the floor as the vase shattered about him. Hurriedly, Cat reached out and switched on the dining room light, gasping again at the sight that met her eyes. The man was knocked out cold, sprawled half on, half off the Oriental carpet laid upon the hardwood floor, shards of the broken vase scattered all around him. For a moment, as she stared at her handiwork, Cat could only think dumbly that she had probably just destroyed a priceless Ming vase. Then she remembered that her father would not have known the Ming Dynasty from Ming of Mongo, and relief that owed a great deal more to her own survival than to the vase's maker flooded her being.

Gingerly stepping over sharp pieces of china, she hastened to the kitchen and picked up the receiver of the telephone, her hands shaking as she dialed 911. Thank God she didn't get a busy signal, that the phone actually rang! Within moments Cat was assured by the dispatcher that the police were en route, and much to her surprise and relief, they actually did arrive approximately ten minutes later, along with paramedics. She admitted them all to the house, explaining the situation to one of the two police officers, while the two paramedics treated the injuries the intruder had sustained from the blow of the heavy vase: minor cuts and bruises and a possible concussion.

After several minutes the second police officer, who had checked the interior pocket of the intruder's sweatpants for identification and then, finding none, had examined the house, returned to the scene in the dining room. His face was puzzled and suspicious now when he looked at her, Cat thought in confusion as he drew his fellow officer aside. They spoke in low tones before turning their attention back to her.

"Ma'am," one of them began, "we seem to have a slight problem here concerning your story. You see, we can't find any signs of the forced entry you described—"

"That's because I let myself in with a damned key!" Morgan interjected surlily as he impatiently waved away the paramedics and hauled himself up into one of the high-backed chairs around the dining table, from where he glared groggily at Cat.

"A *key!*" she cried, stunned by his audacity, his brazen lying to the police. "How could you possibly have a key to my father's house?"

"Your *father!* Damn, damn, *damn!* I knew it! The minute I came to and saw you here, I just *knew* it!" Morgan groaned, shaking his head disbelievingly as he gingerly probed the huge, swollen knot just above his right ear. "Coldcocked by a woman, by God!" he exclaimed sourly. "I'll never live it down." Then he held out his hands to the startled, bemused police officers, as though expecting, indeed *wanting*, to be cuffed and hauled away to jail. "Just clap 'em on and take me in, boys," he drawled mockingly. "I want to wake up in a jail cell tomorrow morning and find out this has all been just another Saturday night in Margaritaville, the product of an imagination unhinged by booze.... Will you *please* get that penlight out of my eyes!" he snapped to the paramedics, who, thinking he was rambling and confused, unaware of the seriousness of his situation, were attempting to recheck the dilation and contraction of his pupils. "I've got a hard head, I've been hit harder in the past and there's nothing wrong with me that a couple of aspirin won't cure!'' Morgan paused for a moment, then addressed Cat again. ''Ms. Devlin...you *are* Ms. Catherine Devlin, are you not?''

''Yes, but how did *you* know that?'' she asked, a strange, sinking feeling of suspicion and mortification suddenly taking hold of her.

''I know...I know because I am your father's friend and business partner, Ms. Devlin...Morgan McCain,'' he announced. Stunned, Cat could only stare at him speechlessly as, in the abrupt silence, the front doorbell rang, accompanied by the high-pitched yapping of dogs, and he continued ruefully, ''And *that* will be Virginia Lorimer, your nosy next-door neighbor—and the cause of this entire damned mess!''

Chapter 5

Getting to Know You

Chuckling with a good deal of amusement, the police and paramedics had left. Apologizing plaintively and defending herself profusely all the while, Virginia Lorimer had finally departed as well, taking away with her the two barking cockapoos, much to Cat's and Morgan's mutual relief. Now they sat alone in the taut, strained silence that had descended in her father's family room, to which they had retired, staring at each other with a mixture of wariness and ruefulness and, still, a measure of disbelief.

Cat could not seem to take in the fact that this man, this cowboy, was her father's friend and business partner, Morgan McCain. In the past, whenever she had thought of Morgan at all, she had, from her father's wild stories and descriptions of him, vaguely envisioned a banty, beer-swilling braggart and brawler who mistakenly believed himself to be God's gift to women, not this tall, rugged, drop-dead-gorgeous man who sat in the chair next to her own, his cool, commanding presence such that he seemed effortlessly to dominate his surroundings.

Morgan was equally slow to absorb the fact that this woman was Frank Devlin's daughter, Catherine...*Cat*, she called herself. He ought to have recognized Frank's Jeep earlier today, he thought dumbly as he gazed at her, feeling like a poleaxed steer and wondering if perhaps he had been too hasty, after all, in refusing to permit the paramedics to take him to the hospital, in case her crack upon his skull had indeed given him a concussion. Then he realized that, of course, there were hundreds of Jeeps in town and that there had been no reason at the time to connect with Frank the one that she had been driving. In fact, Morgan mused, it was just as well he had *not* made the connection, because then his first meeting with her would surely have gone a whole lot differently. His temper would undoubtedly have led him to say things to her he would be deeply regretting at this moment. Awkwardly, Morgan cleared his throat.

"Somehow, we...ah...seem to keep getting off on the wrong foot, don't we?" he observed at last, thinking uncomfortably that Cat was nothing at all as he had imagined her. He had expected someone hard, aloof, sophisticated...cold—not this beautiful, graceful young woman whose dark red hair seemed afire and whose porcelain skin radiated such warmth in the lamplight. Whose green eyes could dance with humor, flash sparks of indignation and harbor shadows of deep anguish all at once when they met his glance. "Why didn't you let me know you were coming to Wichita? I would have been more than happy to pick you up at the airport, to see that you were settled in and had everything you needed."

"Thank you for the thought. But I...needed some time alone...to think, to grieve," Cat responded quietly. "Dad's death was so unexpected, so painful—" She broke off abruptly, tears filling her eyes. Glancing away from him, she bit her lower lip hard, so plainly embarrassed by her uncontrollable display of emotion that Morgan knew it was unfeigned, that despite his previous doubts to the contrary, Ms. Catherine Devlin had, in fact, loved her father wholeheartedly. For a few minutes she fought for composure, finally regaining it. Then she continued. "As you can see, it...hit me pretty hard. I still can't quite believe he's gone. Somehow I keep expecting to hear his voice, his laughter—"

"Yeah, I know what you mean," Morgan admitted, his own voice gruff with emotion.

Cat started a little at his tone, for the first time realizing she was not alone in her sorrow, that Morgan had cared about Frank Devlin, too.

"I'm sorry," she said, after a long moment spent contemplating that fact. "I didn't think about Dad being your business partner, your friend. His death must have been difficult for you, too.... And I haven't even thanked you for—for taking care of him, for making all the funeral arrangements and everything for me when I couldn't get back here from Europe in time."

"Frank was like a father to me. I was glad to do it."

Something about the way Morgan spoke those simple words made Cat understand their truth. It struck her suddenly that although her father had never married again, he might have wanted to. He might have longed for a second wife, a second family...or at least a son, someone to follow in his footsteps, someone to value, hold on to and to build upon all he had worked so hard to achieve in his life. She had not until this moment ever thought of herself as that person, although she had loved her father dearly. Perhaps, she reflected now, surprised and curious and even faintly piqued, her father, despite his own love for her, had not thought of her in that light, either. Perhaps, as he had been like a father to Morgan, Morgan had been to him the son he had never had, the heir apparent, the one to whom the proverbial torch could be safely passed on.

Involuntarily, Cat felt her eyes being drawn to Morgan's hands. They were strong, sure, capable hands, she knew instinctively, callused and accustomed to hard work, despite the fact that they were well shaped and well groomed, with a light dusting of dark hair upon their backs. They were hands to be trusted, she thought. She remembered how they had so easily released her seat belt, had held and supported her so firmly, had unwittingly made her skin tingle—and yet had done nothing untoward.

Yes, her father would have trusted those hands; he would have trusted Morgan McCain.

"Would you—would you like a drink? Or—or some coffee?" Cat asked abruptly on impulse, cursing her wretched tongue for stumbling over the words, for making her feel like a blushing schoolgirl again.

In the space of half a day, this man, this cowboy, had somehow succeeded in affecting her in ways she had not until now thought possible. She did not know why that should be so; she knew only that it was. "I could make some coffee...it would only take a few minutes."

It was late, and Morgan knew he should go. Yet he found himself curiously loath to leave Cat. Was it only this morning he had yearned for just ten minutes of her precious time, so he could tell her exactly what he had thought of her? He wanted to give her something now, but not a piece of his mind—as his sweatpants would certainly reveal if he got to his feet. Damn! Did she know how she looked sitting there, curled up in one of the family room's oversize, stuffed chairs, her hair aflame and one creamy shoulder bared where the sleeve of her caftan had slipped a little down her arm? Just looking at her, just thinking about sweeping her up in his arms, carrying her upstairs and pressing her down upon that big, antique canopy bed he knew Frank had bought for her was making Morgan crazy inside. His groin was tight with desire. He had better go before he made a complete fool of himself again!

"I'd love some coffee," he heard himself answer instead, as though his mouth had without warning disengaged itself from his brain, deliberately and maddeningly hooking up with another portion of his anatomy, a portion notorious for its lack of common sense.

But it was too late now to withdraw his acceptance of Cat's offer. She had already risen from her chair and stepped quickly into the kitchen, as though glad to have something to do. In light of that, he would appear rude and churlish if he left now, Morgan knew. So instead, he joined her in the kitchen, taking a seat at the table, watching her appreciatively as she moved about, grinding aromatic coffee beans for the basket filter in the drip coffeemaker on the counter, adding water, then turning on the machine. From a bag, she took fresh bagels, warming them before arranging them attractively on a platter, along with small bowls of spreadable fruit and low-fat Philadelphia cream cheese. Morgan was not normally much of a bagel eater, thinking of it as an East Coast preference. But he had to admit Cat had somehow made the bagels seem pretty appetizing—even if he was also simultaneously amused by the thought that she might have been laying out a high tea. She might not be the stuck-up, hard-hearted witch he had initially supposed, but he was willing to bet he had been right about one thing: her background and upbringing were such that she would know which fork to use when at a seven-course dinner.

Still, much to his surprise as he watched her preparations, Morgan found it difficult to refrain from imagining Cat belonged to him, that it was his kitchen in which she worked so gracefully and competently, and that after they had drunk their coffee and eaten their bagels, he would have every right to take her upstairs and make love to her. That was only a fantasy, but he suspected something of his thoughts must have shown on his face, because when she joined him at the table, a blush stained her cheeks and she concentrated more than necessary on spreading cream cheese on her bagel.

In fact, Cat was not aware of his thoughts. It was her own that so unsettled her. It had come to her while she worked how at ease Morgan was in her father's house, her father's kitchen, as though he belonged there and she were somehow an interloper. She had felt suddenly out of her milieu and depth, had experienced again that strange sensation she had had in the taxi from the airport—that she had somehow been transported back in time. She had felt as though she were lost somewhere on the wild frontier, with only this cowboy to depend upon for survival. Inexplicably, the image of Robert Redford in the movie she'd just seen kept filling her mind, specifically the scene in which Katherine Ross's character, Etta Place, had been undressing in her bedroom, initially oblivious of the presence of Redford's character, Harry Longbaugh, the Sundance Kid. When Etta had finally spied him, the Kid had drawn his gun and insisted she keep right on taking off her clothes for him—so when Cat had sat down across the table from Morgan, she had been abruptly seized by a crazy notion that he was about to level a revolver at her and demand she undress for him...slowly, very slowly. She had been both mortified and perversely excited by the idea, and she had not dared to look at him in that moment, for fear he might somehow discern her thoughts.

Now, as she glanced up at him surreptitiously from beneath the fringe of her lashes, Cat silently cursed the fact that all the polite conversation she could usually and easily indulge in to entertain a guest seemed to have deserted her. And the suggestion of her college-speech-class professor—to conquer stage fright by imagining one's audience as being totally naked—did not produce the desired effect at all when she envisioned Morgan McCain without any clothes on. In fact, as the image of him nude rose in her mind, Cat's heart beat even faster, and she could hardly swallow the bite of bagel she had chewed into mush. What was the matter with her? Why should this man disconcert her so? He was *only* a man, like any other—and as a professional, independent woman who had just broken off her engagement, it would not be wholly amiss of her at the moment to feel nothing but contempt for the entire male gender. Instead, she was sitting here fantasizing about going to bed with Morgan McCain! There was definitely something wrong with her, Cat decided. Grief and jet lag must somehow have combined to derange her brain!

"The coffee's very good," Morgan said, interrupting her reverie and then repeating his comment when Cat momentarily stared at him blankly.

"Oh...the coffee...thanks. I'm glad you like it. It's a special gourmet blend. I bought it at the grocery store earlier today, and since I'm not familiar with Midwestern brands, I wasn't sure how it would taste. But I thought I'd give it a try, anyway." Jeez Louise, she sounded like a babbling idiot unable to make any intelligent conversation whatsoever! He was probably sitting there thinking, *Ditsy redhead!* and wondering how he could politely escape from her. She could not remember the last time she had felt so awkward, so inadequate, and she did not like the feeling now.

Everything's just been too much for you. You're overwhelmed at the moment, Cat, and therefore off-balance, she told herself sternly. *You need to recover your equilibrium, that's all. You can get through this, one day at a time.*

"I'm sorry," she said then. "I don't normally chatter on so inanely. I've been under a lot of stress, as I'm sure you have, too." She paused for a moment. "I'd like to hear about my father...what kind of service you had for him and where he's—where he's buried. And I'm certain there are things you'd like to discuss as well—business matters..."

"Yes, there are. But it *is* late, and it's been a long day besides—a very long, *befuddled* day." Morgan smiled ruefully, thinking of all the bizarre twists and turns that had led them, finally, to be having coffee in Frank's kitchen. "I'm sure you're tired, and I know *I* am. So tell you what—why don't I meet you here in the morning? That way we can get the Jeep in to be repaired so you'll have a car you can depend on...you won't want to drive the Cadillac, I know, since it's so big. Then I'll take you out to the cemetery. After that, we'll grab some lunch, and I'll see if we can't meet with your father's attorney, Richard Hollis, sometime tomorrow afternoon to take care of all the legalities. How does that sound to you?"

"Fine. That sounds just fine," Cat responded, trying to quell the sudden racing of her pulse at the idea of spending the day with Morgan McCain. He was just a man, like any other, nothing special, she insisted again to herself. Still, the glance he gave her as he finished his coffee and then stood made her heart turn over.

"I'll see you in the morning then," he said as she walked him to the front door.

"I'll—I'll...be here." Jeez Louise, she had almost replied, *I'll be looking forward to it,* as though she were some eager puppy wagging its tail at the sight of a dog biscuit! She had better get hold of herself in a hurry, Cat thought. "Good night, Morgan."

"Good night, Cat."

He jogged off into the darkness, and after she closed the front door behind him, she leaned against it weakly for a moment, her knees trembling.

"Cat Devlin, you're a grieving fool on the rebound!" she declared aloud to herself.

But as she started upstairs to bed, her step was lighter than it had been for many days.

Chapter 6

Hellos and Goodbyes

When Cat awakened in the morning, it was to the sound of what she initially supposed was the digital alarm clock on the nightstand beside her bed, which she had set before retiring. But after she blearily groped for the clock and pressed its Snooze button, and the ringing continued, she realized finally that it was the telephone echoing so jarringly in her ear. Belatedly fumbling for and then lifting the receiver, she spoke.

"Hello." She was still not quite awake. Her voice was soft, smoky, drowsy.

"You know, you can tell an awful lot about a woman from how she sounds when you roust her out of bed in the morning," a low, husky, baritone voice drawled provocatively. "Now you...you sound sleepy—and sexy as hell."

"Who...who is this?" she asked, her pulse leaping suddenly, because she already half suspected her caller's identity, since no one else knew she was in town.

"It's Morgan," he confirmed. "I'll be over in an hour."

Feeling like the world's worst fool, Morgan hung up without giving her a chance to reply. He had not intended to greet her in such a manner; the words had seemed to come from his mouth of their own volition. It was as though, ever since he had met Cat Devlin, he had been possessed by some uncontrollable devil. If he had not rung off, he knew his next line would have been, "And there's nothing I'd like better than to find you still in bed, waiting for me." At the thought, unbidden, the image of Cat lying upstairs in that big canopy bed, half-asleep, wearing a diaphanous negligee that was half slipping from her shoulders rose in his mind, arousing him unbearably. "Get a grip, McCain," he chided himself wryly. "She's just a woman, like any other." But somehow he couldn't seem to make himself believe that.

A cold shower. That was what he needed—a long, cold shower. Groaning at the thought, but resolutely compelling himself to move anyway, Morgan abruptly flung back the sheets and stumbled naked from his bed to his bathroom. He turned on the radio as he passed it, cranking up the volume so he would be able to hear it over the water. Then he opened the shower door, twisted on the Cold tap and forced himself to step inside the tiled enclosure. The sharp, icy spray hit him full blast, effectively quelling his amorous musings. Simultaneously, over the sound of the running water, he made out the opening strains of "What I Did for Love." The irony of that was *not* amusing. Wincing and shivering, he sighed heavily.

It was going to be one of those days.

It's a beautiful day! Cat thought as she scrambled from bed and headed toward her bathroom, flicking on her stereo in passing. The tuner, she had discovered yesterday, was set to a channel called B98-FM, an adult-contemporary station that suited her just fine. As she twisted her dark red hair up on top of her head and, with a French comb, secured the loose ends, she hummed along to the song that was currently playing, "What I Did for Love." The loss of her father still grieved her; she would miss him a lot. But now she felt that, by coming to Wichita, she had somehow encouraged the healing process to begin. It was almost as though, here, her father were still with her in spirit, looking over her shoulder and cheering her on. Involuntarily, she kept thinking of that last line in his letter to her, about her and Morgan being two wildcats, together at last.

"Dad, you old matchmaker, you!" she said ruefully as she turned on the shower and slipped off her negligee. "Why do I have the sneaking suspicion that of all the men you could have picked, this rough-diamond cowboy was the one you thought was right for me, huh? He's nothing at all like Spence—but no doubt you considered that a mark in Morgan's favor, right? Well, we'll see. No matter what you might have thought, the truth is things really haven't gone too smoothly between me and Morgan up until this point—and I'll admit that just for a moment this morning, I was half-afraid he was an obscene caller! He's lucky I didn't hang up on him or, worse yet, blow a whistle in his ear!"

Had Morgan still been lying in bed when he had telephoned her? Cat wondered as the warm spray from the shower head poured over her nude body. And if he had been, what had he been wearing? Pajamas? Boxer shorts? Briefs? Nothing at all?

"What's it to you, Cat? I mean…it's not like you're going to go to bed with the man or anything. Why, you hardly even know him!"

But while there might be some accounting for taste, there was, Cat knew, none at all for chemistry. That was something that just happened. As much as she longed to deny it, and despite the fact that they had twice now got off to a bad start, she knew deep down inside that embers smoldered between her and Morgan, just waiting to be ignited, to explode into something that half frightened and half tantalized her. Still, she was smart enough to realize she was terribly vulnerable right now, not only because of her father's death, but also because of her breakup with Spence. Under the circumstances, a relationship with a man was the last thing she needed to be embarking upon! Her current mental state was assuredly affecting her good judgment.

"Get hold of yourself, Cat!" she told herself sternly as, after stepping from the shower, she toweled herself dry. "Otherwise, you're liable to wind up making a complete fool of yourself! For all you know, Morgan McCain might not want anything more from you than a one-night stand—and your father's shares in the One-Eyed Jacks Oil and Gas Company!"

This last was a sobering thought—one Cat had not previously considered. Of course, Morgan would be concerned about the future of his corporation and its disposition. Abruptly, some of the joy went out of the morning, and it was with a much cooler head and a steadier hand that Cat finished applying her makeup. After that, she dressed in a becoming, peach-colored linen suit and was downstairs, finishing a quick cup of coffee, when Morgan at last rang the doorbell.

When she opened the door, he did a double take at the sight of her, not quite sure for a moment that he was at the right house. There was nothing in her now of the wild, hot-tempered girl-next-door who had nearly run him off the dirt road yesterday, or of the sensuous femme fatale of last night, either. In their place stood a woman who looked every inch the cool, aloof, sophisticated lady Morgan had initially, before meeting her, supposed Cat to be. From her hair done up in a French twist to the stylish Bruno Magli pumps on her feet, this woman personified everything he had ever thought of as a "stuck-up Eastern broad." It struck him in that moment that Cat was, in fact, a carbon copy of Veronica Havers, the one woman he had ever been serious about, who had ditched him in the end for a suave financial investor.

The clever, flirtatious greeting that had sprung to Morgan's lips died unuttered.

"Good morning, Ms. Devlin," he said smoothly, coolly, instead. "If you're ready, you can get your father's Jeep and follow me to the dealership so we can get that damage to the front end squared away."

Cat was frankly puzzled—and not a little piqued and hurt—by his tone and by the fact that he had addressed her as "Ms. Devlin." After all, she had, finally, been "Cat" to him last night, had she not? Was this the same man who had called her only an hour ago and spoken to her so provocatively, tantalizing her? It did not appear so. Yet she could have sworn he had been glad to see her at first. What had happened to change that?

"Just let me get my handbag and lock up the house."

"Fine," Morgan replied tersely. "I'll wait for you outside."

He strode off without another word, leaving Cat staring after him, confused and now a little angry, too, before she closed the front door and made her way to the garage. From there, she backed the Jeep out into the driveway and then onto the street. As she did so, she happened to notice a battered old pickup truck parked alongside the curb a few doors down. Briefly, she frowned at the sight. From what she had seen so far of Vickridge, she knew instinctively the pickup did not belong in the neighborhood. But then she thought that perhaps the truck might be owned by one of the local yard services. She remembered seeing a couple of those around yesterday, their employees mowing lawns and weeding flower beds. She had made a mental note to herself at the time that she herself would need to engage such a service to maintain her father's own grounds if she planned on remaining in his house for any length of time. Otherwise, the grass would soon be waist high and the flower beds full of weeds. Something else to worry about. She supposed she would need a pool service, too. She sighed. There was certainly a lot more to taking care of a house than she had ever before realized—and something to be said for living in an apartment or a town house.

After glancing in his rearview mirror to make certain she was behind him, Morgan drove off in his Bronco. His earlier good mood was now so bad that he burned rubber as he sped away recklessly. Cat could think of nothing she had done to put him in such a foul temper, but whatever the cause, he had no right to take it out on her! she decided, incensed, as she raced after him. From firsthand experience yesterday, he knew she could not drive all that well, so just how did he expect her to keep up with him? Fortunately, this must have occurred to Morgan also, because shortly afterward, he slowed his speed. They turned south onto Rock Road, Cat just managing to get across the two lanes of oncoming traffic, which was at least a little lighter this morning than it had been yesterday afternoon. She glanced at her wristwatch. It was just after nine o'clock. Rush hour here in Wichita must be over, she mused gratefully, having dreaded the idea of trying to make her way through a horde of vehicles. Taxis, buses and subways she knew and could handle. Cars and trucks were another story.

At the busy intersection of Rock Road and what the bright green street sign announced was Kellogg, Morgan stopped at the red light, and as Cat eased the Jeep to a halt behind him, she observed that he was, by means of his rearview mirror, actually *glaring* at her! It was just too much! Her own temper rose accordingly, and for a crazy instant she was strongly tempted to bash his Bronco in the rear end.

After all, the Jeep's front end was already damaged. But then common sense prevailed, and abruptly seized by another wild impulse, one that harkened back to childhood, she instead made a horrible face and stuck out her tongue at him. She saw his eyes widen in sheer surprise, and then, to her satisfaction, he laughed.

"Gotcha!" Cat mouthed to him, grinning.

Morgan had no time to mouth back any equally impudent reply, because just then the light changed from red to green. But as he turned west onto Kellogg, he discovered that his ill mood had vanished as suddenly as it had come upon him. He had been both amazed and amused by Cat's action—not in the least what he would have expected from a woman of her ilk. Not even in fun had Veronica Havers ever resorted to such childish behavior. He found it hard to believe Cat had. It was, however, a stunt Frank might have pulled; and in that moment Morgan realized that while his friend and business partner might be dead and gone, something of him remained behind in his daughter. It was somehow a comforting notion.

Cheered, Morgan pulled the Bronco into the Jeep dealership and parked. Then he walked back toward Cat as she drove in behind him.

"I owe you an apology," he said right off as she rolled down the window. "When I saw you this morning, I was...reminded of someone I'd prefer to forget, and I'm afraid I took it out on you. I was rude and wrong, and I'm sorry. What do you say we try this one last time—and get it right this time?" He held out his hand to her. "Ms. Devlin, I'm Morgan McCain, your father's friend and business partner, and I'm glad to meet you. Frank told me an awful lot about you over the years. He was mighty proud of you."

His explanation of his bad mood both enlightened and intrigued Cat. She had not given any thought to the notion that Morgan might already have a woman in his life. She was strangely glad to learn he did not, even as she thought ruefully that perhaps he was on the rebound, too. Still, he was man enough to admit a mistake and apologize for it, which spoke well of him. And his words about her father touched her deeply. It filled her with happiness to know her father had spoken of her, that he had been proud of her. Tears stung her eyes, although a smile, however tremulous, curved her lips as after a moment she slowly shook Morgan's outstretched hand.

"The pleasure's mine, Mr. McCain. Please…call me Cat."

"Only if you'll call me Morgan."

"That's a deal."

"No, that's a wrap! Cut. Print. There, you see? It might have required a few takes, but I knew we could get it right if only we tried. Pull the Jeep into that garage there—" he pointed toward the body shop "—and I'll meet you inside."

Once they had made the necessary arrangements for the repairs to the vehicle, Morgan escorted Cat to the Bronco. After opening the passenger door for her, he saw that she was comfortably settled inside before going around to slide into the driver's seat beside her.

"I noticed a flower shop—Tillie's, it was called—on the way here," Cat told him as he started up the vehicle. "Would you mind very much if we stopped there first? I'd—I'd like to take some flowers to—to Dad's grave."

"Of course…no problem," Morgan said kindly, silently cursing himself for having been such a cad earlier, for something that had not been Cat's fault and on the morning when she was to visit her father's grave for the first time besides. Morgan thought that if she now believed him to be an insensitive clod, he would have no one but himself to blame for it. Damn! Why was it that in the space of just two short days, the woman sitting beside him appeared to have effortlessly tangled him up in knots, so he now felt as though he did not know whether he was coming or going? Redheads. What was it about redheads?

At the flower shop Cat bought a simple but beautiful sheaf of gladiolus, which she loved but which she had also all her life associated with death and funerals. The scent of the bouquet filled the Bronco as Morgan drove her out east of town, to the cemetery where her father was buried. On the radio, adult-contemporary music played softly…four songs in a row before the deejay spoke and ran the commercials. She recognized the station as B98-FM, because that was its much-touted format.

"Somehow I rather expected you to be a fan of country-and-western music." Cat motioned toward the radio.

"Oh, I am," Morgan confirmed, glancing at her mockingly, as though he suspected she had thought him too much a cowboy to listen to anything else *but* country. "But that's good-time music—for wild days and even rowdier Saturday nights."

"In Margaritaville. Yes, I remember." Cat thought of his words to the two policemen last night. She shook her head disapprovingly, fighting to repress the smile that tugged at the corners of her lips at the memory. "Look, I don't mean to pry or anything...but are you— are you often hauled away to jail? I mean...Dad mentioned he'd bailed you out a couple of times in the past...."

"Yeah, once in a blue moon it's been known to happen, when I've got 'likkered up,' as they say, and got into a brawl at one of the local clubs." Morgan grinned at her sheepishly, a bad-boy grin that made Cat think that in his heart he was truly an outlaw. Then he confessed, "But that was mostly back in my *really* wild days! Now that I'm older and wiser, I'm not nearly as dangerous as I used to be. Too many young guns out there...just looking for an excuse to flatten an old man like me!"

"Uh-huh," Cat drawled sardonically, vividly conscious of the fact that he was not old at all, but a man plainly in his prime. "Wonder why it is, then, that I get the impression you could hold your own against just about anybody?"

"Probably because I can." Morgan flashed her another grin—a smug one this time.

"Well, now we know modesty, at least, is not one of your strong suits!"

"No, ma'am! I make no bones about it—I'm a straight shooter. Right from the hip, too—and so I call 'em as I see 'em. Always have and always will."

"You never learned then that honesty has to be measured out in small doses—and then only to those who can take it?" Cat inquired, arching one brow teasingly.

"Nope. If that's the medicine that'll cure you, I'll cheerfully hog-tie you and spoon it forcibly down your throat whether you want it or not."

"Good heavens! I don't know whether I'm safe alone with you or not!"

"You are...for the moment, at least. And should there ever come a time when you're not, I'll let you know." From beneath lazily hooded eyes, Morgan glanced at her in a way that made Cat's heart pound suddenly hard and fast with excitement.

"Will you?" she asked, softly and a trifle breathlessly, aware there was now a sensual note underlying their banter.

"Yes—and that's a promise."

There was no time to pursue this particular conversation further; they had reached the cemetery where her father was buried. Briefly, Cat again felt a flash of guilt that she had managed, even for a short while, to put her father's death from her mind, to engage in a light-hearted flirtation while she held in her lap the flowers for his grave. But in her heart she knew her father would not have wanted her to feel sorrow for him. He had loved life, and he had lived it to its fullest. He had wanted her to do the same, more than once insisting— and rightly so, she realized now—that she had buried herself in New York and in her work and in a round of social and charitable events.

"When was the last time you took a day off and just walked in the park, Cat?" he would ask her intently during his visits to New York. "New York's got beautiful parks...plenty of 'em. And what about that toy store...F.A.O. Schwarz? Why, if I lived here, I'd roam around in there once a month just to remind myself everybody ought to be a kid again now and then. You know, there *is* such a thing as being *too* adult, Cat. I'll bet that stuffed-shirt Spencer Kingsley doesn't even begin to know how to have fun...*real* fun, the kind that makes you laugh so hard that tears run down your cheeks. Bet he's never just plain silly."

No, Cat thought now as Morgan helped her down from the Bronco. Spence had never been just plain silly. She had never made a face and stuck her tongue out at him. Funny how she had not thought twice about doing that to Morgan McCain.

The cemetery, although lovely, was not what she had expected. It had no headstones in the traditional sense, only flat grave markers, so if Morgan had not accompanied her, she would have wandered around for a long while, searching for her father's grave. As it was, Morgan led her right to it. Despite the tears that filled her eyes at the sight, Cat could not help but smile as she gazed down at the gray, granite marker pressed into the rich, newly turned earth. In the center was engraved an oil derrick, framed by the words *Frank Devlin* and

The Best of the Wildcatters, with the dates of his birth and death below. Shaking her head ruefully, Cat laughed softly.

"Oh, it's perfect. Dad would have loved it," she observed to Morgan, who stood at her side silently and a little defiantly, as though he had expected her to disapprove of the epitaph. She knelt to lay the sheaf of gladiolus tenderly upon her father's grave. Her fingers traced the words written in the granite. "Will you tell me about the service?" she asked. She had taken off the huge, tortoiseshell sunglasses she had donned earlier, and now her eyes squinted a little against the glare of the sunlight as she glanced up at Morgan earnestly.

To his surprise, he realized suddenly that he did not think he had ever seen a woman as beautiful as Cat appeared to him in that moment, kneeling there, her eyes slightly narrowed, glistening with tears, and as green and brilliant as emeralds. The sunlight danced upon her dark red hair, turning it to shimmering waves of upswept flame, and played across her porcelain skin, as lustrous as a pearl. Her moist, wine red mouth was parted in a tremulous smile that spoke of both grief at the loss of her father and gratitude that Morgan had known Frank so well, had, after all, done the right thing.

"Well, as you know," Morgan began quietly, "Frank wasn't much of a churchgoer, so we held the ceremony right here, at the grave side. It was a simple event, with a dignity all its own, although I suppose there are those who might have considered the eulogy I gave more fitting as an opening of 'The Tonight Show.' It *was* rather in the nature of something that might have been given at an Irish wake, actually. I spoke about Frank, about his life, about how he and I got started together in the oil-and-gas business, and I told about some of his wilder exploits. At any rate, it made people laugh, despite their tears, which I think would have pleased Frank, because he always said he didn't want anybody crying over him when he was dead and gone. Afterward the preacher spoke a few words...and quoted that 'dust to dust, ashes to ashes' passage from the Bible. Then, because Frank belonged to the Midian Shrine Temple, I had their bagpipers here to play 'Amazing Grace.' That was pretty much it."

"Thank you," Cat uttered simply. "I know Dad would have approved, because it sounds exactly like what he always insisted he

wanted—'nothing fancy for a plain, good ole boy like me,' he used
to say. I'm so sorry I couldn't get here in time, that I missed it. But
I do have something of my own to add, if you don't mind.'' Slowly,
she stood, opened her handbag and withdrew a folded sheet of paper.
''It's an anonymous poem Dad and I both always liked. He used to
say it summed up his entire philosophy about death and what happens
to you afterward, where you go. I want to read it aloud, if I may.''

''Please do,'' Morgan urged gently.

Cat cleared her throat. Then, after unfolding the paper, she began
to read, her voice faltering a little over the simple but beautiful,
uplifting words:

''Do not stand at my grave and weep....
I am not there. I do not sleep.

I am a thousand winds that blow.
I am the diamond glints on snow.
I am the sunlight on ripened grain.
I am the gentle autumn rain.
When you awake in the morning hush,
I am the swift, up-flinging rush
Of quiet birds in circling flight.
I am the soft star-shine at night.

Do not stand at my grave and cry....
I am not there. I did not die.''

Having ended the poem, she fell silent, lost in her memories of
her father. Then, after a long moment, she slowly folded the paper
and returned it to her purse.

'' 'I am the sunlight on ripened grain,' '' Morgan quoted softly,
suddenly stricken. ''That's what you were doing in the wheat field
yesterday, isn't it? Searching for your father, for his essence, for
whatever it was he meant to you. No wonder my shouting and honk-
ing made you so damned mad. You must have thought I was the
world's biggest jerk—and now I feel like it, too! Worse, I feel like
a real heel! I am so sorry, Cat. I didn't know...I didn't realize....''

''I know you didn't, Morgan. And I'm not angry anymore. I feel pretty awful, too, actually, if you want to know the truth. Mistaking you for a pervert, a stalker, and giving you that crack on the head last night. Why, I'd be willing to bet that wherever he is, Dad's having a great big laugh at our expense right now!''

''Yeah, I can almost hear him! Frank was one of those people who could always find the humor in any situation, and who laughed, really *laughed,* you know, from the belly.''

And then somehow at that memory, Cat and Morgan were both laughing, too. As she spied one of the cemetery's grounds keepers in the distance, she thought the man must think they were crazy, standing there laughing in a graveyard. Or perhaps he was old enough and sensitive enough to understand that some things were just so painful that if you did not laugh, you would start crying and never stop.

But after a while their laughter died away. Still, a trace of companionship and joy remained, and Morgan's voice, when he spoke, was now matter-of-fact.

''Do you like Mexican? Food, I mean. It's getting on toward lunchtime. I don't know about you, but I didn't have any breakfast, and I'm hungry!''

''I adore Mexican,'' Cat answered, thinking that of all the men in the world, it should have been Morgan who had passed by her while she had stood in the wheat field, Morgan who had, during her reading of the poem just moments past, so quickly grasped what she had been doing there yesterday, amid the acres of golden grain. Spence would never have understood, she thought. He had comprehended things like profit-and-loss statements, not people's feelings.

She glanced down at her father's grave.

I love you, and I'll miss you, Dad, she told him silently. *But I hate goodbyes, and I've never believed death was the end, anyway, so I'll just say…until I see you again.*

Chapter 7

Good Ole Boys

The restaurant was called Willie C's Café and Bar, and Cat knew, even before they went inside, that she was going to enjoy it. Its exterior sign was set into a grassy berm at the corner of the parking lot, and behind the sign itself lurked a cutout of a policeman on a motorcycle, hunched over the handlebars, poised to catch imaginary speeders. Sometimes the signboard cop was there and sometimes, he was not, Morgan explained, depending on whether he had been removed for repairs due to wear and tear.

The restaurant itself was one of those fun, trendy places with exposed pipes in the ceiling and old metal signs on the walls. Its claim to fame was its seemingly endless variety of beers from around the world. When the waitress came to their table, Cat and Morgan each, after glancing at the menu, ordered a bottle of dark beer and steak *fajitas.* The beers, when they arrived, were deliciously cold, the bottles dripping ice. While Cat and Morgan waited for their food, they sipped and talked.

"So…did you and Dad *really* name your corporation the One-Eyed Jacks Oil and Gas Company because you started it from your winnings one night at poker?" Cat asked, curious, never having quite believed this wild tale her father had told her.

"Yeah, believe it or not, we did." Morgan grinned at the memory. "It was one of those all-night, back-room games, because gambling, except for a couple of things like the lottery and betting on horse and dog races, is illegal in Kansas. Dawn was just breaking on the horizon, so we were down to the last hand, and since everybody there had been drinking all night long, the betting had got pretty crazy. There was a huge pot at stake. The game that round was five-card draw, and just to make it interesting, the dealer had announced that whoever held the jack with the ax was going to take half the pot, regardless. So even if you didn't win, you still had a chance at drawing the axman." He took a long swallow of beer, then went on.

"It was jacks or better to open—and that was all Frank had. Me…I was bust, didn't have anything worth looking at. Frank drew three cards and got nothing. I drew four and still didn't have anything—except for the last card I'd drawn, which just so happened to be the axman. So I'm running the pot up like crazy, and Frank's running it up, too, because he's putting on a big bluff, hoping to make the others think he's got an unbeatable hand. The next thing we knew, everybody else had dropped out, and it was just Frank and me. He had that pair of jacks—one of which was one-eyed—and I had the one-eyed axman. We split the pot, then pooled our winnings and started the company. Of course, it wasn't really all *that* simple, but we were on our way, at least."

"And now?"

"And now…" Morgan sighed heavily. "Now everything's up in the air until I find out how Frank's left his shares in the corporation. I'm sure he's willed them to you, Cat. We'll find out for certain this afternoon at Richard Hollis's office. But if he has, then the future of the One-Eyed Jacks Oil and Gas Company is going to be pretty much up to you."

"What do you mean? In what way?" Cat was puzzled, because she had thought that when her father and Morgan founded the corporation, they had doubtless made arrangements for the disposition of stock following the death of one partner. Now, however, it seemed from Morgan's words that perhaps they had not.

"Well, since you don't know anything about running an oil-and-gas company, and since you have a life in New York besides, you'll surely want to sell your shares, won't you, Cat?" Morgan prodded, on his tanned visage the expression he wore when playing poker, which was no expression at all and so revealed nothing of his own thoughts and emotions.

"Actually, to tell you the truth, I—I really haven't given Dad's will much thought," Cat confessed after a moment. "I mean…I'm not hard up for money or anything. My grandfather Talbot established a trust fund for me at my birth, and it's grown considerably through the years from a number of investments—besides which, I've never had any reason to touch the principal. So I've been very fortunate in that I've never had to struggle to earn a living. I've never been…you know…existing on my expectations from Dad's estate or anything. Didn't you and Dad have some sort of a buy-out agreement in place in the event of one partner's death?"

"Yes, of course." Morgan nodded. "But it's a first-option clause against the heir's—or heirs', if there are more than one—right to sell, and inheritance of the stock is subject to that condition. So…if Frank *did* will you his shares, I'd have the first option to buy them if you chose to sell them. However, in the event that we couldn't come to terms, you'd be free to sell them elsewhere, or we could opt to dissolve the corporation and liquidate its assets."

"But—but that would mean the end of the One-Eyed Jacks Oil and Gas Company," Cat observed. "Of everything you and Dad worked so hard to build over the years. You surely wouldn't want that, Morgan, would you?"

"No, I wouldn't. Still, even that would be preferable to being compelled to deal fifty-fifty with someone who doesn't know beans about the oil-and-gas business."

By now their *fajitas* had arrived on steaming-hot, traditional cast-iron platters. Cat began studiously to spread sour cream on her tortilla, then to fill the tortilla itself with meat, onions, peppers, cheese, lettuce and tomatoes, ignoring only the guacamole, which she did not care for, having never acquired a taste for avocados.

"You don't like guacamole?" Morgan inquired as he watched her.

"No, not especially."

"Me, neither. There. I knew we were bound to have *something* in common."

"But not One-Eyed Jacks? Is that what you're saying?" She determinedly steered the conversation back to their previous topic, not knowing why it had suddenly become of such importance to her. Morgan was right: she had a life in New York and she knew nothing about the oil-and-gas business. Even so, she found herself protesting, "But I know about buying and selling, about importing and exporting."

"Furniture, antiques, paintings, objets d'art and other such stuff, yes. But not oil and gas," Morgan stated logically as he prepared his own *fajita*, also foregoing the guacamole on the side plate.

Cat shrugged, and her voice, when she replied, was confident, a shade defiant and accompanied by a stubborn, resolute lift of her chin.

"I could learn."

Morgan was silent for a moment, as though he were not quite sure what he was hearing. Then he spoke.

"What about your job in New York, Cat? And Frank had mentioned a boyfriend...a fiancé, now that I think about it." Morgan was abruptly stricken at the memory. He glanced down at her left hand. It was bare of jewelry. "But you're not wearing an engagement ring...?"

"No, I...broke off my engagement to Spence...Spencer Kingsley, my fiancé."

"Wasn't he also your boss or something? Didn't he own the firm where you worked?"

"Yes."

"Well, that must make your job pretty uncomfortable now, I would imagine," Morgan commented dryly, beginning to wonder where all this was leading.

"Actually, I—I...don't have a job anymore. Spence fired me."

"I see."

But the truth was Morgan did not see. He was, in fact, damned if he could figure out her agenda. Was Cat hinting that if Frank had indeed willed her his shares in the One-Eyed Jacks Oil & Gas Company, she intended to remain in Wichita, to step into his shoes at the corporation? Was she pumping him, Morgan, for information about the company so she could somehow attempt to wrest control of it from him, or was she merely interested in discovering what her shares were worth so she could sell them to him or to another investor? He did not know.

He thought suddenly of her background, of her education, of her professional experience, of the fact that she was accustomed to doing business in a city known for its ruthless corporate world, a city that was home to, among other things, Wall Street and Madison Avenue. Other than that, what did he *really* know about her? Upon learning her identity, he had thought she was nothing at all like what he had originally imagined. But what if he had not been so far off the mark after all? Morgan asked himself now, considering all the possible ramifications of having Cat herself as a fifty-fifty partner in the One-Eyed Jacks Oil & Gas Company.

Inwardly, he groaned at the idea. Not only would she prove a monumental distraction to him physically, but also, depending on her aims, either a flat-out nuisance or perhaps one of the cleverest and most dangerous opponents he had ever come up against. After all, she had had the wits, daring and composure to lie in wait for him in the dining room last night and, with that heavy vase, to coldcock him mercilessly, had she not? Perhaps she was actually as beautiful as belladonna. Veronica had been like that. Despite his attraction to Cat, he would have to be on his guard against her, Morgan decided now. To remember that even if she were Frank Devlin's daughter, she was also Julia Talbot's. Julia, who had kept from Frank his only child— and who had done her level best to poison Cat's mind against him.

"Look, I'm real sorry about your breakup and about your losing your job, Cat. But I'm sure that with your abilities, you won't have any trouble finding another position," Morgan asserted, because he would be damned if he'd tell her anything else about the One-Eyed Jacks Oil & Gas Company now, reveal anything that might help her with whatever plans she had in mind—at least not until he discovered whether he must really consider her a threat. He would not be made a fool of again, as Veronica had made a fool of him. It might be that Cat's broken engagement and her firing were somehow related. Perhaps she had attempted to boss Spencer Kingsley around, to grab control of *his* company—and that was what had led to the breakup of her engagement and her subsequent firing, because what man worth his salt would tolerate being dictated to by a woman?

"Oh, I can always find another job," Cat agreed easily, oblivious of Morgan's current thoughts. "It's establishing a *career* that's the hard part. There really is a glass ceiling women come up against in business, you know, a prejudice against our climbing any higher than a few token upper-management positions in the corporate world. We still earn only approximately seventy cents for a man's every dollar— and I think that far too often, we have to work twice as hard as a man to get it, too!"

"That's what you think, is it?" Morgan eyed her skeptically. Damn! A feminist, to boot—and just when, half ashamed of and disgusted by his suspicions, he had almost convinced himself they were unwarranted, that because of his bad experience with Veronica, he was once more and without any good reason leaping to conclusions about Cat.

"Well, it's true, isn't it?" Cat probed, only half teasingly.

Reluctantly, Morgan was compelled to admit it was. After that, however, although she made more than one attempt to continue their conversation, he was strangely taciturn. She did not know what had prompted this new change in his obviously mercurial moods, but she could not help but remember what he had told her earlier—that she reminded him of someone he would prefer to forget.

At that thought, some of Cat's pleasure in their lunch went out of her day, and she was quiet and reflective while Morgan paid their bill, then led her outside to the Bronco. After she was comfortably settled inside, he drove downtown, and she got her first glimpse of the heart of city, which, upon her arrival in Wichita, the taxi driver had avoided by taking her along the meandering Big and Little Arkansas rivers and through various park areas.

The city was small and simple but beautiful, many of its main intersections paved with old-fashioned brick, the sidewalks lined with trees. No building was taller than twenty-six stories, so the skyline was much lower than that of New York, and sunlight slanted down brightly.

Along the way, Morgan pointed out a number of sites to her, among them Naftzger Park and, across the street from that, a pseudohistorical district he said was called Old Town. It reminded her a little, somehow, of the South Street Seaport in New York, with all its shops and restaurants and its turn-of-the-century Victorian air. Here again old-fashioned bricks paved the streets, which were studded with reproduction lampposts and park benches, and there were large, pleasant parking lots to accommodate all the cars.

"I'll bring you down here one evening if you like," Morgan offered as he pulled into one of the Old Town parking lots, "show you some of the city's nightlife." He deftly maneuvered the Bronco into an empty space, then shut off the motor. "Richard Hollis's office is a few blocks from here, but with your being from New York, I didn't think you'd mind if we walked. It's a nice day, and I know ten blocks or more is nothing to a New Yorker."

Cat was glad to see that the mischievous twinkle had returned to his eyes and that his increasingly familiar, crooked grin curved his mouth when he looked over at her.

"That's right," she replied, smiling. "How do you think I stay in such great shape?" She had intended the remark only to be flippant, but as his suddenly heated eyes roamed over her lingeringly, she could not prevent the blush that rose to her cheeks.

"You are definitely that," he agreed appreciatively, wondering what she would think if he told her that in her peach-colored linen suit, she somehow reminded him of a crystal glass of sorbet, that he could almost taste her melting on his tongue. Instead, he forced himself to glance away, pretending to check his wristwatch. "Well, we've got just about fifteen minutes before our appointment with Richard Hollis. So we'd better get a move on."

Once they reached the sidewalk, Cat noticed that Morgan moved around her instinctively so he was curbside—a holdover from previous centuries, when a gentleman always walked on the outside so a lady would not be drenched by the contents of slop jars emptied from upper-story windows. The courtesy seemed somehow quaint in this day and age. Yet it was still the mark of a man with manners, and Cat appreciated the gesture. Even if he *were* a rough-diamond cowboy, Morgan did, after all, have a few smooth edges, it seemed.

"Oh, look! A trolley!" she exclaimed suddenly, laughing aloud with a child's delight as the vehicle trundled past them.

"It's a bus, actually," Morgan corrected, "although it does resemble the old trolleys that did, in fact, used to run here. You can still see the tracks in places. But these days we get the same picturesque effect without all the hassle."

"Well, I still think it's charming and romantic," she insisted.

"Then we'll have to take a ride on one sometime."

"That sounds nice—but, well…look, Morgan, I don't want you to feel obligated to show me the city sights or otherwise entertain me while I'm here in Wichita. I assure you I'm a big girl now, and I've been used to taking care of myself for a long, long time, besides."

Although Cat had striven for a lighthearted tone, Morgan believed he detected a tiny note of bitterness in her last words, nevertheless. For the first time, he wondered what her life, her childhood, must have been like, growing up in the Talbot family mansion and without her father. Instinctively, Morgan sensed that Julia Talbot had not been the closest and most loving and nurturing of mothers. It further occurred to him how often a crowded city like New York could, perversely, emphasize one's own loneliness and isolation. Although Cat had had her family, her fiancé and her work to occupy her, she might in reality have been close to no one. Perhaps even her friends had been more in the nature of business and social acquaintances, as was so frequently the case in the corporate world, rather than true, cross-your-heart-and-hope-to-die friends. There was, he had come gradually to realize, a strange, appealing vulnerability in her that he would not usually have associated with a woman of her ilk.

Morgan's own family had loved him, and Frank had treated him like a son. But now he recognized that perhaps Cat had been alone, even unloved, until adulthood, when Frank and she had set about establishing the relationship they ought to have shared all their lives. Was it any wonder then she had loved her father so deeply?

"I don't feel any obligation toward you whatsoever, Cat," Morgan declared in response to her earlier remarks. "So if I take you any-where or do anything for you, you can rest assured it's because I want to and not because I feel as though I have to. I just thought that since you made the trip here to Wichita, especially when you didn't have to, you'd like to see some of the things I know Frank was planning to show you this summer." Morgan paused for moment, gathering his thoughts. Then he continued.

"Look, Cat, I know that, culturally, Wichita can't begin to compete with New York. But we're not totally backwoods here, either. You see that big round building over there?" He pointed to a huge, sand-colored, circular edifice in the distance, rising from the beautifully landscaped edge of the riverbank, and Cat nodded. "That's Century Two, which contains our convention and exhibition halls, as well as one of our live theaters, where you can see productions to rival any-thing off or *on* Broadway. Musicals are perennially popular here. Robert Goulet performed in *Camelot* at Century Two not too long ago—although I *did* wonder how he felt about playing King Arthur now, when he'd originated the role of Lancelot! As for ballet, well, Gelsey Kirkland has danced *The Nutcracker* there. We've got some awfully fine art in Wichita, too. Just look around you—" his hand swept out, indicating various sculptures on the streets "—and what you see here is equaled or surpassed by what's out at Wichita State University, where the art building alone has a rare mural by Miró on its front. Nor will you see any better Native American art anywhere. Blackbear Bosin's statue *The Keeper of the Plains,* at the confluence of the Big and Little Arkansas rivers, is magnificent."

"Morgan McCain! Are you trying to tell me I'm a snob—or pro-vincial?" Cat inquired tartly.

"No, neither. I'm just saying Frank wanted you to realize Man-hattan Island is not the beginning and end of the world."

"I know that. But it sure is exciting…much more fast paced than downtown Wichita, for example," she retorted, pride demanding she defend her hometown.

"Yes, it is that, I agree. But there's something to be said for life in the slow lane, too. Frank just wanted you to know that." By now they had reached an office building, and Morgan opened one of the heavy glass front doors, ushering Cat into the marble-floored lobby and then toward the bank of elevators in the hallway beyond.

"Don't we have to...you know...sign in or anything?" she asked, glancing around at her surroundings as she and Morgan waited for one of the elevators' doors to open.

He grinned at her. "Like I said, this isn't New York, Cat—although, even here, most of these buildings *do* keep their rest rooms locked!"

She frowned at him with mock reproval. "Aha! So Wichita isn't quite a paradise after all. Is that what you're telling me?"

"Pretty proud of yourself for figuring that out so quick, despite all my efforts to convince you otherwise, aren't you? Yes, it's true—but then, you aren't likely to be mugged on the streets here, either! Now get in the elevator, woman. If the truth were known, you're probably a worse menace to Wichita society than one of the local winos or panhandlers!"

Taking her elbow before she could retort, Morgan steered her past the brass-plated doors that had just glided open. Inside, he pressed the button for the fourth floor, and they rode up in silence, Cat pretending studiously, after his last remark, to ignore him. Whistling under his breath, Morgan watched her openly, not troubling to repress the smile that tugged at his lips or the admiration in his eyes as they traveled over her.

"You look like a peach in that outfit," he commented at last, with feigned nonchalance, "and I'll just bet you're as tasty as one, too. You'd better not sit too close to Hollis in his office...he's the kind liable to take a bite out of you."

Cat was not normally at a loss for words. But before she could think of a suitable rejoinder, Morgan had escorted her into the legal firm and was announcing their names to the receptionist just inside. After speaking into her telephone for a moment, the woman announced that Mr. Hollis would be with them shortly and suggested they have a seat in the meanwhile. Cat settled herself on the reception room's comfortable, overstuffed love seat, somehow agitated when, instead of taking a chair, Morgan sat beside her, his thigh pressing hers almost intimately—and, she half suspected, deliberately, although it was hard to be sure. The love seat was not very wide, and its cushions were so soft and plump that Cat and Morgan both sank into them. He draped his arm over the back of the love seat, too, just brushing her shoulders. For an instant she had a sudden, wild urge to lay her head back, to move into the curve of his body, to feel his arms wrapped around her, holding her safe and secure.

But of course, she did no such thing—especially when she spied the receptionist eyeing her and Morgan surreptitiously, clearly speculating on what, if anything, might be between them. Still, Cat could not suppress the unexpected flash of pride and satisfaction, the inexplicable twinge of jealousy and possessiveness that shot through her at the idea that the receptionist found Morgan attractive—and that she, Cat, should, however mistakenly, be perceived as his woman. Despite herself, she had to admit it was a boost to her ego, particularly after her falling-out with Spence. He had been considered quite a catch by their circle of friends and acquaintances, most of whom had thought Cat was a fool for breaking off her engagement to him.

But however flattering and gratifying the momentary illusion of a relationship between her and Morgan, Cat was nevertheless relieved when her father's attorney made his appearance. Sitting so close to Morgan, she had been vividly aware of his masculinity, of his strength, of the subtle scents of soap and cologne and sweat that emanated from his tanned flesh, involuntarily making her remember the sound of his voice on the telephone earlier that morning, and of how she had wondered afterward if he had been lying—naked—in bed when he had called her. So powerful, in fact, was that image as it rose unbidden in her mind that she was barely aware of Morgan introducing her to Richard Hollis. It was only at the lawyer's complimentary but slyly suggestive remarks that she was jolted from her reverie into the realization that Morgan had perhaps been right, that Mr. Hollis *was* indeed the kind of man who could be expected, if not to take a bite out of her, at least to pinch covertly a woman's derriere. Instinctively, she edged a little closer to Morgan, only to find herself scowling at him and longing to slap the smug smirk off his face when he mouthed, "I told you so," behind Mr. Hollis's back as the lawyer turned to lead them toward his office. She gave Morgan what she hoped was a quelling glare, but it had no visible effect upon him, except to cause him to grin even wider as they followed the congenially chatting attorney.

Still, to her relief, once seated in front of Mr. Hollis's desk, waiting silently but expectantly as he sorted through his papers to withdraw what Cat knew must be her father's last will and testament, Morgan became abruptly all-business. She sensed rather than observed the tension that coiled within him at that moment, so that despite his outwardly calm and relaxed demeanor, she somehow knew he was as alert and wary as a predator. It occurred to her then that he was really not so easygoing as he seemed, that he did have a black temper, that there was possibly a dangerous, maybe even deadly aspect to Morgan's character—and that if her father had willed her his shares in the One-Eyed Jacks Oil & Gas Company, she might be about to see that dark side.

Involuntarily, Cat shuddered at the thought. Her every business instinct warned her she did not want to tangle with Morgan McCain. That, just like her, he went for broke and played to win.

Mr. Hollis began to read her father's will aloud, stopping now and then to explain or elaborate upon a point as he turned the crisp white pages stapled into the traditional blue legal cover. Once he'd finished, Cat sat there for a moment in silence, stunned. Then, her temper rising as she grasped the import of her father's decision, but wanting to be entirely clear about it, she spoke.

"Mr. Hollis—"

"Rich...please, call me Rich, Ms. Devlin," the lawyer drawled.

"Very well...Rich, then. Are you telling me that although my father left me forty-eight percent of his shares in the One-Eyed Jacks Oil and Gas Company, the two percent that he willed to Morgan has given *him* controlling interest in the corporation?"

"Yes, yes, that's the upshot of it exactly, Ms. Devlin." The attorney nodded briskly. "You're an astute woman, I can tell. Still, let's face it—you don't know anything about running an oil-and-gas company, as I'm sure Frank was well aware. So, giving you the power to stalemate any decisions Morgan might want to make with regard to the corporation would hardly have been fair now, would it? After all, along with Frank, Morgan founded the One-Eyed Jacks Oil and Gas Company. He built it over the years into the successful entity it's become. This way it can continue along those lines, under Morgan's aegis, with you still benefiting from Frank's own investment in the company—and, I might add, Ms. Devlin, with your not being compelled to trouble your pretty head about business matters that surely wouldn't have been of any interest to you, in any event.''

At that, it was all Cat could do to restrain herself from exploding, although, in fact, she did not know why she was so damned mad. She had not expected her father to leave her anything, much less the bulk of his estate, including the majority of his shares in the One-Eyed Jacks Oil & Gas Company. Indeed, that he had done so should have gladdened her heart, because it was surely proof of how much she had meant to him. And certainly, ensuring that Morgan, his friend and business partner, had gained controlling interest in the corporation was, as Mr. Hollis had already so logically pointed out, only fair. Still, Cat could not repress the irrational feelings of pique and hurt that rose within her at the thought that no matter how much her father had loved her, he plainly had not trusted her ability to follow in his footsteps at the One-Eyed Jack Oil & Gas Company, either.

Well, and why should he have? she tried to ask herself reasonably. Although she had often chatted with her father about his work, she had never expressed any serious interest in learning about it. She had never indicated she would be willing to give up her life and job in New York to move to Wichita, to take a position in his corporation, with the understanding that he would be training her to step into his shoes upon his retirement or at his death. As a result, she had no cause whatsoever to feel slighted. Yet the incontrovertible fact was she did. It was silly and childish, but there it was all the same—and the smile of satisfaction that now curved Morgan's mouth only made Cat's indignation worse. She knew he was inwardly ecstatic not to have been saddled with her as a fifty-fifty partner, ecstatic to have gained controlling interest in the corporation.

Damn it! She was an intelligent, competent, professional business-woman, confident of her capability to make a success of most anything she chose to put her mind to. That her father and Mr. Hollis, and possibly Morgan, had conspired to rob her of that opportunity was galling and painful. They were men, and they had doubted her, probably—if Mr. Hollis's attitude were any indication—for no better reason than that she was a woman!

Cat believed that deep down inside, regardless of how outwardly liberal any of them might appear, all men harbored macho tendencies, secretly felt themselves to be superior to women. Spence surely had. It was his questioning of her opinion over a purchase for the import-export firm that had led to their terrible argument, which he had ended abruptly with the supercilious statement that he was a man and that, as such, he fully intended to wear the pants in their relationship, both professionally and personally. Incensed by his high-handed dismissal of her judgment, by his pigheaded refusal even to consider she might be right about the acquisition for the firm, Cat had, in the heat of the moment, broken off their engagement. Stung by her rejection, Spence had then coldly informed her she was permitting her personal feelings to interfere with her professional duties, that an invariably emotional response to business matters was why all females were unsuited for top-management positions. He had then suggested that, this being the case, perhaps Cat ought to search for a less-demanding job, one where her bouts of PMS would not prove so disruptive to the orderly, rational workings of the male corporate world.

That had been so low a blow that Cat had not trusted herself to speak further. Instead, with every ounce of willpower she possessed, she had forced herself to clamp her jaws shut and turn and walk away without another word. She had rarely ever suffered from premenstrual syndrome—and she had certainly never, for any cause, behaved irresponsibly on the job. She had hoped and counted on the fact that with their marriage she and Spence would become partners in the import-export firm. Instead, she had found her head slammed against the glass ceiling he himself had erected above her.

Now she felt herself striking another one in Mr. Hollis's office. That she knew nothing about the oil-and-gas industry was irrelevant. She was not stupid, and she ought at least to have been permitted the chance to learn, to prove herself before judgment had been passed upon her. That Mr. Hollis was leering at her from behind his desk only further outraged her. He was unquestionably a sharp lawyer, or her father would not have employed him. But his manner toward women left much to be desired. Cat had no doubt that if Morgan had not been present, Rich Hollis would by now be well on his way to chasing her around his office, wilily passing off his advances as comforting gestures of sympathy for her loss. That because she was a woman she should require the presence of another man to forestall such indignities was the acid icing on an already-bitter cake.

"Thank you for your clarification of that last point, Mr. Hollis," she said as coolly as she could manage, struggling to master her anger. "Now, if you'll just show me what, if any, documents need to be signed, I will be able to settle my father's estate and not be compelled to take up any more of your valuable time."

"I'm sure I don't need to remind you I'm being well paid for that time, Ms. Devlin...Cat." The smile the attorney gave her reminded her of the proverbial fox licking its chops. "However, I can understand your wanting to get matters wrapped up as soon as possible, since you do, after all, have a life in New York. I imagine Doo-dah— that's how we less-provincial locals refer to Wichita—must seem pretty tame and boring to a big-city gal like you. I know I always have to set my watch back at least a decade when I return home from a trip out of town," he declared, only half-jokingly. "So why don't I have my secretary draw up the necessary paperwork by tomorrow morning, and you can either stop by my office to sign on all the dotted lines, or I can have it mailed to you, whichever you prefer." The expression on Mr. Hollis's face left her no doubt as to his own preference.

"Please send it to my father's home address." Cat smiled, falsely sweet, as she rose to her feet, suppressing the urge to snatch away her hand rudely as the lawyer reached out to shake it.

As he ushered them to the door of his office, Mr. Hollis shook Morgan's hand, too, and jovially clapped him on the shoulder, congratulating him on his good fortune. Shortly afterward, Cat and Morgan stood in the hallway outside the legal firm, waiting for an elevator to take them back down to the lobby.

"I simply do *not* understand how my father could have employed such a man," Cat remarked in the silence, her brow knit with disapproval and annoyance.

"Who...Rich?" Morgan quirked one eyebrow upward, grinning at her scowl. "Well, I *did* warn you, didn't I? But don't let him fool you. He may act like he barely scraped through law school, but the truth is he's about as shrewd as attorneys come. It's not his fault he's also a good ole boy with a weakness for anything in skirts."

"Isn't it?" Cat retorted sourly.

"Why, no, darlin'," Morgan drawled, grinning even more hugely at her. "It's the nature of the beast. Some of us are just a little more subtle and a great deal more selective about it than others—although I admit that I would find it hard to fault Rich's eye this afternoon."

"You know, Morgan, you're real lucky there's a floor in there." Cat pointed to the elevator as it clanged to a stop before them and the brass-plated doors slid open. "Otherwise, the way I feel right now, I'd have been sorely tempted to shove you down the shaft!"

His laughter rang in her ears. Yet somehow, despite that, despite everything, she could not halt the sudden, hard thudding of her heart at the unmistakable desire in his glance and at the thought that he had called her "darlin'." Silently, Cat cursed herself for a fool, but it did not help. And all the way down to the lobby, she was discomfited by a wild, unbidden and inexplicable fantasy in which Morgan suddenly pressed her up against one wall of the elevator, pushed her linen skirt up around her thighs and took her urgently in a mutual burst of savage, uncontrollable passion before, outwardly calm and collected, they exited the car.

Chapter 8

Chemistry...the Equalizer

The next few days Cat spent pacing the rooms of her father's house and thinking endlessly, feeling somehow as though she had reached a crossroads, a turning point in her life. For the first time she could remember since childhood, she found herself with time hanging heavily on her hands, with neither school nor a job nor social and charitable engagements to occupy her hours. She had no university classes, no business meetings and no functions of any sort to attend, no deadlines to meet, no appointments to keep, no one to see and no place to go.

For the space of a single day, it was heavenly.

Rather than rising early, she luxuriated in sleeping late. Instead of coffee and a bagel snatched on the run, she ate a leisurely breakfast, lingering over the stock-market section of the daily newspaper, the *Wichita Eagle.* She took a long shower and washed her hair, after which she gave herself a facial, a manicure and a pedicure. She swam in the pool out back and caught up on some of her reading. She watched television and, later that evening, continued the task of sorting through her father's personal papers and belongings, boxing everything up and labeling it neatly with black, felt-tipped markers.

But by the following afternoon, accustomed to long, hard hours of work, Cat was already bored out of her mind, stir-crazy, practically climbing the walls of her father's house. She wondered how her mother had been satisfied to spend her whole life as a social butterfly, attending lunches and brunches, playing bridge, tennis and golf at the local country club and patronizing this social or charitable event or that. With time just to think, to dwell on, among other things, her relationship with Spence, Cat now realized that far from envisioning her as a partner in the import-export firm, he had seen her, following their marriage, as stepping into her mother's shoes instead. Too late Cat recognized that he had said as much on more than one occasion. Wrapped up in her career and her own plans for their future, she had simply chosen not to hear him, had chosen to delude herself into believing he would come around to her point of view once he understood how very important it was to her.

She would *not,* however, she assured herself as she walked back to her father's house from the mailbox at the end of the driveway, make that same mistake with Morgan McCain. Him she had heard loud and clear. He did not want as his partner in the One-Eyed Jacks Oil & Gas Company someone who knew nothing about the oil-and-gas business. Well, that was just fine and dandy with her, Cat reflected crossly as she ripped open the big envelope from Richard Hollis's office and thought again of her father's will, of how he had disposed of his shares in the corporation. She would sell Morgan the forty-eight percent of her father's stock she had inherited and be done with it! Then she would kick Wichita's prairie dust off her heels and head back to the big city, to the real world of New York, where she belonged.

That she no longer had anything, truly, to return to there—no job, no fiancé, no real family and only a few friends—was immaterial. It was her home. That her father had always insisted home is wherever one's heart is, was a thought Cat determinedly shoved from her mind. Despite how much he had loved her, even *he* had not trusted her to follow in his footsteps at the One-Eyed Jacks Oil & Gas Company, had made it clear with the disposition of his shares that he had not expected her to do so.

Once inside the house, Cat made her way to her father's study, where she read and then signed all the documents Richard Hollis had enclosed in the envelope. Then she sat down at her father's laptop computer to compose a letter to Morgan, offering for sale her shares in the One-Eyed Jacks Oil & Gas Company, per the terms of the corporation's buy-out agreement. Then, before she could change her mind, she sealed the envelope, stamped it and drove to the nearest post-office drop box to mail it.

"Forgive me if I seem inordinately slow or confused this morning, but...what do you mean, you can't raise the capital to buy my stock?" Cat's brow was knit with puzzlement as she gazed at Morgan across her father's kitchen table. They had just come back from the Jeep dealership, to which Morgan had driven her earlier to pick up her vehicle, which was now repaired. Knowing from his telephone call of a few days ago that he had received her letter about her wanting to sell him her shares in the One-Eyed Jacks Oil & Gas Company, she had invited him back for coffee and to discuss her offer.

"Just that...just exactly what I said, Cat—there's no way at the moment I can put together the necessary financing to buy you out," Morgan reiterated, slightly defensive and embarrassed. After all his talk to her about not wanting her as a partner in the corporation, it was humiliating to be forced to admit he himself was not in a position to do anything about it, that he could not take her up on her offer, no matter how much he might wish to do so. Nor were matters helped by the fact that she was, this morning, dressed in a simple T-shirt and a pair of plain old jeans, reminding him of how she had looked at their first meeting, of how much he had wanted her in that instant. Inwardly, Morgan groaned. Whether he liked it or not, Cat continued to play havoc with his senses! Every time he glanced at her it was as though he could think of nothing but sleeping with her! It made him feel as though he had regressed to his days as a hormone-driven teenager, was not now a mature man who ought to have better control over himself and a good deal more common sense! "Look, Cat, you've got to understand that the oil-and-gas business is in kind of a bad way right now—"

"Why is that…when you showed profits just a few years back?" she interrupted, oblivious of his unbusinesslike thoughts, letting him know she had done her homework, that to prepare herself for this discussion, she had read, among other things, the corporation's most-recent annual reports.

"Yes, but that was during Desert Storm. As horrible and unconscionable as it might seem, Cat," Morgan explained dryly, "American oilmen, among others, benefited when Iraq swooped down to invade Kuwait and set the Kuwaiti oil fields on fire. With Kuwait burning, and various of the other OPEC nations tied up in the Gulf War besides, oil shipments from the Middle East were curtailed. And since the Arab nations are the world's primary suppliers of oil, that drove the price of oil up worldwide, which meant that North and South American oil companies, for example, made money. Once that situation had ended, things more or less returned to the way they've been for the last several years." He paused for a moment. Then he continued.

"You surely must have some idea of how, practically overnight it seemed, the bottom dropped out of the oil market some years back, Cat, and how cities like Houston and Tulsa, whose economies were fueled by that oil, were left up the financial creek until they could begin attracting and developing other industries. The *Exxon Valdez* incident off the coast of Alaska didn't help matters, either. It stirred up not only the environmentalists, but also the entire country—although not without just cause, mind you…so you needn't go getting up in arms about it yourself! And don't say you weren't, because I could practically see your hackles rising! Believe it or not, I share your concerns, so I'm certainly not about to sit here and defend oil companies that either deliberately or carelessly damage this planet. Still, the fact remains that the American oil business is no longer the booming industry it was in its heyday."

"I see." Cat chewed her lower lip thoughtfully, unaware of the effect this simple gesture produced upon Morgan, of how, as he watched her, he longed to nibble that sultry, sensuous lip himself, and so found that he could hardly concentrate on their conversation. "What you're saying is that, barring another crisis in the Middle East or some other turn of events, the oil industry is more or less bust at the moment, and as a result, you can't get your bank to extend you any credit.''

"No, not precisely." Morgan shook his head, as though that action might clear his thoughts of their decidedly sexual drift. With difficulty he forced his mind back to the discussion at hand, knowing how important it was to the future of the One-Eyed Jacks Oil & Gas Company. "I'm saying that in order to do this deal, I'd either have to liquidate other assets I hold or else put them up as collateral against loans I'd rather not take out right now to begin with, because it just isn't smart ever to put all your eggs in one basket.''

"Then, under the circumstances, it's probably not too likely that any other investor will want to buy my shares in the corporation, either, is it?'' Cat queried, frowning as she mulled over the issue— slowly, unwittingly, running her forefinger back and forth across her lower lip as she contemplated her limited options.

"Frankly, no,'' Morgan answered tersely. "In fact, if you want my advice, you'd be wise to hang on to your stock until the price of oil goes up again, at which time you might make a killing on the market.''

"And let you run the company in the meanwhile, however you see fit?''

"Well…yes, Cat. We've been over this before, and I thought we'd agreed that you sure as heck don't know anything about it.''

"If you remember correctly, I also said I could learn." Abruptly, Cat ceased the unconscious, erotic rubbing of her lower lip and sat up straighter in her chair, her chin lifting stubbornly, her eyes flashing with challenge and defiance, her decision made. "And seeing as how it's just not in my nature to be either a hypocrite or a parasite, if I *am* going to be a partner—even a minority partner—in the One-Eyed Jacks Oil and Gas Company, then a partner I fully intend to be! What time did my father usually arrive at his office in the mornings?''

"Between seven and eight o'clock, but—''

"Then you may expect me there tomorrow morning at the same time.'' Her heart pounding at the darkening expression on Morgan's face, she stood, indicating the door. "Thank you for taking me to retrieve the Jeep, Morgan. But now, if you don't mind, I've got a lot of work to do, and I'm sure you must be busy as well.''

''Cat...'' His voice was low, deceptively silky, but she was not fooled. She knew he was suddenly as angry as she had been some days ago in Richard Hollis's office. ''What do you think you're doing, Cat? If you believe for one single minute that I'm going to let you just walk in and try to take over One-Eyed Jacks—''

''Who said anything about my taking it over? I merely intend to pull my weight, that's all. And you don't have any right to attempt to prevent me from doing that, Morgan—legal or otherwise. I don't believe in taking something for nothing. If I could have sold my shares in the corporation, it might have been different. But I'm accustomed to managing my own business affairs and investments, and whether you like it or not, as a forty-eight-percent stockholder in One-Eyed Jacks, I have obligations to the corporation that go beyond my just sitting around collecting a check I don't need and I didn't earn to begin with!''

''Even if I don't want you at the office?'' Morgan prodded as he, too, rose to his feet, no longer looking in that instant like an easy-going cowboy, Cat thought nervously, but rather like some kind of dangerous predator uncoiling himself and preparing to pounce—on her! Involuntarily, she took a step back, her pulse leaping.

''You don't want me there because I'm a woman, damn it!'' she protested, fighting to control the abrupt impulse she had to turn and run from the kitchen before whatever ominous, explosive thing she now belatedly sensed brewing between them erupted.

''Well, boy howdy, you got that right!'' he retorted.

''So...you admit it! That *is* a surprise. But then I already knew it, so you couldn't have fooled me anyway, even if you'd tried! You think that just because I'm a woman, I can't do the job, and you don't even want to give me the chance to try! And that's so short-sighted and bullheaded and unfair of you! Oh, you're no better than Spence...just another macho man, a male chauvinist pig who thinks women ought to be kept barefoot and pregnant—''

''You'd be wise to hold off on your hotheaded insulting of me until you get your facts straight, Cat.'' Morgan's voice was quiet but lethal, and it sent a shiver of both apprehension and inexplicable anticipation coursing through her as he moved toward her, slowly backing her up against the kitchen counter and placing his hands on either side of her so she could not escape. "I *do* question your ability to do the job, but *that* has nothing to do with your being a woman!"

"Then…I—I don't understand. What—what has my gender got to with it at all then?"

"This."

Before Cat realized what he intended, Morgan caught hold of her, his strong hands burrowing through her dark red hair, deliberately compelling her face up to his. His mouth came down on hers, speaking silently, urgently, of his hunger for her. Taken by surprise, she acquiesced to his kiss, feeling as though the earth had suddenly heaved, had dropped without warning from beneath her feet as he molded her to him. His hands tightened in her hair as he slanted his lips over hers, his mustache tickling her, his tongue tracing the outline of her mouth before parting it, thrusting inside, deepening the kiss, exploring the warm, dark cavern of her.

Deep down inside Cat, desire flickered, the spark flaring quickly and uncontrollably into a flame that swept through her like wildfire, consuming her, as she had somehow sensed it would should Morgan ever touch her, kiss her, make love to her. Of their own volition, her arms crept up his muscular chest, fingers splayed and trembling with the onslaught of passion before they clutched his broad shoulders, nails biting into his flesh, spurring him on as he took her mouth again and again, hotly, eagerly demanding her response.

She moaned low in her throat as his hands slid down her back, provocatively kneading her spine before cupping her buttocks, pressing her against him so she could feel the heat and strength of his arousal. Her knees went weak. She felt as though she were melting, trickling down into a pool of mindless sensation at his feet, and in some dark corner of her mind, she was startled to grasp dimly that she was still standing. She knew it was only because Morgan held her up as his lips burned from her mouth to the pulse fluttering crazily at the delicate hollow of her throat.

Then, at long last, with a low groan of reluctance, he drew away, his eyes like blue fire as he stared down at her, his glance taking in the tangle he had made of her hair; the quiver of her tremulous, parted lips, slightly bruised from his kisses; the rapid, shallow rise and fall of her breasts beneath the butter yellow T-shirt she wore; the sight of her pebbled nipples straining tautly against the thin cotton.

"I have been wanting to do that from the very first moment I saw you, Cat." Morgan's voice was husky with the desire that roiled within him. "And that's the real reason I don't want you at the office. I don't think I'll be able to think clearly with you there, and it's been my experience, besides, that mixing business with pleasure seldom works out. Most people just can't separate their personal feelings from their professional responsibilities."

If Cat had been dazed from his kisses, his words served like a bucket of cold water rudely thrown in her face, abruptly restoring her to her senses. For had not Spence said much the same thing to her during their argument, accused her of letting her emotions get in the way of her job—when in reality it had been *he* who could not keep his love and business lives apart?

"You needn't worry about that, Morgan," she insisted as coolly as she could manage, wishing her heart would stop thudding so fast in her breast, that her breathing would return to normal. "Because if you forget at the office, I'll be sure to remind you."

"Then you're really serious about coming to work at One-Eyed Jacks?"

"Yes…yes, I am," she responded obstinately.

Morgan was silent for a long, tense moment, staring at her intently, his dark visage still, closed, unreadable, revealing nothing of his thoughts and emotions. Then, with a low growl of what might have been displeasure, despair, defiance or all three, he turned away, grabbing his Stetson from the table and clapping it roughly on his head.

"Have it your way then. But be warned, Cat." His eyes traveled over her blatantly, lingering on her lush mouth, her swollen breasts. "You are no longer safe alone with me!"

Then he strode from the kitchen, deliberately slamming the front door behind him.

After he had gone, Cat leaned against the kitchen counter weakly, still shaking from the aftermath of her emotions, the sensations surging wildly through her body. God, how could this have happened? How could she have *let* it happen? That she was vulnerable was no excuse. She had recognized that fact, along with her own attraction to Morgan McCain. She should have guarded against both—against *him!* Instead, she had permitted him to kiss her—and she had reveled in the potent feelings he had unleashed inside her; she had ached for more. If Morgan had not released her when he had, she had no doubt he would even now be carrying her upstairs to her bedroom to make love to her, or simply flinging her down on the kitchen floor—with her complete and eager compliance!

Despite all her bold talk, how *could* she go to work at the One-Eyed Jacks Oil & Gas Company now? Cat asked herself, distressed. Especially after the way things had turned out with Spence, and with Morgan's obvious feelings about mixing business with pleasure? But then she realized he had undoubtedly hoped his parting words to her *would,* in fact, discourage her from coming into the office tomorrow morning; that if she felt he would be so busy pursuing her personally that he would have no time for her professionally, she would give up the whole idea of becoming a working partner in the corporation.

At that thought, Cat's eyes abruptly narrowed and her temper rose.

"Damn you, Morgan!" she snapped indignantly. "I am *not* going to be dissuaded from trying to fulfill my obligations as a stockholder, from trying to take over Dad's position at One-Eyed Jacks just because *you* don't think I can do the job—much less because you think you can't keep your hands to yourself at the office! Once bitten, twice shy—and I've already learned my lesson the hard way from Spence. We'll be business partners, you and I, Morgan—and that's all we'll be!"

But as she involuntarily remembered the feel of his mouth on her own, tasting her, arousing her unbearably, Cat nevertheless had a terrible, sneaking suspicion this was going to prove much more easily said than done.

Chapter 9

Corporate Politics

The following morning, bright and early, Cat drove to the offices of the One-Eyed Jacks Oil & Gas Company. She did not know what she had expected, but it was not the low, sprawling cluster of glass-and-red-brick buildings that lined the man-made waterway at the grassy edge of the office park. As she walked toward the edifice that housed the One-Eyed Jacks offices, she surveyed her surroundings with approval, noting the trees that had been planted and the other landscaping that had been done. That was one thing Cat had to admit she liked about Wichita: it was green, with trees, bushes, flowers and grass all over. Even the downtown area was beautifully landscaped, it was not just the parks. It *was* pleasant, Cat thought, not to be surrounded by towering blocks of steel and concrete, not to walk in shadow on even the sunniest of days. Away from downtown, there were no skyscrapers to speak of. The building she was now entering was only three stories tall.

The heavy glass door closed behind her with a whisper, shutting out the sounds of the early morning traffic, leaving the interior of the edifice so quiet that Cat felt briefly as though she had entered a library. A short staircase rose from the center of the foyer, and a glance at the directory that hung on one brick wall confirmed that the One-Eyed Jacks Oil & Gas Company was on the second floor. Her mouth was suddenly dry from agitation and her heart thudded with excitement as she slowly climbed the steps to the hallway beyond. It was not just the thought of beginning her new job that filled her with such nervous anticipation, but also the prospect of seeing Morgan again and of his reaction to her presence at the corporation they now owned, if not equally, at least jointly.

Of course he had issued that warning to her yesterday merely to prevent her from showing up at the office this morning. Of course he had. It was foolish to think otherwise, to think that perhaps he had been serious. Of course she was safe alone with him. He had been teasing her, that was all. Still, Cat's pulse raced—because what if he had not been? In that case, how could she trust him—or herself in his presence? she wondered as she remembered his kisses and their potent effect upon her. It was not enough to admit she was vulnerable at the moment, because even if she had not been, the simple truth was she was strongly attracted to Morgan.

Reaching the office doors of the One-Eyed Jacks Oil & Gas Company, Cat paused and drew a deep breath. Then she pushed open the wooden door with its brass lettering and went in. The young receptionist, seated at the desk in the reception area, was obviously expecting her.

"Good morning, Ms. Devlin."

"How…how did you know who I was?"

The woman smiled. "Mr. McCain described you very well."

"Indeed?" Cat commented dryly, wondering just *how* he had described her. "Then you probably also know I'll be working here from now on, that I'll be taking my father's place in the business."

"So Mr. McCain has informed us. I'm Josie Kendricks, by the way." The receptionist extended her hand, and Cat shook it firmly. "If you'll follow me, I'll introduce you to Mrs. Whittingdale, who was your father's personal secretary, as well as being Mr. McCain's. She'll show you to your father's office and get you whatever you need."

Despite the perky brunette's engaging friendliness, a puzzled frown knit Cat's brow as she followed the receptionist into a hallway that led to the inner offices of the corporation. Clearly, Morgan had not believed she would heed his warning, but had instead expected her at the One-Eyed Jacks Oil & Gas Company this morning, had even paved the way for her. The mystery was why had he done it? Then, as she remembered their past meetings, a wry smile tugged at the corners of her mouth. No doubt Morgan had thought of her fiery redhead's temper and had sought to avoid any unpleasantness at the corporation. Well, that suited her just fine. She had twice got off on the wrong foot with Morgan. She certainly did not want to do the same with the employees of the One-Eyed Jacks Oil & Gas Company.

"Ms. Devlin, this is Mrs. Whittingdale," Josie announced as they reached the secretary's office, "affectionately known around here as Whitty."

As the older woman rose from her desk, Cat was immediately struck by both the shrewdness and the warmth in her bright, twinkling blue eyes. Gray-haired, plainly but impeccably groomed in a tailored suit, Whitty looked as though she would have been right at home taking tea with the Queen Mum rather than taking dictation. Still, there was a motherly air about her that softened the severity of her appearance and spoke of her kindness. Smiling, sensing she had found not only a friend but also an ally, Cat stretched out her hand, which Whitty shook, then patted in a brisk but caring manner.

"I'll admit I was skeptical at first when Morgan said you were going to take Frank's place here at One-Eyed Jacks," Whitty declared in a no-nonsense fashion. "But now that I've seen you, I can tell there's a good deal of your father in you, Ms. Devlin."

"Cat...please, call me Cat."

"That's a bargain only if you'll agree to call me Whitty in return. Mrs. Whittingdale is too much of a mouthful for anybody!" The secretary chuckled. "My, my...Frank's daughter. Morgan said you were attractive—but then, seeing as how he's said as much about *me* in the past, I didn't pay him a whole lot of mind initially. But now I realize he wasn't exaggerating one iota in his description of you— and from the way he behaved when he talked about you, I have the strangest feeling things are shortly going to get very interesting around here at One-Eyed Jacks, that you're going to liven the place up considerably with your presence. So why don't you come along with me into Frank's office, and we'll have us a cup of coffee and a lovely little chat. Then I'll start showing you some of the ropes of the oil-and-gas business.''

"That would be wonderful, Whitty," Cat declared, meaning her words sincerely, for she sensed the secretary, even more than Morgan, could have proved to be a real stumbling block at the corporation, making things very difficult for her indeed. To have Whitty on her side helped tremendously.

Following coffee with the secretary in what had once been Frank Devlin's office, Cat found herself alone at her father's huge antique desk, examining a towering stack of what Whitty had termed oil-and-gas leases. Leafing through them, Cat could not help but shake her head with both amazement and amusement. Some of the documents were so old that they defined the regions covered in the leases in antiquated language she thought could hardly be legal in this day and age. *That area bounded on the north along a line from Farmer Thomas's well to the boulder known as the Black Rock at the edge of the Widow Piper's property* was just one example she read. She discovered that in many cases not just the rights to the property's oil and gas were leased, but also to its minerals. Cat sighed at the realization, because that meant even more to learn. Still, she became so engrossed in reading the documents that the morning fairly flew by, and she was surprised when Morgan, after knocking on the office door, opened it and stuck his head inside.

"You mean you haven't given up yet and gone home in despair?" he said in greeting, his now-familiar, crooked grin curving his mouth so that she knew he was teasing her—even if he *did* wish she'd never come to the offices of the One-Eyed Jacks Oil & Gas Company to begin with.

"Then this horrendous pile of leases filled—at least in several instances—with delightfully archaic legalese was your idea?" She motioned to the stack of papers before her, wishing her pulse had not begun to leap erratically at just the sight of him, that the memory of his kisses yesterday had not risen in her mind.

"No…if you must know, it was Whitty's idea. She said everybody—including me—had had to start somewhere to learn about the oil-and-gas business, and that you might as well begin with the leases."

"Well, they certainly have been very informative. I have to admit that other than as something that makes automobiles go, I hadn't ever really given much thought to gasoline before—where it comes from, how it's discovered, how it's taken from the ground, how it's refined and marketed, et cetera." As she spoke, Cat stood, sliding around the desk to perch on its front edge, having some notion that this would put her more at Morgan's eye level so she would not be disadvantaged by his looking down at her as he strolled into her father's office…her office now.

But after a moment, she wished she had stayed where she was, for her new vantage point gave her an excellent view of Morgan—of the slow, sexy, subtle swagger of his hips as he walked toward her. There were so few men who moved with such a combination of power and grace, she thought, fascinated despite herself. It was an inherent trait, not something that could be learned. It made her think of a predator on the prowl, muscles rippling and bunching as the animal prepared to spring. So strong was this impression that Cat instinctively leaned back a little as Morgan came to a halt before her, so she wound up looking up at him anyway, her throat bared in an age-old gesture of submission that made her feel inadvertently exposed and vulnerable. She was vividly conscious of the heat that emanated from Morgan's body, and of how his eyes traveled from the tips of her shoes up her hose-clad legs, lingering on the curve of her breasts beneath the jacket of her lemon yellow linen suit before finally coming to rest on her face.

Ill-concealed desire smoldered in the depths of his ice blue eyes, making them appear perversely like blue flame—clear, pure, brilliant—against the bronze of his skin. At the far corners of his eyes, fine laugh lines etched his visage; deeper grooves bracketed his mustache and mouth. Cat had a sudden, wild urge to reach up and trace the contours of those lines, that mustache, that mouth. She wondered what Morgan would do if she did, if that would prove to be the spark to ignite him. She shuddered faintly at the thought, knowing she was playing with fire and that if she did not want to be burned, she must keep things between them on a strictly businesslike basis.

"What...what can I do for you, Morgan?"

"Well, now I believe that if I put my mind to it, I could think of some *very* entertaining answers to that question." He placed one hand on either side of her, on top of the desk, effectively hemming her in so she could not escape. "And it occurs to me that you must want to hear those answers, or you would not have shown up here this morning after my warning to you yesterday."

"Indeed? Then let me disabuse you of that notion," Cat rejoined tartly, heat suffusing her own body despite herself as he leaned over her. "I'm here to do a job, *not* to be seduced! You were right about mixing business with pleasure. I learned that the hard way...with Spence. I thought he and I could be engaged, could even get married and could eventually work together as partners in the import-export firm. But I was wrong—and that's a mistake I don't intend to make again, especially with you! So if your visit to my office is of a personal nature, then I'm afraid I'll have to ask you to leave, *Mr. McCain.*"

He was silent for a long moment, staring down at her. Then he spoke. "What went wrong at the import-export firm? Did you try to take it over, too...to boss Spence around?"

"No, I most certainly did not! But I *did* expect my judgment and decisions to be respected—not to be overruled merely because Spence had the mistaken notion that all women were emotionally unsuited for top-management positions!"

"Well, *I* never said anything like that."

"Didn't you?" Cat snapped, her temper rising—not to mention her temperature at his proximity. "Oh, perhaps not in so many words, but wasn't the message the same?"

"No. As I told you yesterday, I doubt your ability to do the job you've set your mind on, yes—but not because you're a woman. The fact that you're a woman is *my* problem, Cat, because I find you attractive, and you are therefore a distraction. Still, if necessary, I can learn to live with that, I suppose."

"Oh?" She deliberately arched one brow to make her skepticism plain. "Is that why you said I was no longer safe alone with you then?"

"No, I said that in the heat of the moment, just so you'd know that even if you decided to come here to One-Eyed Jacks, it wouldn't necessarily place you off-limits in my mind.... Damn it, Cat! Do you want me to apologize for kissing you yesterday? Is that it?"

She shook her head, because how could she insist on that? Despite Morgan's words, which had seemingly suggested otherwise, she knew he was not the sort of man to force himself on a woman. He would have released her yesterday at any moment she had voiced a protest. Instead, she had remained silent, had reveled in his kisses. How could she insist he apologize, when she was as much to blame as he?

"Yesterday shouldn't have happened." Her voice was softer now. "There are so many reasons why it shouldn't have happened."

"But it *did* happen, Cat." Morgan's own voice was equally low, and underlaid now with a husky note of urgency and desire.

"Yes. But that doesn't mean it has to happen again. Look, Morgan, I'd like for us to be business partners...even friends—"

"But not lovers?" The burning intensity of his gaze scalded her. Tension stretched between them. For a moment Cat was half frightened, half exhilarated by the thought that he meant to kiss her again, such was the passion that darkened his face. But instead, after an instant, with difficulty, Morgan forced a rueful smile to his lips, and when he spoke, his tone was resolutely light. "Now, why did I have the sneaking suspicion you were going to tell me that? Even so, it's not going to work, you know. Feelings—strong feelings—are hard to fight, and I'm not at all sure I want to battle mine anyway. Still, if you insist, I suppose I must try." He paused briefly and, to her perverse disappointment, moved a little away from her, as though he no longer trusted himself to stand so close. Then he continued. "I came to your office to insist upon taking you to lunch. However, you mustn't think of it as an actual date, Cat, but, rather, as a...power lunch. Isn't that what, these days, they call what used to be known as a three-martini lunch?" He smiled once more—an engaging, wicked grin, so she knew that was not how he would have phrased his invitation only a few minutes ago, before she had made her position plain. "I thought we could discuss the business and celebrate your becoming a part of One-Eyed Jacks."

If she had any sense at all, Cat knew she should refuse. After all, she had already laid out the ground rules of their relationship, and she had to adhere to them or Morgan would not take her seriously, about either him or her job at the corporation.

"All right," she heard herself reply instead. "A power lunch it is then."

Cat was astounded by her own response. She must be out of her mind, she thought, dismayed. But then she reasoned that there was nothing wrong with having lunch with a colleague, and she and Morgan really *did* have business to discuss. So what if he had admitted that he was attracted to her, if the way he glanced at her was anything but businesslike? So what if she could not seem to put his kisses from her mind, if every time she looked at him, she wished he would kiss her again? Her breath caught in her throat at the realization. She was being foolish, behaving like some high school girl with a silly crush. She simply had to get hold of herself and her emotions.

Sliding from the edge of the desk, she grabbed her handbag and drew its long leather strap over her shoulder. "Perhaps Whitty would like to join us," she suggested. "After meeting her this morning, I'm sure she knows almost as much as you—if not more—about One-Eyed Jacks and the oil-and-gas business."

"No doubt." Morgan's tone was dry. "But actually, I hadn't planned on making this a threesome. However, if you don't trust yourself alone with me, if you feel you need a chaperon, Cat..."

"Certainly not!" she retorted, flushing, because of course that was precisely why she had suggested asking Whitty to join them.

"Then let's go, shall we?" Taking Cat's arm, he ushered her from the office. "Whitty," he said to the secretary as they passed her desk, "Cat and I will be having lunch at Applebee's if you need us."

"All right, Morgan. You kids have fun," Whitty replied.

"We've...got a lot of business to go over." Cat could feel another blush creeping up her cheeks at the knowing twinkle in the secretary's eyes.

"Of course," Whitty agreed, positively beaming.

"Do you know what she thinks?" Cat hissed, mortified, once they were outside in the parking lot and climbing into Morgan's Bronco.

"Yes. She has been trying to marry me off for years, ever since she started to work at One-Eyed Jacks, in fact." He shook his head ruefully, chuckling. "She thinks I need to give up my wild, wicked ways and settle down. So far her endeavors to procure me a bride have proved unsuccessful—much to her despair. However, as you will come to learn, once Whitty has her mind set on something, she's like a feisty terrier with an old bone—she doesn't let go easily. Rather like you, I should imagine."

Cat had the good grace to laugh at that. "Yes, I'll confess that persistence has always been one of my strong suits. Have you never even come close to marriage then, Morgan?" she inquired curiously.

For a moment she thought he wasn't going to answer her. His lighthearted mood abruptly dissipated, and with more force than was necessary, he jammed the key into the ignition of the Bronco, starting the engine up with a roar. "One near miss," he finally announced tersely, a muscle flexing in his jaw, so Cat knew without even asking that he spoke of the woman he had on a previous occasion said he would prefer to forget, the one of whom she, Cat, had reminded him. "We were engaged, but it...didn't work out."

Cat felt her resemblance to his lost love must be hard for Morgan. At least he did not make her think of Spence.... No, now that she thought about it, that was not quite true. In some ways, he *had* reminded her of Spence. Of course most people did have a particular physical type to whom they were attracted. There were some men who preferred blondes, for example; others who were drawn only to brunettes. Cat herself had always liked tall, dark men. Such as Spence and Morgan.

"Was she a redhead, your fiancée?"

"No, a blonde...but the kind who knew Bach from Beethoven— and old money from new. In the end she decided she preferred the former."

Cat detected a note of bitterness in Morgan's voice, and she knew the breakup had hurt him more than he would ever admit, such was his pride.

"Ouch," she said lightly. "Sounds like your blonde and Spence would have made a go of it. He was…something of a snob, too, I'm afraid."

"And you're not?"

"No…no, I don't think I am—at least, I hope I'm not. I never wanted to be my mother, you see…someone who would throw away a chance at love, at happiness, because the man was poor or lacked social position or whatever. I loved my father, Morgan, no matter what his failings might have been. He was a fine man. The more I knew him, the more I came to understand that. I was proud to be his daughter. I was…I *am* proud of what he accomplished in his life. Nobody ever handed him anything on a plate. He started with nothing, and together with you, he built One-Eyed Jacks. That's why I'm so determined to learn all I can about the oil-and-gas business, why I plan on succeeding at this job—with or without your help and regardless of your personal feelings or mine."

"All right. That seems fair enough," Morgan replied as he pulled into Applebee's parking lot and killed the Bronco's engine. "Why don't we just agree to play things by ear then and see where they go from here?"

"That sounds good."

They went inside the restaurant, which was crowded. Fortunately, Whitty had foreseen this and had prudently phoned ahead for reservations. So after Morgan gave his name to the hostess, they were seated at a table fairly quickly. After glancing at the menu, Cat ordered the Santa Fe chicken salad, while Morgan decided on the Applebee's steak dinner. Then, much to her surprise, he took his Waterman fountain pen from his shirt pocket and, on the back of a napkin, began to draw a diagram that demonstrated the basics of drilling an oil well.

"I think it'd make explaining this a little easier if you'd move around here and sit beside me, Cat, so we can both see what I'm doodling—since, admittedly, I'm no artist.'' He indicated the chair next to him.

She glanced at him suspiciously for some sign that he was flirting with her, testing her resolve not to become involved with him, but she could read nothing of his thoughts. He was wearing what she had come to recognize as his poker face. Still, she *did* want to learn, so after a minute Cat moved around the table to take the chair beside him. Bending her head to study the diagram he had drawn, she missed the smile that curved Morgan's mouth beneath his mustache before he began to tell her all about how to dig black gold from the earth.

Chapter 10

The Play's the Thing

In the weeks that followed, Cat applied herself diligently to learning everything she could about the oil-and-gas industry. She made several trips downtown to the main library to check out books, which she lugged home to read and study at night. During the day, she continued her work at the offices of the One-Eyed Jacks Oil & Gas Company, and although she had as yet to make any real decisions there, she grew more confident in her knowledge as time wore on. She had discovered that in addition to its offices, the corporation had a building at a second location, a corrugated steel structure that resembled a large garage or a small plant, where vehicles, machinery, equipment, parts and other supplies were stored and out of which the pumpers and other employees who handled the actual day-to-day, hands-on operations and on-site labor worked. The main offices were referred to at the company as ''HQ,'' for headquarters, and the second building, managed by a foreman, was called simply ''the shop.''

Much to Cat's surprise, for she had fully expected Morgan to fight her every hard-won step of the way, he instead treated her like a management trainee, making certain her education about the oil-and-gas business was as thorough as possible. He took her out to the shop to show her what went on there. Although a receptionist-secretary worked in a cubbyhole of an office at the back, the shop was clearly a man's milieu. Its green-glassed windows, barricaded with chicken wire and lined with taped alarm wire as a precaution against break-ins, were cracked in places and coated so thickly with grime that it was almost impossible to see through them. The concrete floors were stained with blotches of oil and grease. Next to the time clock hung a giant bulletin board boasting, among other things, a pin-up-girl calendar and a couple of risqué French postcards. Beneath was a long metal table on which sat message bins, untidy piles of dusty brochures and coffee-stained papers, and an ashtray filled to overflowing. In the men's small bathroom, the door of which stood open, Cat spied a stack of *Playboy* magazines on the floor in one corner.

"Good heavens, this place is a pigsty! Why haven't you done something about cleaning it up?" Cat asked Morgan, frowning at him with disapproval.

"Now, darlin', do try to keep that temper of yours under control," he drawled, grinning at her. "Because the one thing you're not going to change at One-Eyed Jacks is the shop, believe me. You could straighten this place up and fix it up as fancy as you pleased and a week later it'd look just like this again. It's mostly men who work here—and the majority of 'em have blue-collar backgrounds and a high school education, if that. Not that I'm knocking 'em, mind. For the most part, they're decent, hardworking men, and I trust 'em to take care of what I need taken care of. But yuppies they just aren't, babe."

"Don't call me that—or 'darlin'' or any other name of that ilk! It's sexist and demeaning in a professional environment!" Cat snapped. "And so are that...that calendar, those postcards, and those magazines! I want them, at least, removed from the premises immediately!"

"The men'd just bring 'em back tomorrow, Cat," Morgan stated matter-of-factly, no longer smiling. "And I reckon you must have thought Frank was pretty 'sexist and demeaning,' too—since he called all the gals at the office, including Whitty, 'sugar.'"

Cat was nonplussed by this discovery. "He—he did?"

"Yeah, he did. On the other hand, the few women who work the wells and pipelines are paid the exact same wages as their male counterparts at One-Eyed Jacks." He pointed to the Equal Employment Opportunity sign encased in glass and hanging prominently on one wall. "Frank believed in that, as do I. And it's true what they say, you know—actions *do* speak louder than words."

"Is that...is that why you're helping me, training me?" she queried curiously.

"Yes. I still don't know whether you'll prove able to take Frank's place at One-Eyed Jacks, Cat. But you were hell-bent-for-leather determined to try, and it wouldn't be right of me not to give you that chance. Besides which, I want you to know that if you wind up blowing it, it for damned sure won't be because you're a woman and because I, a man, stood in your way! It'll be for the simple reason that you just couldn't cut the mustard, Cat—and you won't have anybody but your own sweet self to blame for that!"

She was so astounded by Morgan's words that for a moment she could only stare at him, speechless. Then, at last, she spoke. "I suppose I should thank you for that."

"Yes, you should," he insisted dryly.

"Well, then...thank you."

"You're welcome. Now, can we get out of here and leave the shop in peace? Or do you make it a general policy to give every man you meet a hard time?"

With difficulty, Cat bit back the retort that sprang to her lips. Deep down inside, she knew Morgan was right, that the minute her back was turned, the pin-up-girl calendar and the French postcards would be tacked back onto the bulletin board and the *Playboy* magazines returned to the men's rest room. It was, as Morgan had once told her, simply the nature of the beast. She sighed, shaking her head.

"Fine! But I'm sending a Fabio calendar down here today—and the next time I come here, I expect to see it hanging right up there beside the Vargas Girl!"

Morgan threw back his head and laughed uproariously at that. "Oh, Cat, you're a woman after my own heart, I do believe!"

Together, they exited the shop—much, she felt sure, to the relief of the foreman and his men. After that, Morgan drove her out to tour some of the sites she had read about in the oil-and-gas leases that first day at the company. As she and Morgan rode along, Cat observed herds of cattle and sheep grazing in fields bounded by barbed wire and farmers driving big combines, in the process of harvesting acres of golden wheat. Here and there some of the fields already cleared were being burned. The windows of the Bronco were down, and on the wind that streamed into the vehicle, she smelled the pungent scent of what she thought was marijuana.

"My God, that's pot burning!" she exclaimed, startled.

"That's sure what it smells like, isn't it?" Morgan agreed affably. "And out here in the country, it's certainly a possibility. Sometimes the ranchers and farmers don't even know it's being grown on their land—particularly more-isolated sections—courtesy of would-be drug dealers. However, more than likely it's just what's left of plain old alfalfa that's already been cut. When it burns, it smells just like grass going up in smoke."

They had by now reached some of the oil-well sites, and Morgan turned off onto a narrow dirt path, then parked the Bronco. After they got out of the vehicle and began to walk across the field, he indicated the beam pump that was their goal.

"That's Three of a Kind Number One, and that one over there—" he pointed to another beam pump in the distance "—is Three of a Kind Number Two. Unless a landowner voices some stringent objection, One-Eyed Jacks has a policy of naming its wells after poker hands and cards in general."

"And when the landowner objects?"

"Then we usually wind up calling the well after the landowner...Hank Souther Number One, for instance. All the wells have both names and numbers. That's how we keep them straight. After we choose a name for a lease site, all the wells at that location are numbered in the order they're drilled. So the wells here on Mrs. Williams's property, for example, are named Three of a Kind and numbered one through four, since we have four wells here."

"The beam pumps are so ugly in reality, compared to the diagrams

I've seen," Cat declared as she studied Three of Kind Number One more closely.

"Yeah, these are older wells. Nowadays, since the world's become more conscious of its environment and ecology, we try harder not to disturb the surrounding land so much, to work more in harmony with nature." He went on to explain to her how a well was drilled and machinery operated, the way in which the natural gas was siphoned off and a dozen other things that made her recognize just how vast Morgan's knowledge was, especially compared to her own.

Later on, however, when, in the weeks that passed, he took her to visit one of the local oil refineries to which the One-Eyed Jacks Oil & Gas Company marketed its crude oil, Cat did not feel nearly so ignorant. The principles of marketing she understood backward and forward. A few days after that, she confidently entered Morgan's office to inform him that according to her research, One-Eyed Jacks could make more money by selling its crude to a different refinery.

"Yes, I know," he said.

"Then…I don't understand. We *are* in business to make a profit, aren't we? So why aren't we selling our crude to that refinery?" Cat asked, genuinely puzzled.

"For the simple reason that I refuse to do business with any refinery that dumps toxic waste into the environment, darlin'."

"Do you know for a fact that that particular refinery does that?"

"I do."

"Then why haven't you done anything about it, reported it to the proper authorities?"

"There isn't any need to, that's why. That refinery is under investigation even as we speak. But like those of justice, the wheels of government bureaucracy grind slowly. It'll be years before all the facts are uncovered, a decision is reached and that refinery is fined, forced to clean up its act, and the heads of its management roll. Until that time, however, One-Eyed Jacks' crude goes elsewhere—or do you still want to question that?" Morgan raised one eyebrow inquiringly.

"No, I don't."

"Good. Now, what are your plans for this weekend?"

The abrupt change of topic momentarily threw Cat off stride.

"This—this weekend?" she parroted lamely.

"Yes, I have season tickets to Music Theater, and I thought you might like to accompany me to Friday night's performance." Morgan grinned when Cat, torn by her conflicting emotions, hesitated. "You needn't think of it as an actual socks-on car date, Cat," he declared.

"A socks-on car date? What in the hell is that?"

"Just what it sounds like—a date that requires a man to wear socks with his shoes and to pick his date up in a car."

"As opposed to what, for heaven's sake?"

"As opposed to his throwing a pair of sneakers on his bare feet right before she drives herself over to his house, bringing the beer and pizza with her."

"That's not a date," Cat asserted, disgusted. "That's a delivery service!"

"Only if she delivers," Morgan rejoined, impudently waggling his eyebrows à la Groucho Marx and tapping an imaginary cigar as he spoke, then grinning even more widely at the blush that stained Cat's cheeks crimson.

"Don't you dare ask me if *I* deliver, Morgan McCain!" she warned, doing her best to repress the answering smile that tugged at her lips in response to his antics.

"How *did* you guess that was going to be my next question? Never mind. Don't answer that. You'll only say something insulting about my dubious character—and then I'll be forced to admit it's probably true. Now, about Music Theater..." He determinedly returned to their previous topic of conversation. "Before you decline my invitation, I feel compelled to point out that it is one of *the* places to see and be seen in Wichita. And although I don't give a damn about that—and I'm beginning pleasantly to suspect you don't, either—it *will* offer you a prime opportunity to meet many of this town's movers and shakers, several of whom One-Eyed Jacks does business with. Therefore, if it suits you to do so, you may legitimately think of it as a professional social occasion—and not a real date with me at all," he ended blandly, his thick, spiky black lashes hooding his eyes, so she could not tell what he was thinking at that moment.

Despite her resolve not to get involved in a relationship with Morgan that was other than professional, Cat found herself wanting badly to accept his invitation. Both to her dismay and to her provocation, she had discovered that the more time she spent with him, the more she learned about him, the better she knew him, the more strongly attracted to him she had become. Deep down inside, she knew that if she were honest with herself, she must admit she had already halfway fallen in love with him. He was not only the most ruggedly handsome man she had ever seen, but also intelligent, honest, ethical, compassionate and appealingly down-to-earth. That he was also wild and wicked merely added spice to the mixture.

"What's playing at Music Theater?" she finally asked, telling herself sternly that she would be a fool to turn down an opportunity to mingle with those who belonged to what she had learned was commonly and sometimes scornfully referred to as Wichita's "21 Club." "Something like *Annie, Get Your Gun,* no doubt."

"No, actually, it's *Cabaret.*"

Of course it had to be one of her all-time favorites—slick and witty, socially provocative and insightful.

"All right. I'll go with you," Cat said. "What should I wear?"

"The same thing you'd wear to a performance on Broadway."

"And just how would you know what anybody wears to the theater in New York, Morgan?"

"Just because I choose to live in Wichita doesn't mean I haven't been to the Big Apple, darlin'—several times, in fact. It's a great place to visit...lots of fun and exciting things to do. It's a habit of mine to go there every so often, generally on my way to Europe. I even went with Frank once or twice—although, I'm forced to confess, I foolishly declined the pleasure of making your acquaintance then, having the horribly mistaken notion that you and I wouldn't exactly hit it off. Last time I saw both *Phantom of the Opera* and *Les Misérables.* And that's how I know what's worn to the theater in New York."

"I see. So you're not quite the simple cowboy you sometimes appear. That being the case, may I then safely assume you will *not* be attired in a Stetson hat, Levi's jeans and Tony Lama boots when you pick me up Friday night?'' Cat queried archly.

''You may.''

Nor was he when, at the appointed hour on Friday evening, he arrived to pick her up. In fact, after opening her front door to admit him, Cat could only stand and stare, her breath catching in her throat. From his stylish, European-cut, black Armani suit to the traditional Cole Haans on his feet, Morgan looked not as though he'd stepped from a Marlboro cigarette advertisement, but from the glossy pages of *GQ*. Spence at his best had nothing on Morgan.

''Unless you're waiting for me to kiss you, close your mouth, Cat,'' he said in greeting, grinning at her obvious astonishment. ''Because you look so damned gorgeous that I'm sorely tempted to sample a taste of you!''

Cat blushed at both his compliment and the suggestion that he might kiss her—even though she knew with certainty she had seldom looked better. She had taken inordinate care with her appearance, trying on first one dress and then another before she had finally settled on her ''little black dress,'' which was a basic but dramatic, clinging silk sheath with a halter strap and no back. She had left her dark red hair loose and flowing, and the contrast of it and her pale skin with the dress was vivid. Her jewelry was simple but equally sensational— a pair of dangling gold earrings and a single, heavy gold bangle bracelet on her right wrist.

''Let me just get my handbag and wrap,'' she told him. ''Then we'll go.'' Once outside, she paused momentarily at the sight of the sleek black Corvette parked in the half-circle drive. ''Is this yours?'' She motioned toward the sports car.

''Yeah…a '68 that I rebuilt and restored myself. I got it out of my garage earlier this evening. Somehow I had a sneaking suspicion that I'd be taking a long, cool woman in a black dress to the theater, and the Bronco just didn't seem to fit the occasion.'' He opened the Corvette's passenger door for her. ''Get in.''

Music Theater was held at the Century II's Concert Hall, Morgan informed her during their drive to the downtown area, and the performance of *Cabaret* was sold out. After he had parked the sports car in the circular building's huge parking lot, they strolled toward the edifice itself and up its gently inclined steps. Inside, Cat saw that the continuous, curved hallway that encompassed the interior did double duty by serving as an art gallery. Paintings hung all along the walls, small, discreet white price cards tucked into the right-hand corner of each frame. Greeting people he knew, Morgan ushered Cat into the theater, where she discovered that they had excellent seats front and center. The orchestra was just in the process of tuning up. Drawing off her lacy shawl, then settling into her chair, she leafed through her program, pretending not to notice when Morgan slid his arm along the top of her seat back, lightly brushing her bare shoulders. Still, the sensation was so erotic—especially after the house lights had dimmed—that she could hardly concentrate on the show.

His touch was like fire against her skin, igniting an answering spark in her as she listened to the music she knew by heart. The fact that all through the first half of the performance, Morgan played idly with her hair and caressed her shoulder languidly did not help. It only fanned the initial spark to flame, so that by the time that intermission rolled around and the house lights came up, she felt as though she were burning up with fever. Instead of watching Sally Bowles's plight on stage, Cat had kept drifting away into one fantasy after another—each of which had ended with Morgan making love to her. Prompted by the musical, she had even envisioned herself as a cabaret singer and stuck Morgan in a military uniform! Now she could hardly look at him as he escorted her into the lobby and asked her whether she wanted any refreshments.

"There's no alcohol served here, of course. But I can get you a soft drink and a candy bar if you'd like," he told her.

"A—a cola would be fine," she replied, glad of an excuse to get rid of him for a few minutes until she could force her thoughts into a more orderly channel. Besides, maybe a soft drink would cool her down!

Still, as she watched him stroll over to the refreshment bar, she could not help but admire him. He was undoubtedly the most handsome man present tonight, she thought, noticing—not without a violent twinge of jealousy—how many women eyed him appraisingly and flirted with him invitingly as he made his way through the crowd, pausing now and then to shake hands with various men. When he finally returned, he handed Cat her cola, then proceeded to point out who was who in Wichita, introducing her to several prominent, influential people.

"Why, as I live and breathe, I do believe it's Morgan McCain! You handsome outlaw, you! What in the world are you doing here? Music Theater's not generally *your* particular brand of home brew," a tall, cool blonde drawled as she approached them, towing behind her a man Cat knew intuitively came from generations of old money.

She did not need to hear Morgan greet the woman to know this was his ex-fiancée, Veronica Havers—the whole story of whom Whitty had told her at the office. Now, seeing Veronica, Cat recognized the type instantly. She had seen a hundred Veronicas before at her mother's parties and wherever else social predators were to be found, prowling in their sleek attire and baring their sharp claws. Cat disliked Veronica on sight, and she knew the feeling was mutual.

"Ronnie," Morgan said coolly, then nodded to the man. "Paul."

"Aren't you going to introduce us to your...friend, Morgan?" Veronica prodded.

"Yes, of course. Cat, these are the Stirlings...Ronnie and Paul. And this is Frank Devlin's daughter, Cat. I'm sure you probably heard about Frank's death."

"Yes, such an unexpected tragedy...a heart attack, wasn't it? Our sympathies on your loss, Ms. Devlin." Veronica surveyed Cat assessingly, mentally toting up the cost of her dress, jewelry, shoes and handbag—a process that was not lost on Cat.

It was one of those rare occasions when she was actually grateful to her mother for being such a snob. Because of Julia Talbot, Cat knew how to deal with women who wielded words and glances like the keenest of daggers.

"Thank you, Ms. Stirling. It's very kind of you to say so."

"Cat's down from New York," Morgan explained. "She's taken Frank's place at One-Eyed Jacks. Her extensive experience in importing and exporting coupled with her background in both the European and Asian business markets are giving the company a fresh and exciting perspective.''

"I'm sure that Ms. Devlin has indeed proved a valuable asset—in more ways than one. How…nice for you, Morgan." Clearly, Veronica was in reality insinuating how wonderful it was that Morgan now had a partner with whom he could sleep—*and* keep the stock all in the family, so to speak.

At Veronica's words, Cat could feel her blood pressure skyrocketing. "Actually, Ms. Stirling," she purred in Julia Talbot's best cat fashion, laying her hand lightly on Morgan's arm and gazing up at him seductively before flashing Veronica a brilliant smile, "it's very nice for both of us, isn't it, Morgan?"

His eyes danced with knowing amusement and at the same time smoldered with heat as he glanced down at her. He slipped his arm possessively about her waist and drew her up next to him so her head rested on his shoulder.

"It's better than nice, darlin'," he declared huskily, effectively wiping the tight smile off of Veronica's face. "Much better."

To Cat's relief, the lobby lights flashed on and off then, signaling that intermission was coming to an end, so there was no time for further conversation. Morgan made their goodbyes, then led her away, his arm still clasped around her waist, his head bent near to hers as he whispered in her ear.

"Now *that* was a performance worth the price of admission!" He laughed softly. "Hell! Even *I* half believed we're sleeping together! Ronnie's smile disappeared so fast that she looked like she'd accidentally sucked on an unripe persimmon!"

"You don't agree then that *Cabaret* is worth whatever you paid for the tickets?" Cat asked, pointedly ignoring his latter remarks. "If I recall correctly, Ms. Stirling *did* suggest Music Theater wasn't your particular brand of home brew." She knew instinctively that Veronica was watching them walk away together. Cat could practically feel the daggers aimed at her bare back.

"To the contrary, babe," Morgan insisted, his arm tightening about her in a way that sent a sudden rush of heat and excitement through her. "I can't remember when I've enjoyed a musical more."

Cat felt the same, but she was damned if she was going to admit that to Morgan.

"Why? Do you keep a black leather coat and a pair of jackboots hidden in your closet?" Her double entendre was, on the one hand, a reference to the show's World War II setting and the military uniforms of its German officers.

"Naw...just a lariat for roping high-strung fillies who chafe at being cut out of the herd and branded."

For the life of her, Cat could not think of a satisfactory comeback to that.

Chapter 11

Dances and Dreams

The third time Cat noticed the battered old pickup truck in the parking lot of the One-Eyed Jacks office park, it belatedly occurred to her it was the same truck she had seen in Vickridge on the morning following her arrival in Wichita. She had, in fact, observed it in the neighborhood on several occasions since. As she walked toward the glass-and-red-brick building, now so familiar that it felt like a second home to her, her brow was knit in a puzzled frown. It was entirely possible, she supposed, that the vehicle *did,* in fact, belong to a lawn service that not only mowed yards in Vickridge, but also cared for the landscaping at the office park. But for the first time this morning, she realized that in all the times she had seen the pickup, she had *not* viewed any lawn mowers in its bed or in use in the vicinity. At the very least, the situation was certainly odd. It made her feel anxious now, as though perhaps someone were spying on her. Maybe she should mention it to Morgan, Cat mused. But then she remembered what had happened when she had mistaken *him* for a stalker, and she told herself her uneasiness about the truck was due to nothing more than her imagination working overtime again. In fact, the more she dwelled upon it, the thought that some lone assailant had singled her out almost upon her very arrival in Wichita seemed highly improbable, even downright fantastic.

Shaking her head and shrugging, she dismissed the notion, forcing herself to concentrate instead on the work that lay ahead of her today. Morgan had given her a number of reports to study, after which he planned to ask her what, if any, wells she would recommend shutting down and why. While she did not mind these tasks he set her—in fact, she enjoyed the challenge tremendously—the manner in which he insisted on conducting his "quizzes," as he called them, had proved both discomfiting and exciting. She could not think of it as other than outrageous blackmail, because he was, in effect, talking her into dates in exchange for his teaching her about the oil-and-gas business. Further, she knew learning how to do her job was only half the reason why she continued to prove such a willing victim.

One afternoon he had told her the day's quiz would take place at the Boat House downtown, a replica of the original Riverside Boat House of Wichita's earlier era. There he had proceeded to rent a canoe, in which he had then paddled the two of them leisurely and romantically down the Big Arkansas river—while interrogating her about how much natural gas wells pumping various amounts of barrels of oil per day should be producing. He had interspersed his questions with remarks about how her eyes were greener than the leaves of the trees lining the river and how, in the sundress and hat she had worn to work that day, she looked, reclining in the bow of the canoe, as though she had just stepped from some Victorian painting.

Another day he had taken her to a stables, where he had hired two horses for them to ride, Western style, despite the fact that Cat had always ridden English. Along a secluded bridle path he had tested her knowledge about the mechanics of beam pumps—while telling her how the sunlight slanting through the limbs of the trees turned her dark red hair to flame and made her skin glow with the luster of a pearl. At the end of the trail, he had leaned over from atop his horse and, taking Cat by surprise, had kissed her lingeringly on the mouth, nearly causing them both to be unseated from their saddles when her mare had started, stamping and switching its tail.

From the windows of the Petroleum Club in the Fourth Financial Center, Cat had watched the flaming orange sun go down over the city, raining fire in the sky. She had played tennis at Riverside Park and racquetball at the Racquet Club. She had ridden the old wooden roller coaster at Joyland, exhilarated by the coveted last car's skipping on the tracks. She had batted baseballs in the batting cages and putted golf balls on the miniature golf course at Sports World. From the Farm and Art Market, she had carried home fresh fruits and vegetables, Indian jewelry and local artwork. In Towanda, a small town not far away, she had bought a carousel horse at Two Lions Antiques and had dined at the Blue Moon Saloon. She had gunned down monsters on the arcade machines at Aladdin's Castle and shot up targets at the Bullseye! Indoor Shooting Range. For a $3.00 ticket that Morgan had insisted on buying, she had actually ridden an elephant at the Shrine Circus and for a quarter, she had bought a bag of popcorn to feed the animals at the Sedgwick County Zoo, famous nationwide for its natural habitats. She had won $500 on a trifecta bet at the Greyhound Park Racetrack and had seen a famous rock group perform at the Kansas Coliseum. In Morgan's Piper Cub plane, she had flown to the little Kansas town of Beaumont for lunch at the Beaumont Hotel. She had discovered that the sleek speedboat stored in her father's garage actually belonged to Morgan when he had driven her out to Lake Afton for a cookout and water skiing. Several of his friends had joined them, and while Cat and the other women sunned themselves on the beach, Morgan and the other men, shouting and laughing, had steered the speedboat so close to shore that the women had been sprayed unmercifully by the speedboat's rooster tail, the giant plume of water it spewed behind it. As a result of his antics, Morgan had received a stern warning from the shore patrol.

Although she had on these occasions acquired a good deal of knowledge about the oil-and-gas industry and, with flying colors, passed all her so-called quizzes, Cat knew she was in reality being cleverly seduced. Worse, all the reasons she kept telling herself why she ought not to embark upon an affair with Morgan appeared increasingly lame whenever she thought about them, mere excuses to hide the real truth: she had fallen in love with him, and she was afraid of being hurt again.

Yet, as though he instinctively sensed as much, Morgan did not press her, rarely did more than kiss her. How he held himself in check, Cat did not know—although she suspected he took numerous long, cold showers. To the best of her knowledge, he saw no other women. Nor did she see any other men, although several she had met had called to ask her out, the other "outlaws" in the rowdy crowd Morgan ran with apparently having no scruples about cutting into one another's time if they could. Cat had turned them all down, and she thought Morgan knew both that they had called her and that she had rejected their invitations, although he never mentioned it to her.

Sighing, she tossed the report she had been reading onto her desk, the figures making little or no sense, since she kept drifting off into reverie, thinking about Morgan. Moments later, as though her thoughts had somehow communicated themselves to him, he knocked on her door, then entered her office.

"Are you free for supper Friday night?" he asked.

"*This* Friday?" She groaned at the prospect, rolling her eyes with disbelief. "Morgan, you have simply *got* to be kidding! There's no way I can be ready for one of your damned quizzes this Friday! You only gave me this stuff two days ago!" She indicated the papers scattered over her desk.

"Well...to tell you the truth, Cat, I was thinking we might forget the quiz this time and have an actual socks-on car date for a change. What do you say?"

She said nothing for a long moment—for she knew that, with his words, he was in reality telling her he was tired of playing games, that he wanted to do more than just kiss her good-night at her front door.

"I—I don't know, Morgan—"

"Come on, Cat. You've seen for yourself I don't bite." Wisely, he did not add aloud what he was thinking: that if he had to take one more long, cold shower, he was certain he was going to collapse from hypothermia. "Except that there won't be any quiz, I promise you it won't be different from any of the other times we've gone out—unless you want it to be.'' He groaned inwardly at the thought that she would not.

"Oh…all right then,'' she finally agreed, knowing that to refuse just because he was not planning on quizzing her would be ridiculously hypocritical.

"Great. I'll pick you up at seven. Wear your jeans and your dancing shoes.''

After Morgan had gone, Cat sat staring out her office windows at the winding waterway beyond and thinking she had no sense at all, that she was surely on the road to ruin since she hadn't learned not to make the same mistake twice. Her heart was beating so fast that she wondered if she ought to drive herself to the nearby Minor Emergency Center and insist on having an EKG run—especially since her father had dropped dead of a heart attack. But deep down inside, she knew she was being silly, that there was nothing wrong with her heart except that she had foolishly given it away to Morgan, even if he did not know it yet. Its speed was due solely to the thought of surrendering her body to him as well, of making love with him.

"Cat, you're a damned fool,'' she told herself aloud—both then and later, right before she opened her front door to admit him at the agreed-upon hour.

They ate supper in Old Town, at the River City Brewery, a quiet, charming restaurant Cat found both pleasant and entertaining. The interior was all done in highly polished woods, and behind the elegant bar that ran nearly the length of the south wall were not mirrors, but windows, behind which stood the huge, gleaming vats in which the restaurant's own beer was brewed right on the premises. There were several varieties, with different beers offered on different days, so for starters, Morgan insisted on ordering the samples, which came in containers only slightly bigger than shot glasses. Cat tasted them all before finally settling on the Old Town Brown, a delicious dark beer.

"An excellent choice—since that happens to be my own personal favorite, too,'' Morgan declared as he laid aside his menu. "You have a very discerning palate, Cat.''

"For beer, anyway. I'm still not sure about my taste in men, however. I can't believe I allowed you to talk me into an actual 'socks-on car date,' as you insist upon calling it!''

"Did it ever occur to you that maybe it's because you're as weak willed as I am when it comes to fighting the attraction between us? That it's strong enough to have overpowered whatever common sense or scruples we might both possess? No, don't answer that, because I know you're only going to deny it—and that, I won't permit. What I've suggested is no less than the truth, and deep down inside, you know it, Cat.''

"Do I?''

"Yes, you do. You're just too proud and stubborn to admit it! I believe that just because of what happened between you and Spencer Kingsley, you've got the mistaken notion that we can't be both business partners and lovers—a notion I'll admit that I shared at first. But I was wrong, just as you are. Our circumstances are different. You don't work for me and I'm not looking at cutting you in on my assets, as Spencer was. You're already a co-owner of One-Eyed Jacks, and I've come to respect your judgment besides. In fact, I'm sorry I initially doubted your ability to do the job. In the weeks you've been at the company, you've learned more about the oil-and-gas business than I thought was possible, and we've worked well together, Cat, you and I. To think we, as two mature adults, can't carry that relationship over into our private lives is foolish. We can. We will.''

"Indeed?'' Her tone was dry, and she lifted one brow. "Well, isn't that the height of arrogance? You're pretty damned sure of yourself, Morgan. You're pretty damned sure of me!''

"That's because I'm not Spencer, Cat—and you're not Ronnie. And this isn't something that's happening because we're both on the rebound or tied together by Frank or One-Eyed Jacks, either. It's happening because it was meant to, because the chemistry's not just right, it's damned near explosive between us. You feel it, too, Cat. Every time I look at you, kiss you, I can see in your eyes that you do. You want to make love with me just as badly as I want to make love with you.''

She did not answer—for the simple reason that she *had* no answer.

In her heart of hearts, she knew everything Morgan had said was true. She did not want to go on fighting him, fighting herself and the feelings he stirred so strongly within her. She wanted to go to bed with him, to feel him lying naked beside her in the darkness, to know him intimately, to awaken in the morning and see his head on the pillow next to her own. She was glad that, just then, the waitress appeared with their supper, so their conversation naturally came to a halt while their plates were placed before them.

"Can I get you anything else?" the woman asked.

"Cat?" Morgan glanced at her inquiringly. She shook her head. "No, thank you. That'll be all at the moment," he told the waitress, who smiled and nodded before leaving them alone again.

To Cat's relief, Morgan did not continue their previous discussion, but talked desultorily of this and that, entertaining her with his seemingly endless supply of lighthearted anecdotes, which never failed to amuse her, to make her laugh. That was one of the things that drew her to him, she recognized slowly now—his ability to make her laugh, to make her feel as though she had not a care in the world. It was perhaps that, more than anything, that had helped her through the worst of her initial grief at her father's death, that had made her work at One-Eyed Jacks not just a challenge, but also a pure delight. It occurred to her suddenly how little she had laughed with Spence, how little true pleasure he had taken in the simple things life had to offer. She remembered how, once, when passing by Central Park, she had badgered him into hiring a hansom cab to take them for a drive. No sooner had they got settled in the carriage than, much to her anger and disappointment, Spence had opened up his briefcase and proceeded to use the time to go over some contracts. But Morgan always left his briefcase in the Bronco, and he had devoted his entire attention to her during their trolley ride one afternoon, whispering silly sweet talk in her ear, making her laugh and blush.

Lost in reverie, Cat finished her supper. Then, once Morgan had taken care of the check, they strolled outside beneath the old-fashioned streetlights that lit up the whole of Old Town. Since it was Friday night, the security guards that regularly patrolled the district were out in full force, ensuring that even unescorted females were safe, could park their cars and walk from place to place, if they so chose. There was something for just about everyone in Old Town, Morgan told her, pointing out, among other attractions, the Texas Roadhouse, where live bands entertained Generation X-ers; Heroes, which catered to college jocks, cheerleaders, frat rats and sorority sisters; and the Cowboy.

"That last one's self-explanatory." He grinned.

"And that's where we're going now, I take it."

"Yes, indeed. If you don't already know how, tonight you're going to learn how to dance the cotton-eyed Joe and the two-step."

"Am I?"

"Yes, you are—so don't give me any argument about it."

"Would it surprise you to learn I wasn't planning to—" Cat broke off abruptly, having suddenly spied a battered old pickup truck in one of the parking lots. She was certain the vehicle was the same one she had seen both in Vickridge and outside the offices of the One-Eyed Jacks Oil & Gas Company. She grabbed Morgan's arm, pulling him to a halt. "Do you see that beat-up old truck over there?"

"Yeah...what about it?"

"I've seen it several times before," she said. Then she went on to explain when and where. "Oh, Morgan, I know it sounds crazy, but I'm really beginning to believe whoever owns that truck has been... well...following me around and spying on me."

"But...why, Cat? For what purpose? You say you don't think it's anyone you know. And although you're financially well-off, you're not famous, by any means. So it's hard to imagine you'd be a candidate for kidnapping. Nor are you hiding any skeletons in your closet—at least, so far as I'm aware. So that presumably lets out blackmail, too."

"Maybe the guy's a nut case, a—a stalker!"

"Uh-huh. That's what you thought about me at first, remember? Still, I'd rather be safe than sorry. To be honest, there's something familiar about that truck. I could swear I've seen it before, too." He pulled his fountain pen and one of his business cards from his pocket. Turning the card over and cupping it against his palm, he wrote down the license-plate number of the vehicle. "Monday morning, I'll call a friend of mine at the DMV, see what I can find out. All right?"

"Yes, thanks. I'd appreciate that."

They continued on to the Cowboy, where the bouncer at the door greeted Morgan by name. The place was jam-packed with people and rowdy with music, noise and laughter. Fortunately, because Morgan was tall, he could see over the crowd. After a moment, he located a couple of tables full of employees of the One-Eyed Jacks Oil & Gas Company. Taking Cat's elbow, he steered her deftly through the throng—giving more than one man who stared at her appreciatively a sharp, warning glance that clearly said, "Back off, boys. She's with me and is going to stay that way." It was all Cat could do not to laugh as each man warily sized Morgan up and then turned away, plainly deciding against tangling with his six feet, two inches of lean, hard muscle. Other men he knew he greeted boisterously, shaking their hands and clapping them on the shoulders before, with obvious pride, he introduced Cat to them. All of them paid her flattering, if outrageous and a trifle embarrassing, compliments, the kind Morgan was prone to make himself, so she understood that, as her father had been and as Morgan himself was, his friends were all reckless, rambunctious good ole boys, outlaws at heart.

"I don't think I've ever seen so many Stetsons, jeans and boots all in one place before," Cat commented, "or been called a 'filly' so many times in one night, either. In fact, I don't ever remember anybody—except you, once—referring to me that way before."

Morgan chuckled. "It's those long legs of yours, darlin'," he asserted, still grinning. "They just naturally make a man think of a high-spirited racehorse—among other things."

"What other things?" she queried tartly, glancing up at him sideways. Somehow he had casually managed to slide his arm around her waist possessively, and his head was bent near to hers so he could hear her over the cacophony of the Oakridge Boys belting out "Elvira," while countless pairs of hands clapped in time to the beat and equally countless pairs of boots shuffled and stamped on the dance floor. She could smell the masculine scents of soap and cologne that emanated from his skin, feel the warmth of his body pressed close against her in the crush.

He bent his head even lower to drawl in her ear, "Well, if you absolutely insist on knowing…"

"I do."

"Things like bridling that redheaded temper of yours and riding in your saddle, sweetheart."

"Morgan McCain!" Cat exclaimed, simultaneously indignant and yet perversely as wrought up as a racehorse as it waited in the starting gate, adrenaline pumping wildly. He wanted to sleep with her. He had made that plain more than once—but never before so graphically, conjuring up in her mind an image of his hands tangled in her dark red hair while he rode her, his face buried against her throat, and goaded her to climax as expertly as a jockey rode a thoroughbred, his face bent close against its windswept mane, urging it to the finish line.

"Hey, don't blame me," Morgan said impertinently. "You're the one who insisted."

"Is that what you think about me all day at the office?"

"Yeah…ain't it awful?" Before she realized what he intended, he brushed her mouth hard and swiftly with his own, then sharply pulled away. "Now, get a move on—before I have to beat the hell out one of these good ole boys for ogling you too damned lustfully!"

"Oh! You're—you're impossible!" Cat sputtered lamely.

"And don't you just love it?" Morgan retorted insolently, grinning wickedly.

She had no time to reply, for just then they reached the tables where the employees from the One-Eyed Jacks Oil & Gas Company had congregated, the Cowboy apparently being a favorite watering hole not just of Morgan's. By now Cat knew many of the men and women, and she waved and greeted them by name as they called out to her and Morgan. Drinks and chairs were quickly shifted and two additional seats dragged over from other tables so she and Morgan had a place to sit. He motioned to a nearby waitress, and minutes later Cat had a cold beer in front of her. Hot not only from the heat of so many bodies crowded together, but also from Morgan's proximity, his arm draped across the back of her chair, his hand idly playing with her shoulder, she took a long swallow of the beer. She wondered what their employees thought, seeing them together like this. Although there had been a few joking remarks at their appearance, everybody had just seemed to accept that she and Morgan were together and to think nothing more of it. This was a far cry from the looks she had got and the comments she had overheard when she had accepted Spence's proposal of marriage. She knew that more than one of his employees had gossiped that she had slept her way to the top of the import-export firm. Doubtless they had thought she had got what she deserved when Spence had fired her. Of course, Morgan had been right: she was not *his* employee, but a co-owner of the One-Eyed Jacks Oil & Gas Company. But did that really make a difference? Somehow, Cat fervently hoped that it did, because she knew Morgan was right, and that sooner or later, her will to go on resisting him would totally crumble.

"All right, all you rowdy cowboys and cowgirls," the deejay's voice called over the PA system, "it's time to take a break from all the hootin' and hollerin'. So grab the partner of your choice while we slow things down a little with Restless Heart's 'Tell Me What You Dream.'"

As the opening strains of the tune began, the saxophone wailing, Cat turned to Morgan. "Believe it or not, this is one country-and-western song I actually know—even if I *did* think it was some bluesy pop number the first time I heard it!"

"It's the saxophone and the emphasis on the drums and bass." Pushing his chair back from the table, he stood and held out his hand to her. "Time for your dancing lesson, babe."

He said it so matter-of-factly, taking her acquiescence for granted, that she was almost tempted to retort that he might have asked—and politely. But the truth was she loved this tune, and she wanted to dance to it with him. So instead, she rose without a word and let him lead her out onto the lighted dance floor beneath the mirror-covered saddle suspended from the ceiling. Moments later she was glad she had. Morgan danced divinely, with an uncanny smoothness born of his body's inherent, fluid power, grace and rhythm. Nor was there any doubt about who was leading whom, as was so often the case with some men, who hesitated to take charge on a dance floor—or anywhere else, for that matter. Morgan held her masterfully, trusting, expecting her to follow. In his arms, Cat felt as though she had been transported into a movie or a dream. She seemed to float across the dance floor, her body perfectly in tune with his as she matched him step for step. This was how it would be to make love with him, she thought, half-dazed not only from the beer she had drunk, but also by the images of him naked and poised above her that rose again in her mind.

"Cat, you can dance," he whispered in her ear, his tone both pleased and provocative.

"Yes, Morgan."

He did not speak again, but held her even tighter, his body swaying subtly, sexily against hers as they traversed the dance floor. There was not another couple there to touch them, Cat knew, and she felt the eyes of the crowd upon them, both admiring and jealous, as they moved and whirled together. Morgan's steps grew increasingly more intricate, moving beyond the two-step to an actual swing, but even when he dipped her, Cat did not stumble, her feet lighter and surer than they had ever been in her life. The music filled her being, the saxophone and Morgan himself sending a wild thrill shooting through her as she danced on in his embrace, her eyes closed, instinct alone guiding her. She was hardly aware when the strains of the song faded, segueing smoothly into another slow tune. For the first time, she knew what Eliza Doolittle had felt when she had sung "I Could Have Danced All Night" in the movie *My Fair Lady.* Cat felt as though she could have danced forever in Morgan's arms, with the lights playing about the two of them and the mirror-covered saddle shimmering above them, casting stars beneath their feet.

But at last the deejay livened the mood again with a fast, rough-and-tumble tune, and as one, by mutual, unspoken consent, Cat and Morgan left the dance floor, knowing their own mood had been spoiled by the change of tempo in the music.

"Morgan, would you mind pointing me in the direction of the

cowgirls' room?'' Cat asked as they returned to the table, where she picked up her leather handbag. ''I need to powder my nose.''

''Your nose looks fine to me. But the cowgirls' room is thataway.'' He pointed toward the rest rooms. ''In fact, on second thought, I'll go with you. Otherwise I might wind up having to flatten one or more of the cowboys here tonight.'' He walked her to the door of the ladies' room, saying, ''Wait here for me if you get done before I do,'' as he left her to head into the men's room.

Once inside the ladies' room, Cat used the toilet, then flushed it, washing and drying her hands afterward before opening her purse to search for her makeup bag. As she glanced in the mirror, she decided Morgan had lied, that she looked ghastly. But then she had hardly ever been in a bar's bathroom where the harsh lights did *not* drain every woman's face—no matter how beautiful—of color, emphasizing the dark circles under her eyes and making her resemble a week-old corpse. Cat grimaced at her reflection, then frowned as, after several minutes of rummaging through her handbag, she failed to find her makeup bag. It must have fallen out in Morgan's Bronco, she thought, sighing impatiently, annoyed at herself. That was what she got for continually forgetting to zip her purse. She left the ladies' room to find Morgan waiting for her.

''Could I have the keys to the Bronco?'' she asked.

''Why? Did I dance so badly that you're planning on driving off and leaving me stranded here as punishment?''

''Don't be silly. You dance like a dream—and you know it!'' she replied tartly, then went on to explain about the loss of her makeup bag.

''I'll go look for it, Cat.''

''No, I'll do it. It'll only take a moment, and I could use the fresh air besides. In the meantime, why don't you go on back to the table and order me another beer? All that dancing's made me thirsty. Relax, Morgan,'' she insisted when he still hesitated. ''I'm not going to make off with your Bronco. The parking lots are well lighted and patrolled by security, and I can take of myself, anyway. I'm used to walking around New York—and not always in broad daylight, remember?''

"All right," he agreed reluctantly at last. "But if you're not back here in ten minutes, I'm coming after you."

"It's a deal. See you in five."

He tossed her the keys to the Bronco, and after making her way through the crowd, she left the Cowboy. The night air, although indeed fresh after the smoky atmosphere of the club, was also humid, and it clung to Cat's sweating skin, making her long for a shower as she started across the parking lots toward the Bronco. As she had learned to do in New York, she walked briskly, her head up and alert, her carriage straight and purposeful, sending out the signal that she would not be an easy target. In her hand, she held Morgan's key ring so the ends of keys protruded from between her fingers, in the manner of a makeshift brass knuckles, a trick she had learned in a self-defense course she had taken some years back. Without incident, she reached the Bronco and opened the front passenger door. The vehicle's interior light came on, so she could see her makeup bag had indeed fallen out of her handbag and lay upon the floor inside. She bent to retrieve it, then rose and turned—only to find herself face-to-face with a strange man dressed in a T-shirt and jeans, and looking none too sober as his eyes raked her lewdly.

"Damn! You're a pretty piece! Hard to believe you're ole Frank's daughter—although now that I see you up close, I can tell there's a family resemblance."

"You—you knew my father?" Cat inquired, clutching her makeup bag and wondering if it or the keys would do more damage in the event she required a weapon.

"Oh, yeah, me and Frank, we was good friends." He took a long gulp from the beer bottle he carried, then wiped his mouth off with the back of his hand. "My name's Skeeter Farrell, by the way, and I'm mighty pleased to meetcha. I used to work for One-Eyed Jacks...that is, before McCain fired me, the no-good bastard. He didn't have no call to do that. I'd been there damned near fifteen years! But McCain cut me loose, just like I was nothin'. Frank wouldn't of done that. He would of put things right. But before I ever got a chance to talk to him, he had that heart attack and died. That's why I finally come to you, Ms. Devlin. I been watching you—

ever since the morning I drove out to Frank's house to talk to him. That was before I learned he had keeled over dead, of course. I didn't know who you were at first. I thought you was just some young chick livin' with ole Frank. But when I heard about Frank's death, I thought maybe you'd just bought his house or somethin'. Then one day I seen you out at One-Eyed Jacks, and even though it took me a while to figger out just who you really was, I finally put two and two together after I heard tell you'd stepped into yore daddy's shoes.'' Farrell paused, taking another generous sip of his beer. Then he continued.

"It's thisaway, you see—I want my old job back, Ms. Devlin. I got to have it. Times is hard and money's tight, and nobody's hirin' at the moment, 'specially with the aircraft companies layin' folks off.''

Wichita, Cat had learned, was known as the Air Capital of the world because of all the aircraft manufacturers that had headquarters or plants in town—Boeing, Beech, Cessna and Learjet among them, not to mention all the companies that manufactured aircraft components, engines, instruments and other equipment, parts and supplies. There were also aircraft rebuilders, aircraft upholsterers, aircraft testers, aircraft brokers, aircraft charter, rental and leasing services, aircraft ferriers and transporters and upward of a dozen aircraft schools. More than a few movie and rock stars had learned to fly in Wichita or had bought a plane there. And whenever something happened that affected the aircraft industry for the worse, Wichita's entire economy suffered.

"Look, I'd like to help you, Mr. Farrell. Really, I would,'' Cat declared placatingly. "But I'm afraid I'm not in a position to override Mr. McCain's authority at One-Eyed Jacks.''

"Why not?'' he demanded, his eyes narrowing and an ugly note creeping into his voice. "Frank left you his shares in the company, didn't he? Leastways, that's what I heard through the grapevine. So you got the same rights as McCain then. You can put me back on the payroll if you wanna.''

"No, I can't. Really. Now, if you'll excuse me—''

"No, I *won't* excuse you, Ms. High-'n'-Mighty Devlin! 'Cause I think you're just feedin' me a line of bull, that's what! I seen you tonight at the Cowboy, dancin' with McCain. And if he ain't already inside them sweet britches of yore'n, I'll eat my hat! So the way I figger it is this—all you gotta do is tell him you've rehired me, and it'll be a done deal.''

"I'm sorry. I can't. Now I really do have to go—"

"You're not goin' anywhere, you red-haired witch—leastways, not until you either gimme my job back or gimme what you're givin' McCain.'' With those menacing words, Farrell abruptly flung his beer bottle away, smashing it loudly upon the pavement of the parking lot and causing Cat to jump, startled. Then, before she could collect her wits to defend herself, he grabbed her and forced her backward into the Bronco, the passenger door of which still stood open.

Despite how she struck out at him wildly with both her makeup bag and the key ring she held, scratching and bloodying his weaselly face, Farrell finally managed to compel her down onto the seat by first slapping her hard and then imprisoning her wrists. The next thing Cat knew, he was pressing his slobbering mouth to her throat and tearing roughly at her shirt and jeans. She tried to scream, but he pressed his lips over hers, cutting off the sound. After that, she saved her breath, knowing she needed it for the violent struggle she was waging against him. The longer and harder she fought, the more likely it was that the security patrol or Morgan would come.

At last she somehow got her knee up and slammed it viciously between Farrell's thighs. He half slid, half staggered backward from the Bronco into the parking lot, doubled over and groaning with pain, and as Cat rose shakily, it was to see Morgan towering above Farrell. Morgan's dark visage was terrifyingly murderous as he caught her assailant by the shoulder, jerked him up, spun him around and socked him square in the face. Cat heard the sickening sound of bone and cartilage crunching and saw blood spurt from Farrell's broken nose as he flew backward, to sprawl upon the pavement. Fear glittered in his beady eyes, but his instinct for self-preservation drove him to scramble to his feet and, with his fists, swing out at Morgan wildly. Morgan deftly sidestepped the blows, then set about to give Farrell a thrashing he would not soon forget—one that demonstrated to Cat why Morgan had been hauled away to jail for brawling in the past.

She thought it was a miracle he did not beat Farrell to death, even after the man snatched up the jagged-edged neck of his broken beer bottle and slashed out with it brutally before Morgan kicked the improvised weapon from his hand.

Fortunately, however, it seemed Morgan was not so hotheaded that he did not know when to quit. Farrell was still alive, bleeding and moaning amid the shattered glass and the spilled beer upon the pavement, when Morgan finally stepped back, ending the fight and glaring down at him furiously.

"You ever, *ever* touch her again and I'll kill you, you son of a bitch!" Morgan snarled. Then he bent to retrieve his keys from where they had fallen to the ground during Cat's struggle with Farrell. "You okay?" he asked Cat tersely. Trembling, clutching her torn knit shell to her breasts, her eyes huge in her ashen face, she nodded wordlessly, fighting to hold back the sobs that rose in her throat. "Put your feet back in the Bronco, honey. I'm taking you home—and I want to get out of here before the security patrol shows up. This is one night I don't intend to spend in jail."

"What about—what about him?" She nodded toward Farrell as she settled herself inside the vehicle and, with trembling hands, fastened her seat belt.

"I'll call him an ambulance," Morgan replied curtly, his voice hard.

"Don't...do me...any favors, McCain!" Farrell hissed between rasps for breath.

"Suit yourself." Shrugging, Morgan slammed Cat's door, then strode around the Bronco to slide in beside her. Shoving the key into the ignition, he started up the engine, tires burning rubber as he stepped on the accelerator and wheeled the Bronco from the parking lot. Turning left on Douglas, he sped along the downtown's main street, running more than one yellow light as he did so.

"Morgan, please slow down. You're angry, you're driving too fast and you're not wearing your seat belt," Cat said quietly.

At her words, he abruptly turned the Bronco down a side street, veered over to the curb and pulled to a halt, killing the motor. By then, Cat was so rattled that she burst into tears. Beside her, Morgan growled an imprecation before he unhooked her seat belt and drew her into his arms, cradling her head against his broad chest.

"Shh," he murmured, stroking her hair gently. "Hush now. Don't cry, darlin'." As he held her in his embrace, he noticed for the first time that the knit shell she wore was torn. He swore again softly. "That bastard! I should have killed him!"

"No…I'm—I'm all right. Really, I am."

"Then tell me why in the hell Farrell was trying to rape you, damn it!"

"He was drunk. Somehow he'd—he'd learned who I was—"

"Yeah, he's the one who's been following you, Cat. That battered old pickup truck you pointed out to me earlier belongs to him. That's why it looked so familiar to me."

"Oh, God… He's been spying on me off and on ever since I came to town, trying to find out all about me and—and working up his nerve to approach me. He said he used to be employed at One-Eyed Jacks before you—you fired him—"

"That's right. He was, and I did. He'd always had something of a problem with booze, but he'd managed somehow to keep it under control until recently, when his wife finally divorced him, and it became clear to me he was drinking on the job. He wouldn't admit he was an alcoholic and agree to treatment and counseling, as I advised, so I had to let him go, Cat. Machinery of any kind always poses a potential hazard, and I couldn't have him working the wells and lines, possibly endangering himself or other employees."

"No, of course not," Cat agreed. "But he's—he's terribly angry about your firing him, Morgan. He wanted me to give him his job back, and when I told him I couldn't, he turned mean and ugly. He said he'd seen us dancing together tonight at the Cowboy and that I must be…sleeping with you. And then he—he told me I was either going to rehire him or—or give him what I was giving to—to you. That's when he went berserk and attacked me."

"Well, you don't have to worry about him anymore. After tonight, he won't be bothering you again, I guarantee it."

"Maybe not, but…shouldn't we at least notify the police, Morgan? I mean, what if Farrell's crazy enough to try something else?"

"Like what? The man's a coward, Cat. Only look how long it took him to screw up his courage to approach you—and most of that, he undoubtedly got from a bottle. No, I think we can probably forget about Skeeter Farrell. He had his chance, and he blew it. But…damn it, Cat! When you saw he was drunk and what kind of mood he was in, why didn't you just promise him his job back, then tell me what had happened so I could deal with him?"

"I—I don't know. It all happened so fast that I—I just didn't think. And if you dare say one word about women and their emotions and their being unable to handle a tough situation as well as a man, I'll—I'll get out of this car and walk home!"

"Not down here, you won't. This area's a haven for bums and winos—not to mention hot-rodding teenagers on Friday nights. Besides, I wasn't going to say anything of the sort. Look, Cat, men and women just think differently, and that's a fact. But that doesn't make one way right or even better and the other way wrong. And there are plenty of emotional men, just as there are an equal number of cool-headed women."

"I just don't happen to be one of the latter, right?"

"No, that's not what I'm saying at all. I'm saying everybody's different, and every situation's different, and nobody's behavior is one-hundred-percent predictable or correct one hundred percent of the time. When you thought I was a stalker, you kept your wits and coldcocked me just as cool as you please. And tonight you fought back long and hard enough to save yourself until help could arrive. Neither of those actions was the mark of a woman who can't think on her feet, babe—even if you *are* an emotional female. No, don't go getting all riled up on me now. I just meant you feel things deeply, Cat…here." He laid his hand gently against her heart. "I think you always have and probably always will. It's why in the hell you're weighing yourself down about it by lugging around that gigantic chip on your shoulder that's got me stymied."

Cat could not help but laugh at that. "I suppose you'd like to knock it off, huh?"

"Among other things," Morgan uttered softly, his hands cupping her face, his thumbs tracing the tracks of her tears and brushing them away.

"Oh, no, you don't. After what you said in the Cowboy, I wouldn't touch that line again with a ten-foot pole."

"Is that so? Then I guess I'll just have to show you instead of tell you what I meant," he murmured huskily before he tipped her face up to his and his lips claimed hers, tenderly at first, then more insistently when she did not resist.

She had wanted him to kiss her, Cat realized, to take away the memory of Farrell holding her down and pressing his mouth to hers. As though he sensed her desire, her need, Morgan went on kissing her, his tongue following the contours of her lips, leaving them hot and moist before he parted them to seek the sweetness inside. Lingeringly, he tasted her, explored her, deepening the kiss until Cat moaned low in her throat, heat and longing suffusing her body. Her heart beat fast as her hands crept up to twine about his neck, to caress the thick hair that curled at the edge of his collar. Morgan's own hands still held her face, his fingers wrapped in the strands of hair at her temples as he slanted his mouth over hers, then kissed her cheek, her throat, before at last reluctantly drawing away, much to her disappointment.

"It's getting late, and the weather's starting to act up besides. See that off in the distance?" Morgan pointed to a sudden, wild barrage of flashes that lit the horizon of the night sky. "That's heat lightning. Be some hours or even days before a storm breaks, though. Still, I expect we'd better go."

Not trusting herself to speak, Cat nodded, slowly refastening her seat belt while he hooked his own into place, then started the Bronco. After pulling away from the curb, he made a U-turn in the side street to take them back out onto Douglas, where he headed east again, toward Vickridge. Within minutes, he was turning into the half-circle drive before the house that had belonged to Frank Devlin and that was now Cat's own. Morgan walked her up to the front porch bracketed by a pair of big, brass coach-lantern lights that had come on electronically when darkness had fallen. Taking her key from her outstretched hand, he unlocked the door for her and opened it.

"Do you want me to come inside with you, Cat?"

She wanted desperately to say yes, but instead, she shook her head. "No, I…I think I'd just like to take a shower and then to go to bed, if you don't mind. I'm sorry Farrell wound up spoiling our evening. It was wonderful up until then."

"Yes, it was—and it's all right, I understand about the rest. Good night then."

"Good night, Morgan."

Reaching out with one hand, he caught hold of her nape and gently pulled her to him, kissing her once more as he had done earlier in the Bronco, leaving Cat flushed and weak in the knees when he finally released her—and very much aware of his desire.

"You sure you won't change your mind about my coming inside?" he asked softly.

"No," she whispered, shaking her head.

"No, you're not sure, or no, you won't change your mind?"

"No, I'm…I won't change my mind."

"Well, I won't say I'm not disappointed. But lock up behind me then, and don't forget to set the alarm."

"I will. I won't. Thank you for the dinner and dancing, Morgan."

"Anytime, darlin'."

Whistling softly, melodically, his hands in the pockets of his jeans, he strolled toward the Bronco. It was not until Cat had closed the door behind him and turned the dead bolt that she realized the song he had been whistling was Restless Heart's "Tell Me What You Dream."

Chapter 12

Heat Lightning

Hearing again—although now only in her mind—the saxophone wailing bluesily, remembering how she and Morgan had danced so divinely together to the song, Cat was tempted to open the door and call him back. But in the end, she did not. Instead, after setting the alarm, she trudged slowly upstairs, vividly and uncomfortably conscious of the bigness, the emptiness of the house. With over ten thousand square feet, it really was much too large for one person, although she understood why her father had bought it. It had served as a tangible symbol of his success. But just now she would have given anything to have someone with whom to share the huge house, so it would not be so lonely. And if she were honest with herself, she knew she wanted that someone to be Morgan. Why had she let him go? Had he not already complicated her life? Did he not already haunt her restless dreams at night? So what did further involvement with him matter? He was not Spence; he had told her as much. Could she not put aside her doubts and believe that, trust that their personal relationship would not interfere with their professional one? She could, she knew—and how much she wanted to do just that, how much she wanted him. But it was too late now to change her mind. He had already gone.

Upstairs, she undressed, throwing her torn shirt into the wastebasket, knowing that even if it could be repaired, she would never want to wear it again. Skeeter Farrell had put his hands upon it, upon her. After turning on the shower, she stepped inside the tiled enclosure, soaping and scrubbing herself over and over until, at last, she felt clean, unsoiled by Farrell's touch. When she was done, Cat got out and dried herself off, then donned a long, black silk negligee that felt sinful and sensuous against her naked skin. She had just flicked off the lights and climbed into bed when the telephone rang. She fumbled for the receiver in the darkness.

"Hello."

"You know what I think, Cat?" Morgan's voice sounded in her ear, low and husky, like a long, slow caress along her spine, sending a shiver of excitement and anticipation through her. "I think you didn't really want to be alone tonight. I think you didn't really want me to go. And so now I'm wondering what you'd do if I came back. Cat? Cat...are you still there? Yes, you are. I know you are. I can hear you breathing. It makes me imagine how you'd sound, lying naked against my chest after we'd made love.... Cat?"

"I've...I've already locked up the house for the night," she told him softly, breathlessly, for the picture he evoked in her mind was so strong, so enticing that she longed for it to become a reality, no matter the consequences.

He laughed throatily. "I have a key, remember? After that first night, when you mistook me for a burglar and, with that vase, cracked me over the head, then called the police, you never did ask me for my set of your father's keys. I reckon that in all the excitement, you just forgot about 'em."

"Yes, I did. But it doesn't matter. You see, I've already set the alarm, too."

He laughed again, in the same soft, sexy way as before.

"Do you think I don't know the code to deactivate it, Cat? You're wrong. I do—because I'm sure you never gave a thought to changing it." He paused for a moment, allowing her to absorb that fact. Then he continued. "Are you already in bed, too?"

Cat knew she should deny she was, that she should lie and say she was still up and dressed. But somehow her mouth seemed to have a will of its own, refusing to cooperate with her brain.

"Yes...I'm already in bed, too." Was that really her own voice, so hushed, so sensuous, so tremulous with anticipation and arousal? Her hand trembled on the receiver. Her heart beat fast in her breast. Her entire body felt like molasses melting over a fire, languorous, suffused with a slow-rising, spreading heat.

"What are you wearing?" Morgan asked hoarsely.

"A silk negligee."

"Nothing else, Cat?"

"No."

"What color is it?"

"Black."

His ragged, harshly indrawn breath grated in her ear, sending another shudder through her. She knew without asking that he was envisioning her as she lay in her bed, naked save for the black silk negligee that, like a cocoon, enwrapped her body, contrasting starkly with her porcelain skin, her dark red hair, loose and tumbled about her. She knew that, as she was, he was imagining himself coming into her bedroom, undressing and sliding nude into the bed to take her in his arms, to strip her negligee from her body.

"If I come over, let myself in, will you still be upstairs in bed, Cat, waiting for me? Will you?"

After a taut, provocative, seemingly interminable moment of silence, she answered.

"Yes, I will."

"I'm on my way."

The line went abruptly dead. Cat's hand was still shaking as she placed the receiver back in the cradle. She must be out of her mind, she thought. What had she done? Was this not how her disastrous affair with Spence had begun—with her giving in to him, against all her better judgment? She should turn on the lights, rise from her bed and get dressed at once so she could meet Morgan at her front door, explain she had made a mistake, had changed her mind. Instead, she continued to lie there in darkness broken only by the silver moonlight that filtered in through the half-open louvers of the plantation shutters screening her bedroom windows. The pounding of her heart had not slowed. The heat permeating her body had not dissipated. Cat felt as though she were burning up with fever, that only the coolness of the sheets was keeping her from bursting into flame and melting. She almost got up to lower the thermostat on the central air-conditioning, because the air inside the house seemed as sultry and oppressive as that outside. But a perverse combination of lethargy and nervous suspense held her where she lay. She wished it would rain, but she knew from what Morgan had told her earlier that the lightning that flashed intermittently in the distance was only heat lightning, that any storm, if it broke, was hours or even days away. So she lay in the silence, her ears straining to discern the purring of the Bronco's engine, and waited.

But she heard nothing beyond the sounds of the night, for Morgan was not in his Bronco. Such were the images of Cat that had played in his mind that, after hanging up the telephone, he had grabbed up his set of Frank's keys and headed on foot from the town house. Earlier, upon returning home, he had changed into a T-shirt and sweatpants. Now he jogged along the winding streets of Vickridge, his way lighted by the streetlights, the moonlight and the occasional bursts of lightning on the horizon. The air was so muggy that for all his excellent physical shape, he was having difficulty breathing as he ran. Still, he did not slow his pace.

Within ten minutes, he had reached Frank's house...Cat's house now—and she was upstairs, waiting for him, already in bed and wearing nothing but a black silk negligee. Morgan's groin tightened at the thought. The brass, coach-lantern lights on either side of the front door of the stately Tudor house still glowed in the darkness, making it easy for him to find the proper key on the ring he withdrew from an inside pocket. He was still panting from his run as he unlocked the door and opened it.

Upstairs, Cat heard the click of the dead bolt turning, of the door swinging open, so the distant rumble of thunder sounded louder than before. *Morgan was here!* He was actually here, inside the house! But...how? She had not heard his Bronco. He must have jogged over. Oh, God, what if it was not really him? What if it was a burglar—

or, worse, Skeeter Farrell, come to finish what he had started in the Old Town parking lot? No, her highly strung nerves were causing her imagination to run wild. Of course it was Morgan. Even now she could hear the chime of the alarm as it was deactivated—and no one else but she and Morgan knew the proper code sequence to enter. But maybe whoever was downstairs had not needed the code. Maybe he had located the main box of the alarm system, somehow knocked out its power.... Scenes from every thriller she had ever watched at the movies or on TV or read in a book rose in her mind to haunt her. No, she reassured herself again, she was being silly. It was Morgan bounding so quickly and lightly up the stairs, his every breath a serrated rasp cutting the silence sharply. The next thing she knew, his tall, dark, silhouetted figure was looming in the doorway of her bedroom. She could not see his face.

"Morgan?" she whispered hesitantly, half frightened, half exhilarated, her heart thudding so hard that she thought it would burst. "Morgan?"

He did not answer. Instead, he prowled toward her, moving deeper into the shadows, ripping his T-shirt off over his head as he came, carelessly throwing it aside. Lifting first one foot and then the other, he yanked off his sneakers, not even bothering to untie them, and his socks, dropping them behind him. Then he stepped from his sweatpants and briefs. Naked, he stood at the edge of the bed, staring down at her.

Cat was everything Morgan had ever imagined, lying there, waiting for him, the diffuse moonlight dancing over her, its silvery glow making her appear like some otherworldly enchantress. Her hair looked as though it were aflame, a fiery halo about her head. Her skin gleamed as white and lustrous as a pearl. The black silk negligee she wore was so understated in its elegance that he knew how expensive it must have been. It had spaghetti straps, one of which had slipped from her shoulder, and a heart-shaped bodice cut in a deep V that bared the generous swell of her full breasts, which rose and fell shallowly and as swiftly as the pulse at the hollow of her graceful throat. From its bodice, the negligee continued like a sheath to her ankles. Beginning at the front of the hem, a long slit that reached nearly to her thighs exposed a tantalizing glimpse of her long, racy legs. Morgan had, in his time, seen garments a hell of lot more revealing, but they, and the women in them, had been nothing to compare to Cat in the black silk negligee. He thought she was the sexiest female he had ever seen, and for a moment he was half-afraid he was not going to be able to hold back, that he was going to be finished before he even got started. With iron control, he mastered himself and slipped beside her into the bed.

"Morgan…?" Cat murmured uncertainly once more as his weight sank upon the mattress, the word dying upon her lips, swallowed by his carnal mouth, which without warning seized her own ravenously, devouring her.

She did not ask again, but gave herself up to him as his hands burrowed roughly through her hair, tightening at her temples and pulling her face up to his. He ground his mouth against hers, his mustache grazing her, his teeth nibbling her lower lip before his tongue traced its outline, then plunged deep inside her mouth to tangle and twine with her own tongue. Such were the sensations and emotions Morgan evoked inside her that Cat was not even aware of how her hands had crept up his chest to tunnel through his own hair, to draw him even nearer as she kissed him back with spiraling passion, low whimpers emanating from her throat, spurring him on.

After long minutes during which she ached to feel her skin totally naked and pressed against his, Morgan's hands slid down to her shoulders, tugging the thin straps of her negligee from her arms to bare her breasts. Then, as though he, too, had hungered for their flesh to meet, he crushed her to him, his head buried against her throat, his mouth gently biting the soft, vulnerable spot where her shoulder joined her nape. Like the heat lightning that shattered the night sky beyond the bedroom windows, electricity jolted through her so her back arched, causing her swollen breasts to rub sensuously against his broad chest. He groaned, long and low, his breath hot upon her skin before his tongue darted forth to lick and tease the tiny pulse that jerked erratically at the hollow of her throat. That and the way in which the dark hair that matted his chest brushed the sensitive peaks of her breasts tortured Cat so exquisitely that she was nearly half-mad with desire. Her hands clutched Morgan's back, slick and sheened with sweat in the aftermath of his jog. Her nails dug into his flesh as, at the secret heart of her, the spark he had ignited with his kisses caught flame, searing her.

But although she pressed against him suggestively, so she could feel the hardness of his arousal against her at the juncture of her thighs, he restrained himself, ignoring her silent plea. Instead, his palms glided down to cup her breasts, his thumbs skimming her flushed nipples, rotating slowly, tauntingly, across them. From their tips, pleasure radiated through her in waves that rippled clear to her toes, curling them. But even that reaction paled in comparison to what she felt when, after a moment, Morgan pressed her breasts high, then lowered his head and slowly drew one taut, tingling peak into his mouth, sucking hard. In that moment, Cat ceased to think; she could only feel, becoming a quivering mass of all-consuming sensation. His teeth captured her nipple, holding it in place for the flicking and laving of his tongue as she strained and moaned against him. Her hands, fingers tensed and splayed, moved down his back and buttocks, searching out responsive spots, rubbing and kneading, eliciting another groan from him. His lips scalded the valley between her breasts. His tongue snaked out and, with a long, languorous lick, lapped away the sweat that trickled there before his mouth took possession of her other breast, torturing it as sweetly as he had its twin.

Cat felt as though for the first time in her life she was learning what it was to be seduced by a man. That Morgan still had not spoken, that, in some dark corner of her mind, the tiniest bit of doubt remained about his identity, only added spice and excitement to their lovemaking, giving it a sense of the forbidden, the dangerous. He was big and strong. She could feel his muscles quivering and bunching in his back as he embraced her, his arms like a pair of steel bands imprisoning her, although she was a willing captive. Yet for all his power, all his sensual savagery, his torment of her bore an unmistakably tender edge, so she knew he was aware of her not just as a woman, but also as a person. That this night, this joining, had more meaning for him than just an assuagement of his lust.

That realization, too, heightened the intensity of Cat's feelings, her desire, her longing. She wanted Morgan desperately, had wanted him from the very beginning, she realized, when she had first seen him striding toward her on that dusty country road. She had never before known a man such as he, a man who teased and aroused her as he did, taking his own sweet time with her, despite the fact that his labored breathing told her how he hungered for her, ached for her, as she ached for him.

His mouth claimed hers again with an urgency that sent another electric thrill coursing through her. His tongue plunged deep between her lips, seeking, finding, tasting her as though she were warm honey that trickled enticingly upon his tongue and he could not get enough of her. Her hands moved upon him restlessly. Her fingers tangled in his thick, glossy hair, curled around his neck, crept down to brush the fine, damp strands that dusted his chest, to explore the planes and angles of his body, to trace the outline of muscle and sinew. His sweating flesh was like raw silk beneath her palms, like the sensuous feel of her negligee caressing her own skin as Morgan reached down to push the fabric up about her thighs so the slit in the front of the garment both framed and revealed her womanhood. His hand trailed lingeringly down her belly, coming to rest upon the soft, hidden petals of her. He touched her there, a quick, light stroke that was sweet, wild agony to her. Cat gasped and moaned against his mouth, arched wantonly against his hand. She was fire and ice, burning and melting, helpless against the exigent, instinctive need for fulfillment that had seized her.

This time he did not ignore her imploring whimpers, but slid his fingers deep into the well of her carmine softness, only to withdraw them tormentingly, spreading quicksilver heat, before slipping them into her again. His thumb parted the cleft of her, discovering the key to her pleasure, circling and fondling until she was frantic, nearly sobbing for release. And all the while, his fingers taunted her, and he kissed her, his tongue mimicking the movements of his hand. Cat clutched him fiercely, her nails raking his back as she sought to drag him onto her.

"Please..." she entreated softly, hoarsely. "I want you, Morgan...all of you. I need to feel you inside of me...now...."

He rolled atop her then, suddenly and roughly in his urgency, his need, his hands beneath her knees, spreading her wide for him as, with a low, tortured groan, he drove into her, sure and hard and deep, taking her breath as he filled her. With a gasp, a cry, she arched her hips to receive him, meeting each strong thrust as he moved within her, taking her to the heights of rapture. She clung to him tightly as the tremors built inside her, rocked her violently with their explosion before Morgan's own release came. He shuddered long and hard against her, his face buried against her shoulder, his breath hot upon her slick, dewy skin.

After a while he withdrew from her, turning to lie upon his back and pulling her into his embrace, cradling her against his chest. She could feel his heart pounding as furiously as her own, could hear the rasp of his breath against her ear.

"Morgan?" she whispered.

He laughed, the sound low and wicked with humor.

"What if I told you I wasn't your Morgan, Cat?" he drawled teasingly as he stroked her dark red hair possessively. "That'd be quite a shock to your senses, I would imagine…finding out you'd just made love to a total stranger."

"Is that why you wouldn't answer me…so I'd think you *were* a stranger? I'll admit I did wonder at first, and it *was* exciting, that tiny bit of doubt. But when you kissed me, I knew it was you. So tell me, are you…*my* Morgan, I mean?" Her fingers traced tiny circles and spirals amid the fine hair on his chest.

"If you want me to be."

"I think perhaps I do, you know."

"You *think*?" he rejoined dryly. "What do you mean…you *think*?"

"Well, I haven't quite made up my mind yet. You're going to have to make love to me again before I can decide. You see, I'm afraid the first time was so incredible that I was completely dazed all through it. Next time, I'll have better control of myself, so I'll be in a better position to judge your worth as a lover." A smile tugged at the corners of her lips.

"Oh, you will, will you? Well, we'll just have to see about that, won't we? Come here, you.'' He tightened his hold upon her, turning her over upon her back, his mouth descending to cover hers in the darkness. ''God, how I've wanted you, Cat,'' he muttered against her lips, ''and yet now that you're mine, it seems I want you even more than ever before. I'm already ready and eager for you again.''

''Is that so?'' she inquired archly. Grasping her hand, he showed her it was indeed so, inhaling sharply when she touched him, stroked him. ''What are you waiting for then?'' she murmured, her breath quickening.

He laughed softly, devilishly, once more. ''What's your hurry? We've got all night, don't we?''

''Yes…yes, we do,'' Cat agreed huskily as she wrapped her arms around his neck and drew him down to her again. ''Even so, I don't want to waste a single minute of it. Do you?''

''No…'' Morgan breathed before his mouth closed over hers again, his tongue shooting deep, silencing her fiercely, feverishly, as he once more took her to paradise and back.

Chapter 13

Wildcat

When Cat awoke in the morning, it was to discover she was stark naked and still lying in Morgan's embrace, in her canopy bed, which they had shared last night. He had not slipped away in the wee hours, as some men would have done, to return to his town house, but had stayed with her. She smiled drowsily at the realization, pleased by it. A man who spent the night was more serious about a relationship than one who did not. Yawning, she stirred and stretched like a sinuous cat before snuggling even closer to him.

"Hmm. That felt nice. Do that again," Morgan murmured, his eyes closed and a smile of satisfaction playing about the corners of his lips.

"You're awake!" Cat exclaimed softly.

"Barely. You wore me out last night, woman! I may never be able to get out of this bed."

"Is that so? Well, then you'll be at my utter mercy, won't you? And then I'll show you a thing or two about green-breaking a bronco," she teased.

"So show me—because if memory serves me correctly, sweetheart, for a city girl, you sure as hell know how to ride." As he spoke

these last words, he glanced at her lazily, knowingly, from beneath
half-closed lids, making her blush.

His hand was resting upon her breast, and now he began slowly
to caress her, circling his palm lightly across her nipple. Instantly,
the rosy peak contracted and stiffened in response, and a rush of heat
flooded Cat's entire being. Lowering his head to her other breast,
Morgan sucked its tip, his tongue flicking it until it was as taut and
flushed as its twin, before, at last, he sought her mouth, kissing her
deeply. With his lips and tongue and hands, he quickly brought her
yearning for him to a feverish pitch before he entered her. He thrust
into her once, twice. Then, crushing her to him, he suddenly rolled
them both over so she was astride him. Gasping for breath, Cat gazed
down at him, saw the passion that darkened his eyes, coupled with
the deviltry that danced in them. He opened his mouth to speak.

"Morgan, don't even *think* about hollering, 'Ride 'em, cowgirl!'"
she warned, trying without success to repress the smile that tugged
at her lips at the very idea, before she began to move slowly upon
him.

"I wasn't…going to…do that, darlin'."

"Yes…you…were!"

When they had finally reached their respective pinnacles and finished making love, she collapsed upon him. After a long moment,
her shoulders began to shake with silent laughter.

"Confess!" she demanded, glancing up at him, laughter still bubbling in her throat. "You *were* going to say it!"

"Honey, I was not."

But Cat knew from the grin he could not hold back that she was
right, that he *had* been going to say it. "You were."

"All right," he admitted sheepishly at last, still grinning. "I was,
damn it! You know me too well. Will you forgive me if I fix you
breakfast?"

She kissed him lightly on the nose. "Yes."

They took a long, hot shower together, Morgan thanking God that
the water was steaming for a change, making Cat burst into laughter
again when he told her how many cold showers he had subjected
himself to over the past several weeks. He soaped her and then she

soaped him, and they wound up making love again, with the warm spray from the shower head pouring upon them. After that they dressed and went downstairs. True to his word, Morgan cooked breakfast, while Cat meandered outside to fetch the morning newspaper from the driveway.

"What sections do you want?" she asked him as she slid the newspaper from the clear plastic cover that protected it in case of rain, then poured herself a cup of coffee and sat down at the kitchen table.

"Editorial, Sports and the Stock Market Report."

"Now, that's a man's combination if I ever heard one. Still, I'm afraid I'll fight you for the Stock Market Report, at least."

"No, I'll be a gentleman and let you have it first. Besides, I always read Fred Mann's sports column and Randy Brown's op-ed before I look at the Stock Market Report anyway, because I enter all the figures of the latter into my computer."

"Okay...here's Randy. Hmm. He's quite good-looking," she announced, casting from beneath long, thick lashes a surreptitious glance at Morgan as she studied Brown's picture alongside his column. She leafed through the remaining sections. "And here's Fred. My, he's handsome, too."

"If you say so, Cat. I don't read 'em for their looks. I read 'em because I happen pretty much always to agree with Fred's observations and predictions when it comes to sports, and because Randy's editorials always crack me up. Whenever this town starts filling up with hot air like a balloon, he can always be counted on to have a pin handy. One time, when all the yuppies in Tall Grass were battling a zoning change in order to prevent a Wal-Mart from being built across the street from their neighborhood, and all the equally upscale residents of Eastborough were attempting to prevent anybody from driving through their neighborhood to Towne East Mall, Randy wrote an absolutely hysterical editorial about the Balkanization of Wichita. I almost died laughing when I read it. How do you like your eggs?"

"Over easy. Well, I don't know about their columns, but if these two guys are any example of the men who work there, I believe I'll apply for a job at the *Wichita Eagle* if you wind up throwing me out of One-Eyed Jacks.''

"I don't think you have to worry about that, babe." Glancing up from the stove, Morgan eyed her intently, appreciatively. "You're not only doing a great job, but I've also grown rather attached to you—besides which, you don't know anything about working for a newspaper."

"I could learn," she declared brightly.

"Now where and when did I hear that line before?" he teased. "However, after what I've seen, I no longer doubt it in the slightest. Still, you can forget it, Cat. You're not going to work anywhere but at One-Eyed Jacks, where you belong...with me."

"Is that so?"

"Yeah, that's so. End of discussion. Now, please give me those newspaper sections. Much as I like their columns, I *don't* like the idea of your ogling Fred and Randy over *my* breakfast!"

"That's okay. I've come to prefer a man with a mustache any-way—and neither of them has one."

"Good. I'll buy a razor then for every man you meet."

Cat laughed so hard at that that she nearly choked on her coffee. In fact, during the whole weekend, she laughed more than she could remember laughing in a long time. Morgan both made her laugh and made love to her endlessly. He returned home only once the entire weekend—to get clothes and to pick up his Bronco—and even then he took her with him, so she got to see his town house for the first time. Like her father's house when she had first moved into it, it was beautifully decorated, but obviously a man's domain, lacking a woman's touch. Unlike most bachelor pads, however, it was clean and tidy—but then Cat had expected no less from a man who sent even his jeans to the dry cleaners to be starched and pressed.

On Monday morning—later than either of them normally arrived at work—Morgan drove Cat to the offices of the One-Eyed Jacks Oil & Gas Company, insisting it was silly of them to take two cars, especially when they both lived in the same neighborhood. In the end, she reluctantly agreed, although she still wondered what their employees would think.

"Who cares what they think?" Morgan growled in response to her question. "We don't meddle in their private lives, and I don't expect them to meddle in ours."

When they entered the office, Josie, the receptionist, was already at her desk.

"Could you please hold for a moment?" she said into the telephone receiver she held to her ear. Then, punching the Hold button, she glanced up at Cat. "Cat, this is a long distance call for you...from New York."

"Oh, Jeez Louise, I hope it's not my mother!"

"No." Josie shook her head. "It's a man. He said his name is...wait just a minute, I've got it right here...." From her desk, she picked up the pink telephone message slip she had begun to fill out. "His name is Spencer Kingsley. Do you want me to put him through to your office?"

For a long moment, Cat made no reply. She was shocked that Spence had tracked her down and called her. She was vividly aware of Morgan at her side, of the tension that had abruptly tautened his body at Josie's announcement, so he was like a predator preparing to spring. Cat knew he did not want her to take Spence's call. She was surprised he had not answered Josie's question himself, instructing her to inform Mr. Kingsley that Cat was not yet in. But then she recognized that, for all his seemingly macho talk and behavior, Morgan would never make her own decisions for her unless it were a matter of life and death.

"Yes, put Mr. Kingsley through to my office, Josie," Cat directed at last. Then, glancing at Morgan, she said softly, "I owe him that much, I think."

"If you say so, Cat," he replied tonelessly, a muscle flexing in his jaw, so she knew he was not as unaffected by her decision as he sought to appear. Then he went into his office and closed the door firmly behind him.

Going into her own office and shutting the door, Cat picked up the receiver of her telephone and punched the button of the blinking line.

"Hello, Spence," she said to her ex-fiancé coolly. "What can I do for you?"

They talked for a little more than half an hour. Even so, Cat had no sooner ended the conversation than Morgan appeared in her office, so she knew that all the while, he had been watching his own telephone, waiting for her to hang up and the light on the line she was using to go dark.

"So...what did your former fiancé want?" he asked casually, with just the slightest emphasis on the word *former,* his eyes hooded so she could not guess his thoughts.

"He...ah...wanted to apologize for the argument we had in Europe, the one that led to our breakup. He said he had missed me, and he asked me when I was planning on returning to New York. He intimated that since my departure from the import-export firm, things have not been going as smoothly as they did when I was there, and he offered me not only my old job back, but also a full partnership. And then he told me he would...ah...like very much to—to renew our engagement," she ended quietly.

For a moment silence stretched between them, tense and awkward.

"I see." Morgan's tone was terse. "And what was your response to all that, Cat?"

She never had a chance to reply, for just then Whitty came running into the office, visibly upset, her face stricken.

"Morgan, Quint just called," she announced agitatedly, one hand at her breast. Quint was the shop foreman. "You've got to get out to the Deuces Wild Number Seven right away. That no-good Skeeter Farrell's set it on fire—and it's burning out of control!"

"My God," Cat breathed. "Morgan, wait! I'll go with you!"

Grabbing up her purse, she ran after him as he tore out of the office and raced to the Bronco, pausing just long enough for Cat to slide in beside him as he started up the vehicle. By the time she got her seat belt fastened, he was already speeding down the street, heading north toward the city limits.

"Get Quint on his cellular," he directed tersely, a muscle working in his jaw. "Find out what in the hell happened and what's been done about it so far. Tell him we're en route, that we'll be there as soon as we can."

"Right." Cat nodded, picking up Morgan's cellular telephone and punching in Quint's number. As though he had been expecting the call, he answered almost immediately. "Quint, this is Cat. Morgan and I are on our way to the Deuces Wild. Could you fill us in on what you know and what action you've taken so far?" she asked as Morgan concentrated on driving, weaving in and out of traffic impatiently.

"Well, I don't know much, except for what I already told Whitty." Quint's voice sounded in her ear. "Because we'd been having a problem with some of the equipment, Ty Anders—he's the pumper on the Deuces Wild line—had departed from his usual routine this morning," he explained, "going straight out to Number Seven. By the time he got there, the well was already on fire, but he saw Skeeter's old pickup truck barreling away from the site. That's how come we figured Skeeter was responsible for the fire."

"How did Farrell start it?"

"Who knows? Your guess is as good as mine, Cat. A Molotov cocktail, a pipe bomb, a stick of dynamite.... Hell! He could have used most anything like that. But whatever it was, it blew the beam pump sky-high—Ty says there're pieces of it all over the place—and it set the surrounding field ablaze, too. I've notified the fire department, and they've got trucks on the way even as we speak."

"Was anybody hurt by the explosion?"

"No, although if Ty had arrived a few minutes earlier, he probably would have been killed. He was just lucky his truck had a dead battery this morning."

"Did you call the sheriff's department, Quint?"

"You betcha! They're sending officers.... We'll probably have to have some kind of bomb squad, too, if we find out Skeeter rigged more than one well to blow. I've pulled men off some of the other lines to help out."

"Good." That seemed to cover everything Cat could think of, so she hung up, then relayed all the information to Morgan.

"Quint's a good man, an excellent foreman," Morgan declared. "I feel confident he's done everything that could be done at this point and has the situation in hand. But we'll know for sure when we get to the Deuces Wild site." Without warning, he banged his fist on the steering wheel. ''Damn that Skeeter Farrell! I should have listened to you, Cat, and reported him to the police Friday night when he attacked you! I should have realized then how desperate and crazed he'd grown. Instead, I put his action down to the booze and figured that after our fight, he'd slink away with his tail between his legs and wouldn't pose a threat anymore, either to you or One-Eyed Jacks. My God! What if he hadn't chosen one of the wells as his target? What if he'd come back for you, Cat?''

''But he didn't.''

''That's not the point! He might have!'' Morgan's fingers clenched and unclenched around the steering wheel. ''I would never have forgiven myself if Farrell had harmed you, Cat. I'm not sure he'd have survived when I'd got done with him.''

''Then I'm glad I wasn't his target,'' Cat said, for she suspected Morgan's temper was such that he might have carried out his threat. And while it was exciting to know how deeply he cared for her and that he was more than willing to come to her defense, when she actually thought of his size and strength and remembered the thrashing he had given Farrell in the parking lot of Old Town, she shivered. It was difficult to believe the man who made love to her with such power and passion and yet such tenderness could be so lethal.

In many respects he was like a throwback to the nineteenth century. That was, Cat thought, one of his principal attractions. Now, when she recalled her arrival in Wichita, her awakening in the taxi and feeling as though she had been transported back in time, she envisioned Morgan in her mind as well. She could see him striding out of fire and smoke on the horizon of the prairie, dressed in a long duster, guns in hand.

That image became something of a reality when they finally reached the site of Deuces Wild Number Seven, where chaos reigned. Fire trucks, water trucks, sheriff's cars, One-Eyed Jacks company trucks and other vehicles were already parked haphazardly around the location. A sheriff's officer on the scene stopped the Bronco, but then allowed it to pass after Morgan had identified himself and Cat. Morgan parked the car, and the two of them got out, staring at the sight before them. A long plume of flame roared from the well, billowing smoke into the air. The gas line had ruptured. Fire and smoke swept across the field as well, and it was on this that the firemen were concentrating most of their initial efforts, lest the blaze spread to other wells or to the storage tanks for crude oil. Water spewed from long hoses hooked up to the water trucks. Men operating heavy machinery were digging trenches in the distance, in preparation for starting a backfire if it became necessary.

"Wait here," Morgan ordered Cat firmly.

With a handkerchief, he covered his face against the waves of acrid black smoke, then raced toward the burning well and Quint, who had already arrived. Standing in the middle of the confusion, the foreman was simultaneously talking to a sheriff's officer and shouting orders to employees of the One-Eyed Jacks Oil & Gas Company. Cat chafed fiercely at remaining behind by the Bronco. Still, she had sense enough to realize that, realistically, there was little she could do to help and that, as a result, she would only be in the way if she, too, charged toward the well. Sirens wailing, more fire trucks appeared on the scene, along with additional water trucks. She saw one of the sheriff's officers talking into his radio, and at that, she recognized that there was, after all, some action she could take.

Climbing back into the Bronco, she seized Morgan's cellular telephone and dialed the offices of the corporation.

"Josie, this is Cat," she said when the receptionist answered. "Put me through to Whitty immediately, please." In seconds the secretary was on the line. "Whitty, I need you to take whatever money you need from petty cash and to go to a fast-food restaurant or deli or wherever you think best. Buy enough sandwiches and chips to feed an army, and see what you can do about getting some jugs of cold lemonade and iced tea as well. Between the summer heat and the fire, it's like an inferno out here, and since the situation is awfully bad, I don't think it's going to be resolved anytime soon. I don't know how many of the men have their lunch boxes with them, if any do, or whether they have anything to drink. Turn on the answering machine, and take Josie and Grace with you if you need help." Grace was the general office clerk. "Then head this way. Meanwhile, I'll call Stella at the shop and tell her to close down and meet us here. Between the five of us, we ought to be able to manage.''

"Understood," Whitty replied briskly. "We're on our way."

Thanking God that Whitty was so efficient, Cat rang off, then telephoned Stella, relaying the necessary instructions. In moments Stella, too, was en route. Once Cat had finished her calls, there seemed little else for her to do except sit and wait. More than once, she climbed into the driver's seat and started up the engine to run the Bronco's air conditioner, she was so hot and perspiring. When Morgan returned, she told him she had ordered both the offices and the shop of the One-Eyed Jacks Oil & Gas Company closed, and that Whitty, Josie, Grace and Stella were on their way with food and drink.

"Good idea, Cat. I should have thought of it myself."

"No, you've got enough on your mind as it is, Morgan." She motioned toward the burning well. "What are they going to do about that? Can the fire be put out?"

"Probably. As you've learned, wells requiring beam pumps lack sufficient pressure to force the oil to the surface—which is what necessitates the beam pump in the first place—and the output from Deuces Wild Number Seven has been steadily falling off anyway, so its resources were beginning to be exhausted. It was one of the wells I was thinking about shutting down. So now we're going to try to extinguish the fire and then seal off the well. I don't know how long that will take, however."

In the end, it took several days to bring the fire under control, then put it out and cap off the well and the gas line, as well as clean up the debris from the surrounding area. During that time, Skeeter Farrell was arrested, and evidence was discovered in his garage that, along with the pumper, Ty Anders, having witnessed him fleeing the scene of the fire, linked him definitely to the crime. Farrell was currently cooling his heels in jail, having been unable to raise the bail money he had needed to regain his freedom.

During the days that Morgan had overseen the hectic operations at Deuces Wild Number Seven, he and Cat had had little free time to spend together. Much to her disappointment, he had returned home most nights to his town house—hungry, dirty, in need of food and a shower and utterly exhausted. After calling her to bring her up to date on the status of the well and to tell her good-night, he had hung up and collapsed on his bed, falling asleep almost instantly. By mutual, unspoken agreement, both of them had deliberately avoided mentioning the subject of Spencer Kingsley's telephone call to her.

But Cat had known that once the crisis was past, the topic would arise and she and Morgan must finish the conversation they had started just as Whitty had barged into Cat's office to inform them about Farrell's sabotage of Deuces Wild Number Seven. So, during the passing days, Cat had reflected long and hard about her future. She had felt no desire whatsoever to renew her engagement with Spence, and so she had told him, grasping from his dialogue that his primary interest in her had stemmed not from any real love for her, but from the fact that his import-export firm was not running nearly so smoothly without her.

That he had at last recognized her capabilities had been a gratifying thought. Still, it had not made her long to return to her old job. Since she had started work at the One-Eyed Jacks Oil & Gas Company, she had not missed the import-export firm. Nor, Cat had realized with surprise, had she missed Spence, either. Her father had been right. Spence had been a charming, convenient companion who had fit in with both her crowd and her corporate aspirations. Because of that, she had convinced herself she had fallen in love with him, deliberately blinding herself to the lack of any true passion between them.

These past several days, Cat had recognized that when Spence had gone away without her on business trips, she had felt only a mild sense of relief that she would have some time to herself. Morgan's absence, however, she had felt keenly, tossing and turning alone in her bed at night, missing him lying beside her, making love to her. When he had been injured at the site of Deuces Wild Number Seven, Cat had been stricken with dread and panic until she had learned he was not seriously hurt. She had known with certainty then how much she loved him, how deeply she would regret his loss. She wanted, she had realized then, nothing more than to remain in Kansas, to spend the rest of her life with Morgan McCain.

With that thought in mind, Cat had taken special care with her appearance this evening, as well as with the supper she had offered to prepare for the two of them, feeling that with Morgan having taken her out to so many places, she at least owed him a home-cooked meal in return. He had told her he liked spaghetti, so she had fixed that, making fresh pasta and sauce, along with an Italian salad and crusty garlic bread. When Morgan arrived, just as the sun was beginning to set, he added his own contribution to the meal—a bottle of excellent Beaujolais.

They ate in the kitchen so that, through the French doors and windows that lined the back of the house, they could watch the sun go down, a flaming ball of orange that sank slowly on the western horizon.

"Sunsets are truly beautiful here," Cat uttered softly as she and Morgan cleared the table, stacking the dirty dishes in the dishwasher before sitting back down at the table, cups of espresso in hand. "And at night, you can see the stars in the sky even from the city. They've never looked so close to me before, as though I could just reach up and pluck one from the sky."

"Yeah," Morgan agreed as he sipped his espresso. "There's nothing like the night sky over the prairie." He paused for a moment, gathering his thoughts. Then he continued. "You know, Cat, you never did tell me what your answer to Spencer Kingsley was—and we need to talk about that. But before we do, I thought we might play a little game of poker."

"Poker?" she exclaimed, genuinely surprised. "What kind of poker?"

"Two-card draw."

"What's that? I don't think I've ever even heard of it before."

Reaching into his pocket, he withdrew a box, which he opened to reveal a deck of cards. Removing them, he began to shuffle them expertly, then placed the deck before her, indicating that she should cut. Once she had done so, he fanned the cards out on the table.

"Here's the deal," he announced, eyeing her intently. "We'll each draw two cards and turn them faceup on the table. If, by some chance, you happen to turn up the two one-eyed jacks, I'll give you the two percent of my stock that Frank left me, so we'll be equal partners in the company. If, on the other hand, I happen to draw the two one-eyed jacks, then instead of returning to New York to marry Spencer Kingsley, you'll agree to remain in Wichita...to marry me," he ended quietly.

"M-m-marry you? Did you say,...*marry* you, Morgan?"

"*I* didn't stutter, did I? That's the bet, Cat. Are you in or out?"

She was so astounded by his proposal that she was momentarily speechless. Of course she had fantasized about him asking her to marry him. She had even dared to hope that he might, in time. But she had not expected it to happen so soon, if at all. Her heart thrummed with nervous excitement in her breast. Her hands began to tremble. What if, by some miracle, *she* drew the two one-eyed jacks and he did not? What if neither of them did?

"What—what if neither of us gets the pair of one-eyed jacks?"

Morgan shrugged. "Then the high card wins, and the loser can fix breakfast in the morning. So what do you say, Cat? Here's your chance to get your fair share of the company...*or*—" he grinned at her insolently "—me as a husband. Is it a bet?"

"Yes...yes, it's a bet."

"Then take your best shot, darlin'." He nodded at the cards on the table.

Slowly, her pulse racing, Cat reached out and pulled two cards from the deck.

"Aren't you going to look at 'em?" Morgan inquired, quirking one brow upward.

She shook her head. "Not until you pick yours."

"All right." Swiftly, hardly even glancing at the deck, he, too, drew two cards.

Only then did Cat turn hers over, gasping when she saw that, incredibly, she had drawn the pair of one-eyed jacks.

"That's—that's unbelievable! Do you know what the odds of that are?"

"Yeah, I do. Looks like you'll be getting my stock...*and*—" he turned his own two cards faceup, grinning impudently again "—marrying me, too, sweetheart."

For a long moment Cat stared at his own pair of one-eyed jacks, stunned. Then she realized what he had done, and, her heart pounding harder than ever, she began to turn all the cards over.

"I hadn't a chance at losing, had I? And neither did you, Morgan! They're all one-eyed jacks...all the cards! You rigged the deck! You cheated!"

"Yeah...but you know what they say—all's fair in love and war. And I *do* love you, Cat." His dark visage softened as he looked at her, his eyes smoldering with desire like twin embers and shining unmistakably with love. His voice was husky with emotion. "The day you came into it was the best day of my entire life. I don't want to lose you, darlin'. Please say you'll stay. Say you'll marry me."

"Yes...and again, yes. Oh, Morgan!" Her eyes filled with sudden tears of happiness as she gazed at him. "I love you, too!"

Standing, he swept her up into his arms, kissing her fiercely and deeply as he began to carry her toward the front staircase, which led upstairs, to her bedroom. Clinging tightly to his neck, Cat kissed him back with equal fervor, sure in her heart that, this time, she was feeling that certain special something with a certain special someone. This time she was sure beyond a shadow of a doubt that she had got it right. As though in answer to her thoughts, she seemed to hear from the study, as Morgan bore her past it, the echo of her father's laughter and then the smug, pleased sound of his voice.

My two wildcats—together at last!

Thanks, Dad, she called silently over her shoulder before tightening her hold on Morgan and smiling up at him invitingly, her heart in her eyes. "Well, I suppose this filly's about to be roped and branded permanently!" she said.

"Why, of course, darlin'," Morgan drawled wickedly, his eyes dancing as he carried her down the hallway and into her bedroom. "Don't you know? I've already got my lariat stashed and waiting under your bed!"

She laughed joyously, her heart singing as he tossed her down on the bed, then fell upon her to gather her into his strong and loving arms—then and for always.

Epilogue

The Winning Hand

He ought to have had the flowers delivered, Morgan thought ruefully as he strode through the maze of corridors in HCA Wesley Hospital, his vision almost totally obscured by the huge crystal vase filled nearly to overflowing with beautiful mixed flowers—Cat's favorite kind of arrangement—that he carried. But he had wanted to bring the bouquet himself, along with the big stuffed Teddy bear he had securely tucked under one arm, and the Wranglers baseball cap he had crammed in the back pocket of his jeans.

After an elevator trip and some more long halls, Morgan finally reached Cat's private room in the maternity ward. There, he awkwardly shifted his burdens so he could knock softly on the door. Then, with his shoulder, he pushed open the heavy wooden door and tiptoed inside the room, managing to peek through the towering flowers to see if his wife was asleep. To his delight, she was awake, her hospital bed cranked up so that she was in a sitting position and their newborn son, Frank Devlin McCain, cuddled snugly against her breast. Morgan thought he had never seen her look so beautiful. In the golden sunlight that streamed in through the open blinds of the window, her skin positively glowed in that luminescent way that was peculiar to new mothers, and her dark red hair shone like fire opals.

Spying her husband, Cat's eyes lit up warmly with love, and she smiled with pleasure before holding one finger warningly to her lips.

"Shh," she whispered, glancing down tenderly at their baby. "He's just now finished his feeding and dropped off to sleep." She motioned toward her hospital table. "Set those gorgeous flowers down there before you drop them, Morgan, then wheel that table a little closer so I can see them, please."

"As you wish," he replied, grinning and causing her both to smile again and to blush at the memories that his words evoked. On the evening that they both felt certain that little Frank had been conceived, they had rented a movie, *The Princess Bride,* and watched it together before making love passionately and tenderly long into the night. Ever since then, Morgan had taken to saying teasingly the film's famous line, "As you wish," to Cat's every expressed desire.

He placed the flowers on the table, then moved it to the bed.

"They're just beautiful," Cat declared quietly as she touched the blossoms gently and bent her head to inhale their fragrant scent. "Thank you, my love. And now, since I have a strange, sneaking suspicion that that colossal Teddy bear is for little Frank and not for me, why don't you put it in his bassinet. Then you can kiss us both and hold him for a while."

"There's nothing I'd like better." Morgan propped the big Teddy bear up in one corner of the plastic, hospital bassinet, which one of the nurses had wheeled into the room earlier. Then he bent and kissed his wife lingeringly before taking little Frank into his arms. "Come here, Ace," he said as lifted the sleeping baby, cradling him gingerly.

"Morgan—" Cat eyed him with mock reproval, trying but failing to repress her rueful smile "—I thought we had agreed our son would *not* be called Ace, Deuce, Trey, Jack, King, or any other name connected in any way, shape, or fashion with cards or poker."

"I know we did, Cat. But…well, damn it! You've just got to trust me on this one. No little boy wants to go through life being called Frankie, does he, Ace?" Morgan looked down at his son, and as though in response to his father, little Frank opened his eyes drowsily, waving one tiny fist in the air before yawning widely and drifting back to sleep. "There. You see?" Morgan shot Cat a triumphant glance that quickly turned sheepish as she shook her head and rolled her eyes at him to indicate just what she thought of his perception on little Frank's "answer." "Oh, I almost forgot." Morgan hastily changed the subject, reaching into his back pocket and drawing forth the Wranglers baseball cap, which he placed gently at a cocky angle on the sleeping baby's head.

"Oh, Morgan." Cat laughed softly. "You're incorrigible!"

"Yeah, but you love it—and me."

"I do."

"Good—because I love you, too, and so I'm never going to let you get away from me. You're my queen of hearts. Between you and Ace here, I got dealt the world's winning hand." Taking the cap off little Frank and putting it on the Teddy bear's head, Morgan laid the baby tenderly in the bassinet. Then drawing one of the hospital chairs up next to Cat's bed, her husband sat down, pulling a deck of cards from his shirt pocket. "And since I feel so incredibly lucky, do you feel up to our afternoon poker game?" That was how he had been entertaining her while she was in the hospital.

"Yes. Jacks or better to open?" Cat inquired, lifting one eyebrow archly.

Morgan grinned. "As you wish," he said.

* * * * *

RETURN TO SENDER
Merline Lovelace

This one's for Sherrill and Elisha and Peggy
and all the folks at the S. Penn Post Office—
thanks for your friendly smiles when I show up all drawn and
haggard to put a finished manuscript in the mail. Thanks, too,
for your cheerful professionalism. You're outstanding
representatives of the finest postal system in the world!

Chapter 1

Rio de Janeiro.

Mount Sugarloaf rising majestically above the city.

Streets crowded with revelers in costumes of bright greens and yellows and reds.

The glossy postcard leaped out at Sheryl Hancock from the thick sheaf of mail. Her hand stilled its task of sorting and stuffing post office boxes. The familiar early-morning sounds of co-workers grumbling and letters whooshing into metal boxes faded. For the briefest moment, she caught a faint calypso beat in the rattle of a passing mail cart and heard the laughter of Carnival.

"Is that another postcard from Paul-boy?"

With a small jolt, Sheryl left the South America festival and returned to the Albuquerque post office where she'd worked for the past twelve years. Smiling at the woman standing a few feet away, she nodded.

"Yes. This one's from Rio."

"Rio? The guy sure gets around, doesn't he?"

Elise Hart eased her bulk around a bank of opened postal boxes to peer at the postcard in Sheryl's hand. From the expression in Elise's brown eyes, it was obvious that she, too, was feeling the momentary magic of faraway places.

"What does this one say?"

Sheryl flipped the card over. "'Hi to my favorite aunt. I've been dancing in the streets for the past four days. Wish you were here.'"

Sighing, Elise gazed at the slick card. "What I wouldn't give to dump my two boys with my mother and fly down to Rio for Carnival."

"Oh, sure. I can just see you dancing through the streets, eight months pregnant yet."

"Eight months, one week, two days and counting," the redhead replied with a grimace. "I'd put on my dancing shoes for a hunk like Mrs. Gunderson's nephew, though."

"You'd better not put on dancing shoes! I'm your birthing partner, remember? I don't want you going into premature labor on me. Besides," Sheryl tacked on, "we only have Mrs. Gunderson's word for it that her nephew qualifies as a hunk."

"According to his doting aunt, Paul-boy sports a thick mustache, specializes in tight jeans and rates about 112 on the gorgeous scale." Elise waggled her dark-red brows in an exaggerated leer. "That's qualification enough in my book."

"Paul-boy, as you insist on calling him, is also pushing forty."

"So?"

So Sheryl didn't have a whole lot of respect for jet-setting playboys who refused to grow up or grow into their responsibilities. Her father had been a pharmaceutical salesman by profession and a wanderer by nature. He'd drifted in and out of her life for short periods during her youth, until her mother's loneliness and bitter nagging had made him disappear altogether. Sheryl didn't blame him, exactly. More often than not, she herself had to grit her teeth when her mother called in one of her complaining moods. But neither did she like to talk about her absent parent.

Instead, she teased Elise about her fascination with the man they both heard about every time the frail, white-haired woman who'd moved to Albuquerque some four months ago came in to collect her mail.

"Don't you think Mrs. Gunderson might be just a bit prejudiced about this nephew of hers?"

"Maybe. He still sounds yummy." Sighing, Elise rested a hand on her high, rounded stomach. "You'd think I would have learned my lesson once and for all. My ex broke the gorgeous scale, too."

Sheryl had bitten down hard on her lip too many times in the past to keep from criticizing her friend's husband. Since their divorce seven months ago, she felt no such restraints.

"Rick also weighed in as a total loser."

"True," Elise agreed. "He was, is and always will be a jerk." She traced a few absent circles on her tummy. "We can't all find men like Brian, Sher."

At the mention of her almost-fiancé, Sheryl banished any lingering thoughts of Elise's ex, Latin American carnivals and the globe-trotting Paul Gunderson. In their place came the easy slide of contentment that always accompanied any thought of Brian Mitchell.

"No, we can't," she confirmed.

"So have you two set a date yet?"

"We're talking about an engagement at the end of the year."

"You're engaged to get engaged." Her friend's brown eyes twinkled. "That's so...so Brian."

"I know."

Actually, the measured pace of Sheryl's relationship with the Albuquerque real estate agent satisfied her almost as much as it did him. After dating for nearly a year, they'd just started talking about the next step. They'd announce an engagement when the time was right, quite possibly at Christmas, and set a firm date for the wedding when they'd saved up enough to purchase a house. Brian was sure interest rates would drop another few points in the next year or so. Before they took the plunge into matrimony, he wanted to be in a position to buy down their monthly house payments so they could live comfortably on her salary and his commissions.

"I think that's what I like most about him," Sheryl confided. "His dependability and careful planning and—"

"Not to mention his cute buns."

"Well..."

"Ha! Don't give me that Little Miss Innocent look. I know you, girl. Under that sunshine-and-summer exterior, you crave excitement and passion as much as the next woman. Even fat, prego ones."

"What I crave," Sheryl replied, laughing, "is for you to get back to work. We've only got ten minutes until opening, and I don't want to face the hordes lined up in the lobby by myself."

Elise made a face and dipped into the cardboard tray in front of her for another stack of letters. She and Sheryl had come in early to help throw the postal box mail, since the clerk who regularly handled it was on vacation. They'd have to scramble to finish the last wall of boxes and get their cash drawers out of the vault in time to man the front counter.

Swiftly, Sheryl shuffled through the stack in her hand for the rest of Mrs. Gunderson's mail. Today's batch was mostly junk, she saw. Coupon booklets. Advertising fliers. A preprinted solicitation from the state insurance commissioner facing a special runoff election next week. And the postcard from Paul-boy, as Elise had dubbed him. With a last, fleeting glance at the colorful street scene, Sheryl bent down to stuff the mail into Mrs. Gunderson's slot.

It wouldn't stuff.

Frowning, she dropped down on her sneakered heels to examine the three-by-five-inch box. It contained at least one, maybe two days' worth of mail.

Strange. Mrs. Gunderson usually came into the post office every day to pick up her mail. More often than not, she'd pop in to chat with the employees on the counter, her yappy black-and-white shih tzu tucked under her arm. Regulations prohibited live animals in the post office except for those being shipped, but no one had the heart to tell Inga Gunderson that she couldn't bring her baby inside with her. Particularly when she also brought in homemade cookies and melt-in-your-mouth Danish spice cakes.

A niggle of worry worked into Sheryl's mind as she shoved Mrs. Gunderson's mail into her box. She hoped the woman wasn't sick or incapacitated. She'd keep an eye out for her today, just to relieve her mind that she was okay. Pushing off her heels, she finished the wall of boxes with brisk efficiency and headed for the vault. She had less than five minutes to count out her cash drawer and restock her supplies.

She managed it in four. She was at the front counter, her ready smile in place, when the branch manager unlocked the glass doors to the lobby and the first of the day's customers streamed in.

Sheryl didn't catch a glimpse of Mrs. Gunderson all morning, nor did any of her co-workers. As the day wore on, the unclaimed mail nagged at Sheryl. During her lunch break, she checked the postal box registry for the elderly renter's address and phone number.

The section of town where Inga Gunderson lived was served by another postal station much closer to her house, Sheryl noted. Wondering why the woman would choose to rent a box at a post office so far from her home, she dialed the number. The phone rang twice, then clicked to an answering machine. Since leaving a message wouldn't do anything to assure her of the woman's well-being, Sheryl hung up in the middle of the standard I-can't-come-to-the-phone-right-now recording.

Having come in at six-thirty to help "wall" the letters for the postal boxes, she got off at three. A quick check of Mrs. Gunderson's box showed it was still stuffed with unclaimed mail. Frowning, Sheryl wove her way slowly through the maze of route carriers' work areas and headed for the women's locker room at the rear of the station. After peeling off her pin-striped uniform shirt, she replaced it with a yellow tank top that brightened up the navy shorts worn by most of the postal employees in summer. A glance at the clock on the wall had her grabbing for her purse. She'd promised to meet Brian at three-thirty to look at a property he was thinking of listing.

After extracting a promise from Elise to go right home and get off her feet, Sheryl stepped outside. Hot, dry heat hit her like a slap in the face. With the sun beating down on her head and shoulders, she crossed the asphalt parking lot toward her trusty, ice-blue Camry. She opened the door and waited a moment to let the captured heat pour out. As she stood there in the hot, blazing sun, her nagging worry over Mrs. Gunderson crystallized into real concern. She'd swing by the woman's house, she decided. Just to check on her. It was a little out of her way, but Sheryl couldn't shake the fear that something had happened to the frail, white-haired customer.

With the Toyota's air conditioner doing valiant battle against the heat, she pulled out of the parking lot behind the post office and headed west on Haines, then north on Juan Tabo. Two more turns and three miles took her to the shady, residential neighborhood and Inga Gunderson's neat, two-story adobe house. She didn't see a car in the driveway, although several were parked along the street. Maybe Mrs. Gunderson's car was in the detached rear garage. Or maybe she'd gone out of town. Or maybe...

Maybe she was ill, or had fallen down the stairs and broken a leg or a hip. The woman lived alone, with only her precious Button for company. She could be lying in the house now, helpless and in pain.

More worried than ever, Sheryl pulled into the driveway and climbed out of the car. Once more the heat enveloped her. She could almost feel her hair sizzling. The thick, naturally curly mane tended to turn unmanageable at the best of times. In this soul-sucking heat, it took on a life of its own. Tucking a few wildly corkscrewing strands into the loose French braid that hung halfway down her back, Sheryl followed a pebbled walk to the front porch. A feathery Russian olive tree crowded the railed porch and provided welcome shade. Sighing in relief, she pressed the doorbell.

When the distant sound of a buzzer produced a series of high, plaintive yips and no Mrs. Gunderson, Sheryl's concern vaulted into genuine alarm. Inga Gunderson wouldn't leave town without her Button. The two were practically joined at the hip. They even looked alike, Elise had once joked, both possessing slightly pug noses, round, inquisitive eyes and hair more white than black.

Sheryl leaned on the doorbell again, and heard a chorus of even more frantic yaps. She pulled open the screen and pounded on the door.

"Mrs. Gunderson! Are you in there?"

A long, piteous yowl answered her call. She hammered on the door in earnest, setting the frosted-glass panes to rattling.

"Mrs. Gunderson! Are you okay?"

Button howled once more, and Sheryl reached for the old fashioned iron latch. She had just closed her hand around it when the door snapped open, jerking her inside with it.

Gasping, she found herself nose to nose with a wrinkled linen sport coat and a blue cotton shirt that stretched across a broad chest. A *very* broad chest. She took a quick step back, at which point several things happened at once, none of them good from her perspective.

Her foot caught on the door mat, throwing her off balance.

A hard hand shot out and grabbed her arm, either to save her from falling or to prevent her escape.

A tiny black-and-white fury erupted from inside the house. Gums lifted, needle-sharp teeth bared, it flew through the air and fastened its jaws on the jean-clad calf of her rescuer-captor.

"Ow!"

The man danced across the porch on one booted foot, taking Sheryl with him. Cursing, he lifted his leg and shook it. The little shih tzu snarled ferociously and hung on with all the determination of the rat catcher he was originally bred to be. Snarling a little herself, Sheryl tried to shake free of the bruising hold on her arm. When the stranger didn't loosen his grip, she dug her nails into the back of his tanned hand.

"Dammit, let go!"

She didn't know if the command shouted just above her ear was directed at her or the dog, and didn't particularly care. Pure, undiluted adrenaline pumped through her veins. She had no idea who this man was or what had happened to Mrs. Gunderson, but obviously *something* had. Something Button didn't like. Sheryl's only thought was to get away, find a phone, call the police.

Her attacker gave his upraised leg another shake, and Sheryl gouged her nails deeper into his skin. When that earned her a smothered curse and a painful jerk on her arm, she took a cue from the shih tzu and bent to bite the hand that held her.

"Hey!"

Still half-bent, Sheryl felt herself spun sideways. Her captor released his grip, but before she could bolt, his arm whipped around her waist. A half second later, she thudded back into the solid wall of blue oxford.

Her breath slammed out of her lungs. The band around her middle cut off any possibility of pulling in a replacement supply. As frantic now as the dog, she kicked back. One sneakered heel connected with the man's shin.

"Oh, for...!" Lifting her off her feet, her attacker grunted in her ear. "Calm down! I won't hurt you."

"Prove...it." she panted. "Let...me...go!"

"I will, I will. Just calm down."

Sheryl calmed, for the simple reason that she couldn't do anything else. Her ribs felt as though they'd threaded right through one another and squeezed out everything in between. Red spots danced before her eyes.

Thankfully, the excruciating pressure on her waist eased. She drew great gulps of air into her starved lungs. The sounds of another snarl and another curse battered at her ears. They were followed by a wheezy whine. When the spots in front of her eyes cleared, she turned to face a belligerent male, holding an equally belligerent shih tzu by the scruff of its neck.

For the first time, she saw the man's face. It was as hard as the rest of his long, lean body, Sheryl decided shakily. The sun had weathered his skin to dark oak. White lines fanned the corners of his eyes. They showed whiskey gold behind lashes the same dark brown as his short, straight hair and luxuriant mustache.

His mustache!

Sheryl whipped her gaze down his rangy form. Beneath the blue cotton shirt and tan jacket, his jeans molded trim hips and tight, corded thighs. She made the connection with a rush of relief.

The hunky nephew!

She'd have to tell Elise that Mrs. Gunderson wasn't all that far-off in her description. Although Sheryl wouldn't quite rate this rugged, whipcord-lean man as 112 on the gorgeous scale, he definitely scored at least an 88 or 90. Well, maybe a 99.

Wedging the yapping shih tzu under his arm like a hairy football, he gave Sheryl a narrow-eyed once-over. "Sorry about the little dance we just did. Are you all right?"

"More or less."

"Be quiet!"

She jumped at the sharp command, but realized immediately that it was aimed at Button. Thankfully, the shih tzu recognized the voice of authority. His annoying, high-pitched yelps subsided to muttered growls.

Swinging his attention back to Sheryl, Button's handler studied her with an intentness that raised little goose bumps on her arms. She couldn't remember the last time a man had looked at her like this, as though he wanted not just to see her, but into her. In fact, she couldn't remember the last time any man had *ever* looked at her like this. Brian certainly didn't. He was too considerate, too polite to make someone feel all prickly by such scrutiny.

"What can I do for you, Miss…?"

"Hancock. Sheryl Hancock. I know your aunt," she offered by way of explanation. "I just came by to check on her."

Those golden brown eyes lasered into her. "You know my aunt?"

"Yes. You're Paul Gunderson, aren't you?"

He was silent for a moment, then countered with a question of his own. "What makes you think so?"

"The mustache," she said with a tentative smile. And the thigh-hugging jeans, she added silently. "Your aunt talks about you all the time."

"Does she?"

"Yes. She's really proud of how well you're doing in the import-export business." Belatedly, Sheryl recalled the purpose of her visit. "Is she okay? I was worried when I didn't see her for a day or two."

"Inga's fine," he replied after a small pause. "She's upstairs. Resting."

Sheryl didn't see how anyone could rest through Button's shrill yapping, but then, Mrs. Gunderson was used to it.

"Oh, good." She started for the porch steps. "Would you tell her I came by, and that I'll talk to her tomorrow or whenever?"

Paul moved to one side. It was only a half step, a casual movement, but Sheryl couldn't edge past him without crowding against the wrought-iron rail.

"Why don't you come inside for a few minutes?" he suggested. "You can give me the real lowdown on what my aunt has to say about me, and we can both get out of the heat for a few minutes."

"I wish I could, but I'm running late for an appointment."

"There's some iced tea in the fridge. And a platter of freshly baked cookies on the kitchen table."

"Well..."

The cookies decided it. And Button's pitiable little whine. Obviously unhappy at being wedged into Paul's armpit, the dog snuffled noisily through its pug nose. The rhinestone-studded, bow-shaped barrette that kept his facial fur out of his eyes had slipped to one side. His bulging black orbs beseeched Sheryl to end his indignity.

She felt sorry for him but didn't make the mistake of reaching for the little stinker. The one time she'd tried to pet him at the post office, he'd nipped her fingers. As he now tried to nip Paul's. His sharp little teeth just missed the hand that brushed a tad too close to him. With a muttered oath, Paul jerked his hand away.

"How anyone could keep a noisy, bad-tempered fur ball like this as a pet is beyond me."

Somehow, the fact that Inga Gunderson's nephew disliked his aunt's obnoxious little Button made Sheryl feel as though they were allies of sorts. Smiling, she accepted his invitation and preceded him into the house.

Cool air wrapped around her like a sponge. The rooftop swamp cooler, so necessary to combat Albuquerque's dry, high-desert air, was obviously working overtime. As Sheryl's eyes made the adjustment from blazing outside light to the shadowed interior, she looked about in some surprise. The house certainly didn't fit Mrs. Gunderson's personality. No pictures decorated the walls. No knick-knacks crowded the tables. The furniture was a sort of pseudo-Southwest, a mix of bleached wood and brown Naugahyde, and not particularly comfortable looking.

Turning, she caught a glint of sunlight on Paul's dark hair as he bent down to deposit Button on the floor. To her consternation, she also caught a glimpse of what looked very much like a shoulder holster under the tan sport coat. She must have made some startled sound, because Paul glanced up and saw the direction of her wide-eyed stare. He released the dog and straightened, rolling his shoulders so that his jacket fell in place. The leather harness disappeared from view.

Sheryl had seen it, though.

And he knew she had.

His face went tight and altogether too hard for her peace of mind. Then Button gave a shrill, piercing bark and raced across the room. With another earsplitting yip, he disappeared up the stairs. He left behind a tense silence, broken only by the whoosh of chilled air being forced through the vents by the swamp cooler.

Sheryl swallowed a sudden lump in her throat. "Is that a gun under your jacket?"

"It is."

"I, uh, didn't know the import-export business was so risky."

"It can be."

She took a discreet step toward the door. Guns made her nervous. Very nervous. Even when carried by handsome strangers. Especially when carried by handsome strangers.

"I think I'll pass on the cookies. It's been a long day, and I'm late for an appointment. Tell your aunt that I'll see her tomorrow. Or whenever."

"I'd really like you to stay a few minutes, Miss Hancock. I'm anxious to hear what Inga has to say about her nephew."

"Some other time, maybe."

He stepped sideways, blocking her retreat as effectively as he had on the porch. But this time the movement wasn't the least casual.

"I'm afraid I'll have to insist."

Chapter 2

She knew about Inga Gunderson's nephew!

As he stared down into the blonde's wide, distinctly nervous green eyes, Deputy U.S. Marshal Harry MacMillan's pulse kicked up to twice its normal speed. He forgot about the ache in his gut, legacy of a roundhouse punch delivered by the seemingly frail, white-haired woman upstairs. He ignored the stinging little dents in his calf, courtesy of her sharp-toothed dust mop. His blood hammering, he gave the new entry onto the scene a thoroughly professional once-over.

Five-six or -seven, he guessed. A local, from her speech pattern and deep tan. As Harry had discovered in the week he'd been in Albuquerque, the sun carried twice the firepower at these mile-high elevations than it did at lower levels. It had certainly added a glow to this woman's skin. With her long, curly, corn-silk hair, tip-tilted nose and nicely proportioned set of curves, she looked more like the girl next door than the accomplice of an escaped fugitive. But Harry had been a U.S. marshal long enough to know that even the most angelic face could disguise the soul of a killer.

His jaw clenched at the memory of his friend's agonizing death. For a second or two, Harry debated whether to identify himself or milk more information from the woman first. He wasn't about to jeopardize this case, which had become a personal quest, by letting a suspect incriminate herself without Mirandizing her, but this woman wasn't a suspect. Yet.

"Tell me how you know Inga Gunderson."

Her eyes slid past him to the door. "I, uh, see her almost every day."

"Where?"

"At the branch office where I work."

"What branch office?"

She started to answer, then forced a deep, steadying breath into her lungs. "What's this all about? Is Mrs. Gunderson really all right?"

She had guts. Harry would give her that. She was obviously frightened. He could detect a faint tremor in the hands clenched at the seams of her navy shorts. Yet instead of replying to Harry's abrupt demands for information, she was throwing out a few questions of her own.

"Are you her nephew or not?"

He couldn't withhold his identity in the face of a direct question. Lifting his free hand, he reached into his coat pocket. The woman uttered a yelp every bit as piercing as the damned dog's, and jumped back.

"Relax, I'm just getting my ID."

He pulled out the worn brown-leather case containing his credentials. Flipping it open one-handed, he displayed the five-pointed gold star and a picture ID.

"Harry MacMillan, deputy U.S. marshal."

Her gaze swung from him to the badge to him and back again. Her nervousness gave way to a flash of indignation.

"Why didn't you say so?!"

"I just did." Coolly, he returned the case to his pocket. "May I see your identification, please."

"Mine? Why? I've told you my name."

Her response came out clipped and more than a little angry. That was fine with Harry. Until he discovered her exact relationship to the fugitive he'd been tracking for almost a year, he didn't mind keeping her rattled and off balance.

"I know who you said you were, Miss Hancock. I'd just like to see some confirmation."

"I left my purse in the car."

"Oh, that's smart."

The caustic comment made her stiffen, but before she could reply Harry cut back to the matter that had consumed his days and nights for so many months.

"Tell me again how you know Inga Gunderson."

Sheryl had always thought of herself as a dedicated federal employee. She enjoyed her job, and considered the service that she provided important to her community. Nor did she hesitate to volunteer her time and energies for special projects, such as selling T-shirts to aid victims of the devastating floods last year or coordinating the Christmas Wish program that responded to some of the desperate letters to Santa Claus that came into the post office during the holidays. She'd never come close to any kind of dangerous activity or bomb threats, but she certainly would have cooperated with other federal agencies in any ongoing investigation…if asked.

What nicked the edges of her normally placid temper was that this man didn't ask. He demanded. Still, he was a federal agent. And he wanted an answer.

"Mrs. Gunderson stops in almost every day at the station where I work," she repeated.

"What station?"

"The Monzano Street post office."

"The Monzano post office." He shoved a hand through his short, cinnamon-brown hair. "Well, hell!"

Sheryl bristled at the unbridled disgust in his voice. Although her friendly personality and ready smile acted as a preventive against the verbal abuse many postal employees experienced, she'd endured her share of sneers and jokes about the post office. The slurs, even said in fun, always hurt. She took pride in her work, as did most of her co-workers. What's more, she'd chosen a demanding occupation. She'd like to see anyone, this lean, tough deputy marshal included, sling the amount of mail she did each day and still come up smiling.

"Do you have a problem with the post office?" she asked with a touch of belligerence.

"What?" The question seemed to jerk him from his private and not very pleasant thoughts. "No. Have a seat, Miss Hancock. I'll call my contacts and verify your identity."

"Why?" she asked again.

His hawk's eyes sliced into her. "You've just walked into the middle of an ongoing investigation. You're not walking out until I ascertain that you're who you say you are...and until I understand your exact relationship with the woman who calls herself 'Mrs. Gunderson.'"

"*Calls* herself 'Inga Gunderson'?"

"Among other aliases. Sit down."

Feeling a little like Alice sliding down through the rabbit hole, Sheryl perched on the edge of the uncomfortable, sand-colored sofa. Good grief! What in the world had she stumbled into?

She found out a few moments later. Deputy U.S. Marshal Mac-Millan dropped the phone onto its cradle and ran a quick, assessing eye over her yellow tank top and navy shorts.

"Well, you check out. The FBI's computers have your weight at 121, but the rest of the details from your background information file substantiate your identity."

Sheryl wasn't sure which flustered her more, the fact that this man had instant access to her background file or that he'd accurately noted the few extra pounds she'd put on recently. Okay, more than a few pounds.

MacMillan's gaze swept over her once more, then settled on her face. "According to the file, you're clean. Not even a speeding ticket in the past ten years."

From his dry tone, he didn't consider a spotless driving record a particularly meritorious achievement.

"Thank you. I think. Now will you tell me what's going on here? Is Mrs. Gunderson...or whoever she is...really all right? Why in the world is a deputy U.S. marshal checking up on that sweet, fragile lady?"

"Because we suspect that sweet, fragile lady of being involved in the illegal importation of depleted uranium."

"Mrs. *Gunderson?*"

The marshal, Sheryl decided, had been sniffing something a lot more potent than the glue on the back of stamps!

"Let me get this straight. You think Inga Gunderson is smuggling uranium?"

"Depleted uranium," he corrected, as though she should know the difference.

She didn't.

"It's the same heavy metal that's used in the manufacture of armor-piercing artillery shells," he explained in answer to her blank look. Almost imperceptibly, his voice roughened. "Recently, it's also been used to produce new cop-killer bullets."

Sheryl stared at him, stunned. For the life of her, she couldn't connect the tiny, chirpy woman who brought her and her co-workers mouthwatering spice cakes with a smuggling ring. A uranium smuggling ring, for heaven's sake! Of all the thoughts whirling around in her confused, chaotic mind, only one surfaced.

"I thought the Customs Service tracked down smugglers."

"They do." The planes of MacMillan's face became merciless. "We're working with Customs on this, as well as with the Nuclear Regulatory Commission, the FBI, the CIA and a whole alphabet of other agencies on this case. But the U.S. Marshals Service has a special interest in the outcome of this case. One of our deputies took a uranium-tipped bullet in the chest when he was escorting Inga Gunderson's supposed nephew to prison."

"Paul?" Sheryl gasped.

The hazy image she'd formed of a handsome, mustached jet-setter lazing on the beach at Ipanema among the bikinied Brazilians surfaced for a moment, then shattered forever.

She shook her head in dismay. She should have known better than to let herself become intrigued, even slightly, by a globe-trotting wanderer! Her father hadn't stayed in one place long enough for anyone, her mother included, to get to know him or his many varied business concerns. For all Sheryl knew, he could have been a smuggler, too. But not, she prayed, a murderer.

At the memory of her father's roving ways, she gave silent, heartfelt thanks for her steady, reliable, soon-to-be-fiancé. Sure, Brian occasionally fell asleep on the couch beside her. And once or twice he'd displayed more excitement over the prospect of closing a real estate deal than he did over their plans for the future. But Sheryl knew he would always be there for her.

As he was probably there for her right now, she realized with a start. No doubt he was waiting in the heat at the house he wanted to show her, flicking impatient little glances at his watch. She'd promised to be there by three-thirty. She snuck a quick look at her watch. It was well past that now, she saw.

"What do you know about Paul Gunderson?"

The curt question snapped her attention back to Deputy Marshal MacMillan.

"Only what Inga told me. That he's a sales rep for an international firm and that he travels a lot. From his postcards, it looks like his company sends him to some pretty exotic locales."

MacMillan dropped his hands from his hips. His well-muscled body seemed to torque to an even higher degree of tension.

"Postcards?" he asked softly.

"He sends her bright, cheery cards from the various places he travels to. They come to her box at the Monzano branch. We—my friends at the post office and I—thought it was sweet the way he stayed in touch with his aunt like that."

"Yeah, real sweet." His face tight with disgust, MacMillan shook his head. "We ordered a mail cover the same day we tracked Inga Gunderson to Albuquerque. The folks at the central post office assured us they had the screen in place. Dammit, they should have caught the fact that she had another postal box."

Sheryl's defensive hackles went up on behalf of her fellow employees. "Hey, they're only human. They do their best."

The marshal didn't dignify that with a reply. He thought for a moment, his forehead furrowed.

"We didn't find any postcards here at the house. Obviously, Inga

Gunderson destroyed them as soon as she retrieved them from her box. Did you happen to see the messages on the cards?"

Sheryl squirmed a bit. Technically, postal employees weren't supposed to read their patrons' mail. It was hard to abide by that rule, though. More than one of the male clerks slipped raunchy magazines out of their brown wrappers for a peek when the supervisors weren't around. *Cosmo*s and *Good Housekeeping* had been known to take a detour to the ladies' room. The glossy postcards that came from all over the world weren't wrapped, though, and even the most conscientious employee, which Sheryl considered herself, couldn't resist a peek.

"Well, I may have glanced at one or two. Like the one that arrived this morning, for instance. It—"

The marshal started. "One came in this morning?"

"Yes. From Rio."

"Damn! Wait here. I'm going to get my partner." He spun on one booted heel. His long legs ate up the distance to the hallway. "Ev! Bring the woman down!"

Sheryl heard a terse reply, followed by a series of shrill yaps. A few moments later, she recognized Mrs. Gunderson's distinctive Scandinavian accent above the dog's clamor. When she made out the specific words, Sheryl's jaw sagged. She wouldn't have imagined that her smiling, white-haired patron could know such obscenities, much less spew them out like that!

She watched, wide-eyed, as a short, stocky man hauled a handcuffed Inga Gunderson into the living room.

"Get your hands off me, you fat little turd!"

The elderly lady accompanied her strident demand with a swing of her foot. A sturdy black oxford connected with her escort's left shin. Button connected with his right.

Luckily, the newcomer was wearing slacks. As MacMillan had earlier, he took several dancing hops, shaking his leg furiously to dislodge the little dog. Button hung on like a snarling, bug-eyed demon.

The law enforcement officer sent MacMillan a look of profound disgust. "Shoot the damned thing, will you?"

"No!"

Both women uttered the protest simultaneously. As much as Sheryl disliked the spoiled, noisy shih tzu, she didn't want to see it hurt.

"Button!" she commanded. "Down, boy!"

The dog ignored Sheryl's order, but its black eyes rolled to one side at the sound of its mistress's frantic pleas.

"Let go, precious. Let go, and come to Mommy."

The warbly, pleading voice was so different from the one that had been spitting vile oaths just moments ago that both men blinked. Sheryl, who'd heard Inga Gunderson carry on lengthy, cooing conversations with her pet many times before, wasn't as surprised by the abrupt transition from vitriol to syrupy sweetness.

"Let go, sweetie-kins. Come to Mommy."

The shih tzu released its death grip on the agent's pants.

"There's a pretty Butty-boo."

With his black eyes still hostile under the lopsided rhinestone hair clip, the little dog settled on its haunches beside its mistress. In another disconcerting shift in both tone and temperament, Inga Gunderson directed her attention to Sheryl.

"What are you doing here? Don't tell me you're working with these pigs, too?"

"No. That is, I just stopped by to make sure you were all right and I—"

"She's been telling us about some postcards," MacMillan interrupted ruthlessly.

Inga's seamed face contorted. Fury blazed in her black eyes. "You just waltzed in here and started spilling your guts to these jerks? Is that the thanks I get for baking all those damn cookies for you and the other idiots at the post office, so you wouldn't lose my mail like you do everyone else's?"

Shocked, Sheryl had no reply. Even Button seemed taken aback by his mistress's venom. He gave an uncertain whine, as if unsure whom he should attack this time. Before he could decide, MacMillan reached down and once again scooped the dog into the tight, restraining pocket of his arm.

"Get her out of here," he ordered his partner curtly. "Call for backup and wait in the car until it arrives. I'll meet you at the detention facility when I finish with Miss Hancock.''

The older woman spit out another oath as she was tugged toward the front door. ''Hancock can't tell you anything. She doesn't know a thing. *I* don't know a thing! If you think you can pin a smuggling rap on me, you're pumping some of that coke you feds like to snitch whenever you seize a load.''

Yipping furiously, Button tried to squirm free of the marshal's hold and go after his mistress. MacMillan waited until the slam of the front door cut off most of Mrs. Gunderson's angry protests before releasing the dog. Nails clicking on the wood floor, the animal dashed for the hallway. His grating, high-pitched barks rose to a crescendo as his claws scratched frantically at the door.

Sheryl shut out the dog's desperate cries and focused, instead, on the man who faced her, his eyes watchful behind their screen of gold-tipped lashes.

''She's right. I don't know anything. Nothing that pertains to uranium smuggling, anyway.''

''Why don't you let me decide what is and isn't pertinent? Tell me again about these postcards.''

''There's nothing to tell, really. They come in spurts, every few weeks, from different places around the world. The messages are brief—from the little I've noticed of them,'' Sheryl tacked on hastily.

''Can you remember dates to go with the locations?''

''Maybe. If I think about it.''

''Good! I want to take a look at the card that arrived this morning. If you don't mind, we can take your car back to the branch office.''

''Now?''

''Now.''

''But I have an appointment.''

''Cancel it.''

''You don't understand. I'm supposed to meet my fiancé.''

The marshal's keen gaze took in her ringless left hand, then lifted to her face.

''We're, uh, unofficially engaged,'' Sheryl explained for the second time that day.

"This shouldn't take long," MacMillan assured her, taking her elbow to guide her toward the door. "You can use my cell phone to call your friend."

His touch felt warm on her skin and decidedly firm. They made it to the hall before a half whine, half growl stopped them both in their tracks. The shih tzu blocked the front door, his black eyes uncertain under his silky black-and-white fur.

"We can't just leave Button," Sheryl protested.

"I'll have someone contact the animal shelter. They can pick him up."

"The shelter?" Her brows drew together. "They only keep animals for a week or so. What happens if Mrs. Gunderson isn't free to claim him within the allotted time?"

"We'll make sure they keep the mutt as long as necessary."

A touch of impatience colored MacMillan's deep voice. He reached for the door, and the dog gave another uncertain whine. Sheryl dragged her feet, worrying her lower lip with her teeth.

"He doesn't understand what's happening."

"Yeah, well, he'll figure things out soon enough if he tries to take a chunk out of the animal control people."

"I take it you're not a dog lover, Mr....Sheriff... Marshal Mac-Millan."

"Call me 'Harry.' And, yes, I like dogs. Real dogs. Not hairy little rats wearing rhinestones. Now, if you don't mind, Miss Hancock, I'd like to get to the post office and take a look at that postcard."

"We can't just let him be carted off to the pound."

The marshal's jaw squared. "I don't think you understand the seriousness of this investigation. A law enforcement officer died, possibly because of Inga Gunderson's complicity in illegal activity."

"I'm sorry," she said quietly. "But that's not Button's fault."

"I didn't say it was."

"We can't just leave him."

"Yes, we can."

With her sunny disposition and easygoing nature, Sheryl didn't find it necessary to dig in her heels very often. But when she did, they stayed dug.

"I won't leave him."

Some moments later, Sheryl stepped out of the adobe house into the suffocating heat. A disgruntled deputy U.S. marshal trailed behind her, carrying an equally disgruntled shih tzu under his arm.

She slid into her car and winced as the oven-hot vinyl seat covers singed the backs of her thighs. Trying to keep the smallest possible portion of her anatomy in direct contact with the seat, she keyed the ignition and shoved the air-conditioning to max.

With the two males eyeing each other warily in the passenger seat, Sheryl retraced the route to the Monzano station. She was pulling into the parking lot behind the building when she realized that she'd forgotten all about Brian. She started to ask Harry MacMillan if she could use his phone, but he had already climbed out.

He came around the car in a few man-sized strides. Opening her door, he reached down a hand to help Sheryl out. The courteous gesture from the sharp-edged marshal surprised her. Tentatively, her fingers folded around MacMillan's hand. It was harder than Brian's, she thought with a little tingle of awareness that took her by surprise. Rougher. Like the man himself.

Swinging out of the car, she tugged her hand free with a small smile of thanks. "We can go in the back door. I have the combination."

Button went with them, of course. They couldn't leave him in the car. Even this late in the afternoon, heat shimmered like clear, wavery smoke above the asphalt. Stuffed once more under MacMillan's arm and distinctly unhappy about it, the little dog snuffled indignantly through his pug nose.

Sweat trickled down between Sheryl's breasts by the time she punched the combination into the cipher lock and led the way into the dim, cavernous interior. Familiar gray walls and a huge expanse of black tile outlined with bright-yellow tape to mark the work areas welcomed her. As anxious now as MacMillan to retrieve the postcard from Mrs. Gunderson's box, she wove her way among hampers stacked high with outgoing mail toward her supervisor's desk, situated strategically in the center of the work area.

"You do have a search warrant, don't you?" she asked Harry over one shoulder.

He nodded confidently. "We have authority to screen all mail sent to the address of Inga Gunderson, alias Betty Hoffman, alias Eva Jorgens."

"Her home address or her post office box?"

"Does it make a difference?"

At MacMillan's frown, Sheryl stopped. "You need specific authority to search a post office box."

"I'm sure the warrant includes that authority."

"We'll have to verify that fact."

Impatience flickered in his eyes. "Let's talk to your supervisor about it."

"We will. I'd have to get her approval before I could allow you into the box in any case."

Sheryl introduced Harry to Pat Martinez, a tall, willowy Albuquerque native with jet-black hair dramatically winged in silver. The customer service supervisor obligingly called the main post office and requested a copy of the warrant. It whirred up on the fax a few moments later.

After ripping it off the machine, Pat skimmed through it. "I'm sorry, this isn't specific enough. It only grants you authority to search mail addressed to Mrs. Gunderson's home address. It'll have to be amended to allow access to a postal box."

Sheryl politely kept any trace of "I told you so" off her face. Harry wasn't as restrained. He scowled at her boss with distinct displeasure.

"Are you sure?"

"Yes, Marshal, I'm sure," Pat drawled. With twenty-two years of service under her belt, she would be. "But you're welcome to call the postal inspector at the central office for confirmation."

He conceded defeat with a distinct lack of graciousness. "I'll take your word for it." Still scowling, he shoved Button at Sheryl. "Here, hold your friend."

He pulled a small black address book out of his pocket, then punched a number into the phone. His face tight, he asked the person who answered at the other end about the availability of a federal judge named, appropriately, Warren. He listened intently for a moment, then requested that the speaker dispatch a car and driver to the Monzano Street post office immediately.

Sheryl watched him hang up with a mixture of relief and regret. Her part in the unfolding Mrs. Gunderson drama was over. She certainly didn't want to get any more involved with smugglers and kindly old ladies who spewed obscenities, but the trip to Inga's house had certainly livened up her day. So had the broad-shouldered law enforcement officer. Sheryl couldn't wait to tell Brian and Elise about her brush with the U.S. Marshals Service.

MacMillan soon disabused her of the notion that her role in what she privately termed the post office caper had ended, however.

"I'll be back in forty-five minutes," he told her curtly. "An hour at most. I'm sorry, but I'll have to ask you to wait for me here."

"Me? Why?"

"I want you to take a look at the message on this postcard and tell me how it compares with the others."

"But I'm already late for my appointment."

He cocked his head, studying her with a glint in his eyes that Sheryl couldn't quite interpret.

"Just out of curiosity, do you always make appointments, not dates, with this guy you're sort of engaged to?"

Since the question was entirely too personal and none of his business, she ignored it. "I'm late," she repeated firmly. "I have to go."

"You're a material witness in a federal investigation, Miss Hancock. If I have to, I'll get a subpoena from Judge Warren while I'm downtown and bring you in for questioning."

She hitched Button up on her hip, eyeing MacMillan with a good deal less than friendliness.

"You know, Marshal, your bedside manner could use a little work."

"I'm a law enforcement officer, not a doctor," he reminded her. Unnecessarily, she thought. Then, to her astonishment, his mustache lifted in a quick, slashing grin.

"But this is the first time I've had any complaints about my bedside manner. Just wait for me here, okay? And don't talk about the case to anyone else until I get back.''

Sheryl was still feeling the impact of that toe-curling grin when Harry MacMillan strode out of the post office a few moments later.

Chapter 3

With only a little encouragement, the Albuquerque police officer detailed to Harry's special fugitive task force got him to the Dennis Chavez Federal Building in seventeen minutes flat. Luckily, they pushed against the rush-hour traffic streaming out of downtown Albuquerque and the huge air force base just south of I-40. The car had barely rolled to a stop at the rear entrance to the federal building before Harry had the door open.

"Thanks."

"Any time, Marshal. Always happy to help out a Wyatt Earp who's lost his horse."

Grinning at the reference to the most legendary figure of the U.S. Marshals Service, Harry tipped him a two-fingered salute. A moment later, he flashed his credentials at the courthouse security checkpoint. The guard obligingly turned off the sensors of the metal detector to accommodate his weapon and waved him through.

Harry took the stairs to the judge's private chambers two at a time. Despite his impatience over this detour downtown for another warrant, excitement whipped through him. He was close. So damned close. With a sixth sense honed by his fifteen years as a U.S. marshal, Harry could almost see the fugitive he'd been tracking for the past eleven months. Hear him panting in fear. Smell his stink.

Paul Gunderson. Aka Harvey Millard and Jacques Garone and Rafael Pasquale and a half-dozen other aliases. Harry knew him in every one of his assumed personas. The bastard had started life as Richard Johnson. Had gone all through high school and college and a good part of a government career with that identity. His performance record as an auditor for the Defense Department described him as well above average in intelligence but occasionally stubborn and difficult to supervise. So difficult, apparently, that a long string of bosses had failed to question the necessity for his frequent trips abroad.

While conducting often unnecessary audits of overseas units, Johnson had also used his string of aliases to establish a very lucrative side business as a broker for the sale and shipment of depleted uranium, a by-product of the nuclear process. As Harry had discovered, most of the uranium Johnson illegally diverted went to arms manufacturers who used it to produce armor-piercing artillery and mortar shells for sale to third-world countries. But recently a new type of handgun ammunition had made an appearance on the black market, and the U.S. government had mounted a special task force to find its source.

When he was arrested a little over two years ago, Johnson had claimed that he didn't know the product he brokered was being used to manufacture bullets that shredded police officers' protective armor like confetti. The man who gunned down the marshals escorting Johnson to trial certainly knew, though. He left one officer writhing in agony. In the ensuing melee, Johnson finished off the other.

Harry had lost a friend that day. His best friend.

He'd been tracking Johnson ever since. After months of frustrating dead ends, chance information from a snitch had established a tenuous link between Johnson and the Gunderson woman. She'd slipped through their fingers several times before Harry finally traced her to Albuquerque. Through the damned dog yet! Harry didn't even want to think about all the calls they'd made to veterinarians and grooming parlors before they got a lead on an elderly woman with a Scandinavian accent and a black-and-white shih tzu!

They'd no sooner found her than she'd almost slipped away again. Harry had barely set up electronic surveillance of her home when the same dog groomer who IDed her alerted him that Inga Gunderson had canceled her pet's regularly scheduled appointment. She was, according to the groomer, going out of town. Harry had been forced to move in…and had gotten nothing out of the woman.

Then Sheryl Hancock had stumbled on the scene.

With her tumble of blond hair and sunshine-filled green eyes, she would have made Harry's pulse jump in the most ordinary of circumstances. The fact that she provided a definitive link to Paul Gunderson sent it shooting right off the Richter scale. He shook his head, still not quite believing that the Gundersons had been using the U.S. mail to coordinate their activities all this time.

The mail, for God's sake!

In retrospect, he supposed it made sense. Phones were too easily tapped these days. Radio and satellite communications too frequently intercepted by scanners set to random searches of the airwaves. For all the heat the postal system sometimes took, it usually delivered…which was more than could be said for a good many other institutions, private or public. The card sitting in Inga Gunderson's box right now could very well hold vital information. Every nerve in Harry's body tightened at the thought of studying its message.

He cornered the judge and did some fast talking to obtain an amended warrant. A quick call to his partner to check on Inga Gunderson's status confirmed what Harry already suspected. The woman refused to talk until her lawyer arrived. Since the man was currently cruising the interstate somewhere on the other side of Amarillo, it would be some hours yet before he arrived and they could confront the suspect.

"Everything we've got on her is circumstantial," Ev warned. "I don't know if it's enough to hold her unless we establish a hard connection between her and Richard Johnson or Paul Gunderson or whatever he's calling himself now."

"I'm working on it. Just sit on the woman as hard as you can. Maybe she'll crack. And give me a call when her lawyer shows."

"Will do."

Harry hung up, more determined than ever to get his hands on that postcard.

"Box 89212?"

Buck Aguilar glanced from Sheryl and Pat Martinez to the man facing him across a sorting rack. Oblivious to the tension radiating from the marshal, the postal worker handed Pat back the amended warrant.

"Closed that box this afternoon."

He picked up the stack of mail he'd been working before the interruption. Letters flew in a white blur into the sorting bins.

His face a study in disbelief, Harry leaned forward. "What do you mean, you closed it?"

At the fierce demand, Buck lifted his head once again. Slowly, his gaze drifted from the marshal's face to his boots and back up again. From the expression on the mail carrier's broad, sculpted face, Sheryl could tell that he didn't take kindly to being grilled.

"Got a notice terminating the box," Buck replied in his taciturn way. "Closed it."

The clatter of wheels on concrete as another employee pushed a cart across the room drowned Harry's short, explicit reply. Sheryl caught the gist of it, though. The marshal was *not* happy. She waited for the fireworks. They weren't long in coming.

"What did you do with the contents of the box? Or more specifically—" Harry sent a dagger glance at Sheryl and her supervisor "—what did you do with the postcard that was in there?"

"Returned to sender. Had to. BCNO."

"What the hell does that mean?"

Buck glanced at the marshal again, his eyes flat. Spots of red rose in his cheeks, darkening the skin he'd inherited from his Jacarillo Apache ancestors. Sheryl and the other employees at the Monzano branch office knew that look. Too well. It settled on her co-worker's face whenever he was about to butt heads with another employee or an obnoxious customer. Since Buck stood six-four and carried close to 250 pounds on his muscled frame, that didn't occur often. But when it did, the results weren't pretty.

Pat Martinez replied for him. "*BCNO* means 'Box closed, no order.' Without a forwarding order, we have no choice but to return the mail to sender."

"Dammit!"

"You got a problem with that, Sheriff?"

Buck's soft query lifted the hairs on Sheryl's neck.

"Yeah, I've got a problem with that. And it's 'Marshal.'"

The two men faced each other across the bin like characters in some B-grade Western movie. *The Lawman and the Apache.* At any minute, Sheryl expected them to whip out their guns and knives. Even Button sensed the sudden tension. Poking his nose through the straps of Sheryl's purse, he issued a low, throaty growl.

Hastily, she stepped into the breech. "Maybe it's not too late to retrieve the card. What time did you close the box, Buck?"

His gaze shifted once again. Infinitesimally, his expression softened. "'Bout three-thirty, Sher."

"Oh, dear."

Although it seemed impossible, the marshal bristled even more. "What does 'oh, dear' mean?"

She turned to him, apology spilling from her green eyes. "I'm afraid it means that the contents of Mrs. Gunderson's box went back to the Processing and Distribution Center on the four o'clock run."

"You mean that postcard left here even before I went chasing downtown after the blasted amended warrant?"

"Well...yes."

Harry stared at her, aggravation apparent in every line of his body. For a moment, she wasn't quite sure how he'd handle this new setback. Finally, he blew out a long, ragged breath.

"So where is this distribution center?"

"The P&DC is on Broadway, but..."

"But what?"

Sheryl shared a look with her supervisor and co-worker. They were more than willing to let her handle the thoroughly disgruntled marshal. Bracing herself, she gave him the bad news.

"But the center uses state-of-the-art, high-speed sorters. It also makes runs to the airport every half hour. Since we rent cargo space on all the commercial carriers, your postcard would have gone out—" she glanced at the clock on the wall "—an hour ago, at least. Depending on how it was routed, it's halfway to Dallas or Atlanta or New York right now."

A muscle twitched on the side of MacMillan's jaw. "I suppose there's no way to trace the routing?"

"Not unless it was certified, registered or sent via Global Express, which it wasn't."

"Great!"

A heavy silence descended, broken when Pat Martinez handed Harry his useless warrant.

"I'm sorry about sending you downtown on a wild-goose chase, Marshal, but I won't apologize for the fact that my employees followed regulations. If you don't need me for anything else, I'll get back to work."

"No. Thanks."

Buck moved off, too, rolling his empty hamper away to collect a full one from the row at the back of the box area. Sheryl and Button waited while Harry rubbed a hand across the back of his neck, flattening his cotton shirt against his stomach and ribs.

At the sight of those lean hollows and broad surfaces, a sudden and completely unexpected tingle of awareness darted through Sheryl. Content with Brian, she hadn't looked at other men in the year or so they'd been dating. She'd certainly never let her gaze linger on a set of washboard ribs or a flat, trim belly. Or noticed the tight fit of a pair of jeans across muscled thighs and...

"Are you hungry?"

Sheryl jerked her gaze upward. "Excuse me?"

"Are you hungry? I skipped breakfast, and Ev and I were too busy taking physical and verbal abuse from the Gunderson woman to grab lunch. Why don't we have dinner while we talk about these postcards?"

"Tonight?"

The tightness left his face. A corner of his thick, luxuriant mustache tipped up in a reluctant smile. "That was the general idea. I know I made you miss your... appointment...with this guy you're sort of engaged to. Let me make it up to you by feeding you while I squeeze your brain."

"Squeeze my brain, huh? Interesting approach. Does it get you a lot of dinner dates?"

"It never fails." His smile feathered closer to a grin. "Another example of my charming bedside manner, Miss Hancock. So, are you hungry?"

She was starved, Sheryl realized. She was also obligated to provide what information she could to the authorities, represented in this instance by Deputy U.S. Marshal Harry MacMillan.

Still, she hesitated. When she'd called Brian a while ago to apologize for standing him up, he'd sounded more than a little piqued. Sheryl couldn't blame him. In an attempt to soothe his ruffled feathers, she'd promised to cook his favorite chicken dish tonight. They'd fallen into the routine of eating at her apartment on Tuesdays and his on Fridays. This was supposed to have been her night. Oh, well, she'd just have to make it up to him next week.

"I need to make a phone call," she said, hitching her purse and its furry passenger up on her shoulder.

Graciously, MacMillan handed her his mobile phone. With both dog and man listening in, Sheryl conducted a short, uncomfortable conversation with Brian.

"I'm sorry I've kept you waiting all this time, but something's come up. I'm going to be tied up awhile longer. Yes, I know it's Tuesday night. No, I can't put this off until tomorrow."

She caught MacMillan's speculative gaze, and turned a shoulder. "Yes. Maybe. I'll phone you when I get home."

Sheryl ended the call on a small sigh. Brian's structured approach to life usually gave her such a comfortable feeling. Sometimes, though, it made things just a bit difficult.

"Trouble in almost-paradise?" Harry inquired politely, slipping his phone back into his pocket.

"Not really. Where would you like to eat?"

"You pick it. I don't know Albuquerque all that well."

She thought for a minute. "How about El Pinto? They have the best Mexican food in the city and we can get a table outside, where we can talk privately."

"Sounds good to me."

Sheryl led the way to the rear exit, absorbing the fact that he was apparently a stranger to the city.

"Where's home? Or can you say?"

As soon as she articulated the casual question, she wondered if he would...or should...answer. She had no idea what kind of security U.S. marshals operated under. He'd told her not to talk about the case. Maybe he wasn't supposed to talk about himself, either.

Evidently, that wasn't a problem.

"I'm assigned to the fugitive apprehension unit of the Oklahoma City district office," he replied, "but I don't spend a whole lot of time there. My job keeps me on the road most of the time."

Another wanderer! They seemed to constitute half the world's population. Sheryl's minor annoyance with Brian's inflexibility vanished instantly. He, at least, wouldn't take off without warning for parts unknown. She led the way outside, blinking at the abrupt transition from dim interior to dazzling sunlight.

"I'd better meet you at the restaurant. I'll have to go by my apartment first to drop off Button. Unless you want to take him back to your place?" she finished hopefully.

"I can't," he replied without the slightest hint of regret. "I'm staying in a motel."

She sighed, resigning herself to an unplanned houseguest. "Do you know how to get to El Pinto?"

"Haven't got a clue. Just give me the address. I'll find it."

She chewed her lip, thinking perhaps she should suggest a more accessible place. "It's kind of hard to locate if you're not familiar with Albuquerque."

He sent her a look of patented amusement. "U.S. marshals have been tracking down bad guys since George Washington pinned gold stars on the original thirteen deputies. I'm pretty sure I can find this restaurant."

"I stand corrected," Sheryl said gravely.

She drove out of the parking lot a few moments later, with Button occupying the seat beside her. Harry trailed in a tan government sedan. Following her directions, he turned south at the corner of Haines and Juan Tabo, and she headed north.

By this late hour, Albuquerque's rush-hour traffic had thinned to a steady but fast-moving stream. The trip to her apartment complex took less than fifteen minutes. As always, the cream-colored adobe architecture and profusion of flowers decorating the fountain in the center of the tree-shaded complex gave her a quiet joy. Sheryl had moved into her one-bedroom apartment soon after her last promotion and loved its cool Southwestern colors and high-ceilinged rooms. It was perfect for her, but the pale-mauve carpet hadn't been pet-proofed. After unlocking the front door, she set the shih tzu down in the tiled foyer.

"We have to establish a few ground rules, fella. No yapping, or you'll get me thrown out of here. No taking bites out of me or my furniture. No accidents on the rug."

Busy sniffing out the place, Button ignored her.

"I'm serious," she warned.

Once she'd plopped her purse down on the counter separating the kitchen from the small dining area, she pulled a plastic bowl from the cupboard and filled it with water.

"It's either me or the pound, so you'd better... Hey!"

With regal indifference to her startled protest, the shih tzu lifted his raised leg another inch and sprayed the dining table.

Obviously, Button didn't believe in rules!

Sheryl went to work with paper towels, then scooped up the unrepentant dog. A moment later, she set him and the water dish down on the other side of the sliding-glass patio doors. Hands on hips, she surveyed the small, closed-in area. The leafy Chinese elm growing on the other side of the adobe wall provided plenty of shade. The few square yards of grass edging the patio tiles provided Button's other necessary commodity.

"This is your temporary residence, dog. Make yourself comfortable."

After sliding the patio door closed behind her, she heeled off her sneakers and padded into the bathroom to splash cold water on her face. Then she shucked her shorts and tank top and pulled on a gauzy sundress in a cool mint green. She had her hair unbraided and was pulling a brush through its stubborn curls when a series of high-pitched yips told her Button wanted in.

Too bad. He'd better get used to outdoor living.

She soon learned that what Button wanted, Button had his own way of getting. Within moments, the yips rose to a grating, insistent crescendo.

The brush hit the counter with a thud. Muttering, Sheryl retraced her steps and cut the dog's protests off with a stern admonition.

"I guess I didn't make myself clear. You've lost your house privileges. You're going to camp out here on the patio, Buttsy-boo, or take a trip to the pound."

Ten minutes later, Sheryl slammed the front door behind her and left a smug Button in undisputed possession of her air-conditioned apartment. It was either cave in to his hair-raising howls or risk eviction. In desperation, she'd spread a layer of newspapers over the bathroom floor. She could only hope that the dog would condescend to use them. The next few days, she thought grimly, could prove a severe strain on her benevolence toward animals in general and squish-faced lapdogs in particular.

As she shoved the car key into the ignition, a sudden thought struck her. If even half of what Harry had told her about Mrs. Gunderson's activities was true, Sheryl could be stuck with her unwanted houseguest for a lot longer than a few days.

Groaning, she backed out of the carport. No way was she keeping that mutt for more than a day or two. Harry had to have stumbled across some relative or acquaintance of Mrs. Gunderson during his investigation, someone who could take over custody of her pet. She put the issue on the table as soon as they were seated in El Pinto's shaded, colorful outdoor dining area. Harry stretched his long legs out under the tiled table and graciously refrained from pointing out that it was her insistence on taking the dog with them that had caused her dilemma in the first place.

"There's nothing I'd like better than to identify a few of Inga Gunderson's friends and acquaintances."

Sheryl had to scoot her chair closer to catch his reply over the noise of the busy restaurant. A fountain bubbled and splashed just behind them, providing a cheerful accompaniment to the mariachi trio strumming and thumping their guitars as they strolled through the patio area. Harry had chosen the table deliberately so they could talk without raising the interest of other diners. Even so, Sheryl hadn't counted on practically sitting in his lap to carry on a conversation.

"As far as we know," he continued, "Inga doesn't have any acquaintances here. She made a few calls to local businesses, but no one's phoned her or visited her." His gold-flecked eyes settled on his dinner partner. "Except you, Miss Hancock."

"'Sheryl,'" she amended absently. "So what will happen to her?"

"We have sufficient circumstantial evidence to book her on suspicion of smuggling. The charge might or might not stick, but she's not the one I really want. It's her supposed nephew I'm after."

Despite Harry's relaxed pose, Sheryl couldn't miss the utter implacability in his face. He slipped a pen and small black-leather notebook out of his jacket pocket, all business now.

"Tell me about the postcards."

She waited to reply until the waitress had placed a brimming basket of tortilla chips on the table and taken their drink orders.

"They usually come in batches," she told Harry. "Two or three will arrive within a week of each other, then a month might go by before another set comes in."

"I figured as much," the marshal said, almost to himself. "He'd have to send backups in case the first didn't arrive. Have any others come in with this one from Rio?"

"Two. The first was from Prague. The second from Pamplona."

"Pamplona?" His brow creased. "Isn't that where they run bulls through the streets? With the locals running right ahead of them?"

"That's what the scene on the card showed." Sheryl hunched forward, recalling the vivid street scene with a shake of her head. "Can you imagine racing down a narrow, cobbled street a few steps ahead of thundering, black bulls?"

"I can imagine it, but it's not real high on my list of fun things to do," Harry admitted dryly. He loaded a chip with salsa. "How about you?"

"Me? No way! I have enough trouble staying ahead of my bills, let alone a herd of bulls. Uh, you'd better go easy on that stuff. I heard the green chili crop came in especially hot this year."

"Not to fear, I've got a lead-lined stom— Arrggh!"

He shot up straight in his chair, grabbed his water glass and downed the entire contents in three noisy gulps. Blinking rapidly, he stared at the little dish of salsa in disbelief.

"Good Lord! Do you New Mexicans really eat this stuff?"

"Some of us do," Sheryl answered, laughing. "But we work up to it over a period of years."

The waitress arrived at that moment. Harry shot her a look of profound gratitude and all but snatched the Don Miguel light he'd ordered out of her hand. The ice-cold beer, like the water, went down in a few long, gulping swallows.

The waitress turned an amused smile on Sheryl. "Didn't you warn him?"

"I tried to."

Winking, she picked up her tray. "Another gringo bites the dust."

Sheryl eyed the marshal, not quite sure she'd agree with the waitress's assessment. His golden brown eyes watered, to be sure. A pepper-induced flush darkened his cheeks above the line of his mustache. He drained his mug with the desperation of a man who'd just crawled across a hundred miles of burning desert.

She would categorize him as down, but certainly not out. He showed too much strength in those broad shoulders. Carried himself with too much authority. Even in his boots and jeans and casual open-necked shirt, he gave the impression of a man who knew what he wanted and went after it.

For an unguarded moment, Sheryl wondered if he would pursue a woman he desired with the same single-minded determination he pursued the fugitives he hunted. He would, she decided. He'd pursue her, and when he caught her, he'd somehow manage to convince her she'd been the hunter all along. The thought sent a ripple of excitement singing through her veins. She shook her head at her own foolishness.

Still, the tingle stayed with her while Harry dragged the heel of his hand across his eyes.

"Remind me to listen to your warnings next time."

The offhand remark made Sheryl smile, until she realized that there probably wouldn't be a next time. As soon as she filled Marshal MacMillan in on the details from the postcards, he'd ride off into the sunset in pursuit of his quarry.

How stupid of her to romanticize his profession. She'd better remember that he lived the same life-style her father had. Here today, gone tomorrow, with never a backward glance for those he left behind.

Recovering from his bout with the green chilies, Harry got back to business.

"Prague, Pamplona and Rio," he recited with just a hint of hoarseness. "We've suspected all along that our man is triangulating his shipments."

"Triangulating them?"

"Sending them through second and third countries, where they're rebundled with other products like coffee or bat guano, then smuggled into the States."

"Why in the world would someone bundle uranium with bat guano and…? Oh! To disguise the scent of the metal containers and get them past the Customs dogs, right?"

"You got it in one." He leaned forward, all business now. "Can you remember any of the words on the cards?"

"On two of them. I didn't see the one from Prague. My friend Elise described it to me, though."

"Okay, start with Rio. Give me what you can remember."

"I can give it to you exactly." She wrinkled her brow. "'Hi to my favorite aunt. I've been dancing in the streets for the past four days. Wish you were here.'"

Harry stared at her in blank astonishment. "You can recall it word for word?"

"Sure."

"How?" he shot back. "With the thousands of pieces of mail you handle every day, how in the hell can you remember one postcard?"

"Because I handle thousands of pieces of mail every day," she explained patiently. "The white envelopes and brown flats—the paper-wrapped magazines and manila envelopes—all blur together. Not that many postcards come through, though, and when they do, they catch our attention immediately.''

She decided not to add that the really interesting postcards got passed from employee to employee. The male workers particularly enjoyed the topless beach scenes that American tourists loved to send back to their relatives. Some cards went well beyond topless and tipped into outright obscenity. Those they were required to turn into the postal inspectors. Sheryl had long ago ceased being surprised at what people stuck stamps on and dropped in a mailbox.

Harry had her repeat the message. He copied the few sentences in his pad, then studied their content.

''I don't think this is Carnival season. I'm sure that happens right before Lent in Rio, just as it does in New Orleans.''

He made another note to himself to check the dates of Rio's famous festival. Sheryl was sitting so close she could make out every stroke. His handwriting mirrored his personality, she decided. Bold. Aggressive. Impatient.

''Maybe the four days has some significance,'' she suggested.

''It probably does.'' He frowned down at his notes. ''I don't know what yet, though.''

''Do you want to know about the picture on the front side?'' she asked after a moment.

''Later. Let's finish the back first. What else do you remember about it?''

''What do you want to start with? The handwriting? The color of ink? The stamp? The cancellation mark?''

He sat back, his eyes gleaming. He looked like a man who'd just hit a superjackpot.

''Start wherever you want.''

They worked their way right through sour cream enchiladas, smoked charro beans, rice and sopapillas dripping with honey. The mariachi band came to their table and left again, richer by the generous tip Harry passed them. The tables around them emptied, refilled. They were still working the Rio postcard when Harry's phone beeped.

"MacMillan." He listened for a moment, his brow creasing. "Right. I'm on my way."

Snapping the phone shut, he rose to pull out Sheryl's chair. "I'm sorry. Inga Gunderson's lawyer just showed up and wants to see his client. We'll have to go over the rest of the cards tomorrow. I'll call you to set up a time."

A small, unexpected dart of pleasure rippled through Sheryl at the thought of continuing this discussion with Marshal MacMillan. Shrugging, she chalked it up to the fact that she still had something worthwhile to contribute to his investigation.

She drove out of the parking lot a few moments later, thinking that she'd better reschedule the last-minute layette shopping spree she and Elise had planned for tomorrow night. As determined as Harry was to extract every last bit of information from her, they might have to work late.

She couldn't know that he would walk into the post office just after nine the next morning and reschedule her entire life.

Chapter 4

"**I**'m sorry, sir," Sheryl repeated for the third time. "I can't hand out a DHS check over the counter. Even if I could, I wouldn't give you a check addressed to someone else."

The runny-eyed scarecrow on the other side of the counter lifted an arm and swiped it across his nose. His hand shook so badly that the tattoos decorating the inside of his wrist were a blur of red and blue.

"That's my old lady's welfare check," he whined. "I gotta have it. I want it."

Yeah, right, Sheryl thought. What he wanted was another fix, courtesy of the Department of Human Services. She wondered how many other women this creep had bullied or beaten out of their food and rent money over the years to feed his drug habit.

"I can't give it to you," she repeated.

"My old lady's moved, I'm tellin' ya, and she didn't get her check this month. She sent me in to pick it up."

"I'm sure someone explained to her that the post office can't forward a DHS check. We're required by regulations to deliver it to the address where she physically resides or send it back."

"Send it back? Why, dammit?"

The angry explosion turned the heads of the other customers who'd come in with the first rush of the morning. In the booth next to

Sheryl's, Elise glanced up sharply from the stamps she was dealing out.

Holding on to her patience with both hands, Sheryl tried again. "We have to send the checks back to DHS because a few people abused the system by moving constantly and collecting checks from several different counties at once. Now everyone has to pay the price for their fraud."

The lank-haired junkie fixed her with a malevolent glare. "Yeah, well, I don't give a rat's ass about them other people. I just want my old lady's money. You'd better give it to me, bitch, or I'm gonna—"

"You're going to what?"

At the dangerous drawl, both Sheryl and her unpleasant customer jerked around.

The sight of Harry MacMillan's broad-shouldered form sent relief pinging through her. Relief and something else, something far too close to excitement for Sheryl's peace of mind. Swallowing, she ascribed the sudden flutter in her stomach to the fact that the marshal looked particularly intimidating this morning.

As he had yesterday, he wore jeans and a well-tailored sport coat, this one a soft, lightweight, blue broadcloth. As it had yesterday, his jacket strained at the seams of his wide shoulders. Adding to his overall physical presence, his jaw had a hard edge that sent off its own silent warning. The gold in his eyes glinted hard and cold.

Sheryl could handle nasty characters like the one standing in front of her at this moment. She'd done it many times. But that didn't stop her from enjoying the pasty look that came over the druggie's face when he took in Harry's size and stance.

"Nah, no problem," he replied to Harry, but his mouth pinched when he turned back to Sheryl. "Me 'n' my old lady need that money."

"Tell her to contact DHS," She instructed once again. "They'll issue an emergency payment if necessary."

His thin, ravaged face contorted with fury and a need she could only begin to guess at. "I wouldn't be here if it wasn't necessary, you stupid—"

He broke off, slinging a sideways look at Harry.

The marshal jerked his head toward the lobby doors. "You'd better leave, pal. Now."

The watery eyes flared with reckless bravado. "You gonna make me, *pal?*"

"If I have to."

Like waves eddying around a rock, the other customers in the post office backed away from the two men. A tight, taut silence gripped the area. Sheryl's knee inched toward the silent alarm button just under her counter.

The thin, pinch-faced junkie broke the shimmering tension just before she exerted enough pressure to set off the alarm. With another spiteful glance at Sheryl, he pushed past Harry and shouldered open the glass door. A collective murmur of relief rose from the other customers as the door thumped shut behind him.

Harry didn't relax his vigilance until the departing figure had stalked to a battered motorcycle, threw a leg over the seat, jumped on the starter and roared out of the parking lot.

"Nice guy," one of the women in line murmured.

"Wonder what his problem was?" another groused.

"Do you get many customers like that?" Harry inquired, moving to Sheryl's station.

No one objected to the fact that he cut ahead of them in line, she noticed.

"Not many. What are you doing here? I thought you were going to call and set up a time for us to meet?"

"I decided to come in person, instead. Can you get someone to cover for you here? I need to talk to you privately."

"Yes, of course. Wait for me in the lobby and I'll let you in through that door to the back area."

With a nod to the other customers, Harry turned away. Elise demanded an explanation the moment the glass doors swung shut behind him.

"Who *is* that?"

"He's—"

Sheryl caught herself just in time. Harry had told her not to discuss the case with anyone other than her supervisor. She hadn't, although the restriction had resulted in another uncomfortable phone conversation with Brian after she'd driven home from El Pinto.

"He's an acquaintance," she finished lamely, if truthfully.

"Since when?"

"Since last night."

Elise's dark-red brows pulled together in a troubled frown. "Does Brian know about this new acquaintance of yours?"

"There's nothing to know." With an apologetic smile at the lined-up customers, Sheryl plopped a Closed sign in front of her station. "I'll send Peggy up to cover the counter with you."

She found the petite brunette on the outside loading dock, pulling in long, contented drags of cigarette smoke mixed with diesel fumes from the mail truck parked next to the ramp.

"I know you're on break, but something's come up. Can you cover for me out front for a few minutes?"

"Sure." Peggy took another pull, then stubbed out her cigarette in the tub of sand the irreverent carriers always referred to as the butt box. Carefully, she tucked the half-smoked cigarette into the pocket of her uniform shirt.

"I have to conserve every puff. I promised myself I'd only smoke a half a pack today."

"I thought you decided to quit completely."

"I did! I will! After this pack. Maybe." Smiling ruefully at Sheryl's grin, she strolled back into the station. "How long do you think you'll be? I'm supposed to help Pat with the vault inventory this morning."

"Not long," Sheryl assured her. "I just need to set up an appointment."

Contrary to her expectations, she soon discovered that Harry hadn't driven to the Monzano station to make an appointment.

She stared at him, dumbfounded, while he calmly informed her and her supervisor that Albuquerque's postmaster had agreed to assign Miss Hancock to the special fugitive apprehension task force that Harry headed.

"Me?"

Sheryl's startled squeak echoed off the walls of the stationmaster's little-used private office.

"You," he confirmed, pulling a folded document out of his coat pocket. "This authorizes an indefinite detail, effective immediately."

"May I see that?" her supervisor asked.

"Of course."

Pat Martinez stuck her pencil into her upswept jet-black hair and skimmed the brief communiqué he handed her.

"Well, it looks like you're on temporary duty, Sheryl."

"Hey, hang on here," she protested. "I'm not sure I want to be assigned to a fugitive apprehension task force, indefinitely or otherwise. Before I agree to anything like this, I want to know what's required of me."

"Basically, I want your exclusive time and attention for as long it takes to extract every bit of information I can about those postcards."

"Exclusive time and attention? You mean, like all day?"

"And all night, if necessary."

Sheryl gaped at him. "You're kidding, right?"

He didn't crack so much as a hint of a smile. "No, Miss Hancock, I'm not. My team's been at it pretty much around the clock since we tracked Inga Gunderson to Albuquerque. I won't ask that you put in twenty-four hours at a stretch, of course, but I will ask that you work with me as long as necessary and as hard as possible."

"Look, I don't mind working with you, but we're shorthanded here. The box clerk is on vacation and Elise could go out on maternity leave at any moment."

"So the postmaster indicated." Calmly, Harry nodded to the document held by Sheryl's supervisor. "We took that into consideration."

"The postmaster is sending a temp to cover your absence," Pat explained. "If Elise goes out, he'll cover that, too." Her eyes lifted to Harry. "You're thorough, MacMillan."

"I learned my lesson after the fiasco with the warrant," he admitted. "This time, I made sure we dotted every i and crossed every t."

Sheryl wasn't sure she liked being lumped in with the i's and t's, but she let it pass. Now that she'd recovered from her initial surprise, she didn't object to the detail. She just didn't care for Harry's high-handed way of arranging it.

As if realizing that he needed to mend some bridges with his new detailee, the marshal gave her a smile that tried for apologetic but fell a few degrees short. Sheryl suspected that MacMillan rarely apologized for anything.

"I didn't have time to coordinate this with you and Ms. Martinez beforehand. My partner and I were up most of the night running air routes that service Prague, Pamplona and Rio through the computers. We're convinced our man is bringing in a shipment soon, and we're not going to let it or him slip through our fingers. We've got to break the code that was on those postcards, and to do that we need your help, Sheryl."

Put like that, how could she refuse?

"Well, if you're sure someone's coming out here to cover for me…"

"The postmaster assured me that wasn't a problem."

Sheryl looked to Pat, who nodded. "We'll manage until the temp gets here. Go close down your station."

Still a little bemused by her sudden transition from postal clerk to task force augmentee, Sheryl headed for the front. Naturally, her curious co-workers peppered her with questions.

"What's going on, Sher?" Elise wanted to know. "Why are you closing out?"

Peggy grinned wickedly over the divider separating the stations. "And who's the long, tall stud with the mustache? Tell us all, girl."

"I can't right now. I'll tell you about it later."

When she could, Sheryl amended silently, hitting a sequence of keystrokes to tally her counter transactions. The printer stuttered out a report for her abridged workday. Another quick sequence shut down the computer.

Her hand resting on her mounded tummy, Elise waited for the next customer. "Where are you going now?"

That much at least Sheryl could reveal. "Downtown. The postmaster has assigned me to a special detail."

"With the stud? No kidding?" Peggy waggled her brows. "How do I go about getting assigned to this detail?"

"By stopping by to check on little old ladies on your way home from work."

"Huh?"

"I'll tell you about it later," Sheryl repeated.

With swift efficiency, she ejected her disk from her terminal and removed her cash drawer. After stacking her stock of stamps on top of the drawer, she carried the lot to the vault. A quick inventory tallied her cash receipts with the money orders, stamps and supplies she'd sold so far this morning. She scribbled her name across the report, then left it for the T-6 clerk who had the unenviable task of reconciling all the counter clerks' reports with the master printout produced at the end of each day. That done, she hurried back to her counter to retrieve her purse and extract a promise from Elise.

"Brian's supposed to pick me up at eleven-thirty. He wanted to show me a house during lunch that he's going to list. He needs a woman's opinion about the renovations that might be necessary to the kitchen. Would you go with him? Please? You know how he always raves about what you did with your kitchen."

Brian wasn't the only one who raved about the miracles Elise had performed with the small fixer-upper he'd found for her after her divorce. With two kids to house and a third about to make an appearance, she'd taken wallpapering and sheet curtains to a higher plane of art. She'd also turned a dilapidated kitchen into a marvel of bleached cabinets, hand-decorated tiles and artfully disguised pipes.

"I'll be happy to go with him, but..."

"Thanks! Tell him I'll call him tonight."

Sheryl left Elise with a frown still creasing her forehead and hurried toward the back. Now that she'd gotten used to the idea, she had to admit the prospect of taking part in a criminal investigation sent a little thrill of excitement through her. The Wanted posters tacked to the bulletin board in the outer lobby and the occasional creeps who came into the post office, like the one this morning, were the closest she'd come to the dark, seamy side of life. Besides, she was only doing her civic duty by helping Harry piece together the puzzle of the postcards.

Which didn't explain the way her pulse seemed to stutter with that strange, inexplicable excitement when she saw the marshal. Hands shoved into his pockets, ankles crossed, he lounged against one of the carriers' sorting desks as though he had nothing else in the world more important to do than wait for her. The pose didn't fit his character, she now knew. Harry MacMillan was anything but patient. She'd just met him yesterday—fallen into his arms, more correctly—and now he'd pulled her off her job to work on his team.

At the sound of her footsteps, he glanced up, and Sheryl's excitement took on a deeper, keener edge. His toffee-colored eyes swept her with the same intent scrutiny that had raised goose bumps on her skin yesterday. Suddenly self-conscious, she glanced down at her pin-striped shirt with its neat little cross tab tie and her navy shorts.

"Should I change out of my uniform?"

His gaze skimmed from her nose to her knees and back again. "You're fine."

She was a whole lot better than fine, Harry thought as he followed her to the exit. He'd never paid much attention to postal uniforms, but Sheryl Hancock filled hers out nicely. Very nicely.

Her pin-striped shirt with its little red tab was innocuous enough, but the long, curving stretch of leg displayed by those navy shorts pushed his simple observation into swift, gut-level male appreciation. It also put a knot in his belly that didn't belong there right now.

Frowning, Harry gave himself a mental shake. He'd better keep his mind focused on the information Sheryl could supply, not on her tanned legs or the seductive swing of her hips. And he'd darn well better remember why he'd yanked her from her workplace and put her on his team. She held the key to those damned postcards. He felt it with every instinct he possessed. He wasn't going to rest until he'd pulled every scrap of information out of this woman.

Despite his stern reminder that his business with Sheryl was just that, business, his pulse tripped at the thought of the hours ahead. On the advice of her lawyer, Inga Gunderson flatly refused to talk to the investigators. Harry and Ev had spent several frustrating hours with the woman last night. Finally, they'd left her stewing in her own venom. The clerk of the court had assured them that she wouldn't get a bail hearing until late tomorrow, if then, given the overloaded court docket.

Earlier this morning, Ev had left to drive up to the labs at Los Alamos to talk to one of the government's foremost experts on the use and physical properties of depleted uranium. The New Mexico state trooper assigned to the task force was now out at the local FAA office, compiling a list of secondary airstrips within a hundred-mile radius. The Customs agent working with them on an as-needed basis had returned to his office to cull through foreign flight schedules. For the next few hours at least, Harry would have the task force headquarters—and Sheryl—to himself.

He intended to make good use of that time.

"Why don't I drive, since my vehicle is cleared for the secure parking at the Chavez Federal Building? We can come back for your car later."

"Okay. Just let me open my windows a bit to keep from baking the seats."

A moment later, Sheryl buckled herself into the blast furnace heat of the tan sedan. "So you're operating out of the downtown court-house?"

"We've set up task force headquarters in the U.S. Marshals' offices."

Task force headquarters!

A vague image formed in her mind of a busy, high-tech command post, complete with wall-sized screen satellite maps displaying all kinds of vital information, humming computer terminals, beeping phones and a team of dedicated, intense professionals. The idea of becoming a part, however briefly, of the effort kindled a sense of adventure.

Reality came crashing down on her the moment she stepped inside the third-floor conference room in the multistory federal building in the heart of the city. Hand-scribbled paper charts decorated the non-descript tan walls. Foam coffee cups and cardboard boxes of records littered the long conference table. Wires from the phones clustered

in the center of the table snaked around the cups and over the boxes
like gray streamers. A faint, stale odor drifted from the crushed pizza
cartons that had been stuffed into metal wastebaskets in a corner.
Sheryl looked around, gulping.

"This is it? Your headquarters?"

"This is it." Harry shrugged off the clutter with the same ease he
shrugged out of his jacket. "Make yourself comfortable."

She might have been able to do just that if her gaze hadn't snagged
on the blue steel gun butt nestled against his left side. Even holstered,
the weapon looked ugly and far too dangerous for her peace of mind.

Harry tossed his jacket over a chair back and turned, catching her
wary expression. "Don't worry. I know how to use it."

Somehow, that didn't reassure her.

"I don't like guns," she admitted, dropping her shoulder bag into
a chair. "They make me nervous. Very nervous."

Calmly, he rolled up the cuffs of his white cotton shirt. "They
make me nervous, too. Especially when they're loaded with uranium-
tipped bullets. Ready to get to work?"

After that unsubtle reminder of the reason she was here, Sheryl
could hardly say no. Pulling out one of the chairs, she rolled up to
the table.

"I'm ready."

"We pretty well took apart the postcard from Rio last night. Let's
start with the one from Pamplona today. We'll reverse the process
and work the front side first. Can you describe the scene?"

She shot him an amused glance.

"Of course you can," he answered himself. "You talk, I'll listen."

Summoning up a mental image of the card, Sheryl painted a vivid
word picture that included a narrow, cobbled street lined with two-
story stone houses. Geranium-filled window boxes. White-shirted
young men racing between the buildings, looking over their shoulders
at the herd of black bulls just visible at a bend in the street.

Harry copied down every word, so intent on searching for simi-
larities with the card from Rio that it was some time before he noticed
the subtle difference in Sheryl's voice. It sounded softer, he realized
in surprise, almost dreamy. He glanced up to find her staring at the

wall, her mouth curving slightly. She'd gotten lost somewhere on a high, sunny plain in Spain's Basque province.

Harry got a little lost himself just looking at her. The faint trace of freckles across the bridge of her nose fascinated him, as did the mass of tawny hair tumbling down her back. She'd pulled the hair at her temples back and caught it in one of those plastic clips with long, dangerous-looking teeth. His hand itched to spring the clip free, to let those curls take on a life of their own.

"There was a cathedral in the background," she murmured, drawing his attention away from the curve of her cheek. "An old Gothic cathedral complete with flying buttresses and a huge rose-colored window in the south transept. One of man's finest monuments to God."

Sighing, she shifted in her seat and caught Harry staring at her. "I've read a little bit about medieval Gothic cathedrals," she confessed with an embarrassed shrug. "Some people consider them the architectural wonders of the modern world."

"Have you ever been inside one?"

"No. Have you?"

He nodded. "Notre Dame."

"In Paris?"

Her breathless awe made Harry bite back a grin. He'd visited the majestic structure on a wet, dreary spring day. All he could recall were impenetrable shadows, cold dampness and thousands of votive candles flickering in the darkness. Of course, he was a marine gunny sergeant on leave at the time, and far more interested in the *filles de joie* working the broad embankments along the Seine than in the gray stone cathedral

"Maybe your sort-of fiancé will spring for a trip to Paris for a honeymoon," he commented casually.

He saw at once that he'd said the wrong thing. The soft, faraway look disappeared from her green eyes. She sat up, a tiny frown creasing her brow.

"Brian isn't interested in traveling, any more than I am. We prefer to save our money for something more practical, like a house or a new car or the kids' college education."

Without warning, a thought rifled through Harry's mind. If he wanted to stake his claim to a woman like this one, he'd whisk her off to a deserted island, peel off her clothes and make love to her a dozen times a day before either of them started thinking about a house and a new car and the kids' college education.

His belly clenched at the image of Sheryl sprawled in the surf, her tanned body offered up to the sun like a pagan sacrifice. Her arms reached for him. Her eyes...

Dammit!

A quick shake of his head banished the crashing surf. He had to remember why he was here. And that Sheryl was spoken for...almost. Pushing aside her vague relationship with the jerk who made appointments instead of dates, he brought them both back to the matter at hand.

"Let's talk about the message on the back."

She blinked at his brusque instruction, but complied willingly enough.

"As best I recall, it was short and sweet. 'Hi, Auntie. I've spent two great...'" She paused, chewing on her lower lip. "No, it was three. 'I've spent three great days keeping a half step ahead of the bulls. See you soon, Paul.'"

"Run it through your mind again," Harry ordered. "Close your eyes. See the words. Picture the—"

One of the phones on the table shrilled. He grabbed the receiver, listened for a few minutes and hung up with a promise to call back later.

"Close your eyes, Sheryl."

Obediently, she blanked out the chart-strewn walls.

"Visualize the words. Follow every curl of every letter. Describe them to me."

Like a dutiful disciple of a master mesmerizer, she let Harry's deep, slow voice lull her into a state of near somnolence. Slowly, lines of dark swirls began to take shape.

She didn't even notice when morning faded into afternoon, or when the uninspiring conference room began to take on an aura of a real live operations center. She did note that the phones rang constantly, and that a seemingly steady stream of people popped in to talk to Harry or pass information.

Sometime around the middle of the afternoon, the short, stocky Everett Sloan returned from Los Alamos Laboratories. Sheryl soon discovered that, unlike Harry, he was assigned to the Albuquerque office of the U.S. Marshals and had been tapped as the local coordinator for the task force. Shedding his wrinkled suit jacket, Ev informed his temporary partner that he'd collected more information than he'd ever wanted to know about the properties and characteristics of the heavy metal known as U-235.

A short time later, a slender, striking brunette in the brown shirt, gray pants and Smoky the Bear hat of a New Mexico state trooper joined the group. After brief introductions, Fay Chandler tossed her hat on the table and unrolled a huge aerial map showing every airstrip, paved or otherwise, within a hundred-mile radius. The three-letter designation code for each strip had been highlighted in yellow. If their suspect intended to bring his contraband in someplace other than Albuquerque International, Fay would coordinate the local response team.

In the midst of all this activity, Harry somehow remained focused on Sheryl and the postcards. After hours of work, he reduced the sheets of information he'd pulled from her to a few key words and phrases. He repeated them now in an almost singsong mantra.

"Rio...Carnival...April...four."

Sheryl picked up the chorus. "Pamplona...bulls...July... three."

"Prague...Wenceslas Square...September...two."

MacMillan stared at the words, as though the sheer intensity of his scrutiny would solve the riddle they represented. "I know there's a pattern in there somewhere. A reverse order of numbers or letters or something!"

"Maybe the computers will find it." Ev Sloan slid his thumbs under his flashy red-and-yellow Bugs Bunny suspenders to hitch up his pants. "I'll go down to the data center and plug the key words in. The airstrip designation codes, too. Be back in a flash with the trash."

Harry caught Sheryl's smile and put a more practical spin on Ev's blithe remark. "You'll think it's trash, too, when you see the endless combinations the computers will kick out. It'll take us the rest of the evening, if not the night, to go over them."

Sheryl's smile fizzled. Good grief! He hadn't been kidding about working day and night. She snuck a peek at the clock on the wall. It was after five. They'd worked right through lunch. The Diet Pepsis and bags of Krispy Korn Kurls Harry had procured from the vending machines down the hall had long since disappeared. Practical considerations such as real food and a cool shower and retrieving her car from the post office parking lot crept into Sheryl's mind.

As if to echo her thoughts, a loud, rolling growl issued from her tummy.

"I'm a creature of habit," she offered apologetically when Harry glanced her way. "I tend to crave food…real food…a couple of times a day."

He speared a look at the clock, then reached for the jacket he'd tossed over a chair back hours ago. "Sorry. I didn't intend to starve you. There's a decent Italian sub shop across the street. Ev, Fay, you two up for another round of green peppers and sausage?"

Ev shook his head. "I want to get the computers rolling. Bring me back a garlic sausage special."

"I'll pass, too," Fay put in. "My youngest has a T-ball game at six-thirty and I swore on his stack of Goosebumps that I'd make this one. I'll come back here after the game's over, Harry."

MacMillan shrugged into his jacket. "You've been at this hard for the past three days and nights. Relax and enjoy the game."

Laughing, Fay rerolled her aeronautical maps. "Your single status is showing, Marshal. Anyone with kids would know better than to advise a parent to relax at a T-ball game."

"I stand corrected."

So he was single. Without knowing why she did so, Sheryl tucked that bit of information away for future reference. She'd noticed that he didn't wear a wedding ring. A lot of men didn't, of course, but the confirmation that the marshal was neither married nor a parent added a new dimension to the man…and triggered a whole new set of questions in her mind. Was he divorced? Currently involved with someone? Seeing someone who didn't mind the fact that he spent almost all his time away from home, chasing fugitives?

Sheryl shook off her intense curiosity about the marshal with something of an effort. His personal life had nothing to do with her, she reminded herself, or with her part in his investigation. She shifted her attention to Fay, who winked and settled her hat on her sleek, dark hair.

"Some people think that high-speed chases in pursuit of fleeing suspects and cement-footed drunks are tough, but I'm here to tell you that keeping up with my four rug-rats takes a whole lot more stamina."

"I don't have any rug-rats at home, but I can imag—" Sheryl stopped abruptly, her eyes widening. "Oh, no! I do!"

"If you're referring to the obnoxious rodent you insisted on taking home with you," Harry drawled, "I can't think of a more perfect description."

She grabbed her purse, trying not to think of the damage the shih tzu might have done to her dining-room chairs and pale-mauve carpet during his long incarceration.

"I have to swing by the post office to get my car, then go home to let Button out," she said worriedly.

"Good enough. We can grab some dinner on the way."

The thought of sharing another meal with Harry sent a tingle of anticipation down Sheryl's spine......followed by an instant rush of guilt. Belatedly, she realized that she hadn't even thought of Brian since early morning. The marshal's forceful personality and fierce determination to bring Richard Johnson-Paul Gunderson to justice had swept her right into the stream of the investigation, to the exclusion of all else.

"I'd better pass on dinner, too," she said. "I'll grab a sandwich at home."

And call Brian.

The task force leader conceded the point with a small shrug. "Whatever works."

Just as well, Harry thought as he waited beside Sheryl for the elevator to the underground parking. This manhunt had consumed him for almost a year, yet today he'd had to fight to stay focused on the information his newest team member was providing. Harry knew damn well that Sheryl didn't have any idea of the way his muscles had clenched every time she'd leaned over to check his notes. Or the havoc she'd caused to his concentration whenever she'd stretched out those long, tanned legs. After almost eight hours of breathing her scent and registering every nuance in her voice and body language, Harry figured he'd better put some distance between them. He needed to regain his sharp-edged sense of purpose, which was proving more difficult than he would have imagined around Sheryl.

They turned into the Monzano station well after six. To the east, the jagged Sandia Mountains were beginning to take on the watermelon-pink hue that the Spaniards had named them for. To the west, the sun blazed a fiery gold above the five volcanoes that rose from the lava fields like stubby sentinels.

The station's front parking lot had long since emptied, and a high, sliding gate blocked the entrance to the fenced-in rear lot. Rows of white Jeeps with the postal service's distinctive red-and-blue markings filled the back parking area. Sheryl spied her ice-blue Camry at the far end of the lot.

"You can let me out here," she told Harry. "I have a key card to activate the gate. I'll see you back at the courthouse in an hour or so."

"I'll wait here until you drive out."

She didn't argue. Although the station was located in a quiet, residential neighborhood, it took in large amounts of cash every day. They'd never had a robbery at the Manzano station, but postal bulletins regularly warned employees to stay alert when coming in early or leaving late. After keying the gate, Sheryl waited while the metal wheels rattled and bumped across the concrete. Her footsteps made little sucking noises as she crossed asphalt still soft from the scorching afternoon sun.

She was almost to her car when she heard a clink behind her. It sounded as though someone or something had bumped into a parked Jeep. Sheryl glanced over her shoulder. Nothing moved except the elongated shadow that floated at an angle behind her. Frowning, she dug in her purse for her keys and wound through the last row of vehicles at a brisk pace. Relief rippled through her as she approached her trusty little Camry. When she got her first full look at the car, relief melted into instant dismay. The vehicle sat low to the ground. Too low. Keys in hand, Sheryl stood staring at its board-flat tires.

Slowly, she moved closer and bent to examine the front tire. It hadn't just gone flat, she saw with a sudden, hollow sensation. It had been slashed. She was still poking at the gaping wounds in the rubber with her finger when another sound cut through the stillness like a knife.

Her heart leaping into her throat, Sheryl spun around. The slanting rays of the sun hit her full in the face…and blurred the dark silhouette of the figure looming over her.

Chapter 5

"What the hell...?"

Sheryl recognized Harry's broad-shouldered form at almost the same moment his voice penetrated her sudden, paralyzing fear.

Without stopping to think, without taking a breath, she flowed toward him. She didn't expect him to curl an arm around her and draw her hard against his body, but she certainly didn't protest when he did. She closed her eyes, taking shameless comfort in his presence. It was a moment before she managed to murmur a shaky explanation.

"Someone slashed my tires."

"So I see," he rasped, his voice low and tight above her head. "I got antsy about letting you walk back here alone. Looks like I had reason to."

His muscles twisting like steel under her cheek, he turned to survey the parking lot and the wire fence surrounding it.

"Not a security camera in sight," he muttered in disgust.

Slowly, Sheryl disengaged from his hold. She was still shaken enough to miss the security of his arms, but not so much that she didn't realize the feel of his body pressed against hers wasn't helping her regain her equilibrium. Swallowing, she tried to steady her nerves while he completed a scowling survey of the area.

The vista on the other side of the fence didn't afford him any more satisfaction than the lack of outside cameras in the parking lot. A tumbleweed-strewn field cut by a jagged arroyo separated the station from the residential area. The landscape shimmered with a silvery beauty that only someone used to New Mexico's serene, natural emptiness could appreciate. At this moment, all Sheryl could think of was how easily someone could have crossed the emptiness and scaled the wire link fence.

Echoing her thoughts, Harry scanned the residences in the distance and shook his head. "Those houses are too far away for anyone to spot a fence climber. The post office should have better security."

"That's assuming whoever cut my tires climbed the fence. He could've just walked into the lot. With all the carriers coming and going, we don't keep the gates locked during the day."

"I know."

Belatedly, she remembered that Harry had driven in and out of those open gates with her several times. She wasn't thinking clearly, she realized.

He went down on one knee to examine the tires. "We're also assuming that an outsider caused this damage."

A new series of shocks eddied through Sheryl. "You can't think anyone at the post office would cut my tires like that."

He rose, dusting his hands. "Why not?"

"They're my friends as well as my co-workers!"

"All of them?"

"Well..."

She could name one carrier whose coarse, barroom style of humor had resulted in a couple of private and very heated discussions about what was considered acceptable language in the workplace. Then there was that temporary Christmas clerk who'd pestered her for dates long after she and Brian started seeing each other. Neither of those men had ever shown any animosity toward her, however. Certainly not the kind of animosity that would lead to something like this.

"Yes," she finished. "All of them."

Harry lifted a skeptical brow but didn't argue. "Well, I suspect you can't say the same about all of your customers."

"No." She shuddered, thinking of the thin, hostile doper who'd confronted her across the counter this morning. "I can't."

"That's why I followed you into the parking lot. I got to thinking about the crackhead who'd threatened you." He hesitated, then continued slowly. "I also got to thinking about the fact that right now you're my only link to Inga Gunderson's nephew."

Sheryl stared up at him in confusion. "What could that have to do with my slashed tires?"

"Maybe nothing," he answered, his face tight. "Maybe everything."

Before she could make any sense of that, he pulled out his phone. "Let's get the police out here to check the area before I call Ev."

Her mind whirling, Sheryl listened while he contacted the Albuquerque police and asked them to send a patrol car to the Monzano station right away. A moment later, he made a short, succinct call to his partner.

"Find out if the Gunderson woman contacted anyone other than her lawyer, or if she sent out any messages, written or otherwise. I want every second of her time accounted for since we brought her in yesterday afternoon."

Yesterday afternoon? Sheryl shook her head in disbelief. Was it only yesterday afternoon that she'd driven to Inga Gunderson's house, worried about the woman's well-being? Just a little more than twenty-four hours since she'd practically fallen into Harry MacMillan's arms? It seemed longer. A whole lot longer!

No wonder, considering all that had happened in those hours. She'd stood Brian up not once but twice. She'd gained a thoroughly obnoxious houseguest. She'd transitioned from postal clerk to task force augmentee without so much as five minutes' notice. And she'd just lost four tires that she'd planned to squeeze another thousand miles out of, despite the fact that the tread had pretty well disappeared. She was wondering if her insurance would cover the cost of replacements when she caught the tail end of Harry's conversation.

"Finish up at Miss Hancock's apartment. I'll call you when I get through." He snapped the phone shut.

"Finish up what at my apartment?"

"I'm going to follow you home after we get done here. I want to check your locks."

"Check my locks? Why?"

"Just in case the person who did this also knows where you live."

"Oh."

Harry's eyes narrowed at the sudden catch in her voice. Sliding the phone into his pocket, he nodded toward the loading dock.

"Let's wait over there, out of the heat."

Sheryl trailed beside him, but she didn't need the shade offered by the overhanging roof to cut the effects of the sun. The idea that the person responsible for the damage to her car might also know her home address had cooled her considerably. Harry's carefully neutral expression only added to that chill.

"I'm not trying to scare you," he said evenly, "but this wasn't a random act. The perpetrator didn't vandalize any of the other vehicles. Only yours."

"I noticed that."

"He could have done it out of spite." He slanted her a careful look. "Or he might have been trying to disable your car so you couldn't drive off when you came back to the post office…although there are certainly less obvious ways of doing that."

"For someone who isn't trying to scare me, you're doing a darn good job of it!"

"Sorry."

Blowing out a long breath, he tried to recover the ground he'd just lost.

"Look, all cops are suspicious by nature, and most of us are downright paranoid. I'm reaching here, really reaching, to even imagine a connection between this incident and the fact that Inga Gunderson knows you're providing us information about her postcards."

"I hope so!"

The near panic in her voice brought his brows down in a quick frown. Cursing under his breath, he backpedaled even more.

"I'll wait to see if the police can lift any prints from the car before I speculate any further. In the meantime, try to think of anyone who might hold a grudge against you or want to get even over something."

"Other than the creep this morning, I can't think of anyone. I lead a pretty quiet life aside from my work."

"That doesn't say a lot for your fiancé," MacMillan offered as an aside. "Correction, sort-of fiancé."

A tinge of heat took some of the chill from Sheryl's cheeks. "Brian and I are very comfortable together."

His brow went up. "That says even less."

"Yes, well, not everyone wants to go chasing all over the world after bad guys, Marshal. Some of us prefer a more settled kind of life, not to mention unslashed tires."

"We'll get the tires fixed and put a—"

He broke off, his head lifting at the sound of a siren in the distance. It drew closer, the wail undulating through the evening stillness. Sheryl gave a little breath of relief.

"They got here fast."

Harry pushed away from the dock. "That's one of the benefits of having a representative from the Albuquerque Police Department on the task force. Come on, let's go direct them to the crime scene."

Hearing her trusty little Camry described as a "crime scene" didn't exactly soothe the victim's ragged nerves. She trailed after MacMillan, sincerely wishing Mrs. Inga Gunderson had never brought her melt-in-your-mouth cookies and yappy little dog into the Monzano Street station.

The reminder that the yappy little dog had no doubt spent the day demolishing Sheryl's apartment didn't particularly help matters, either.

By the time the police finished their investigation of the scene and a twenty-four-hour roadside service had replaced the Camry's tires, the spectacular light show that constituted a New Mexico sunset had begun. The entire western horizon blazed with color. Streaks of pink and turquoise layered into vibrant reds and velvet purples. The sun hovered like a shimmering gold fireball just above the Rio Grande. As Sheryl drove up the sloping rise toward her east-side apartment with Harry following close behind, the city lights twinkled like earth-bound stars in her rearview mirror.

The serenity and beauty of the descending night helped loosen the tight knot of tension at the back of her neck. The police hadn't found anything that would identify the slasher. No prints, no footprints, no personal item conveniently dropped at the scene as so often occurred in movies and detective novels. The police had promised to canvas the houses that backed onto the fields around the station, but didn't hold out any more hope than Harry had that someone might have witnessed the vandalism. Tomorrow, they would interview Sheryl's co-workers. Rumors would speed like runaway roadrunners around the post office with this incident coming on top of her sudden detail. Elise must be wondering what in the world her friend had gotten herself into.

She'd call her tonight, Sheryl decided. And Brian. Despite the marshal's orders, she had to tell them something. They were her best friends.

When she caught her train of thought, Sheryl's hands tightened on the steering wheel. When had she started thinking of Brian as a friend, not a lover, for goodness' sake? And why did Harry's little editorial comments about their relationship raise her hackles?

Frowning, she waited for the easy slide of comfort that always accompanied any reminder of Brian and their future together. It came, but it brought along with it another traitorous thought. Was comfort really what she wanted in a marriage?

Oh, great! As if escaped fugitives, smuggled uranium and slashed tires weren't enough, Sheryl had to pick now of all times to question a relationship that she'd happily taken for granted until this minute.

The events of the past two days had rattled her, she decided. Both her home and her work schedule had been thrown off-kilter, as had the comfortable routine she and Brian had fallen into. As soon as she finished this detail and Harry MacMillan went chasing after his fugitive, her life would return to its normal, regular pace.

Sheryl pulled into her assigned parking slot, wondering why in the world the prospect didn't cheer her as much as it should have. A car door slammed in the area reserved for visitor parking, then Harry appeared beside the Camry. As he had before, he opened Sheryl's door and reached down a hand to help her out.

Oddly reluctant, she put her hand in his. The small electrical jolt that raced from her palm to her wrist to her elbow did *not* help resolve the confusion that welled in her mind. With a distinct lack of graciousness for the small courtesy, Sheryl yanked her hand free and led the way through the two-story adobe buildings.

While she fumbled through the keys for the one to her front door, Harry swept an appreciative eye around the tiled courtyard shared by the eight apartments in her cluster. Soft light from strategically placed luminaria bathed the little bubbling fountain and wooden benches carved with New Mexico's zia symbol. Clay pots spilled a profusion of flowers that hadn't yet folded their petals for the night. Their fragrance hung on the descending dusk like a gauzy cloud.

"This is nice," he commented. "Very nice. A place like this might tempt even me into coming home once in a while."

Once in a while.

The phrase echoed in Sheryl's head as she shoved the key into the lock. If she'd needed anything more to banish the doubts that had plagued her a few moments ago, that would have done it. She had no use for men who returned home every few weeks or months and stayed only long enough to get their laundry done.

"It's comfortable," she replied with deliberate casualness. "And I like the view. From the back patio, you can see— Oh, no!"

She halted in the entryway, aghast. Dirty laundry trailed in a colorful array from the foyer to the living room. Bras, panties, socks, tank tops and uniform shirts decorated the tiles, along with what looked like every shoe she owned.

"Button?" Harry inquired from behind her.

"No," Sheryl said in a huff. Slamming the door, she tossed her purse and her keys on the kitchen counter and bent to scoop up an armful of underwear. "This is the latest decorating scheme for working women who have to dress on the run."

"It works for me."

At his amused comment, she shot a glance over her shoulder. Her face heated when she spied the filmy, chocolate-and-ecru lace bra dangling from his hand. She'd splurged on the bra and matching panties just last week. As any woman who'd ever had to wear a uniform to work could attest, a touch of sinfully decadent silk under the standard, company-issued outer items did wonders for one's inner femininity.

"I'll take that." She snatched the bra out of his hand. "Why don't you wade through this stuff and go into the living room. Since we haven't heard a peep out of Butty-boo, he's obviously—"

"Butty-boo?"

"That's what Inga called him, among other, similarly nauseating names. He must be hiding." She started down the hall. "You check the living room. I'll check the bedroom."

She found the shih tzu stretched out in regal abandon on her bed. He'd made a nest of the handwoven Zuni blanket she used as a spread. His black-and-white fur blended in with the striking pattern on the blanket, and she might have missed him completely if he hadn't lifted his head at her entrance and given a lazy, halfhearted bark.

"That's it?" Sheryl demanded indignantly. "Two people walk into the house who could be burglars for all you know, and that's the best you can do? One little yip?"

In answer, Button yawned and plopped his head back down.

"Had a hard day, did you?"

Disgusted, she used one foot to right the overturned straw basket she used as a clothes hamper.

"Well, so did I, and I'm telling you here and now that I'd better not come home to any more messes like this one."

With that totally useless warning, Sheryl dumped her laundry in the basket and steeled herself to check the bathroom. To her surprise and considerable relief, Button had used the newspapers she'd spread across the tiles. She hoped that meant he hadn't also used the living-room carpet.

She took a few moments to swipe a little powder on her shiny nose and tuck some stray tendrils of hair back behind her ear, then headed for the living room. Button's black eyes followed her across the room. With another yawn and an elaborate stretch, he climbed out of his nest, leaped down from the bed and padded after her.

Sheryl had taken only a step or two into the living room when the dog gave a shrill bark that seemed to pierce right through her eardrums. Like a small, furry cannonball, Button launched himself across the mauve carpet at the figure jimmying the locks on the sliding-glass patio doors.

This time, Harry met the attack head-on. Jerking around, he growled at the oncoming canine.

"Take another bite out of my leg and you're history, pal!"

The shih tzu halted a few paces away, every hair bristling.

His target bristled a bit himself. "If it were up to me, you'd be chowing down at the pound right now, so back off. Back off, I said!"

Button didn't take kindly to ultimatums. His black lips drew back even farther. Bug eyes showed red with suppressed fury. The growls that came from deep in his throat grew even more menacing. Guessing that the standoff might break at any second, Sheryl hurried forward and scooped the dog into her arms.

"This is Harry, remember? He's one of the good guys. Well, not a good guy to you, since he sent your mistress off in handcuffs, but he's okay. Really."

Murmuring reassurances, she stroked the small, quivering bundle of fur.

"Helluva watchdog," the marshal muttered in disgust. "What was he doing back there, anyway? Trying on the rest of your underwear?"

Despite the fact that she herself didn't feel particularly benevolent toward the animal, Sheryl didn't have the heart to expose him to more criticism. Harry didn't need to know that Button had sprawled in indolent indifference while persons unknown had entered her apartment. Besides, the dog had leaped to the attack quickly enough once roused. Deciding to treat the marshal's question as rhetorical, she didn't bother to answer.

"How are the locks?"

"The dead bolt on the front door is sturdy enough. These patio doors are another story. If you don't mind, I'd like to get some security people up here to install a drop bar and kick lock, as well as a rudimentary alarm system. I'll have them wire your car while they're at it. They can be here in an hour or so."

"Tonight?"

"Tonight."

Sheryl's fingers curled into the dog's silky topknot. The fear that had gripped her for a few paralyzing moments in the parking lot reached out long tentacles once more. She shivered.

Harry's keen glance caught the small movement. He gave a smothered oath. "My paranoia's working overtime. The alarm probably isn't necessary, but I'd feel better with it in."

"Probably?" she repeated hollowly.

Harry cursed again and closed the short distance between them. Button issued a warning growl, which the marshal ignored. Lifting a hand, he smoothed an errant curl back from her cheek.

"I'm sorry, Sher. I didn't mean to scare you again."

The touch of his palm against her cheek startled Sheryl so much that she barely noticed his use of her nickname. She did, however, notice the tiny bits of gold warming his brown eyes. And the way his mustache thickened slightly at the corners, as if to disguise the small, curving laugh lines that appeared whenever his mouth kicked into one of his half-rogue, all-male grins.

The way it did now.

Except this grin was more rueful than roguish. It matched the look in his eyes, Sheryl thought, as his hand slid slowly from her cheek to curl back of her neck.

She shivered once more, but this time it wasn't from fear. This time, she realized with something close to dismay, it was from delight. Caught on a confusing cross of sensations, she could only stand and watch the way Harry's grin tipped from rueful into a smile that trapped her breath in the back of her throat.

He shouldn't do this! Harry's mind shouted the warning, even as his fingers got lost in the silky softness of her hair. He knew better than to mix business with personal desire. But suddenly, without the least warning, desire had grabbed hold of him and wouldn't let go.

She felt so soft. Smelled so intoxicating, a mixture of hot sun and powdery talcum, with a little shih tzu thrown in for leavening. She was also scared, Harry reminded himself savagely. Off balance from all that had happened in the past few days. Almost engaged.

Another man might have drawn back at that sobering thought. Someone else might have respected the territory this Brian character

had tentatively staked out. Instead of deterring Harry, the very neb-
ulousness of the other man's claim angered him. Any jerk who kept
a woman like Sheryl dangling in some twilight never-never land
didn't deserve her.

So when she didn't draw back, when her lips opened on a sigh
instead of a protest, Harry bent his head and brushed them with his
own. She tasted so fresh, so irresistible, that he brought his mouth
back for another sample.

The kiss started out slow and soft and friendly. Within seconds, it
powered up to fast and hard and well beyond friendship. A dozen
different sensations exploded in Harry's chest and belly. The urge to
pull Sheryl into his arms, to feel every inch of her against his length,
clawed at him. He started to do just that when another, sharper sensation bit into his lower right arm.

"Dammit!"

He jumped back, almost yanking the stubby little monster locked
onto his jacket sleeve out of Sheryl's arms. She caught the dog just
in time and held on to it by its rear legs. It hung there between them,
a growling, snarling mop with one end firmly attached to Harry's
sleeve and the other to the woman who held him.

"You misbegotten, mangy little..."

"He was just trying to protect me," Sheryl got out on a gasp. "I
think."

Harry thought differently, but he was too busy working his fingers
onto either side of the dog's muzzle to say so at that moment. Ex-
erting just enough pressure to spring those tiny, steel jaws open, he
pulled his coat sleeve free. He then reached over and extracted the
animal from Sheryl's unresisting arms.

Two long strides took him back to the sliding doors. A moment
later, the glass panel slammed shut. Buggy black eyes glared at him
from the outside. Ignoring the glare and the bad-tempered yips that
accompanied it, Harry turned back to Sheryl.

His fierce, driving need to sweep her into his arms once more took
a direct hit when he caught her expression. It held a combination of
regret and guilt...and not the least hint of any invitation to continue.

Chapter 6

"I'm sorry."

The apology came out with a gruffer edge than Harry had intended, for the simple reason that he couldn't think of anything he felt less sorry about than taking Sheryl into his arms. Yet that kiss ranked right up there among the dumbest things he'd ever done.

That said something, considering that he'd pulled some real boners in his life. Two in particular he'd always regret. The first was succumbing to a bad case of lust and marrying too young, much too young to figure out how to get his struggling marriage through the stress of his job. The second occurred years later, when he decided to take a few long-overdue days off to go fishing in Canada. That fateful weekend his best buddy was gunned down. By the time Harry had returned and taken charge of the operation to track down Dean's killers, the trail had gone stone cold.

Now it had finally heated up, and he couldn't allow himself to get sidetracked by a moss-eyed blonde who raised his blood pressure a half-dozen points every time she glanced his way. Nor, he reminded himself with deliberate ruthlessness, could he afford to confuse her by coming on to her like this. He needed her calm and rational and able to concentrate on the task she'd been detailed to do. She still had information Harry wanted to pull out of her.

"That was out of line," he admitted, less gruffly, more firmly. "It won't happen again."

"N-no. It won't."

The guilt in her voice rubbed him raw. Cursing the predatory instincts that had driven him to poach so recklessly on another man's territory, he tried to recapture her trust.

"I guess this damned investigation has sanded away the few civilized edges I possessed."

It had sanded away a few of Sheryl's edges, too. She couldn't remember the last time a kiss had seared her like that. Dazed, she struggled to subdue the runaway fire racing through her veins. A massive dose of guilt helped speed the process considerably.

She was almost engaged, for heaven's sake! How could she have just stood there and let Harry kiss her like that? How could she have been so shallow, so disloyal to Brian? She'd never even looked at another man in all the time they'd been seeing each other. What's more, she'd certainly never dreamed that a near stranger could generate this combination of singing excitement and stinging regret with just the touch of his mouth on hers. She stared at Harry, seeing her own consternation in his frown.

"We've got a good number of hours of work ahead of us yet," he got out curtly. "You can't concentrate if you're worried that I might pounce at any minute. I won't, I promise."

A small sense of pique piled on top of Sheryl's rapidly mounting guilt. She knew darn well she was as much to blame for what had just happened as Harry. Her instinctive, uninhibited response to his touch shook her to her core, and she didn't need him to tell her it wouldn't happen again. She wouldn't do that to Brian or to herself. Still, it rankled just a bit that the marshal regretted their kiss as much as she did, if for entirely different reasons.

Feeling flustered and thoroughly off balance, Sheryl had a need to put some distance between her and Harry. She moved into the kitchen, where she snatched up Button's plastic water dish and shoved it under the faucet to rinse it out.

"Why don't you head back downtown," she suggested with what

she hoped was a credible semblance of calm. "I'll follow after I feed Button, and we can put in a few more hours' work."

Harry looked as though there was nothing he'd like better than to get back to business, but he shook his head. "I'd like to stay here until the security folks arrive and do their thing, if you don't mind."

Sheryl stared at him while water ran over the sides of the dish. In the aftermath of his shattering kiss, she'd totally forgotten what had led up to it.

"No, of course I don't mind."

"I'll call them and get them on the way."

With brisk efficiency, he mobilized the necessary specialists. Another quick call alerted Ev to the fact that he'd have to scrounge his own dinner.

"I guess I could make us some sandwiches," Sheryl said slowly when he snapped the phone shut. "Or I could cook lemon chicken. I have all the fixings. We can eat and work while we wait."

The idea of preparing Brian's favorite meal for Harry disconcerted Sheryl all over again. Honestly, she had to get a grip here. Harry had certainly recovered his poise fast enough. He'd faced the awkwardness head-on and moved beyond it. She could do the same. Briskly, she swiped a paper towel around the bowl and filled it with the dried dog food she'd picked up yesterday.

"I'll feed Button and get something started."

"I have a better idea." Harry shrugged out of his coat, then rolled up his sleeves. "You feed the rodent while I pour you a glass of wine or whatever relaxes you. Then I'll cook the chicken."

"There's some wine in the fridge," Sheryl said doubtfully, "but you don't have to fix dinner."

"I don't have to, but I'd like to."

He flashed her a grin that strung her tummy into tight knots. Good grief, what in the world was the matter with her?

"Being on the road so much, I don't get to practice my culinary skills very often. But my ex-wife trained me well. She never opened a can or flipped on a burner when I was home."

"Well..."

He traded places with Sheryl, taking over the kitchen with an easy

competence that put the last of her doubts to rest. A quick investigation of her cupboards and fridge produced skillet, chicken, flour,
lemons, onions, cracked pepper, butter and a half-full bottle of chilled
Chablis.

While Harry assembled the necessary ingredients, Sheryl fed Button. Naturally, the dog displayed his displeasure over his banishment
to the patio by turning up his pug nose at the dry food. She left him
and his dinner outside, then occupied one of the tall rawhide-and-
rattan counter stools. Sipping slowly on the wine Harry had poured
for her, she tried to understand the welter of confused emotions this
man stirred in her.

She gave up after the second or third sip and contented herself
with just watching. He hadn't been kidding about his culinary skills.
Within moments, he had the floured chicken fillets sizzling in the
skillet. While they browned, he made short work of dicing the onion.
Seconds later, the onion, more butter and a generous dollop of Chablis went into the pan. Sheryl sniffed the delicious combination of
scents, conscious once more of the inadequacy of the Korn Kurls
she'd eaten for lunch.

"My compliments to your ex-wife," she murmured. "You really
do know your way around a kitchen."

"Unfortunately, cooking is my one and only domestic skill...or so
I've been told."

"How long were you married?" she asked curiously.

He squeezed a wedge of lemon over the chicken. The drops spurted
and spit in the hot pan, adding their tangy scent to the aroma of
butter and onions rising from the cooktop.

"Eight years by calendar reckoning. Three, maybe four, if you
count the time my wife and I spent at home together. She's an account executive for a Dallas PR firm now, but when we met she was
just starting in the business. Her job took her on the road as much
as mine did, and..."

"And constant absences don't necessarily make the heart grow
fonder," she finished slowly.

He shrugged, but Sheryl had been in this man's company enough
by now to catch the tight note in his voice. Harry MacMillan didn't

give up on anything easily, she now knew, whether it was a marriage or the relentless pursuit of a fugitive.

"Something like that," he concurred, sending her a keen glance through the spiraling steam. "You sound as though you've been there, too."

"In a way."

She traced a circle on the counter with her glass. She rarely spoke about the father whose absence had left such a void in her heart, but Harry's blunt honesty about his divorce invited reciprocation. Reluctantly, she shared a little of her own background.

"My father traveled a lot in his job, too. My mother stewed and fretted every minute he was gone, which didn't make for happy homecomings."

"I imagine not. Is he still on the road?"

"As far as I know. He and Mom divorced when I was six. He showed up for a Christmas or two, and we wrote each other until I was about ten. The letters got fewer and farther between after he took an overseas position. Last I heard, he was in Oman."

"Want me to track him down for you? It would only take a few calls."

He was serious, Sheryl saw with a little gulp.

"No, thanks," she said hastily. "I don't need him wandering in and out of my life anymore."

"Well, the offer stands if you change your mind," he replied, flipping the slotted wooden spoon into the air like a baton. He caught it with a smooth ripple of white shirt and lean muscle. "Do you have any rice in the cupboard? I'm even better at rice Marconi than lemon chicken."

"And so modest, too."

He grinned. "Modesty isn't one of the skills they emphasize in the academy. Relax, enjoy your wine and watch a master at work."

Maybe it was the Chablis. Or the sight of this tall, rangy man moving so matter-of-factly about her little kitchen. In any case, Sheryl relaxed, enjoyed her wine and managed to ignore the fact that the master chef sported a leather shoulder holster instead of a tall, white hat. Her prickly sense of guilt stayed with her, though, and kept her from completely enjoying the meal Harry served up with a flourish.

It also kept her on the other side of the dining-room table after they finished eating and got down to work. Button, released from his banishment, perched on the back of the sofa and watched the marshal with unblinking, unwavering hostility. With the wine and food to soothe the nerves made ragged by Harry's kiss, Sheryl was able to recall the details on several batches of postcards.

"Venice, the Antibes, Barbados." Harry tapped his pen on the tabletop. "You're sure the cards that arrived before the Rio set came from those three locations?"

"I'm sure. It's hard to mistake gondolas and canals. I remember Antibes because of the little gold emblem in the corner of the card that advertised the Côte d'Azur. And Barbados..."

Sheryl gazed at the wall, seeing in its wavy plaster a sea so polished it glittered like clear, blue topaz, and white beaches lined with banyan trees whose roots hung downward like long, scraggly beards.

"If the picture on the card came anywhere close to reality," she murmured, "Barbados must have the most beautiful beaches in the world."

Harry's pen stilled. Against his will, against his better judgment, he let his glance linger on Sheryl's face. Damn, didn't the woman have any idea what that soft, dreamy expression did to a man's concentration? Or how much of herself she revealed in these unguarded moments? Despite her assertions to the contrary, Harry suspected that the daughter had inherited more than a touch of her father's wanderlust. She tried hard to suppress it, but it slipped out in moments like this, when she mentally transported herself to a white sweep of beach.

Despite *his* intentions to the contrary, Harry mentally transported himself there with her.

The sound of a low, rumbling growl wrenched him back to Albuquerque. A quick look revealed that Button had shifted his attention from Harry to the front door. The dog's entire body quivered as he pushed up on all four paws and stared at the entryway. His gums pulled back. Another low growl rattled in his throat.

Carefully, Harry laid down his pen. "Are you expecting anyone?"

Sheryl's eyes widened at his soft query. Gulping, she shifted her gaze to the door. "No," she whispered.

"Stay here!"

Harry moved toward the door, his mind spinning with possibilities. The dog might have alerted on a neighbor arriving home. Maybe the security team was outside. Whoever it was, Harry had been a cop too long to take a chance on mights and maybes. He waited in the entryway, his every sense straining.

He heard no murmur of voices, no passing footsteps, no doorbell. Only Button's quivering growls...and a small, almost inaudible scrape.

Pulse pounding, back to the wall, Harry edged toward the door. With no side windows to peer out, he had to resort to the peephole. He made out a bent head, a pale blur of a shirt, a glint of moonlight on steel.

With a kick to his gut, he saw the dead bolt slowly twist.

His hand whipped across his chest. The Smith & Wesson came out of its leather nest with a smooth, familiar slide. He reached for the doorknob and waited until the dead bolt clicked open.

The knob moved under his palm. He exploded into action at the exact instant Button flew off the sofa, snarling, and Sheryl shouted at him.

"Harry! Wait!"

Her cry was still echoing in his ears when he yanked the door open with his free hand. A second later, the stranger standing on the other side of the door slammed up against the hallway wall. The Smith & Wesson dug into his ribs.

His cheek squashed into the plaster, the tall, slender man couldn't do much more than gape over his shoulder at his attacker.

"Wh— What's going on here?" he stuttered. "Who are you?"

In response, Harry torqued the stranger's arm up his spine another few inches. His adrenaline pumped like high-octane jet fuel. Button's high-pitched yaps scratched on his strung-tight nerves like fingernails on a chalkboard.

"You first," he countered roughly. "Who the hell are you?"

Before he got an answer, Sheryl locked both hands on his arm. "It's Brian," she shouted, yanking at his bruising hold. "Let go, Harry. It's Brian. Brian Mitchell."

Slowly, he released his grip and stepped back. Button didn't give up as readily. It took Sheryl's direct intervention before the still-snarling dog retired from the field. A good-sized strip of gray twill pants dangled from his locked jaws.

The two men faced each other, blood still up and faces flushed. Sheryl dumped the dog on the sofa and hurried back to calm the roiled waters.

"Brian, I'm so sorry! I didn't expect you, and it's been such a crazy day. Are you okay? Button didn't break the skin on your leg, did he?"

"No." Jaw clamped, the younger man watched his attacker holster his gun. "Who's this?"

"This is, er…" She turned, her face a study in frustration. "I can tell him, can't I?"

Harry took his time replying. Now that he knew the man didn't pose an immediate threat, his sharp-edged tension should have eased. Instead, Sheryl's fluttering and fussing raised his hackles all over again. It didn't take any great deductive skills to identify the man as Brian, her almost-fiancé.

Eyes glinting, he assessed the newcomer. An inch or two shorter than Harry's own six-one, he carried a good deal less weight on his trim frame. He also, the marshal noted, didn't take kindly to having his face shoved up against the wall.

"Elise said someone came into the station this morning and pulled you for a special detail. I take it this is the guy."

"Yes."

His gaze sliced from Sheryl to Harry. "Working kind of late, aren't you?"

She answered for them, a tinge of pink in her cheeks. "Yes, we are. Why don't you come in? I want to check your leg to make sure Button didn't do any serious damage."

Unmoving, Brian looked the marshal up and down. His lip curled. "I wouldn't have picked you for a shih tzu owner."

"You got that much right, anyway," Harry replied with a careless shrug. "I would have dumped the mutt in the pound. Sher insisted on bringing it home."

He used the nickname deliberately, not exactly sure why he wanted to get a rise out of the younger man. Whatever the reason, Brian's scowl sent a spear of satisfaction through his belly.

Sheryl listened to their terse exchange with increasing consternation flavored with a pinch of irritation. They sounded like two boys baiting each other. She could understand why Brian might feel antagonistic, given Harry's rough handling and his presence in her apartment so late at night, but she could do without the marshal's deliberate provocation.

"Let's go into the living room," she said firmly. "Harry will explain what we're doing while I check your leg."

The remains of the meal still sitting on the table didn't help matters, of course. Nor did the empty wine bottle on the kitchen counter. Frowning, Brian took in the littered table, the half-empty wineglasses and the dog once more stretched along the back of the sofa, his duty done. Slowly, he turned to face Sheryl.

"My leg's fine," he said quietly, all trace of antagonism gone now. "But I can certainly use a little explaining."

Before she could reply, Harry stepped forward. The gold star gleamed from the leather credentials case lying in his palm.

"I'm Deputy U.S. Marshal Harry MacMillan. Since Sheryl vouches for you, I'll tell you that I'm tracking a fugitive who escaped while being transported for trial a year ago. His trail led to Albuquerque and, obliquely, to the Monzano branch of the post office."

Brian's face registered blank astonishment, followed by swift concern. "Is this fugitive dangerous?"

"He's suspected of killing the marshal escorting him to trial."

"And you pulled Sheryl into a hunt for a cop killer?"

"I requested that she be assigned to my team, yes."

"Well, you can just unrequest her," Brian declared. "I don't want her taking part in any manhunt for a cop killer."

Sheryl gave a little huff of exasperation. "Ex-cuse me. I'm getting a little tired of this two-sided conversation. In case you've forgotten, this is my apartment and my living room, and it's my decision whether or not I'm going to work on this detail."

Brian conceded her point stiffly. "Of course it's your decision, but I don't like it. Aside from the possible danger, this detail of yours has already disrupted our schedule. I waited almost an hour for you yesterday afternoon, and we missed our Tuesday night together."

As she looked up into his gray eyes, Sheryl's momentary irritation disappeared, swept away by a fresh wave of guilt. She loved Brian. She'd loved him for almost a year now. Yet she'd gotten so caught up in Harry's investigation that she hadn't spared much thought to this kind, considerate man—until the marshal kissed her.

She felt a sudden, urgent need to fold herself into Brian's arms and feel his mouth on hers. She turned, offering Harry a forced smile. "Would you keep Button entertained for a few minutes? I'm going to walk Brian to his car."

"You stay here and talk," he countered. "Much as I hate to be seen in public with this sorry excuse for a dog, he can keep me company while I reconnoiter the outside layout for the security folks."

Sheryl grabbed the leash she'd purchased when she bought the dog food and shoved it in his hand gratefully. Frowning, Brian watched the oversized marshal depart with the undersized mop of fur at the end of a bright-red lead.

"Security folks?" he echoed as the door closed. "What security folks?"

Sighing, Sheryl abandoned her need to be held in favor of Brian's need to know. Taking a seat beside him on the sofa, she tucked a foot under her and recapped the events of the past few days. When she got to the part about the slashed tires, Brian voiced his growing consternation.

"At the risk of repeating myself, I have to say I don't like this. I wish you'd take yourself off this detail."

"We don't know that my slashed tires had anything to do with my participation on the task force. Anyone could have done it, but Harry insists it's better not to take chances. He's got a team coming out to install new locks and an alarm system."

"I still don't like it," Brian repeated stubbornly.

Sheryl bit back the retort that she'd didn't particularly like that part, either. She probably should feel flattered by Brian's protective streak. Instead, she resented it just a little bit. No, more than a little bit.

Suddenly, Sheryl remembered that she'd curled into Harry's side for protection only this afternoon, without feeling the least hint of resentment.

Guilt, confusion and a desperate need to reestablish her usual sense of comfortable ease with Brian brought her forward. Sliding her arms around his neck, she smiled up at him.

"I'm sorry you don't like it, and I appreciate your concern. I want to be part of this team, though. If I have any knowledge that could lead to the capture of a murderer, I have to share it. After this detail, we'll get back to our regular routine. I promise."

Conceding with his usual good-natured grace, he bent his head and met her halfway. Their mouths fit together with practiced sureness...and none of the explosive excitement that Sheryl had experienced only a half hour ago.

Dismayed, she rose up on her knees. Her body melted against Brian's. Her fingers tunneled through his hair. Brian was more than willing to deepen the embrace. His arms went around her waist, drawing her closer.

Afterward, she could never sort out whether he pulled back first or she did. Nor would she ever forget the look in his eyes. Puzzled. Surprised. Not hurt, but close. Too close.

"I guess I'd better leave," he said slowly. "So you and—what's his name?—Harry can get back to work."

When his arms dropped away, her ache spread into a slow, lancing pain. Deep within her, she knew that she would never find her usual comfortable satisfaction in his embrace again. She'd changed. Somehow, she'd become a different person.

She loved Brian. She would always love him. But she knew now that she'd mistaken the nature of that love. Comfort didn't form the basis for a marriage. Security couldn't ensure happiness. For either of them.

If nothing else, Harry's searing kiss had demonstrated that. Sheryl didn't fool herself that she'd fallen in love with Harry MacMillan, or even in lust. She'd barely known the man for thirty-six hours. Yet in that brief period, he'd knocked the foundations right out from under Sheryl's nice, placid existence.

Aching, she wet her lips and tried to articulate some of her confused thoughts.

"Brian..."

He shook his head. "I need to do some thinking. I guess you do, too. We'll talk about it when you finish this detail, Sher."

He pushed himself off the sofa. Miserable, Sheryl followed him to the door. He paused, one hand on the knob, as reluctant to walk out as she was to let him.

"Elise said you rescheduled your shopping expedition for a bassinet for tomorrow night. You need to call her if you're going to be working late again."

"I will." She grabbed at the excuse to delay his departure for another few moments. "Or maybe you could take her?"

He nodded. "Sure, if you can't make it. And don't forget to call your mother. You know she expects to hear from you every Thursday."

"I won't."

He opened the door, and a small silence fell between them. Sheryl felt her heart splinter into tiny shards of pain when he curled a hand under her chin.

"Bye, Sher," he said softly.

"Goodbye, Brian."

He tilted her head up for a final kiss.

Harry watched from the shadows across the courtyard. He needed to see this, he thought, his jaw tight. He needed the physical evidence of Brian's claim. Of Sheryl's affection.

It made Harry's own relationship with her easier, clearer, sharper. She was part of his team.

Nothing more.

Nothing less.

Which didn't explain why he had to battle the irrational temptation to unclip Button's leash and turn the man-eating fur ball loose on Brian Mitchell again.

Chapter 7

Sheryl walked into the task force operations center twenty minutes late on Thursday morning. A taut, unsmiling Harry greeted her.

"Where the hell have you been? I was about to send a squad car up to your place to check on you."

"Button set the darn alarm off twice before I figured out how to bypass the motion detectors."

The marshal bit back what Sheryl suspected was another biting comment about hairy little rodents. Instead, he raked her with a glance that left small scorch marks everywhere it touched her skin.

"Call in the next time you have a problem."

The curt order raised her brows and her hackles. "Yes, sir!"

Harry narrowed his eyes but didn't respond.

Tossing her purse onto a chair, Sheryl headed for the coffeepot in the corner of the conference room. She didn't know what had gotten into Harry this morning, but his uncertain mood more than matched her own. She felt grouchy and irritable and unaccountably off-kilter in the marshal's presence.

Much of her edginess she could ascribe to the fact that she hadn't gotten much sleep last night. She'd spent countless hours tossing and turning and thinking about Brian. She'd spent almost as many hours trying *not* to think about Harry's shattering kiss. She couldn't, wouldn't, allow herself to dwell on the sensations the marshal had roused in her, not when she owed Brian her loyalty.

To make matters even worse, Button had added his bit to her restless night. The mutt insisted on burrowing under the covers and curling up in the bend of her knees. Every time Sheryl had tried to straighten her legs, she'd disturbed his slumber...a move that Button didn't particularly appreciate. He'd voiced his displeasure in no uncertain terms. Between the dog's growls and her own troubled thoughts, Sheryl was sure she'd barely closed her eyes for an hour or so before the alarm went off.

Grumbling, she'd dragged out of bed, pulled on a pair of white slacks and a cool, sleeveless silk blouse in a bright ruby red, then grabbed a glass of juice and a slice of toast. She still might have made it down to the federal building by eight if she'd hadn't had to struggle with the unfamiliar alarm system. Twenty minutes and three calls to the alarm company later, she'd slammed the door behind her and headed for her car.

Her day hadn't gotten off to a good start, even before Harry's curt greeting. As she greeted the assembled team members, she guessed that it wouldn't get much better.

Crisp and professional in her New Mexico state trooper's uniform, Fay Chandler shook her head in response to Sheryl's query about her son's T-ball game.

"They got creamed," she said glumly. "I had to take the whole team for pizza to cheer them up. They perked up at the first whiff of pepperoni, but my husband was still moping when I left the house this morning. He's worse than my seven-year-old."

Folding her hands around the hot, steaming coffee, Sheryl took cautious injections of the liquid caffeine. She carried the cup with her to the conference table and greeted Everett Sloan. The poor man was almost buried behind a stack of computer printouts.

"Hi, Ev. Looks like you're hard at it already."

The short, barrel-chested deputy marshal waved a half-eaten chocolate donut. "'Hard' is the operative word. The computers crunched the numbers and words you gave us from the first set of postcards. Take a look at what they kicked out."

Sheryl's eyes widened at the row of cardboard boxes stacked along one wall, each filled with neatly folded printouts.

"Good grief! Do you have to go through all those?"

"Every one of them."

"What in the world are they?"

"We bounced the numbers and letters of the words you gave us against the known codes maintained by the FBI and Defense Intelligence Agency to see if there's a pattern. So far, no luck." Grimacing, he surveyed the boxes still awaiting his attention. "It'll take until Christmas to find a needle in that haystack…if there is one."

"We don't have until Christmas," Harry put in from the other end of the table. "We've got to break that code fast. We caught Inga Gunderson with her bags packed, remember? We have to assume the drop is scheduled for sometime soon…if it hasn't already gone down," he added grimly.

Fay hitched a hip on the edge of the conference table. "My bet is that Inga sent a message through her lawyer. She probably alerted either the sender or the receivers to the fact she's been tagged. If they didn't call off the shipment, they've no doubt diverted it to an alternate location."

Ev shook his head. "I know her lawyer. Several of us in the Albuquerque Marshals' office had to provide extra courtroom security when he defended one of his skinhead clients against a charge of communicating a threat against a federal law enforcement official. The scuzzball swore his buddies would blow up the Federal building if he was found guilty."

Since the Oklahoma City bombing, Sheryl knew, those threats were taken very, very seriously. She remembered the tension that had gripped the city during that trial.

"Don Ortega gave the guy one helluva defense," Ev continued, "but he told me afterward he fully expected to go up in smoke with his client. He's tough but straight. He wouldn't knowingly aid an escaped prisoner or contribute to the commission of a crime."

"But he might do it unknowingly," Fay argued. "Maybe Inga and company used some kind of a coded message. They're certainly handy enough at that sort of thing."

Ev shook his head emphatically. "Not Don. He's too smart to act as a courier for a suspected felon. Besides, the supervisor of the women's detention center swears Inga hasn't made any calls to anyone other than her attorney. So the odds are that the drop is still on…for a time we've yet to determine at a place we haven't identified."

"We'll identify both," Harry swore, his face as tight and determined as his voice. "Keep working those computer reports. If you don't find anything that makes sense, run them again with the day-month combinations for the next five days."

His partner groaned. "I'm going to need more energy for this."

Polishing off his donut, Ev dug another out of the box in the center of the table. While he munched his way through the report in front of him, Harry turned to the state trooper.

"I want you to drive out to all the airports we've IDed as possible landing sites. Talk to the Customs people and airport managers personally. Ask them to info us on any flight plans with South America as originating departure point or cargo manifests showing transport from or through Rio. Also, tell them to notify us immediately of any unscheduled requests for transit servicing on aircraft large enough to carry this kind of a cargo load."

Fay reached for her Smoky the Bear hat. "Will do, Chief."

Topping off his coffee, Harry walked back to his seat. "All right, Sheryl, let's get to work."

She shot him a quick glance as she settled in the chair next to his. He'd shed his jacket, but otherwise wore his standard uniform of boots, jeans and button-down cotton shirt, this one a soft, faded yellow. His clean-shaven jaw and neatly trimmed mustache looked crisply professional, but the lines at the corners of his eyes and mouth suggested that he'd hadn't slept much more than she had.

No doubt his investigation had kept him awake. It certainly seemed to consume him this morning. He gave no sign that he even remembered brushing a hand across her cheek last night or sending her into a shivering, shuddering nosedive with the touch of his mouth on hers. Not that Sheryl wanted him to remember, of course, any more than she wanted him to kiss her again.

Not until she'd sorted out her feelings for Brian, anyway.

"Where do you want to start?" she asked briskly.

"Let's go over the wording from the Venice-Antibes-Barbados cards again. Start with Barbados."

"Fine."

They worked for several hours before Harry was satisfied that he'd extracted all the information he could on that set of postcards. After sending the key words down to the computer center for analysis, they moved on to other cards that had arrived during Inga Gunderson's four months in Albuquerque. The further back Sheryl reached into her memory, the hazier the dates and stamps and messages got. The scenes on the front side of the cards remained vivid, however.

"Give me what you can on this one from Heidelberg," Harry instructed.

"It came in early April, a week or so before the fifteenth. I remember that much, because it provided such a colorful counterpoint to all the dreary income tax returns we had to sort and process."

Harry scribbled a note. "Go on."

"It was one of my favorites. It had four different scenes on the front. One showed a fairy tale castle perched above the Neckar River. Another depicted the old bridge that spans the river. Then there was a group of university students lifting their beer steins and singing, just like Mario Lanza and his friends did in the *Student Prince*."

At the other end of the table, Ev groaned. "Mario Lanza and the *Student Prince*. I can just imagine what the computers will do with that one!"

Harry ignored him. "What about the fourth scene?"

"That was the best." Sheryl assembled her thoughts. "It showed a monstrous wine cask in the basement of the castle. According to Paul's note, the cask holds something like fifty thousand gallons. Supposedly, the king's dwarf once drained the whole thing."

Harry stared at her. A slow, almost reluctant approval dawned in his eyes, warming them to honey brown. "Fifty thousand gallons, huh? That gives us an interesting number to work with. Good going, Sher."

For the first time that morning, Sheryl relaxed. A sense of partnership, of shared purpose, replaced her earlier irritation with Harry's brusque manner. When he wasn't glowering at her or barking out orders, the marshal had his own brand of rough-edged charm.

As she'd discovered last night.

From the other end of the table, Ev whistled softly. "How the heck can you remember that kind of detail?"

"A good memory is one of the primary qualifications for a postal worker," she replied, smiling. "Especially those of us who are scheme qualified."

"Okay, I'll bite. What's 'scheme qualified'?"

"Although I primarily work the front counter, I'm also authorized to come in early and help throw mail for the carrier runs. Everything arrives in bulk from the central distribution center, you see, then we have to sort it by zip."

"I thought you had machines to do that."

"I wish!" Sheryl laughed. "No, most of the mail is hand-thrown at the branch level. I worked at two different Albuquerque stations before I moved to the Monzano branch. I can pretty well tell you the zip for any street you pick out of the phone book," she finished smugly.

"No kidding?"

Ev looked as though he wanted to put her to the test, but Harry intervened.

"Unless they're pertinent to this investigation, I'm not interested in any zips but the ones on these postcards. Let's get back to work."

"Yes, sir!" Ev and Sheryl chorused.

Harry grilled her relentlessly, extracting every detail she could remember about Mrs. Gunderson's correspondence and then some. They worked steadily, despite constant interruptions.

The phones in the task force operations center rang frequently. In one call, the DEA advised that the informant who'd tipped them to Paul and Inga Gunderson had just come up with another name. They were working to ID the man now. Just before noon, the CIA came back with an unconfirmed field report that six canisters of depleted uranium had indeed passed through Prague four days ago. Their contact was still working Pamplona and Rio to see if he could pick up the trail. His face alive with fierce satisfaction, Harry reported the news to his small team.

"Hot damn!" Ev exclaimed. "Prague! Good going, Sheryl."

A thrill shot through her. She couldn't believe the information she'd provided only yesterday had already borne fruit. Her eyes met Harry's above his latest ream of notes.

"I owe you," he said quietly. "Big time."

Her skin tingled everywhere his gaze touched it. She smiled, and answered just as softly.

"All in the line of duty, Marshal."

The call that came in from their contact in the APD a little later took some of the edge off Sheryl's sense of satisfaction. The police hadn't turned up any leads regarding her slashed tires, nor had they located the man who'd hassled her yesterday morning over his girl-friend's welfare check. The woman had moved, and none of the neighbors knew her or her boyfriend's current address.

"They're going to keep working it," Harry advised.

"I hope so."

In addition to the many incoming calls, the task force also had a number of visitors, including the deputy U.S. district attorney work-ing the charges against Inga Gunderson. Harry and Ev conferred with the man in private for some time. Just before noon, the three of them went downstairs for Inga Gunderson's custody hearing. The marshals returned an hour later, elated and more determined than ever. The government's lawyer had convinced the judge to hold Inga pending a grand-jury review of the charges against her, they reported. The good guys had won another two, possibly three days while the woman remained in custody.

"That's great for you," Sheryl said with a sigh, "but it looks like I've got Button for at least two, possibly three, more days."

"There's always the pound," Harry reminded her.

When she declined to reply, Ev picked up on the conversation.

"Inga's attorney asked about the dog. Said his client was worried about her precious Butty-Boo. We assured him the mutt was in good hands." His pudgy face took on a thoughtful air. "Maybe we should check the mutt out again."

Harry's head jerked up sharply. "You said you went over him while we were at Inga's house."

"I took his collar apart and searched what I could of his fur without losing all ten of my fingers. I might have missed something."

"Great."

"Or he could be carrying something internally," Ev finished with a grimace. He eyed the other marshal across the table. "I'll let you handle this one, MacMillan. You lugged the mutt around under your arm for most of yesterday. He knows you."

"I've done a lot of things in the pursuit of justice," Harry drawled, "but I draw the line at a body cavity search of a fuzz ball with teeth. If you don't mind giving me your house keys and the alarm code, Sheryl, I'll send a squad car out to pick him up and take him to the vet who works the drug dogs. He's got full X-ray capability."

Sheryl dug her keys out of her purse, then passed them across the table. Poor Button. She suspected he wouldn't enjoy the next hour or so. Neither would the vet.

Harry dispatched the squad car, resumed his seat next to hers and reviewed his notes. "Okay, we've got details on eight postcards now. Can you remember any more?"

Sheryl sorted through her memory. "I think there were two, perhaps three, more."

They worked steadily for another hour. A uniformed police officer returned Sheryl's keys and a report that the dog was clean. Fay Chandler called in from Farmington, where she was waiting for the manager of the local airport to make an appearance. Ev went downstairs to confer with his buddies in the computer center.

Finally, Harry leaned back in his chair and tapped his stub of a pencil on his notes. "Well, I guess that's it. We've covered the same ground three times now, with nothing new to add to our list of key words or numbers."

"I wish I could remember more."

"You've given us and the computer wizards downstairs enough to keep us busy the rest of the night. If we don't break whatever code these cards carried, it won't be from lack of trying."

Feeling oddly deflated now that she'd finished her task, Sheryl swept the empty conference room with a glance. After only two days, the litter of phones and maps and computerized printouts seemed as familiar to her as her own living room.

"Do you need me for anything else?"

Harry's gaze drifted over her face for a moment. "If...when...we make sense of what you've told us, I'll give you a call. We might need you to verify some detail. In the meantime, I want you to stay alert...and let me know if any more postcards show up, of course."

"Of course."

"Preferably *before* you return them to sender."

"We'll try to be less efficient," she said gravely.

A small silence gripped them, as though neither wanted to make the next move. Then Harry pushed back his chair.

"I know I've put you through the wringer for the past couple of days. I appreciate the information you've provided, Sheryl. I'll make sure the postmaster knows how much."

He held out his hand. Hers slipped into it with a warm shock that disturbed her almost as much as the realization that she might not see him again after today.

"You'll let me know when...if...Inga gets out of custody, so I can send Button back to her?"

"I will, although if I have my way, that won't occur for seven to ten years, minimum."

"Well..." She tugged her hand free of his.

"I'll walk you down to your car."

Their footsteps echoed in the tiled corridor. Side by side, they waited for the elevator.

Why couldn't he just let her go? Harry wondered. Just let her walk away? There wasn't any need to prolong the contact. He'd gotten what he wanted out of her.

No, his mind mocked, not quite all he wanted.

With every breath he drew in he caught her scent and knew he wanted more from this woman. A lot more. He'd spent most of last night thinking about the feel of her mouth under his, tasting again her wine-flavored kiss. And most of today trying not to notice how her tawny hair curled at her temples, or the way her red silk blouse showed off her golden skin.

If Harry hadn't witnessed the scene in her doorway last night, he might have come back to Albuquerque after he cornered his quarry and given this Brian character a run for his money. But the aching tenderness in Sheryl's face when she'd bid her almost-fiancé good-night had killed that half-formed idea before it really took root. His predatory instincts might allow him to challenge another male for a woman's interest, but he wouldn't loose those instincts on one so obviously in love with another man…as much as he burned to.

The elevator swooshed open, then carried them downward in a smooth, silent descent. With a smile and a nod to the guard manning the security post, Harry escorted Sheryl to the underground parking garage.

Her little Camry sat waiting in the numbered slot Harry had arranged for her. She deactivated the newly installed alarm with the remote device, unlocked the door and tossed her purse inside. Then she unclipped her temporary badge and handed it to him.

"I guess I won't need this anymore."

His hand fisted over the plastic badge. "Thanks again, Sheryl. You've given me more to work with than I've had in almost a year."

"You're welcome."

Let her go! Dammit, he had to let her go! Deliberately, he stepped back.

"I'll keep you posted on what happens," he said again, more briskly this time. "And what to do with Button."

She took the hint and slid into the car. "Thanks."

Harry closed the door for her and stood in a faint haze of exhaust while Sheryl backed out of the slot and drove up the exit ramp. Turning on one heel, he returned to the conference room.

He made a quick call to the task force's contact in the APD to confirm that they'd keep an eye on the Monzano Street station and Miss Hancock's apartment for the next few days. Then he got back to the glamorous, adventurous work of a U.S. marshal.

"All right, Ev, let me have some of those computer printouts."

They worked until well after midnight. Wire tight from the combination of long hours and a mounting frustration over his inability to break the damned code of the postcards, Harry drove to his motel just off of I-40.

The door slammed shut behind him. The chain latch rattled into place. The puny little chain and flimsy door lock wouldn't keep out a determined ten-year-old, but the .357 Magnum Harry slid out of its holster and laid on the nightstand beside his bed provided adequate backup security.

Enough light streamed in through curtains the maid had left open to show him the switches on the wall. He flicked them on, flooding the overdone Southwestern decor with light. The garish orange-and-red bedspread leaped out at him. Decorated with bleached cattle skulls, tall saguaro cacti and stick figures that some New York designer probably intended as Kachinas, it was almost as bad as the cheap prints on the wall. The room was clean, however, which was all Harry required.

He closed the curtains and headed for the shower, stripping as he went. Naked, he leaned back against the smooth, slick tiles and let the tepid water sluice over him.

They were close. So damned close. He and Ev had winnowed the thousands of possible combinations of letters and numbers on the postcards down to a hundred or so that made sense. Tomorrow, they'd go over those again, looking for some tie to the local area, some key to a date, a time, a set of coordinates.

They'd worked hard today. Tomorrow, they'd work even harder. The drop had to happen soon. If Paul Gunderson had passed the stuff through Prague four days ago and was triangulating the shipment through Spain and Rio, he had to bring it into the States any day now. Any hour.

Frustration coiled like a living thing in Harry's gut. Prague. Pamploma. Rio. At last he had a track on the bastard. He wouldn't let him slip through his fingers this time.

He lifted his face to the water, willing himself to relax. He needed to clear his mind, so he could start fresh in a few hours. He needed sleep.

Not that there was much chance of that, he acknowledged, twisting the water off. If last night was any indication, he'd spend half of tonight trying not to think of Sheryl Hancock naked and heavy eyed with pleasure from his kisses, the other half thoroughly enjoying the image.

He slung a towel around his neck and padded into the bedroom. Just as well she had such an amazing memory, he thought grimly. Two days in her company had done enough damage to his concentration. Tomorrow, at least, he wouldn't have to battle the distraction of her smile and her long, endless legs.

Harry almost succeeded in putting both out of his mind. After a short night and a quick breakfast of coffee and *huevos rancheros* in the motel's restaurant, he entered the conference room just after six. Ev arrived at six-thirty, Fay a little later. They slogged through the remaining reports for a couple of hours and had just been joined by an FBI agent with a reputation as an expert in codes and signals when one of the phones rang.

Impatiently, Harry snatched it up. "MacMillan."

"This is Officer Lawrence with the APD. I have a note here to keep you advised of any unusual activity at the Monzano Street post office."

He went still. "Yes?"

"A call came into 911 a few minutes ago, requesting an ambulance at that location."

Ev's desultory conversation with the FBI agent faded into the background. Harry gripped the phone, his eyes fixed on an aeronautical map tacked to the far wall.

"For what reason?"

"I didn't get the whole story. Only that they needed an ambulance to transport a white female to the hospital immediately."

"Did you get a name?"

"No, but I understand it's one of the employees."

His pulse stopped, restarted with a sharp, agonizing kick. "What hospital?"

"University Hospital at UNM."

In one fluid motion, Harry slammed the phone down, shoved back his chair and grabbed his jacket. Throwing a terse explanation over his shoulder to the others, he raced out of the conference room.

Chapter 8

Sheryl called in to work early the next morning to let her supervisor know that Harry had released her from the special task force. Things were quiet for a Friday, Pat Martinez informed her. The temp had her counter station covered, but they could use her help throwing mail on the second shift.

Feeling an unaccountable lack of enthusiasm for a return to her everyday routine, Sheryl decided to run a few errands on her way in. She indulged Button with a supply of doggie treats and herself with a new novel by her favorite romance author before pulling into the parking lot of the Monzano Street station.

The moment she walked through the rear door and headed for the time clock, Sheryl got the immediate impression that things were anything but quiet. Tension hung over the back room, as thick and as heavy as a cloud. The mail carriers who hadn't already started their daily runs crowded around the station supervisor's desk. In the center of the throng, Pat paced back and forth with a phone glued to her ear, her face grave as she spoke to the person on the other end. Peggy, who should have been on the front counter with Elise, was hunched on a corner of Pat's desk. Even Buck Aguilar stood with arms folded and worried lines carved into his usually impassive face.

Sheryl punched in and wove her way through the work stations toward the group clustered around Pat. The station manager's worried voice carried clearly in the silence that gripped her audience.

"Yes, yes, I know. I'll try to reach her again. Just keep us posted, okay?"

The receiver clattered into its cradle.

"They don't know anything yet," she announced to the assembled crowd. "Brian's going to call us as soon as he gets word."

"Brian?" Sheryl nudged her way to the front. "What's Brian going to call about?"

"Sheryl!" Pat sprang up, relief and worry battling on her face. "I've been trying to reach you since right after you called to tell me you were coming in this morning."

"Why? What's going on?"

"Elise fell and went into labor."

"Oh, no!" A tight fist squeezed Sheryl's heart. "Is she okay? And the baby?"

"We don't know. They took her to the hospital by ambulance an hour ago. She was frantic that we get hold of you, since you're her labor coach. I tried your house, then Brian's office, thinking he might know where you were. He didn't, but he went to University Hospital to stay with Elise until we found you."

"Get hold of Brian at the hospital," Sheryl called, already on the run. "Tell him I'll be there in fifteen minutes."

It took her a frustrating, anxious half hour.

She sped down Juan Tabo and swung onto Lomas quickly enough, only to find both westbound lanes blocked by orange barrels. A long line of earthmovers rumbled by, digging up big chunks of concrete. Dust flew everywhere, and Sheryl's anxiety mounted by the second as she waited for the last of them to pass. Even with one lane open each way, traffic crawled at a stop-and-go, five-mile-an-hour pace.

Cursing under her breath, she turned off at the next side street and cut through a sprawl of residential neighborhoods. The Camry's new tires squealed as she slowed to a rolling stop at the stop signs dotting every block, then tore across the intersections. By the time the distinctive dun-colored adobe architecture of the University of New Mexico came into view, she trembled with barely controlled panic.

Elise wasn't due for another two weeks…if then. The baby's sonogram had showed it slightly undersized, and the obstetrician had revised the due date twice already. With the stress of her divorce coming right on top of the discovery that she was pregnant, Elise hadn't been vague about the possible date of the baby's conception. She and Rick had split up and reconciled twice before finally calling it quits. She could have gotten pregnant during either one of those brief, tempestuous reconciliations.

And Pat had said that Elise had fallen! Every time Sheryl thought of the hard, uncarpeted tile floors at the post office, the giant fist wrapped a little tighter around her heart. Offering up a steady litany of prayers for Elise and her baby, she squealed into the University Hospital parking lot, slammed out of the Camry, and ran for the multistory brown-stucco building.

Since she and Elise had toured the facility as part of their prenatal orientation, she didn't need to consult the directory or ask directions to the birthing rooms. The moment the elevator hummed to a stop on the third floor, she bolted out and ran for the nurses' station in the labor and delivery wing.

"Which room is Mrs. Hart in? Is she all right? I'm her birthing partner—I need to be with her."

A stubby woman in flowered scrubs held up a hand. "Whoa. Slow down and catch your breath. Mrs. Hart's had a rough time, but the hemorrhaging stopped before she went into hard labor."

"Hemorrhaging! Oh, my God!"

"She's okay, really. Last time I checked, she was about to deliver."

"Which room is she in?"

The nurse hesitated. "You'll have to scrub before you can go in, but I'm not sure it's necessary at this point. Her husband's with her. From what I saw a little while ago, he's filling in pretty well as coach."

Sheryl's brows shot up. "Rick's here?"

"I thought he said his name was Brian."

Belatedly, Sheryl remembered the hospital rule restricting attendance in the birthing room during delivery to family members and/ or designated coaches.

"We, er, call him 'Rick' for short. Look, I won't burst in, I promise, but I need to be with Elise. Where can I scrub?"

"I'll show you."

A few moments later, a gowned-and-masked Sheryl entered the birthing sanctuary. Doors on either side of the long corridor revealed rooms made homelike by reclining chairs, plants, pictures and low tables littered with magazines. Most of the doors stood open. Two were shut, including Elise's. Mindful of the nurse's injunction, she approached it quietly.

An anguished moan from inside the room raised the hairs on the back of her neck. She nudged the door open an inch or two, and stopped in her tracks.

A trio of medical specialists stood at the foot of the bed, poised to receive the baby. Brian leaned over a groaning, grunting Elise. At least, she thought it was Brian. He was gowned and masked and wearing a surgical cap to keep his auburn hair out of his eyes, and she barely recognized him. She recognized his voice, though, as hoarse and ragged as it was.

"You're doing great. One more push, Elise. One more push."

Sweat glistened on his forehead. His right hand clenched the laboring woman's. With his left, he smoothed her damp hair back from her forehead.

"Breathe with me, then push!"

"I...can't."

"Yes, you can."

"The baby's crowning," the doctor said from the bottom of the bed. "We need a good push here, Mom."

"Breathe, Elise." The command came out in a desperate squeak. Brian swallowed and tried again. "Breathe, then push. Puff. Puff. Puff."

"Puff. Puf...arrrgh!" Elise lifted half off the mattress, then came down with a grunt. Limp and panting, she snarled out a fervent litany.

"Damn Rick! Damn all men! Damn every male who ever learned how to work a zipper!"

Startled, Brian drew back. Elise grabbed the front of his gown and dragged him down to her level.

"Not you! Oh, God, not you! Don't... Don't leave me, Brian. Please, don't leave me."

"I won't, I promise. Now push."

Sheryl peered through the crack in the door, her heart in her throat. After sharing the ups and downs of her friend's divorce and training with her for just this moment, she longed to rush into the room, shove Brian aside and take Elise's hand to help her through the next stage of her ordeal. But her friend's urgent plea and Brian's reply kept her rooted in place. The two of them had bonded. The drama of the baby's imminent birth had forged a link between them that Sheryl couldn't bring herself to break or even intrude on.

"The head's clear," the doctor announced calmly. "Relax a moment, Mom, then we'll work the shoulders. You're doing great. Ready? Okay, here we go."

Sheryl felt her own stomach contract painfully as Elise grunted, then gave a long, rolling moan.

"We've got him."

One of the nurses smiled at the two anxious watchers. "He's a handsome little thing! The spitting image of his dad."

Brian started, then grinned behind his mask. With a whoop of sheer exhilaration, he bent and planted a kiss on Elise's forehead.

She used her death grip on the front of his hospital gown to drag him down even farther. Awkwardly, Brian took her into his arms. She clung to him, sobbing with relief and joy. A second later, the baby gave a lusty wail.

"Don't relax yet," the doctor instructed when Elise collapsed back on the bed, wiped out from her ordeal. "We've still got some work to do here."

Elated, relieved and hugely disappointed that she hadn't participated in the intense drama except as an observer, Sheryl watched Brian smooth back Elise's hair once more. A fierce tenderness came over the part of his face that showed above the mask. The sheer intensity of his expression took Sheryl by surprise. Swiftly, she thought back through the months she and Brian had been dating. She couldn't ever remember seeing him display such raw, naked emotion.

The realization stunned her and added another layer to the wrenching turmoil that had plagued her for two nights now. If she'd had any doubts about the decision she'd made in the dark hours just before dawn this morning, she only needed to look at his face to know it was the right one.

She loved Brian, but she wasn't *in* love with him. Nor, apparently, was he in love with her. Never once had she roused that kind of intense emotion in him. Never had she caused such a display of fierce protectiveness.

Slowly, Sheryl let the door whisper shut and backed away...or tried to. A solid wall of unyielding flesh blocked her way. Turning, she found herself chest to chest with Marshal MacMillan.

"Harry!" She tugged off her face mask. "What are you doing here?"

"I got word that EMS was transporting a female employee from the Monzano Street post office to the hospital. I thought..."

A small muscle worked on one side of his jaw. He paused, then finished in a voice that sounded like glass grinding.

"I thought it might be you."

"Oh, no! Did you think the slasher had come back?"

"Among other things," he admitted, taking Sheryl's elbow to move her to one side as an orderly trundled by with a cart. "By the time EMS verified the patient's identity, I was already in the parking lot, so I came up to see what the problem was."

"Did they tell you? My friend Elise fell and went into labor."

He nodded. "They also told me you were on the way down here, so I waited. How's she doing?"

Sheryl relaxed against the hallway wall, strangely comforted by Harry's presence. "Okay, I think. She and the baby both."

"Good! The nurse said her husband was in with her. From the glimpse I had over your shoulder a moment ago, he's certainly a proud papa."

"Well, there's a little mix-up about that: Elise is divorced. I was supposed to act as her coach, but I didn't get here in time, so Brian filled in for me.''

"Brian?" A puzzled frown flitted across his face. "That was your Brian in there?"

So Harry had seen it, too. The raw emotion. The special bond Brian had forged with Elise.

Sheryl fumbled for an answer other than the one her aching heart supplied. No, he wasn't her Brian. Not any more. Maybe he never had been. But until she talked to him, she wouldn't discuss the matter with anyone else.

Thankfully, one of the nurses walked out of Elise's room at that moment and spared her the necessity of a reply. Sheryl sprang away from the wall and hurried toward her.

"Is everything okay? How are Elise and the baby?"

"Mother and son are both fine," she answered with a smile. "And Dad's so proud, he's about to pop. Give them another few minutes to finish cleaning up, then you can go in."

Their voices must have carried to the occupants of the birthing room, because Brian came charging out a second later. His dark-red hair stuck straight up in spikes. The hospital gown had twisted around his waist. Huge, wet patches darkened his underarms and arrowed down his chest. Sheryl had never seen him looking so ruffled...or so excited.

"Sher! You missed it!" He tore off his mask. "It was so fantastic! Elise is wonderful. And the baby, he's...he's wonderful!"

"Yes, I..."

"Look, can you call the school? Elise is worried about the boys. Tell them I'll pick them up this afternoon and bring them down to see their new brother."

"Sure, I—"

"Thanks! I have to go back in. The doc says it'll be a few minutes yet before you can come in. You, too..."

He blinked owlishly, as if recognizing for the first time the man who stood silently behind Sheryl. If Brian wondered why Harry had turned up at the hospital, he was too distracted to ask about it now.

"You, too, MacMillan."

He turned away to reenter the birthing room, then spun back. "You're never going to believe it, Sher! He's got my hair. Elise's is sort of sorrel, but this little guy has a cap of dark red fuzz." He grinned idiotically. "Just like mine."

"Brian!" Sheryl caught him just before he disappeared. "Do you want me to call your office? If you're going to pick the boys up from school, should I tell your secretary to reschedule your afternoon appointments?"

He flapped a hand. "Whatever."

The door whirred shut behind him.

"Well, well," Harry murmured in the small, ensuing silence. "Is that the same man who had to schedule everything, even his meetings with his almost-fiancée?"

"No," Sheryl answered with a sigh. "It isn't."

Turning, she caught a speculative gleam in the marshal's warm brown eyes. Unwilling to discuss her relationship with Brian until she'd had time to talk to him, she deliberately changed the subject.

"If you want to go in and see Elise and the baby, I'll show you where to find a gown and mask."

"I'd better pass. They don't need a stranger hovering over them right now."

"No, I guess not."

She hesitated, torn between the need to join Elise and a sudden, surging reluctance to say goodbye to Harry for the second time in as many days.

"Thanks for coming down to check on me, even if it wasn't me who needed checking."

"You're welcome."

It took some effort, but she summoned a smile. "Maybe I'll see you around."

The gleam she'd caught in his eyes a moment ago returned, deeper, more intense, like the glint of new-struck gold.

"Maybe you will."

Sheryl spent the rest of the morning and most of the afternoon at the hospital. Brian left after lunch, promising to be back within an hour with Elise's other two boys. His jubilation had subsided in the aftermath of the birth, but his eyes still lit with wonder whenever he caught a glimpse of the baby.

Lazy and at peace in the stillness of the afternoon, Elise cradled her son in her arms and smiled at the woman perched on the edge of her bed. The friendship that had stretched across years of shared work and a variety of family crises, big and small, cocooned them.

"I'm sorry you missed your tour of duty as birthing partner, Sher. I could have used your moral support. The others were easy, but I was a little scared with this one after my fall."

"We were all scared."

Elise brushed a finger over the baby's dark-russet down. "I was going to call him Terence, after my grandfather, but I think I'll name him Brian, instead. Brian Hart. How does that sound to you, little one?"

It must have sounded pretty good, as the baby pursed its tiny lips a few times, scrunched its wrinkled face, then settled once more into sleep.

"I don't know what I would have done without Brian," Elise murmured. "He's…wonderful."

Sheryl found a smile. "He says the same thing about you and little Red here."

Her friend's gaze lifted. "I know I've told you this before, but you're so lucky to have him. There aren't many like him around."

"No, there aren't."

Sheryl's smile felt distinctly ragged about the edges. She had to talk to Brian. Soon. This burden of confusion and guilt and regret was getting too heavy to lug around much longer.

As it turned out, she didn't have to talk to Brian.

He talked to her.

They met at the hospital later that evening. Elise's room overflowed with flowers and friends from the post office. Murmurs of laughter filled the small room as Peggy and Pat and even Buck Aguilar cooed and showered the new arrival with rattles and blankets and an infant-sized postal service uniform.

Deciding to give the others time and space to admire Baby Brian, Sheryl slipped out and went in search of a vending machine. A cool diet soda fizzed in her hand as she paused by a window, staring out at the golden haze of the sunset.

"Sher?"

She turned and smiled a welcome at Brian. He looked very different from the man who'd rushed out of Elise's room this morning, his face drenched with sweat and his eyes alive with exultation. Tonight, he wore what Sheryl always teasingly called his real-estate-agent's uniform—a lightweight blue seersucker jacket, white shirt, navy slacks. His conservative red tie was neatly knotted.

Leaning against the window alcove, Sheryl offered him a sip of her drink. He declined. His gaze, like hers, drifted to the glorious sunset.

"Have you been in to see Elise and the baby yet?" she asked after a moment.

He nodded. "For a few minutes. I could barely squeeze in the room."

"Did she tell you what she'd decided to name him?"

"Yes."

The single word carried such quiet, glowing pride that Sheryl's heart contracted. God, she hated to hurt this man! They'd shared so many hours, so many dreams. Caught up in her own swamping guilt and regret, she almost missed his next comment.

"I need to talk to you, Sher. I don't know if this is the right time... I don't know if there is a right time." He raked a hand through his hair. "But this morning, when I saw what Elise went through, when I was there with her, I realized what marriage is really about."

Sheryl wanted to weep. She set her drink on the window ledge and took his hands in hers.

"Oh, Brian, I..."

He gripped her fingers. "Let me say this."

"But..."

"Please!"

Miserable beyond words, she nodded.

He took a deep breath and plunged ahead. "Marriage means...should mean...sharing sharing everything. Giving everything. Joining together and, if it's in the picture, holding on to each other at moments like the one that happened this morning.''

''I know.''

He swallowed, gripping her hands so tightly Sheryl thought her bones would crack. ''It shouldn't be something comfortable, something easy and familiar or something we just drift into because it's the next step.''

''What?''

His words were so unexpected she was sure she hadn't heard him right.

''Oh, God, Sher, I'm sorry. This hurts so much.''

''What does?''

''When I was with Elise this morning, I realized that…that I love you. I'll always love you. But…''

That small ''but'' rang like a gong in her ears. In growing incredulity, Sheryl stared up at him.

''But what?''

''But maybe… Maybe I don't love you enough,'' he finished, his eyes anguished. ''Maybe not the way a man who might someday stand beside you and hold your hand while you give birth to his children should. I think… I think maybe we shouldn't see each other for a while. Until I sort through this awful confusion, anyway.''

Sheryl wouldn't have been human if she'd hadn't experienced a spurt of genuine hurt before her rush of relief. After all, the man she'd spent the better part of the past year with had just dumped her. But she cared for him too much to let him shoulder the entire burden of guilt.

''I love you, too, Brian. I always will. But…''

He went still. ''But?''

She gave him a weak, watery smile. ''But not in the way a woman who might someday cling to your hand while she gave birth to your children should.''

Chapter 9

Sheryl arrived home well after nine that night. Wrung out from the long, traumatic day and her painful discussion with Brian, she dropped her uniform in the basket of dirty clothes that Button, thankfully, had left unmolested.

She thought about crawling into bed. A good cry might shake the awful, empty feeling that had dogged her since she woke up this morning. Arriving at the hospital too late to share the miracle of birth with Elise after all those months of anticipation had only added to her hollowness. The subsequent breakup with Brian had taken that lost feeling to a new low.

As if those disturbing events weren't enough, another lowering realization had hit her as she'd driven home through the dark night. Just twenty-four hours off the task force, and she missed Harry Mac-Millan as much as she missed her ex-almost.

If not more.

Sighing, Sheryl pulled on a pair of cutoffs and a well-worn pink T-shirt adorned with a covey of roadrunners. Try as she might, she couldn't seem to get her mind off the marshal. As soon as he bagged Paul Gunderson, which she sincerely hoped he would soon do, he'd be off after the next fugitive. That was his job. His life. Chances were that she'd never see him again. Utterly depressed by the thought, she scooped Button out of the nest he'd made in the middle of her bed.

"Come on, fella. You're going to keep me company while I sob my way through a schmaltzy movie or two." She knuckled his head around the topknot she'd tied with a red ribbon. "Since I don't have to work tomorrow, we might just make it an all-nighter."

They were halfway through *Ghost,* her all-time favorite tearjerker, when the doorbell rang. Treating Sheryl to an ear-shattering demonstration of newly awakened watchdog instincts, Button dug his claws into her bare thighs and sprang off her lap. Yapping furiously, he raced for the foyer.

Sheryl swiped at her tear-streaked cheeks with the bottom of her T-shirt and followed. To her surprise and instant, bubbling pleasure, she identified Harry MacMillan's unmistakable form through the peephole. Reaching for the door chain, she shouted a command at the dog.

"Quiet!"

Naturally, Button didn't pay the least attention to her. His ear-shattering barks bounced off the walls.

"Will you hush! It's Harry."

She jerked the chain off, flicked the alarm switch and threw open the door. If anything, Button's shrill yips went up a few decibels when he recognized his nemesis, but the marshal had come armed this time. Flashing a grin at Sheryl, he knelt down and wafted a cardboard carton under the dog's nose.

"Like pizza, pug-face? I got double pepperoni for you, pineapple and Canadian bacon for us."

The nerve-shredding barking ceased as if cut off with a knife. To Sheryl's astonishment, Button plopped down on the tiles, rolled all the way over, then scrambled back onto his paws. Jumping up on his hind legs, he danced backward, inviting Harry and the pizza in.

The marshal rose, smirking. "Even hairy little rodents can be bribed. It was just a matter of finding the right price."

Sheryl stood aside, her heart thumping at the crooked grin. "Did you come all the way over here just to bribe your way into Button's good graces?"

"That, and to cheer you up."

Palming the pizza high in the air, he followed her into the apartment. He placed the carton on the whitewashed oak dining table and shrugged out of his jacket. The leather holster followed his sport coat onto the back of a chair. Sheryl turned away from the gun and drank in the sight of Harry's broad shoulders and rugged, tanned face. The smile in his warm brown eyes acted like a balm to her spirits, pulling her out of her depression like a fast-climbing roller coaster.

"What made you think I needed cheering up?" she asked curiously.

"Let's just say my cop's instincts were working overtime again. I also want to go over the info you gave us on the Rio card one more time. Even the FBI's so-called expert can't crack the damned code."

Ahhh. Now the real reason for his visit was out. She didn't mind. Working a few hours with Harry would do her more good than sobbing while Patrick Swayze tried to cross time and space to be with Demi Moore. Or lying in bed, thinking about Brian.

"Have a seat," the marshal instructed, heading for the kitchen. "I think I remember where everything is."

Button trailed at his heels, having abandoned all pride in anticipation of a late-night treat. Sheryl settled into one of the rattan-backed dining-room chairs as instructed and hooked her bare feet on the bottom rung. With a little advance notice of this visit, she might have traded her cutoffs and T-shirt for something more presentable. She might even have pulled a brush through her unruly hair. As it was, Harry would just have to put up with a face scrubbed clean of all makeup and a tumble of loose curls spilling over her shoulders.

He didn't seem to mind her casual attire when he emerged a moment later with plates, napkins and a wineglass filled with the last of the leftover Chablis. In fact, his eyes gleamed appreciatively as his gaze drifted over her.

"I like the roadrunners."

A hint of a flush rose in Sheryl's cheeks. She definitely should have changed…or at least put on a bra under the thin T-shirt.

"We have a lot of them out here," she said primly, then tried to divert his attention from the covey of birds darting across her chest. "Why do you want to go over the Rio card again?"

The glint left his eyes, and his jaw took on a hard angle that Sheryl was coming to recognize.

"I'm missing something. It's probably so simple it's staring me right in the face, but I'll be damned if I can see it."

"Maybe we'll see it tonight."

"I hope so. My gut tells me we're running out of time."

He passed her the wine and plates, then dug in his jacket pocket for a dew-streaked can of beer. The momentary tightness around his mouth eased as he popped the top and hefted the can in the air.

"Shall we toast the baby?"

"Sounds good to me."

Smiling, Sheryl chinked her wineglass against the can. She sipped slowly, her eyes on the strong column of Harry's throat as he satisfied his thirst. For the first time that day, she felt herself relax. Really relax. As much as she could in Harry's presence.

Sure enough, she enjoyed her sense of ease for ten, perhaps twenty, seconds. Then he set his beer on the table, brushed a finger across his mustache and dropped a casual bomb.

"So did you give Brian his walking papers?"

Sheryl choked. Her wineglass hit the whitewashed oak tabletop with more force than she'd intended. While she fought to clear her throat, Harry calmly served up the pizza.

"Well?"

"No, I didn't give Brian his walking papers! Not that it's any of your business."

"Why not?"

She glared at him across the pizza carton. Getting dumped by Brian was one thing. Telling Harry about it was something else again.

"What makes you think I would even want to?"

He leaned back in his chair, his expression gentle. As gentle as someone with his rugged features could manage, anyway.

"I was there, Sheryl. I saw him with Elise. I also saw your face when he went dashing back into her room."

"Oh."

A small silence spun out between them, broken only by the noisy, snuffling slurps coming from the kitchen. Button, at least, was enjoying his pizza.

Sheryl chipped at the crust with a short, polished nail. She wanted…needed…to talk to someone. Normally, she would have shared her troubled thoughts with Elise. She couldn't burden her friend with this particular problem right now, though, any more than she could call her own mother in Las Cruces to talk about it. Joan Hancock adored Brian, and had told her daughter several thousand times that she'd better latch onto him. Men that reliable, that steady, didn't grow in potato patches.

Maybe… Maybe Harry was just the confidant Sheryl needed. He knew her situation well enough to murmur sympathetically between slices of pineapple and Canadian bacon, but not so well that he'd burden her with unsolicited advice, as her mother assuredly would.

She stole a glance at him from beneath her lashes. Legs stretched, ankles crossed, he lounged in his chair. He looked so friendly, so relaxed that she couldn't quite believe this was the same man she'd almost taken a bite out of on Inga Gunderson's front porch. His air of easy companionship invited her confidence.

"Brian and I had a long talk tonight in the hospital waiting room," she said slowly. "I didn't give him his walking papers, as you put it. I, uh, didn't get the chance. He gave me mine."

A slice of pizza halted halfway to Harry's mouth. "What?"

"He said that his time with Elise this morning changed every thought, every misconception, he'd ever formed about marriage." She nudged a chunk of pineapple with the tip of her nail. "And about love. It shouldn't be easy, or comfortable, or something we just sort of drift into."

Snorting in derision, the marshal dropped his pizza onto his plate. "No kidding! He's just coming to that brilliant conclusion?"

Sheryl couldn't help smiling at the utter disgust in his voice. Harry MacMillan wouldn't drift into anything. He'd charge in, guns blazing…figuratively, she hoped!

"Don't come down on Brian so hard," she said ruefully. "It took me a while to figure it out, too."

Across the table, golden brown eyes narrowed suddenly. "Are you saying that's all this guy was to you? Someone easy and comfortable?"

"Well..."

The single, hesitant syllable curled Harry's hands into fists. At that moment he would have taken great pleasure in shoving the absent real-estate-agent's face not just into the hallway wall but through it. Hell! It didn't take a Sherlock Holmes, much less a U.S. marshal, to figure out that the jerk hadn't fully committed to Sheryl. If he'd wanted her, really wanted her, he wouldn't have moved so slowly or made any damned appointments! He would've staked his claim with a ring, or at least with a more definitive arrangement than their sort-of engagement.

But after seeing them in each other's arms the other night, Harry had assumed...had thought...

What?

That Sheryl loved the guy? That she wanted Brian Mitchell more than he showed signs of wanting her?

The idea that she might be hurting was what had brought Harry to her apartment tonight. That and the sudden lost look in her eyes when the idiot had rushed back into her friend's hospital room and left her standing there. That look had stayed with Harry all afternoon, until he'd startled Ev and Fay and the FBI expert still struggling with the key words from the postcards by calling it a night. Driven by an urge he hadn't let himself think about, he'd stopped at a pizzeria just a few blocks from Sheryl's apartment and come to comfort her.

He now recognized that urge for what it was. Two parts sympathy for someone struggling with an unraveling relationship: anyone who'd gone through a divorce could relate to that hurt. One part concern for the woman he'd worked with for two days now and had come to like and respect. And one part...

One part pure, unadulterated male lust.

Harry could admit it now. When she'd opened the door to him in those short shorts and figure-hugging T-shirt, a hot spot had ignited in his gut. He knew damned well that the slow burning had nothing to do with any desire to comfort a friend or to grill a team member yet again about the postcards.

It had taken everything he had to return her greeting and nonchalantly set about feeding her and the mutt. He couldn't come anywhere close to nonchalant now, though. Any more than he could keep his gaze from dipping to the thrust of her breasts under the thin layer of pink as she rose and shoved her hands into her back pockets.

"I don't know why I didn't see it sooner, Harry." She paced the open space between the dining and living rooms. "I loved Brian. I still do. But I wasn't *in* love with him. I guess I let myself be seduced by the comfortable routine he represented."

Thoroughly distracted by the sight of those long, tanned legs and bare toes tipped with pink nail polish, Harry forgot his self-assigned role of friend and listener.

"Comfortable routine?" He snorted again. "The man has a helluva seduction technique."

"Hey, it worked for me."

The way she kept springing to Brian's defense was starting to really irritate Harry. Almost as much as her admission that she still loved the jerk.

"Right," he drawled. "That's why you're pacing the floor and ole Bry's off on his own somewhere, pondering the meaning of life and love."

She turned, surprise and indignation sending twin flags of color into her cheeks. "Whose side are you on, anyway?"

"Yours, sweetheart."

He rose, barely noticing the way the endearment slipped out. Three strides took him to where she stood, all stiff and bristly.

"You deserve better than routine, Sheryl. You deserve a dizzy, breathless, thoroughly exhausting seduction that shakes you right out of predictable and puts you down somewhere on the other side of passion."

"Is… Is that right?"

"That's right." He stroked a knuckle down her smooth, golden cheek. "You deserve kisses that wind you up so tight it takes all night to unwind."

Harry could have fallen into the wide green eyes that stared up at him and never found his way out. Her lips opened, closed, opened again. A slow flush stole into her cheeks.

"Yes," she whispered at last. "I do."

Her breasts rose and fell under their pink covering. A pulse pounded at the base of her throat. Slowly, so slowly, her arms lifted and slid around his neck.

"Kiss me, Harry."

He kissed her.

He didn't think twice about it. Didn't listen to any of the alarms that started pinging the instant her arms looped around his neck. Didn't even hear them.

He'd hold her for a moment only, he swore fiercely. Kiss her just once more. Show her that there was life after Brian. That life *with* Brian hadn't come close to living at all. Then his mouth came down on hers, and Sheryl showed him a few things, instead.

That her taste had lingered in his mind for two days. But not this sweet. Or this wild. Or this hot.

That her lips were softer, firmer, more seductive than he remembered.

That her body matched his perfectly. Tall enough that he didn't have to bend double to reach her. Small enough to fit into the cradle of his thighs.

At the contact, he went instantly, achingly, hard. He jerked his head up, knowing that one more breath, one more press of her breasts against his chest, would drive him to something she couldn't be ready for. Not this soon after Brian.

Or maybe she could.

Her eyes opened at his abrupt movement. Harry saw himself in the dark pupils. Saw something else, as well. The passion he'd taunted her about. It shimmered in the green irises. Showed in her heavy eyelids. Sounded in the short, choppy rush of her breath.

This time, she didn't have to ask for his kiss. This time, he gave it, and took everything she offered in return.

By the time she dragged her mouth away, gasping, every muscle in Harry's body strained with the need to press her down on the nearest horizontal surface. With an effort that popped beads of sweat out on his forehead, he loosened his arms enough for her to draw back.

"Harry, I..."

She stopped, swiped her tongue along her lower lip. The burning need in Harry's gut needled into white, hot fingers of fire.

"You what, sweetheart?"

"I want to wind up tight," she whispered, her eyes holding his. "And take all night to unwind."

Few saints would fail to respond to that invitation, and Harry had no illusions that anyone would ever nominate him for canonization. Still, he forced himself to move slowly, giving her time to pull back at any move, any touch.

He lifted a hand to her throat and stroked the smooth skin under her chin. "I think we can manage a little winding and a lot of unwinding. If you're sure?"

A wobbly smile tugged at lips still rosy from his kiss. "Who's being cautious and careful now? What happened to breathless and dizzy and thoroughly exhausting?"

Grinning, he slid his arm under the backs of the thighs that had been driving him insane for the past half hour. Sweeping her into a tight hold, he headed for the hall.

"Breathless and dizzy coming right up, ma'am. Thoroughly exhausting to follow."

Sheryl barely heard Button's startled yip as Harry swept past with her in his arms. She didn't think about the idiocy of what she'd just asked this man to do. Tomorrow, she'd regret it. Maybe later tonight, when Harry left, as he inevitably would.

At this moment, she wanted only to end the swirling confusion he'd thrown her into the first moment he'd appeared in her life. To get past the pain of her break with Brian. To do something insane, something unplanned and unscheduled and definitely unroutine.

She buried her face in the warm skin of his neck. When he crossed the threshold to her bedroom, he twisted at the waist. With one booted heel, he kicked the door shut behind him. Sharp, annoyed yips rose from the other side.

"I might not hesitate at a little bribery," he told her, his voice a rumble in her ear, "but I draw the line at voyeurism."

"He'll bark all night," Sheryl warned, lifting her head. "Or however long it takes to unwind."

"Let him." His mustache lifted in a wicked grin. "And in case there's any doubt, it's going to take a long time. A very long time."

The husky promise sent ripples of excitement over every inch of her skin. The way he lowered her, sliding her body down his, turned those ripples into a near tidal wave. Her T-shirt snagged on his buttons. It lifted, baring her midriff. Cooled air raised goose bumps above her belly button. Harry's hard, driving kiss raised goose bumps below.

Her shirt hit the floor sometime later. His jeans and boots followed. In a tangle of arms and legs, they tumbled onto the downy black-and-white blanket that covered her bed. Gasping, Sheryl let Harry work the same magic on her breasts that he'd worked on her mouth. His soft, silky mustache teased. His fingers stroked. His tongue tasted. His teeth took her from breathless to moaning to only a kiss or two away from spinning out of control.

Sheryl wasn't exactly a passive participant in her unplanned, unroutine seduction. Her hands roamed as eagerly as his. Her tongue explored. Her body slicked and twisted and pressed everywhere it met his. She was as wet and hot and eager as he was when he finally groaned and dragged her arms down.

"Wait, sweetheart. Wait! Let me get something to protect you."

He rolled off her. Wearing only low-slung briefs and the shirt she'd tugged halfway down his back, he padded across the room to his jeans.

Sheryl flung an arm up over her head, almost as dizzy and befuddled as he'd predicted. Harry's posterior view didn't exactly unfuddle her. Lord, he was magnificent! All long, lean lines. Bronzed muscles. Tight, trim buttocks.

When he scooped up his jeans and turned, she had to admit that his front view wasn't too shabby, either. Her heart hammered as he dug out his wallet and rifled through it with an impatience that fanned

the small fires he'd lit under her skin. A moment later, several packages of condoms fell onto the blanket.

Sheryl eyed the abundant supply with a raised brow. Harry caught
her look and his mustache tipped into another wicked grin.

"U.S. marshals always come prepared for extended field operations."

"So I see."

Still grinning, he sheathed himself and rejoined her on the bed. He
settled between her legs smoothly, as if she were made to receive
him. His weight pressed her into the blanket. With both hands, he
smoothed her hair back and planted little kisses on her neck.

"I don't want to give you the wrong impression," he murmured
against her throat. "Dedicated law enforcement types have all kinds
of uses for those little packages."

Torn between curiosity and a wild, blazing need to arch her hips
into his, Sheryl could only huff a question into his ear.

"Like…what?"

"Later," he growled, nipping the cords of her neck. "I'll tell you
later."

Would they have a later? The brief thought cut through her searing,
sensual haze. Then his hand found her core and there was only now.
Only Harry. Only the incredible pleasure he gave her.

The pleasure spiraled, spinning tighter and tighter with each kiss,
each stroke of his hand and his body. When Sheryl was sure she
couldn't stand the whirling sensations a moment longer without shattering, she wrapped her legs around his and arched her hips to receive
him. It might have been mere moments or a lifetime later that she
exploded in a blaze of white light.

Another forever followed, then Harry thrust into her a final time.
Rigid, straining, joined with her at mouth and chest and hip, he filled
her body. Only later did she realize that he'd filled the newly empty
place in her heart, as well.

The realization came to her as she hovered between boneless sa-
tiation and an exhausted doze. Her head cradled on Harry's shoulder,
she remembered sleepily that they hadn't gotten around to the

postcards. They'd get to them tomorrow, she thought, breathing in the musky scent of their lovemaking.

Tomorrow came crashing down on them far sooner than Sheryl had anticipated. She was sunk in a deep doze, her head still cradled on a warm shoulder, when the sound of a thump and a startled, pain-filled yelp pierced her somnolent semiconsciousness.

Instantly, Harry spun off the bed. Sheryl's head hit the mattress with a thump

"Wh...?"

"Stay here!"

With a pantherlike speed, he dragged on his jeans and yanked at the zipper. They rode low on his hips as he headed for the door. Gasping, Sheryl pushed herself up on one elbow. Still groggy and only half-awake, she blinked owlishly.

"What is it?"

"I don't know, and until I do, stay here, okay? No heroics and no noise."

Before his low instructions had even sunk in, he'd slipped through the door and disappeared into the shadowed hallway. Sheryl gaped at the panel for a second or two, still in a fog. Then she threw back the sheet and leaped out of bed. She had her panties on and her T-shirt half over her head when the door swung open again.

She froze, her heart in her throat.

To her infinite relief, Harry stalked in. Disgust etched in every line of his taut body, he carried a tomato-and-grease-smeared Button under his arm.

"The greedy little beggar climbed up onto the table. He and our half of the pizza just took a dive."

Chapter 10

Although the little heart-shaped crystal clock on her nightstand showed just a few minutes before eleven, by the time Sheryl finished dressing she was experiencing all the awkwardness of a morning-after.

Button's noisy accident had shaken her right out of her sleepy, sensual haze. Like a splash of cold water in her face, reality now set in with a vengeance. She couldn't quite believe she'd begged Harry to kiss her like that. To seduce her, for pity's sake!

She walked down the hall to the living room, cringing inside as she realized how pathetic she must have sounded. First, by admitting that Brian had dumped her. Then, by practically demanding that the marshal take her to bed as a balm to her wounded ego. She couldn't remember when she'd ever done anything so rash. So stupid. So embarrassing to admit to after the fact.

Heat blazed in both cheeks when she found Harry in the dining room. Hunkered down on one knee, he was scrubbing at the grease stains in her carpet with a sponge and muttering imprecations at the dog that sat a few feet away, watching him with a show of blasé interest.

"You don't have to do that," Sheryl protested, her discomfiture mounting at the sight of Harry's naked chest. Had she really wrapped her arms and legs and everything else she could around his lean, powerful torso?

She had, she admitted with a new flush of heat. She could still feel the ache in her thighs, and taste him on her lips. How in the world had she lost herself like that? She hardly knew much more about this man than his name, his occupation, his marital status and the fact that he logged more travel miles in a month than most people did in two years. That alone should have stopped her from throwing herself at him the way she had! Hadn't she learned her lesson from her parents?

Obviously not. Even now, she ached to wrap her arms around him once again. Smart, Sheryl! Real smart. Dropping to her knees, she reached for the sponge.

"I'll do that while you get dressed."

He looped an arm across his bent knee and regarded her with a lazy smile.

"Unwound already, Sher? And here I promised that it would take all night."

His teasing raised the heat in her cheeks to a raging inferno. She attacked the pizza stain, unable to meet his eyes.

"Yes, well, I know you came here to work, not to, uh, help me get past this bad patch with Brian, and you don't have all night for that."

His hand closed over her wrist, stilling her agitated movements. When she looked up, his air of lazy amusement had completely disappeared.

"Is that what you think just happened here? That I played some kind of sexual Good Samaritan by taking you to bed?"

She wouldn't have put it in quite those words, but she couldn't deny the fact that he'd done exactly that.

"Don't think that I'm not…" She swallowed. "That I'm not grateful. I needed a…a distraction tonight and you—"

With a swiftness that made her gasp, he rose, bringing her up with him. Sudden, fierce anger blazed in his brown eyes.

"A distraction?" he echoed in a tone that raised the fine hairs on the back of her neck. "You needed a distraction?"

Sheryl knew she was digging herself in deeper with every word, but she didn't have the faintest idea how to get out of this hole. She'd only wanted to let Harry know that she didn't expect him to continue the admittedly spectacular lovemaking she'd forced on him. Instead, she'd unintentionally ruffled his male ego. More embarrassed than ever, she tugged her wrist free.

"That didn't come out the way I meant it. You were more than a distraction. You were..." Her face flaming, she admitted the unvarnished truth. "You were wonderful. Thank you."

Harry stared at her, at a total loss for words for one of the few times in his life. Anger still pounded through him. Incredulity now added its own sideswiping kick. He couldn't believe that Sheryl had just *thanked* him, for God's sake! If this whole conversation didn't make him so damned furious, he might have laughed at the irony of it. He couldn't remember the last time he'd lost himself so completely, so passionately, in a woman's arms. Or the last time he'd drifted into sleep with a head nestled on his shoulder and a soft, breathy sigh warming his neck.

Harry hadn't exactly sworn off female companionship in the years since his divorce, but neither had he ignored the lessons he'd learned from that sobering experience. As long as he made his living chasing renegades, he couldn't expect any woman to put up with his here-today, gone-tonight lifestyle. Deliberately, he'd kept his friendships with women light and casual. Even more deliberately, he dated women whose own careers or interests coincided with the transitory nature of his. In any case, he sure as hell had never jeopardized an ongoing investigation by seducing one of the key players involved.

He'd broken every one of his self-imposed rules tonight. Deep in his gut, Harry knew damned well that he'd break them again if Sheryl turned her face up to his at this moment and asked him in that sweet, seductive way of hers to kiss her. Hell, he didn't need asking. Wide-awake now and still tight from the crash that had brought him springing out of bed, he had to battle the urge to sweep Sheryl into his arms and take her back to bed to show her just how much of a *distraction* he could provide. Just the thought of burying himself in her slick, satiny heat once again sent a spear of razor-sharp need through him.

With something of a shock, Harry realized that he wanted this woman even more fiercely now than he had before she'd given herself to him. And here she was, brushing him off with a polite thank-you.

Despite her red cheeks, she met his gaze with a dignity that tugged at something inside him. Something sharper than need. Deeper than desire.

"I'm sorry," she said quietly. "I didn't mean to insult you or cheapen what happened between us. It *was* wonderful, Harry. I just didn't want you to think that I want...or expect...anything more. I know why you're in Albuquerque, and that you'll be gone as soon as something breaks on your fugitive."

She had just put his own thoughts into words. Harry didn't particularly like hearing them.

"Sheryl..."

Her eyes gentled. Her hand came up to stroke his cheek. "It's all right, Marshal. Some men are wanderers by nature as much as by profession. My father was one. So, I think, are you. I understand."

Harry wasn't sure he did. He heard what she was saying. He agreed with it completely. So why did he want to—

The muted shrill of his cellular phone interrupted his chaotic thoughts. Frowning, he extracted the instrument from the jacket he'd left hanging on the back of a dining-room chair.

"MacMillan."

"Harry!" Ev's voice leaped out at him. "Where the hell are you?"

"At Sheryl's apartment." He didn't give his partner a chance to comment on that one. "Where are you?"

"Outside your motel room. I was on my way home when I got the news. I swung by your place to give you the word personally."

"What word?"

"The Santa Fe airport manager just called. He's got a small, twin-engine jet about two hours out, requesting permission to land."

Harry's gut knotted. "And?"

"And the pilot also requested that Customs be notified. He wants to off-load a cargo of Peruvian sheepskin hides destined for a factory just outside Taos that manufactures those Marlboro-man sheepskin coats. From what I'm told, the hides stink. Like you wouldn't believe. Customs isn't too happy about processing the cargo tonight.''

''This could be it,'' his listener said softly.

''I think it is. The FAA ran a quick check on the aircraft's tail number and flight plan. This leg of the flight originated in Peru, but the aircraft is registered in Brazil, Harry. Brazil!''

''Get a helo warmed up and ready for us.''

''Already done. It's on the pad at State Police headquarters. Fay's on her way there now.''

''I'll meet you both in ten minutes.''

Harry snapped the phone shut and jammed it into his jacket. Every sense, every instinct, pushed at him to race into the bedroom and grab his clothes. To slam out of the apartment, jump into his car and hit the street, siren wailing.

For the first time that he could remember, his cop's instincts took second place to a stronger, even more urgent demand. In answer to the question in Sheryl's wide eyes, he paused long enough to give her a swift recap.

''We've got a break, Sher. A plane registered in Brazil is coming into the Santa Fe airport in a couple of hours.''

''No kidding!''

She was still standing where he'd left her when he came running back, shoving his shirttail into his jeans. He grabbed his holster and slipped into it with a roll of his shoulders. Then he snatched up his jacket and strode to where she stood. His big hands framed her face.

''I've got to go.''

''I know. Be careful.''

He gave himself another second to sear her eyes and her nose and the tangled silk of her hair into his memory. Then he kissed her, hard, and headed for the door.

''Harry!''

''What?''

''Come back when you can. I, uh, want to know what happens.''

''I will.''

* * *

The nondescript government sedan squealed out of the apartment complex. With one eye on the late-night traffic, Harry fumbled the detachable Kojak light into its mounting and flipped its switch. The rotating light slashed through the night like a sword. A half second later, he activated the siren and shoved the accelerator to the floor. The unmarked, unremarkable vehicle roared to life.

Ten minutes later, the car squealed through the gates leading to the headquarters of Troop R of the New Mexico Highway Patrol. Grabbing the duffel bag containing his field gear from the trunk, Harry raced for the helo pad. Ev and Fay met him halfway, both jubilant, both lugging their own field gear.

"Give me a rundown on who we've got playing so far," Harry shouted over the piercing whine of the helicopter's engine.

"Our Santa Fe highway patrol detachment is pulling in every trooper they've got to cordon off the airport," Fay yelled. "The Santa Fe city police have alerted their SWAT team. They'll be in place when we get there."

They ducked under the whirring rotor blades and climbed aboard through the side hatch. The copilot greeted them with a grin and directed them to the web rack that stretched behind the operators' seats.

Panting, Ev buckled himself in. "Customs has a Cessna Citation in the air tracking our boy as we speak. They've also got two Black-hawks en route from El Paso, with a four-man bust team aboard each."

Fierce satisfaction shot through Harry at the news. The huge Sikorsky UH-60 Blackhawk helicopters came equipped with an arsenal of lethal weapons and enough candlepower to light up half of New Mexico.

"Good. We might just give them a chance to show their stuff."

While the copilot buckled himself in, the pilot stretched around to show the passengers where to plug in their headsets.

"What's the flying time to Santa Fe?" Harry asked, his words tinny over the static of the radio.

"Twenty minutes, sir."

"Right. Let's do it."

The aviator gave him a thumbs-up and turned her attention to the controls. Seconds later, the chopper lifted off. It banked steeply, then zoomed north.

Harry used the short flight to coordinate the operation with the key players involved. The copilot patched him through to the Customs National Aviation Center in Oklahoma City, which was now tracking the suspect aircraft, the New Mexico state police ops center and the Santa Fe airport manager.

"Our boy is still over an hour out," he summarized for Ev and Fay. "That gives us plenty of time to familiarize ourselves with the layout of the field and get our people into position. No one moves until I give the signal. No one. Understood?"

Harry didn't want any mistakes. No John Waynes charging in ahead of the cavalry. No hotshot Rambos trying to show their stuff. If the man he'd been tracking for almost a year was flying in aboard this aircraft, the bastard wasn't going to get away. Not this time.

The short flight passed in a blur of dark mountains to their right and the sparse lights of the homes scattered along the Rio Grande valley below. The helo set down at the Santa Fe airport just long enough for Harry and the two others to jump out. Bent double, they dashed through the cloud of dust thrown up by the rotor wash. As soon as they were clear, Harry shed his coat and pulled his body armor out of his gear bag. A dark, lightweight windbreaker with "U.S. Marshal" emblazoned on the back covered the armor and identified him to the other players involved. After shoving spare ammo clips into his pockets, he checked his weapon, then went to meet the nervous airport manager waiting for him inside the distinctive New Mexico-style airport facility.

In a deliberate attempt to retain Santa Fe's unique character and limit its growth, the city planners had also limited the size of the airport that serviced it. To make access even more difficult, high mountain peaks ringed its relatively short runway. Consequently, no large-bodied jetliners landed in the city. The millions of tourists a year who poured into Santa Fe from all over the world usually flew into Albuquerque and drove the fifty-five-mile scenic route north.

Even the legislators who routinely traveled to the capital to conduct their business did so by car or by small aircraft.

The inconvenient access might have constituted an annoyance for some travelers, but it added up to a major plus for Harry and the team members who gathered within minutes of his arrival. With only one north-south runway and the parallel taxiway to cover, he quickly orchestrated the disposition of his forces. They melted into the night like dark shadows, radios muted and lights doused.

After a final visual and radar check of their handheld secure radios, Ev headed for the tower to coordinate the final approach and take-down. Harry and Fay climbed into the airport service vehicle that would serve as their mobile command post. When the truck pulled into its customary slot beside the central hangar, Harry stared into the night.

A million stars dotted the sky above the solid blackness of the mountains. Richard Johnson, aka Paul Gunderson, was out there somewhere. With any luck, that somewhere would soon narrow down to a stretch of runway in the high New Mexico desert.

A shiver rippled along Harry's spine, part primal anticipation, part plain old-fashioned chill. Even in mid-June, Sante Fe's seven-thousand-foot elevation put a nip in the night air. He zipped his jacket, folded his arms. His eyes on the splatter of stars to the south, the hunter settled down to await his prey.

The minutes crawled by.

The secure radio cackled as Ev gave periodic updates on the aircraft's approach. Forty minutes out. Thirty. Twenty.

The Blackhawks swept over the airport, rotors thumping in the night, and touched down behind the hangars. One would move into position to block any possible takeoff attempt should anything spook the quarry once it was on the ground. The second would come in from the rear.

Quiet settled over the waiting, watching team. Even Ev's status reports were hushed.

Fifteen minutes.

Ten.

This was for Dean, Harry promised the dark, silent night. For the man who'd razzed him as a rookie, and stood beside him at the altar, and asked him to act as godfather to his son. And for Jenny, who'd cried in Harry's arms until she had no more tears left to shed. For every marshal who'd ever died in the line of duty, and every son or mother or husband or wife left behind.

Without warning, an image of Sheryl formed in Harry's mind. Her hair tumbling around her shoulders. Her eyes wide with excitement and the first, faint hint of worry on his behalf. It struck him that he'd left Sheryl, as Dean had left Jenny, to chase after Paul Gunderson.

Dean had never returned.

Harry might not, either. Dammit, he shouldn't have made that rash promise to Sheryl. Even without the hazards inherent in his job, success bred its own demands. If Gunderson stepped off an airplane in Santa Fe in the next few minutes, as Harry sincerely prayed he would, he'd climb right back on a plane, this time in handcuffs and leg irons. Harry would go with him. He wouldn't be driving back to Sheryl's place to give her a play-by-play of the night's events...or to redeem the promise of the hard, swift kiss he'd left her with.

He had no business making her any kind of promises at all, he thought soberly.

Even if he wanted to, he couldn't offer her much more than a choice between short bursts of pleasure and long stretches of loneliness. And a husband whose job might or might not leave her weeping in someone's arms, as Dean's had left Jenny.

Suddenly, the radio cackled. "He's on final approach. Check out that spot of light at one o'clock, 'bout two thousand feet up."

Harry blanked his mind of Sheryl, of Jenny, even of Dean. His eyes narrowed on the tiny speck of light slowly dropping out of the sky.

The takedown was a textbook operation.

Following the tower's directions, the twin-engine King Air rolled to a stop on the parking apron, fifty yards from where Harry waited in the service vehicle. As soon as the engines whined down and the hatch opened, the Blackhawks rose from behind the adjacent hangar like huge specters. They dropped down, their thirty-million-candlepower spotlights pinning the two figures who emerged from the King Air in a blinding haze of white light. The helo crews poured out.

Harry clicked the mike on the vehicle's loudspeaker and shouted a warning. "This is the U.S. Marshals Service. Hit the ground. Now!" He was out of the vehicle, his weapon drawn, before the echoes had stopped bouncing off the hangar walls.

The two figures took one look at the dark-suited figures converging on them from all directions and dropped like stones.

Harry reached them as they hit the pavement. Disappointment rose like bile in his throat. Even from the back, he could see that neither of the individuals spread-eagled on the concrete fit Paul Gunderson's physical description.

Ev Sloan reached the same conclusion when he panted up beside Harry a moment later.

"He's not with 'em. Damn!"

"My sentiments exactly," Harry got out through clenched jaws. Raising his voice, he issued a curt order. "All right. On your feet. We need to inspect your cargo."

A two-man Customs team went through the King Air's cargo with dogs, handheld scanners and an array of sophisticated chemical testing compounds. A second team searched the plane itself, which had been towed into a hangar for privacy.

By the time the first streaks of a golden dawn pierced the darkness of the mountain peaks outside, unbaled sheepskin hides lay strewn along one half of the hangar. Barely cured and still wearing a coat of gray, greasy wool, they gave off a stench that had emptied the contents of several team members' stomachs and put the drug dogs completely out of action.

The plane's guts lay on the other side of the hangar floor…along with a neat row of plastic bags. Even without the dogs, the stash in the concealed compartment in the plane's belly had been hard to miss.

The senior Customs agent approached Harry, grinning. Sweat streaked his face, and he carried the stink of hides with him.

"Five hundred kilos and a nice, new King Air for the Treasury Department to auction off. Not a bad haul, Marshal. Not bad at all."

"No. Just not the one we wanted."

The agent thrust out his hand. "Sorry you didn't get your man this time. Maybe next time."

"Yeah. Next time."

Leaving the other agency operatives to their prizes, Harry walked out into the slowly gathering dawn. Ev leaned against the hood of a black-and-white state police car, sipping coffee from a leaking paper cup. Then he tossed out the dregs of his coffee and crumpled the cup.

"Well, I guess it's back to the damned computer printouts and postcards. You get anything more from Sheryl when you were up at her place last night?"

"No."

And yes.

Harry had gotten far more from her than he'd planned or hoped for. The need to return to her apartment, to finish this damnable night in her arms, tore through his layers of weariness.

He thought of a thousand reasons why he shouldn't go back...and one consuming reason why he should.

Chapter 11

Sheryl curled in a loose ball on top of the black-and-white blanket. Button lay sprawled beside her. She stroked his silky fur with a slow, light touch, taking care not to wake him while he snuffled and twitched in the throes of some doggie dream. Her gaze drifted to the small crystal clock on the table beside her bed.

Five past six.

Seven hours since Harry had left. Seven hours of waiting and worrying. Of wondering when…if…he'd come back. He'd been gone for only seven hours, yet it seemed as though days had passed since he'd rolled out of this bed and raced into the kitchen in response to Button's attack on the pizza.

Until tonight, Sheryl had never really appreciated the loneliness that had turned her mother into such a bitter, unhappy woman. She'd seen it happening, of course. Even as a child, she'd recognized that her father's extended absences had leached the youth from her mother's face and carved those small, tight lines on either side of her face. Mentally, she'd braced herself every time her father walked out the door. She'd shared her mother's hurt and dissatisfaction, but she'd never *felt* the emptiness deep inside her, as she had these past hours. Never experienced this sense of being so alone.

Despite the hollow feeling in her chest, Sheryl could summon no trace of bitterness. Instead of hurt, a lingering wonder spread through her veins every time she thought of the hours together with Harry. Her breasts still tingled from his stinging kisses. One shoulder still carried a little red mark from his prickly mustache. She'd never experienced anything even remotely resembling the explosions of heat and light and skyrocketing sensation the marshal had detonated under her skin. Not once but twice.

Recalling her fumbling attempt to thank him for services rendered, Sheryl almost groaned aloud. Talk about putting her foot in it! Harry had bristled all over with male indignation. For a moment, he'd looked remarkably like Button with his fur up.

Smiling, she combed her fingers through the soft, feathery ruff decorating the paw closest to her. The shih tzu snuffled and jerked his leg away. One black eye opened and glared at her though the light of the gathering dawn.

''Sorry.''

He gave a long-suffering look and rolled onto his back, all four paws sticking straight up in the air. Sheryl speared another glance at the clock. Six-fifteen.

Too restless to even pretend sleep any longer, she tickled the dog's pink belly. ''Want to get up? You can finish off the pizza for breakfast.''

Black gums pulled back. A warning growl rumbled up from the furry chest. Hastily, Sheryl pulled her fingers out of reach.

''Okay, okay! You don't mind if I get up, do you?''

Silly question. Before she'd was halfway across the bedroom, Button was already sunk back into sleep.

A quick shower washed away the grittiness of her sleepless night. Since it was Saturday, Sheryl didn't even glance at the uniforms hanging neatly in her closet. Instead, she pulled out her favorite denim sundress. With its thin straps, scooped neck and loose fit, it was perfect for Albuquerque's June heat. Tiny wooden buttons marched down the front and stopped above the knee, baring a long length of leg when she walked. The stonewashed blue complemented her tan and her streaky blond hair, she knew. Now all she had to do was erase the signs of her sleepless night. Making a face at her reflection in the mirror, she applied a little blush and a swipe of lipstick.

A few determined strokes with the brush subdued her hair into a semblance of order. Clipping it back with a wooden barrette that matched the buttons on the dress, she padded barefoot into the kitchen.

The first thing she saw was the pizza carton on the counter. Instantly, she started worrying and wondering again.

Where was Harry? What had happened after he'd left her last night?

Leaning a hip against the counter, she filled the automatic coffeemaker and waited while it brewed. Slowly, a rich aroma spread through the kitchen. Even more slowly, the soft, golden dawn lightened to day.

The sound of Button's nails clicking on the tiles alerted her to the fact that he'd decided to join the living. He wandered into the kitchen and gave her a disgruntled look, obviously as annoyed with her early rising as he'd been with her tossing and turning.

"Do you need to go out? Hold on a sec. I'll get the paper and pour a cup of coffee and join you on the back patio."

Sheryl flicked off the alarm and went outside to hunt down her newspaper. As usual, the deliveryman had tossed it halfway across the courtyard. She didn't realize Button had slipped out the front door with her until his piercing yip cut through the early morning quiet.

Startled, Sheryl spun around. From the corner of one eye, she saw Button charge across the courtyard toward the silver-haired Persian that had been sunning itself at the base of the small fountain. The cat went straight up in the air, hissing, and came down with claws extended.

"Oh, no!"

Oblivious to her dismayed exclamation, Button leaped to attack. His quarry decided that discretion was the better part of valor. Streaking across the tiled courtyard, it disappeared through the arched entryway that led to the parking lot. The shih tzu followed in noisy pursuit.

The darned dog was going to wake every person in the apartment complex with that shrill bark. Dropping the paper, Sheryl joined in the chase.

"Button! Here, boy! Here!"

She rounded the entryway corner just in time to see both cat and dog dart across the parking lot. Another cluster of apartments swallowed them up. Sheryl started across the rough asphalt. Suddenly, her bare heel came down on a pebble. Pain shot all the way up to the back of her knee.

"Dammit!"

Wincing, she took a few limping steps, then ran awkwardly on the ball of her injured foot. To her consternation, the noisy barking grew fainter and fainter. A moment later, it disappeared completely, swallowed up by the twisting walkways, picturesque courtyards and multistory buildings of the sprawling complex.

Seriously concerned now, Sheryl ran through archway after archway. Button would never find his way back through this maze. Stepping up the pace as much as the pain in her heel would allow, she searched the apartment grounds. Her dress skirt flapped around her knees. The wooden barrette holding her hair back snapped open and clattered to the walkway behind her. Sweat popped out on her forehead and upper lip.

"Button!" she called in gathering desperation. "Here, boy! Come to Sheryl!"

Her breath cut through her lungs like razor blades when she caught the sound of a crash, followed by a yelp. She tore down another path and through an archway, then came to a skidding, one-heeled halt. If she'd had any breath left, Sheryl would have gasped at the scene that greeted her. As it was, she could only pant helplessly.

An oversized clay pot had been knocked on its side. It now spilled dirt and pink geraniums onto the tiles. Beside the overturned pot lay a tipped-over sundial. Colorful fliers and sections of a newspaper littered the courtyard. In the midst of the havoc, not one but two silver Persians now stood shoulder to shoulder. Fur up, backs arched, they hissed for all they were worth. Their indignant owner stood behind them, flapping her arms furiously at the intruder. Button was belly to the ground, but hadn't given up the fight.

By the time Sheryl had scooped up the snarling shih tzu, apologized profusely to the cats' owner, offered to pay for the damages and listened to an irate discourse on dog owners who ignore leash laws, the sun had tipped over the apartment walls and heated the morning. Limping and hot and not exactly happy with her unrepentant houseguest, she lectured him sternly as she retraced her steps to her apartment. She took a wrong turn twice, which didn't improve her mood or Button's standing. Unconcerned over the fact that he was in disgrace, the dog surveyed the areas they passed through, ears up and eyes alert for his next quarry.

Sheryl was still lecturing when she rounded the corner of her building. The sight of two squad cars pulled up close to the arch leading to her courtyard stopped her in midscold. Curious and now a little worried, she hurried through the curving entrance. Worry turned to gulping alarm when she saw a uniformed officer standing just outside her open apartment door.

Oh, God! Something must have gone wrong last night! Maybe Harry was hurt!

Her heart squeezed tight. So did her arms, eliciting an indignant squawk from Button.

"Sorry!"

Easing the pressure on the little dog, she ran across the courtyard. "What's going on? What's happened?"

"Miss Hancock?"

"Yes. Is Harry all right?"

"Harry?"

"Harry MacMillan. Marshal MacMillan."

"Oh, yeah. He's inside. He's the one who called us when he found your front door open."

Sheryl fought down an instant rush of guilt. She'd forgotten all about the security systems in her worry over Button.

"Are you all right, Miss Hancock?"

"Yes, I'm fine."

"Then where the hell have you been?"

The snarl spun Sheryl around. Harry filled her doorway, his body taut with tension and his eyes furious. Another uniformed police officer hovered at his shoulder.

She took one look at his face and decided this wasn't the time to tell him about the wild chase Button had led her through the apartment complex. In the mood he was obviously in, he'd probably skin the dog whole.

"I, uh, went out to get the newspaper."

His blistering look raked her from her sweat-streaked face to her bare toes, then moved to the rolled newspaper lying a few yards away…right where Sheryl had dropped it.

"You want to run that by me one more time?"

She didn't care for his tone. Nor did she appreciate being dressed down like a recruit in front of the two police officers.

"Not particularly."

Although she wouldn't have thought it possible, his jaw tightened another notch. Turning to the police officer, he held out a hand.

"Looks like I called you out on a false alarm. Sorry."

"No problem, Marshal."

"Thanks for responding so quickly."

"Anytime."

With a nod to Sheryl and Button, the two policemen departed the scene. Harry turned to face her, his temper still obviously simmering. In no mood for a public fracas, Sheryl brushed past him and headed for the cool sanctuary of her apartment.

Harry trailed after her, scowling. "Why are you limping?"

"I stepped on a stone."

For some reason, that seemed to incense him even further. He followed her inside, lecturing her with a lot less restraint than she'd lectured Button just a few moments ago.

"That could have been glass you stepped on."

"Well, it wasn't."

"Running around barefoot is about as smart as leaving your front door wide-open! Speaking of which…"

The oak door slammed behind her, rattling the colorful Piña prints on the entryway wall.

"You want to tell me what good a security system is if you don't even bother to close the damned door?"

Enough was enough. Sheryl had run a good mile or more after the blasted mutt. She was hot and sweaty. Her hair hung in limp tendrils around her face. Her heel still hurt like hell. And she'd spent most of the night worrying about a U.S. marshal who, judging from his foul temper, obviously hadn't apprehended the fugitive he wanted.

Bending, she released the dog. Button promptly scampered off, leaving her to face the irate Harry on her own. She turned to find him standing close. Too close. She could see the stubble darkening his cheeks and chin...and the anger still simmering in his whiskey-gold eyes.

Drawing in a deep breath, she decided to go right to the source of that anger. "I take it Paul Gunderson wasn't aboard the plane you intercepted."

"No, he wasn't."

"I'm sorry."

"Yeah," he rasped. "Me, too. And it didn't exactly help matters when I arrived to find your apartment wide-open and you gone."

"Okay, that was careless."

"Careless? How about idiotic? Irresponsible?

"How about we don't get carried away here?" she snapped back.

Her spurt of defiance seemed to fuel his anger. He stepped even closer. Sheryl refused to back away, not that she could have if she'd wanted to. Her shoulder blades almost pressed against the wall as it was.

"Do you have any idea what I went through when I found the door open and you missing?"

The savagery in his voice jolted through her like an electrical shock. In another man, the suppressed violence might have frightened her. In Harry, it thrilled the tiny, adventurous corner of her soul she'd never known she possessed until he'd burst into her life.

How could she have fooled herself into believing she wanted safe and secure and comfortable? The truth hit her with devastating certainty.

She wanted the fierce emotion she saw blazing in this man's eyes.

She wanted the fire and excitement and the passion that only he had stirred in her.

She wanted Harry...however she could have him.

"No," she whispered. "I don't know what you went through. Tell me."

He buried his hands in her hair and pulled her head back. "I'll show you."

This kiss didn't even come close to resembling the ones they'd shared last night. Those were wild and tender and passionate. This one was raw. Elemental. Primitive. So powerful that Sheryl's head went back and her entire body arched into his.

Nor did Harry display any of the teasing finesse he'd used on her before. His mouth claimed hers. Rough and urgent, his hands found her hips and lifted her into him. Sweat-slick and breathless and instantly aroused, Sheryl felt him harden against her.

He dragged his head up. Nostrils flaring, he stared down at her. Raw male need stretched the skin over his cheekbones tight and turned the golden lights in his eyes to small, blazing fires.

Sheryl wasn't stupid. She knew that this barely controlled savagery sprang as much from his frustration over his failure to nab Paul Gunderson last night as from the worry and anger she'd inadvertently sparked in him this morning. She didn't care. Wherever it sprang from, it consumed her.

Wanting him every bit as fiercely as he wanted her, she slid an arm around his neck and dragged his head back down. She knew the instant his mouth covered hers that a kiss wasn't enough. She fumbled for his belt buckle. He stiffened, then attacked the wooden buttons on her denim sundress. The little fasteners went flying. They landed on the tiles with a series of sharp pops. The dress hit the floor somewhere between the entryway and the bedroom. His jeans and shirt followed.

On fire with a need that slicked her inside and out, Sheryl pushed Harry to the bed and straddled him. He was ready for her. More than ready. But when he reached for her hips to lift her onto his rigid shaft, she wiggled backward.

"Oh, no! Not this time. This time, I want to give you what you gave me last night."

"Sheryl..."

"I'm going to wind you up tight," she promised. "And leave you breathless and dizzy and wanting more."

Much more. So much more.

Her fingers combed the hair on his belly. Moved lower. At her touch, his stomach hollowed. Hot, velvety steel filled her hand. Sheryl's throat went dry. She ran her tongue over her lips.

His shaft leaped in her hand. With a wicked smile that surprised her almost as much as it did Harry, she bent and proceeded to leave him breathless and groaning and wanting more.

Much more.

She was still smiling when she and Harry both dropped into an exhausted stupor.

A bounce of the bedsprings woke her with a jerk some time later. Harry shot straight up, his face a study in sleep-hazed confusion.

"Oh, God!" she moaned. "What now?"

"Did you just—"

He broke off, his entire body stiffening. An expression of profound disgust replaced his confusion. Yanking back the rumpled black-and-white Zuni blanket, he glared at the animal wedged comfortably between their knees.

Button lifted his head and snarled, obviously as displeased at having his rest disturbed as Harry was. The two males wore such identical expressions of dislike that Sheryl fell back on the bed, giggling helplessly.

"You should see your face," she gasped.

Harry didn't share her amusement. "Yeah, well, you should try waking up to a set of claws raking down your thigh."

"I have," she told him, still giggling. "Believe me, I have."

For a moment, he looked as though he intended to take Button on for undisputed possession of the bed. Bit by bit, the light of battle went out of his eyes. Rasping a hand across his chin, he let out a long breath.

"I've got to go."

Sheryl's giggles died, but she managed to keep her smile going. "I know."

"Even though we didn't get Gunderson, we've still got some matters to clear up from last night. Ev will be waiting for me."

She nodded.

"Mind if I use your shower?"

"Be my guest," she said with deliberate nonchalance. "I've even got a razor in there. It's contoured for a woman's legs, but I think it'll scrape off everything but your mustache."

While the water pelted against the shower door, Sheryl slipped out of bed and retrieved her sundress. She wouldn't regret his leaving, she repeated over and over, as if it were a mantra. She wouldn't try to hold him.

She couldn't, even if she wanted to.

She could only keep her smile fixed firmly in place when he walked out of the shower, his chest bare above his jeans and his dark hair glistening.

He gathered his clothes. By the time he buckled on his holster, a frown creased his brow. He crossed to where she sat on the edge of the bed.

"I'll call you."

"Ha! That's what they all say."

Her feeble attempt at humor fell flat. If anything, the line in his forehead grooved even deeper.

"I'll call you. That's all I can promise."

Sheryl sympathized with the wrenching conflict she saw in his eyes. He wanted to leave. Needed to leave. Yet something he couldn't quite articulate tugged at him. That something gave her the courage to rise slowly and lift her palms to his cheeks.

Like Harry, she'd gone through a bit of wrenching herself in the past few days. Without wanting to, without trying to, she'd slipped out of her nice, easy routine and discovered that she wanted more of life than comfort and security.

Harry had shown her what life could…should…be. He'd given her a taste of excitement, of adventure. Of something that she was beginning to recognize as love. She wasn't sure when she'd fallen for this rough-edged marshal, but she had. She suspected it had happened last night, when she'd opened the door and found him standing there with his pineapple-and-Canadian-bacon pizza. She'd known it this morning, when he pinned her against the wall and everything inside her had leaped at his touch.

She was willing to take a chance that what she felt could withstand the test of time. The trial of separation and the tears of loneliness. She wanted to believe that what she could share with Harry was special, different…unlike what her parents had shared.

He hadn't reached that point yet. She saw the hesitation in his eyes. Heard it in his voice. Maybe he'd never reach it. Maybe he'd walk out the door, get caught up in his investigation and forget her.

And maybe he wouldn't.

Sheryl would risk it.

"I didn't ask for any promises, Marshal," she said softly. "I don't need them."

Her smile gentling, she rose on tiptoe and brushed his mouth with a kiss.

"Call me when you can."

For the next few hours, she jumped every time the phone rang…which didn't make for a restful morning, considering that it rang constantly.

Elise called first. After a glowing recount of the baby's first night, she mentioned that the doctor had cleared them both to go home tomorrow.

"So soon?"

"It'll be forty-eight hours, Sher. That's long enough for either of us."

"I'll drive you."

"Thanks, but Brian said he would take us home. Do you suppose you could swing by my house to pick up some clean clothes, though? Mine got a little messed up when I fell."

"Sure." Wedging the phone between her ear and her shoulder, Sheryl reached for a pad and pen. "Tell me what you need."

She scribbled down the short list and hung up, promising to see Elise and the baby later this morning. Just seconds after that, the phone rang again. Her heart jumping, she snatched up the receiver.

It took some doing, but she finally managed to convince the telemarketer at the other end that she did *not* want to switch her long distance carrier.

The third call came shortly after that. Her mother wanted to hear about Elise's delivery.

Sheryl sank onto the sofa. This conversation would take a lot longer than the one she'd just had with the telemarketer, she knew. Scratching Button's ears absently, she told her mother what had happened at the hospital…and afterward. The news that Sheryl had failed to perform her coaching duties surprised Joan Hancock. The news of her breakup with Brian left her stuttering.

"But…but…you two were almost engaged!"

"'Almost' is the operative word, Mom."

"I don't understand. What happened?"

Sighing, Sheryl crossed her ankles on the sturdy bleached-oak plank that served as her coffee table. She'd abandoned her now almost buttonless denim dress for a cool, gauzy turquoise top and matching flowered leggings. With Button snuggled against her thighs, she tried to explain to her mother the feelings she'd only recently discovered herself.

"We decided that we wanted more than what we had together."

"You don't even know *what* you had! You'd better think twice, Sheryl Ann Hancock, before you let a man like Brian slip through your fingers."

Joan's voice took on the brittle edge her daughter recognized all too well. Mentally, Sheryl braced herself.

"He's so nice," her mother argued. "So reliable. He'd never leave you to lie awake at night wondering where he was, or make you worry about whether he had a decent meal or remembered to take his blood pressure medicine."

Recalling the near-sleepless night she'd just spent wondering and worrying about Harry, Sheryl could only agree.

"No, he wouldn't."

"Call him," Joan urged. "Brian loves you. I know he does. Tell him you made a mistake. Tell him you want to patch things up. And I suggest you do it before that so-called friend of yours sinks her claws in him."

Sheryl blinked at the acid comment. "What are you talking about?"

"Oh, come on! I may get up to Albuquerque only a few times a month, but that's more than enough for me to see that Elise knows very well what a prize Brian is, if you don't. She's been mooning after him ever since her divorce."

Struck, Sheryl thought back over the past few months. Elise hadn't exactly mooned over Brian, but she, like Joan, was forever singing his praises. Then there was that kiss at the hospital to consider, when Elise had dragged the man down by his tie. And the substitute father's wide-eyed wonder in the baby.

A huge grin tracked across Sheryl's face. Harry had all but wiped away the ache in her heart caused by her breakup with Brian. She and the marshal might or might not ever reach the "almost" point she'd reached with Brian. Right now, though, she couldn't think of anything that would please her more than for her two best friends to find the same passion, the same wild need, that she'd discovered in Harry's arms.

She sprang up, dislodging the sleeping dog in the process. He gave her a disgusted look and plopped down again.

"I've gotta go, Mom. I have to swing by Elise's house to pick up some clothes for her. Then I'm heading for the hospital. She and I need to talk."

"Yes," her mother sniffed. "You do."

Still grinning, Sheryl hung up and headed for the bedroom. She was halfway across the room when the phone rang again. She spun around, ignoring the protest of her bruised heel, and grabbed the phone.

It had to be Harry this time!

"Miss Hancock?"

She swallowed her swift disappointment. "Yes?"

"My name is Don Ortega. I'm an attorney representing a woman you know as Mrs. Inga Gunderson."

"Oh! Yes, I think I heard your name mentioned."

"I understand from Marshal Everett Sloan that you're keeping my client's dog."

She eyed the animal sprawled in blissful abandon on her sofa.

"Well, I'm not sure who's keeping whom, but he's here. Why? Does Mrs. Gunderson want me to take him to someone else?"

She frowned, wondering why the thought of losing her uninvited houseguest didn't fill her with instant elation. The mutt had chewed up her underwear, sprayed her dining-room chair and led her on a not-so-merry chase through the apartment complex this morning. Even worse, his sharp claws had brought Harry jerking straight up this morning, as they had her more than once the past few nights. She ought to be dancing with joy at the prospect of dumping him on some other unsuspecting victim.

Instead, she breathed an inexplicable sigh of relief when the lawyer responded to her question with a negative.

"No, my client doesn't have any close friends or acquaintances in Albuquerque. She's just worried about her, er, Butty-boo. She asked me to check with you and find out if you'd given him his heartworm pill," he finished on a dry note.

"I didn't know he needed one."

"According to my client, he has to have one today. She was quite insistent about it. Evidently, her dog almost died last year when the worms got into his bloodstream and wrapped around his heart."

The gruesome description made Sheryl gulp.

"She says that he could pick up another infestation if he misses even one dose of the medication," Ortega advised her.

"So where can I get this medication?"

"If you wouldn't mind going to the pet store on Menaul, where Mrs. Gunderson does business, you can pick up the pills and charge them to her account. My client has instructed me to call ahead and authorize the expenditure."

"Well..."

She hesitated, wondering if she should contact Harry or Ev Sloan before she acceded to the attorney's request. But Ev had vouched for the lawyer himself, she recalled, swearing that he was tough but straight. Evidently, he also cared enough about his clients to relay their concern for their pets.

"I don't mind," she told Ortega. "Give me the address of this store."

She jotted it down just below the list of items Elise had asked her to bring to the hospital.

"I was just leaving to visit a friend at University Hospital. I'll stop at the pet store on my way."

"Thank you, Miss Hancock. I'm sure my client will be most grateful."

His client, Sheryl discovered when she walked out of the pet store a little over an hour later, was more than grateful. She was lying in wait for her...in the form of two men with slicked-back hair, unsmiling eyes, shiny gray suits and black turtlenecks that must have made them miserable in Albuquerque's sweltering heat.

One of the men appeared at Sheryl's side just as she unlocked her car door. The other materialized from behind a parked car. Before she had done more than glance at them, before she could grasp their intent, before she could scream or even try to twist away, the shorter of the men slapped a folded handkerchief over her mouth.

She fought for two or three seconds. Two or three breaths. Then the street and the car and the gray suits tilted crazily. Another breath, and they disappeared in a haze of blackness.

Chapter 12

"Dammit, where is she?"

Harry paced the task force operations center like a caged, hungry and very irritated panther. He'd been trying to reach Sheryl since just after ten, and it was now almost three.

Ev Sloan leaned back in his chair and watched his partner's restless prowling. Like Harry's, his face showed the effects of his previous long night in the tired lines and gray shadows under his eyes.

"Want me to call central dispatch and have them put out an APB?"

Harry shoved his hands in his pockets and jiggled his loose change. His gut urged him to agree to the all-points bulletin, but this morning's fiasco held him back. He didn't want to use up any more chits with the Albuquerque police than he already had. Sheryl was probably out shopping or visiting friends. A patrol car had already swung by her apartment and verified that her car wasn't in its assigned slot...and the door to her place was shut!

"We'll hold off on the APB," he growled.

"Whatever you say." Ev scraped a hand across the stubble on his chin. "I'm getting too old for this kind of work. I used to get an adrenaline fix from a takedown like last night's that would last me for weeks. Now all I want to do is to nail this bastard Gunderson, go home, kick off my shoes and grab the remote."

"I'll settle for seeing my son's T-ball team bring in just one run," Fay put in with a smile.

The other two men at the conference table took up the refrain. They'd joined the team this morning, each an expert in his own field. While they tossed desultory comments about the best way to ease the strain that gripped them all, Harry paced the length of the room again, his change jingling.

Why the hell couldn't he shake this edgy, unfinished feeling that had been with him almost since he'd left Sheryl this morning?

Because he'd left Sheryl this morning.

He had to face the truth. The way he'd walked out of her arms and her apartment was eating at him from the inside out. It didn't do any good to remind himself that he'd had to get back to the command center and attend to the up-channel reports from the drug bust last night. Or that he'd wanted another go at Inga Gunderson. The blasted woman still refused to talk, except to pester Harry and Ev and her lawyer, Don Ortega, with repeated instructions on the care and feeding of her precious Button. Harry had come out of this morning's session at the detention center so tight jawed with frustration that his back teeth ached.

A flash message from the CIA with the news that they'd traced the six canisters of depleted uranium to Rio de Janeiro had only added to his mounting tension. The shipment had to be heading for the States any day now.

Any hour.

As a result of that message, the task force had redoubled its efforts. Fay had asked the FAA to send out an alert to every airport manager in the four-state area, then contacted her highway patrol counterparts. Ev had pulled in two more deputy marshals from the Albuquerque office. The added personnel were following up every lead, however tenuous, including an unconfirmed report of a visit to the city by two thugs who supposedly strong-armed for a known illegal arms dealer.

Harry had plenty to occupy his mind...yet he'd interrupted his work a half-dozen times in the past five hours to call Sheryl. Between calls, he'd find himself thinking of her at every unguarded moment.

His fists closed around the loose coins. He shouldn't have just walked out like that. After what they'd shared, his refusal to make any promises must have hit her like a slap in the face.

What the hell kind of promises could he make? he thought savagely. That he'd return to her apartment tonight? Tomorrow night? For however long he was in town? That he'd swing through Albuquerque every few months and take her up on the offer that shimmered in her green eyes when he'd left this morning? That he'd ask her to share his life...or at least the few weeks of relatively normal life he enjoyed before he hit the road again?

The thought of sharing any kind of a life with Sheryl grabbed at Harry with a force that sucked the air right out of his lungs. He stared at the wall, the edge of the coins cutting into his palm. For a moment, he let himself contemplate a future that included nights like last night. Mornings like the one he'd woken up to today.

He wouldn't even mind the hairy little mutt digging his claws into his groin again just to hear Sheryl's laughter. His throat closed at the memory of those helpless giggles and the way she'd fallen back on the bed, her hair spilling across the blanket and her rosy-tipped breasts peaking in the cool air-conditioning.

Angrily, he shook his head to clear the erotic image. Why in the world was he putting himself through this? He'd learned the hard way that fugitive operations and a stable home life didn't make for a compatible mix. Sheryl, too, had seen firsthand her parents' inability to sustain a long-distance marriage. Harry had damned well better stop thinking about impossible futures and concentrate on right here, right now.

Which brought him back full circle to the question of where Sheryl was at this moment. More irritable and edgy than ever, he strode back to the conference table and reached for the phone.

"Maybe her friend in the hospital knows where she is," he said curtly in answer to Ev's quizzical look. "I'll make one more call, then we need to go over today's scheduled flights into every major airport in the four-state area. I want copies of all passenger lists and cargo manifests as soon as they're filed."

The operator patched him though to University Hospital, which in turn connected him with Elise Hart's room. Harry recognized instantly the male voice that answered on the second ring. What did Sheryl's former boyfriend do—live at the damned hospital?

Curtly, he identified himself. "This is Harry MacMillan. I'm trying to reach Sheryl."

Just as curtly, Brian Mitchell responded. "She's not here."

"Do you know where she is?"

"No." Mitchell hesitated, then continued in a less abrupt tone. "As a matter of fact, I was thinking of calling you, Marshal. Sheryl told Elise that she'd swing by her house to pick up some clean clothes before she came to the hospital this morning. She hasn't shown up and doesn't answer her phone."

Harry stiffened. The prickly sixth sense that had been nagging at him all day vaulted into full-fledged alarm.

"We're a little worried about her," Brian finished.

A little worried! Christ!

"I'll check it out."

The real-estate-agent's voice sharpened once again. "She's okay, isn't she? This manhunt you pulled her into hasn't put her in danger."

"I'll check it out."

"I want you to notify me immediately when you find her!"

Yeah, right. Harry palmed him off with a half promise and slammed the phone down. Then he snatched his jacket off the back of a chair and headed for the door.

"Call the APD, Ev. Ask them to put out that all-points. And ask them to have their locksmith meet me at Sheryl's apartment."

Ev took one look at his partner's face and grabbed for the phone. "Right away!"

Harry wheeled the souped-up sedan out of the underground parking garage. The tires whined on the hot asphalt. Merging the vehicle into the light weekend traffic flow, he willed himself into a state of rigid control. He'd carried a five-pointed gold star too long to give in to the concern churning like bile in his belly.

Adobe-fronted strip malls and tree-shaded residences whizzed by. Ahead, the Sandia Mountains loomed brownish gray against an endless blue sky. The stutter of a jackhammer cut through the heat of the afternoon.

The sights and sounds registered on Harry's consciousness, but didn't penetrate. His mind was spinning with possibilities. Sheryl could have gone in to work. No one had answered at the Monzano Branch when he'd called earlier, but they might not answer the phones during off-hours.

She could be running errands. The time could have slipped away from her, and she'd forgotten her promise to stop by the hospital this morning.

Or she might have taken off on another jaunt with that damned dog. Hell, she'd chased him barefoot around the whole complex only this morning and left her door open to all comers.

His hands fisted on the steering wheel. He'd strangle her! If she'd ignored all security measures again and scared the hell out of him like this, he'd strangle her...right after he locked the door behind them, tumbled her onto the bed and told her just how much he'd hated leaving her this morning!

Assuming, a small, cold corner of his mind countered, that Sheryl was in any state to hear him.

At that moment, she wasn't.

Her stomach swirled with nausea. Her throat burned. Black spots danced under her closed lids.

In a desperate effort to clear her blurred vision, Sheryl lifted her head an inch or two. Even that slight movement brought an acrid taste into her dry, parched throat and made her senses swim. Moaning, she let her head fall. It hit the bare mattress with a soft plop, raising a musty cloud of dust motes.

"Ya back with us, sweetheart?"

The thin, nasal voice drifted through the sickening haze. Sheryl's clogged mind had barely separated the words enough to make sense of them when a deeper, almost rasping voice came from somewhere above and behind her.

"The next time you do a broad, you idiot, cut the dosage."

"Hey, enough already! You been on my back for hours about that."

"Yeah?"

The vicious snarl scraped across Sheryl's skin like a dull knife. "Who do you think is gonna be on our backs if we miss this drop?"

"She's coming 'round, ain't she?"

"It's about damn time."

Without warning, a palm cracked against Sheryl's cheek.

"Come on, wake up."

Gasping at the pain that splintered across her face, she fought to bring the figure bending over her into focus. A greasy shine appeared…black hair, slicked back, reflecting the light of the single overhead bulb.

She blinked. Her lids gritted like sandpaper against her eyes. Slowly, she made out a wide, unshaven jaw above a black turtleneck. A pair of unsmiling eyes in a face some people might have considered handsome.

"We ain't gonna hurt you."

"You…" She swiped her tongue around her cottony mouth. "You…just…did."

"That little love tap?" The stranger snorted and dug a hand into her armpit. "Come on, sit up and take a drink. We gotta talk."

The mists fogging Sheryl's mind shredded enough for her to grasp the fact that her wrists were tied behind her. Fear spurted like ice water through her veins. Her feet dropped to the floor with a thump, first one, then the other. She swayed, dizzy and confused and more scared than she'd ever been before. The grip on her arm held her upright.

Another figure appeared from the dimness to her side, holding a glass. When he shoved it at her lips, Sheryl shrank away. A fist buried itself in her hair, yanked her head back.

"It's just water. Drink it."

With the glass chinking against her teeth, she didn't have a whole lot of choice. Most of the tepid liquid ran down her chin, but enough got through her teeth to satisfy the pourer.

The fist loosened. Sheryl brought her head up and eased the ache in her neck. Gradually, the black swirls in front of her eyes subsided

"Wh…? Where am I?"

The words came out in a croak, but Slick Hair understood them. He flicked an impatient hand.

"It don't matter where you are. What matters is where you're going."

She swallowed painfully. Her heart thumping with fear, she met her kidnapper's unsmiling gaze.

"Where am I going?"

A snigger sounded beside her. "That's what you're gonna tell us, sweetheart."

She swung her head toward the second man. Like Slick Hair, this one also wore a black turtleneck and a shiny gray suit. It must be some kind of uniform, she thought with a touch of hysteria. He had small, pinched eyes and a nasal pitch that grated on her ears. He came from somewhere east of New Mexico, obviously. Or maybe he owed that whine to the fact that someone or something had flattened his nose against his face.

Slick Hair scraped a chair across the bare wood floor, twisted it around and straddled the seat. With Broken Nose hovering at his shoulder, he smiled thinly.

"We need to have us a little chat, Sheryl." At her start of surprise, his smile took on a sadistic edge. "What? You don't think we know your name? Of course we know it. We got it from Inga this morning."

Despite her fear and the pain lancing through her face and wrists, her head had cleared enough by now for her to grasp that the men confronting her had some connection to Harry's investigation. She just hadn't expected them to admit it so readily.

"How...?" She swallowed. "How did you talk to Inga? She's in..."

"In jail?" Slick Hair waved a hand, dismissing the small irritation of police custody. "Those bastards at the detention center wouldn't allow her more than her one damn call to her lawyer, but Inga's a shrewd old broad. She got this Ortega guy to call the shop and let our little friend there know you were coming."

"The pet shop?"

"Yeah," Broken Nose put in. "We been hangin' out there, waiting for Inga to show. We was worried when we heard the cops snatched her, but like Big Ja—'' He caught himself. ''Like my friend here says, she's a smart old broad. We just waited, and sure enough, she sent you.''

Slick Hair folded his forearms across the back of the chair. His eyes settled on her face.

''So, you wanna tell us about the postcard?''

She tried to bluff it out. ''What postcard?''

''The one that come in from Rio, Sheryl. The one from Rio.''

''I don't know what you're talking about. No one sent me any postcards, from Rio or anywhere else.''

''Come on, sweetheart,'' Broken Nose whined. ''We got contacts, ya know. It didn't take no undercover dick to find out you work at a post office. Since Inga sent you to the shop, you gotta have the information we want.''

''No, I—''

In a move so swift that Sheryl didn't even see it coming, Slick Hair's arm whipped out. The backhanded blow sent her tumbling sideways onto the bare mattress. She lay there for endless seconds, biting her lip against the pinwheeling pain. She wouldn't cry! She wouldn't give in to the fear coursing through her!

Harry was looking for these men or their partner in crime. He'd soon come looking for her, too. She didn't know how long she'd been out, or where she was now, or what was going to happen next, but she just had to hold on. Find out what she could. Get word to Harry somehow.

Slowly, awkwardly, she pushed herself up on one elbow and faced her captors.

''Now, tell us about the card from Rio, Sheryl.''

''Wh…?'' She wet her lips. ''What do you want to know?''

Slick Hair smiled again, his thin lips slicing across the strong planes of his face. ''Smart girl. Just tell me what Paul wrote on the back.''

Bitterly regretting that she'd ever peeked at Inga Gunderson's mail, much less harbored any concern for her welfare, Sheryl summoned a mental picture of the bright, gaudy Carnival street scene. The words on the back of the card formed, went hazy, reformed.

"'Hi to my favorite aunt,'" she recited dully. "'I've been dancing in the streets for the past five days. Wish you were here.'"

"Five days!"

Broken Nose did a quick turn about the room. It was empty of all but a rickety table, the two chairs and the cot she sat on, Sheryl saw. A blanket covered the only window.

"Five days past the date of the last drop," the smaller man continued excitedly. "Lessee. Last time, we picked up the stuff on the third. Five days past that would make it the eighth. Tomorrow. Damn! We got another whole day to wait."

Slick Hair didn't move, didn't take his eyes off Sheryl's face. With everything in her, she tried not to flinch as he reached out and twisted a hand through her hair.

"I don't think you're giving it to us straight," he said softly, bringing her face to within inches of his own. "You sure that postcard said 'five' days, Sheryl? Think hard. Real hard."

"Yes," she gasped. "Yes, I'm sure."

Slick Hair looked into her eyes for another few moments. "Get the needle," he told his partner quietly.

She tried to jerk away. "No!"

His painful grip kept her still.

"It's just a little drug we got from a friendly doc, Sheryl. It'll help you remember. Help you get the details right."

There was no way she was going to allow these men to stick a needle in her. God only knows who had used it before or what drug they'd pump into her.

"Maybe… Maybe it said 'four days.'"

Satisfaction flared in the eyes so close to her own. "Maybe it did, Sheryl."

"Jesus!" Broken Nose thumped his fist against his shiny pantleg. "That's tonight!"

"So it is," Slick Hair mused. "That must be why Inga sent you to us, Sheryl. She was probably in a real sweat, knowin' Paul was coming in tonight and no one would be there to greet him. Well, we'll be there.''

Sheryl closed her eyes in an agony of remorse. Harry! I'm sorry! I'm so sorry.

''You'll be there, too,'' Slick Hair finished, easing his grip on her hair. ''If Paul doesn't show, we're gonna be real, real unhappy with you.''

The threat should have paralyzed her with fear. Instead, it slowly penetrated her despair and lit a tiny spark of anger. She hoped Paul Gunderson *did* show. She hoped he walked off a plane tonight and found not only these creeps, but a small army of law enforcement officials waiting for him. She hoped to hell she was there to see it when Harry took Gunderson and these two goons down.

Which he would! She knew he would! These men didn't realize that Harry would tear the city apart when he discovered she was missing. He'd find her car, trace her to the pet store. It wouldn't take him long to tie that visit back to Inga Gunderson. Maybe he already had.

He'd find a way to make Inga talk.

He had to!

Chapter 13

Ev Sloan waited for Harry on the steps of the Bernalilo County Detention Center. Even though the sun had dropped behind the cluster of downtown buildings and shadows stretched across the street, sweat streaked Ev's face and plastered his shirt to his chest. As he'd told Fay just before he'd left her at the operations center, he sincerely hoped he'd never have to go through again what he'd experienced since the Albuquerque police had located Sheryl Hancock's abandoned car three hellish hours ago.

His gut had twisted at the realization that the woman he'd worked with for the past couple of days had been snatched right off the street. As deep as it went, his worry over Sheryl's status didn't begin to compare with Harry's. Not that MacMillan's wrenching desperation showed to anyone who didn't know him. Ev had worked with him long enough to recognize the signs, though. The stark fury, quickly masked. The fear, even more quickly hidden. The cold, implacable determination that had driven him every minute since they'd found the car.

Thank God for the crumpled piece of paper under the Camry's front seat. Sheryl's hand-scribbled list had led them to the pet shop and to the nervous shop owner, who'd IDed the two men who'd followed their victim out of the store. The process of identifying them might have taken a whole lot longer than it had if Harry hadn't instantly connected them to the two strong-arms rumored to have been sighted in Albuquerque. With the FBI's help, they now had names, backgrounds and mug shots of both men. Through a screening of Sheryl's phone calls this morning, they also had a link to Don Ortega.

Attorney and client were waiting inside for them now. Ev didn't kid himself. This interview was going to be a rough one. He'd known that since Harry had stalked out of the task force command center a half hour ago, instructing Ev to meet him at the detention center. But he didn't realize how rough until he saw MacMillan climbing out of the sedan that squealed to a stop in front of the steps.

Ev's eyes bugged at the bundle of black-and-white fur wedged under his partner's arm. "Why did you bring that thing down here?"

The car door slammed. "Everyone's got a weak spot in their defenses. Butty-boo here is Inga's."

Spinning around, Ev followed Harry up the steps. "Christ, Mac-Millan, you're not going to do something stupid like strangle the mutt in front of the old woman to get her to talk?"

"That's one possibility."

"You can't! You know you can't! Ortega will have the DA, the IG, the SPCA and everyone else he can contact down on our heads!"

"Ortega's going to have his hands full dodging a charge of accessory to a kidnapping," Harry shot back.

He shoved through the glass doors, leaving Ev to trail him into the cavernous lobby. The dog tucked under his arm looked around, black eyes bright with interest. He must have spotted something that he didn't like across the lobby because he promptly let loose with a series of shrill yips that ricocheted off the marble walls and hit Ev's eardrums like sharp, piercing arrows.

"Think, man!" he urged over the noise. "Think! You can't hurt the animal, as much as we'd both like to. You can't even threaten to hurt it. You'll jeopardize our case against both Inga and Paul Gunderson if we ever get them to court. They'll say Inga confessed under duress. That she—"

Harry swung around, his eyes blazing. "Right now, our case takes second place to Sheryl Hancock's safety."

His barely contained fury cut Button off in midbark The sudden silence pounded at all three participants in the small drama.

"I dragged her into this," Harry said savagely. "I'm damned well going to get her out."

"By strangling the mutt?"

He blew out a long breath. Some of the fury left his face, but none of the determination. His gaze dropped to the dog. Someone had drawn its facial hair up and tied it with a pink bow. Sheryl, Ev supposed. MacMillan looked about as ridiculous as a man could with the prissy thing tucked under his arm.

"I won't hurt him. I couldn't. If I did, Sheryl would be on my case worse than the old woman. Beats me what either of them sees in the little rat."

Despite his professed dislike for the creature, he knuckled the furry forehead with a gentleness that made Ev blink.

"Then why did you bring him here?"

Harry's hand stilled. When he looked up, his eyes were flat and hard once again.

"If nothing else, I'm going to make damned sure Inga Gunderson knows what happens to animals left unclaimed at the pound for more than three days."

They were heading south on I-25.

That much Sheryl could see from the back floor of the panel truck. Every so often an overhead highway sign would flash in the front windshield where her two captors sat. She'd catch just enough of it to make out a few letters and words.

She shifted on the hard floor, trying to ease the burning ache in her shoulder sockets. The movement only sharpened the pain shooting from her shoulders to her fingertips. She'd long ago given up her futile attempts to twist free of the tape that bound her wrists together behind her back.

All in all, she was more miserable and frightened than she'd ever been in her life. She hadn't drunk anything except the water Slick Hair had poured down her throat hours ago. Hadn't eaten anything since the poppy-seed muffin she'd gulped down before heading out the door this morning. She needed to go to the bathroom, badly, but she'd swallow nails before she asked her kidnappers to stop the truck, escort her to a bathroom and pull down her flowered leggings!

Not that she could ask them even if she wanted to. The bastards had slapped a wide strip of duct tape over her mouth before hauling her outside and hustling her into the waiting truck.

Her physical discomfort sapped her strength. The constant battle to hang on to to her desperate belief that Harry would find her drained it even more.

How long had it been now? Nine hours since she'd walked out of the pet shop on Menaul Avenue? Ten?

How long since Harry had realized that she was missing?

Bright highway lights flashed by in the windshield. Sheryl tried to concentrate on them, tried to keep her mind focused on the tiny details that might help if she had to reconstruct events for Harry after this was all over.

Despite her fierce concentration, doubts and sneaking, sinking fear ate away at her. What if Harry hadn't called her, as he'd promised he would? What if he'd gotten so caught up in his investigation that he didn't have time? Oh, God, what if he didn't even know she was missing?

She closed her eyes, fighting the panic that threatened to swamp her.

He said he'd call. He'd promised he would. What Harry promised, he'd do. She'd learned that much about him in the short, intense time they'd been together. He'd called her sometime today. She knew he had. And when she hadn't answered, he'd started looking.

He'd find her.

Battling fiercely with her incipient panic, she almost missed the click of directional signals. A moment later, the truck slowed and banked into a turn. Signs flashed by overhead, but Sheryl couldn't catch the lettering.

After another mile or so, Broken Nose twisted around. "It's show time, doll. You'd better hope our star performer shows."

Dragging a folded moving pad from under his seat, he shook it out and tossed it over her. Total blackness surrounded her, along with the stink of mildew and motor oil. Sheryl closed her eyes and prayed that she'd see Harry when she opened them.

She didn't.

When the pad was jerked away, Broken Nose loomed over her once more. His face was a grotesque mask of shadows in the diffused light of the truck's interior.

"Come on, sweetheart," he whined. "You're gonna wait inside. We don't want no nosy Customs inspectors catchin' sight of you in the truck, do we?"

Wrapping his paw around her elbow, he hauled her out of the truck. Pain zigzagged like white, agonizing lightning up and down Sheryl's arm. She couldn't breathe, let alone groan, through the duct tape sealing her mouth.

Broken Nose hauled her to her feet outside the truck and hustled her toward one of the rear doors in a corrugated steel hangar. Sheryl stumbled along beside him, trying desperately to clear her head of the pain and get her bearings. The air she dragged in through her nostrils carried with it the unmistakable bite of jet fuel fumes. The distant whine of engines revving up confirmed she was at the airport.

The moment her captor shoved her inside the huge, steel-sided building, she recognized the cavernous, shadowy interior. She could never forget it! She'd worked at rotation at the airport cargo-handling facility as a young rookie, years ago, and had counted the months until she'd gained enough seniority to qualify for another opening. Palletizing the sacks of mail that came into this building from the central processing center downtown for air shipment was backbreaking, dirty work.

Sure enough, she spotted a long row of web-covered pallets in the postal service's caged-off portion of the hangar. Desperately, she searched the dimly lit area for someone she might know, someone who might see her. Before she could locate any movement in the vast, echoing facility, Broken Nose shouldered open a door and pushed her into what looked like a heating/air-conditioning room. In the weak moonlight filtering through the single, dust-streaked window, Sheryl saw a litter of discarded web cargo straps, empty crates and broken chairs amid the rusted duct pipes.

Her captor surveyed the dust-covered floor and grunted in satisfaction. "Ain't nobody been in since I scouted this place out two days ago."

Roughly, he dragged Sheryl across the room and shoved her down onto a tangle of web cargo straps. She landed awkwardly on one knee. A hard hand in her back sent her tumbling onto her hip. Her elbow hit the concrete floor beneath the straps. Searing pain jolted into her shoulder, blinding her. Tears filled her eyes. She barely heard the snap as Broken Nose pulled another length of tape from his roll, barely felt her ankles jammed against a pipe and lashed together.

She felt the fist that buried itself in her hair, though, and a painful jerk as he brought her face around to his.

"We're gonna be right outside, see? Pickin' up our cargo soon's the lamebrain from Customs clears it. Everything goes okay, I'll come back for you."

His fist tightened in her hair.

"Anything goes wrong, I might or might not come back for you. If I don't, maybe someone'll find you in a week or a month. Or maybe they won't. You won't be so pretty when they do."

Grinning maliciously, he stroked a finger down her cheek. Sheryl couldn't move enough to flinch from his touch, but she put every drop of loathing she could into the look she sent him. Laughing, he left her in the musty darkness.

She lay, half on her side, half on her back, breathing in dust motes and the acrid scent of her own fear. Her relief that they'd left her for even a few moments was almost as great as her discomfort. Her shoulder was on fire. Her elbow throbbed. The metal clasp on one of the web straps gouged into her hip.

She didn't care. For the first time since she'd walked out of the pet store this morning, she was out of her captor's sight. Ignoring her various aches and pains, she twisted and turned, pulling at the tape binding her ankles to the pipe. The metal pole didn't budge, nor did the tape give, but she did manage to generate a small shower of rust particles and bugs. Praying that none of the insects that dropped down on her were of the biting variety, she tugged and twisted and pushed and pulled.

By the time she conceded defeat, she was filmed with sweat and rust and wheezing in air through her nose. For a moment, the panic she'd kept at bay for so many hours almost swamped her.

Where was Harry? Why hadn't he tracked her down? He was a U.S. marshal, for God's sake? He was supposed to be able to find anyone. Where was he?

Gradually, she fought down her panic. Slowly, she got her breath back. Blinking the sweat from her eyes, she shifted on the pile of straps to try again. Another pain shot up from her elbow. The edge of a strap buckle dug into her hip.

Suddenly, Sheryl froze. The strap buckles! The metal tongue of the clasp that connected the web straps had sharp edges. She'd cut herself on the damned things often enough as a rookie. If she could get a grip on one of the buckles, get the clasp open…

Sweating, straining, wiggling as much as her ankles would allow, Sheryl groped the pile underneath her. Her slick fingers found a metal apparatus, pulled open the hasp. It slipped away from her and closed with a snap. She grabbed the buckle again, holding it awkwardly with one hand.

Grimly determined now, she fumbled one of the thick straps into her hand. If she could just pry the buckle open enough…

Yes!

Too excited for caution, she slid a fingertip along the edge of the hasp. Instantly, warm blood welled from the slicing cut.

The thing was as sharp as she remembered!

Her heart thumping, she went to work on the duct tape. She'd freed her wrists and was working on her ankles when a sharp rap shattered the glass in the dusty window. Pieces fell to the concrete. The small tinkles reverberated like shots in Sheryl's head.

An arm reached inside and fumbled for the lock.

With a burst of strength, Sheryl pulled apart the remaining half inch of duct tape. She scrambled to her feet, still gripping the metal clasp. It wasn't much of a weapon, but it was all she had.

Slowly, the window screeched upward. A moment later, a figure covered in black from head to toe climbed through. Even before he holstered his weapon and whipped off his ski mask, Sheryl had recognized the lean, muscular body.

"Harry!"

She threw herself across the room, broken glass crunching like popcorn under her feet. He crushed her against his chest.

"Are you all right?" he asked, his voice urgent in her ear.

She dismissed burning shoulders and aching wrists and cut fingers. "Yes."

"Thank God!"

His fierce embrace squeezed the air from Sheryl's lungs. She didn't care. At this moment, breathing didn't concern her. All that mattered was the feel of Harry's arms around her. Which didn't explain why she promptly burst into tears.

"It's all right, sweetheart," he soothed, his voice low and ragged. "It's all right. I'm here."

She leaned back, swallowing desperately, and stared up at him through a sheen of tears. "What took you so darned long?"

"It took me a while to convince Inga to talk."

"How…?" She gulped. "How did you do that?"

A small, tight smile flitted across Harry's face. "I got a little help from Button."

"From Button!"

He hustled her toward the window. "I'll tell you about it later. Right now, I just want to get you out of here. Then I'm going after the bastards who kidnapped you. My whole team's outside, ready to move in as soon as you're clear."

"No!" Sheryl spun around and grabbed at him with both hands. "You can't take those two down. Not yet! They're waiting for Paul Gunderson. He's coming in tonight, Harry. Tonight!"

"I know."

His slow, satisfied reply sent a shiver down her back. For a moment Sheryl almost didn't recognize the man who stared at her. His face could have been cut from rock.

Almost as quickly as it appeared, the fierceness left his eyes. In its place came a look that made her blink through the blur of her tears.

"Come on, sweetheart. Let's get you out of here."

Her fingers dug into the sleeves of his black windbreaker. She had to tell him. Had to let him know before he shoved her through the window and turned back into danger.

"Harry, I love you. I…I know it's too soon for commitments and promises and almost-anythings between us, but I—"

He cut off her disjointed declaration with a swift, hard, soul-shattering kiss.

"I love you, too. I suspected it this morning, when all I could think about was getting back to you. I knew it this afternoon, when we found your car." His jaw worked. "I don't *ever* want to go through that again, so let's get you the hell out of here. Now!"

They almost made it.

Her heart singing, Sheryl started for the window once more. Broken glass crunched under her feet and almost covered the sound of the door opening behind them.

"What the hell…?"

Harry spun around, yanking her behind him. Off balance and flailing for a hold, Sheryl didn't see him reach for his gun. Broken Nose did, though.

"Don't do it!" he shouted. Desperation added an octave to his high-pitched whine. "Your hand moves another inch and I swear to God, I'll put one of these hot slugs through you and the bitch both!"

Harry froze. A single glance at the oversized barrel on the weapon in the man's hand confirmed that it was engineered to fire uranium-tipped cop-killer bullets. The same kind of bullets that had ripped right through his best friend's body armor. Harry was willing to stop a bullet to protect Sheryl, but he couldn't, wouldn't, take the chance that it might plow right through him and into her, as well.

His pulse hammering, he lifted both hands clear of his sides. His Smith & Wesson sat like a dead weight in its holster just under his armpit.

"Yeah, yeah! That's better."

Even in the dim moonglow, Harry recognized the man whose flattened nose and jet-black hair he'd memorized from a mug shot less than an hour ago.

"All right, D'Agustino. Don't get crazy here and maybe we can work a deal."

"Jesus! You know who I am?"

"You and your partner both. You might as well give it up now. We've got this place surrounded."

"I knew it! I knew them guys in the coveralls weren't no wrench benders, not with them bulges under their arms. That's why I come running back for the broad. She's my ticket outta here."

Harry felt Sheryl go rigid against his back. Her fingers gripped his shirt. The image of her pinned helplessly against this killer raised a red haze in front of his eyes. Coldly, he blinked it away.

"She's not going anywhere with you, D'Agustino."

"Oh, yeah! Guess again."

The snick of a hammer cocking back added emphasis to the sneering reply.

Harry started to speak, and almost strangled on an indrawn breath. His whole body stiffened at the feel of a hand sliding around his rib cage. Without seeming to move, he brought his arms in just enough to cover Sheryl's reach for his holstered weapon.

Sweat rolled down his temples as her fingers slid under his arm. Sheryl hated guns! They made her nervous. She'd told him so more than once. She probably didn't have the faintest idea how to use one!

At that moment, Harry figured he had two options. He could throw himself at D'Agustino and hope to beat a bullet to the punch, or he could trust the woman behind him to figure out which end of a .357 was which.

It didn't even come close to a choice. He'd take his chances with Sheryl over this punk any day.

"Think about it D'Agustino," he said, trying desperately to buy her some time. "We know who you are. We know you've been working with Paul Gunderson. I have two dozen men waiting to greet him when his plane touches down a few minutes from now."

"Yeah, well, me and Sheryl ain't waiting around for that. Get over here, bitch!"

Harry could smell the man's fear. Hear it in his high, grating whine.

"You might get away this time, but we'll come after you. All of us. The FBI. The U.S. Marshals Service. Customs. Better give yourself up now. Talk to us."

"Don't you understand! I'm a dead man if Big Jake hears I cut a deal with the feds!"

"You're a dead man if you don't."

"No! No, I ain't!"

He knew the instant D'Agustino's gun came up that time had just run out.

He dived across the room.

A shot exploded an inch from his ear.

Sheryl didn't kill the little bastard. She didn't even wound him. But she startled him just enough to throw off his aim.

His gun barrel spit red flame. A finger of fire seared across Harry's cheek. The wild shot ricocheted off a pipe and gouged into the ceiling at precisely the same instant his fist smashed into an already flattened nose with a satisfying, bone-crunching force.

D'Agustino reared back, howling. A bruising left fist followed the right. The man crumpled like a sack of stones.

His chest heaving, Harry reached down and jerked the specially crafted .45 out of his hand. Although the thug showed no signs of moving any time soon, he kept the gun trained at his heart. Over the prone body, his anxious gaze found Sheryl.

"You okay?"

She nodded, her face paper white in the dimness. Then, incredibly, she produced a shaky, strained smile.

"You'd better cuff him or...or do whatever it is you marshals do. We've got a plane to meet."

Chapter 14

"I'm not leaving."

Sheryl folded arms encased in the too-long sleeves of a black windbreaker and glared at Deputy Marshal Ev Sloan. He fired back with an equally stubborn look.

"It could get nasty around here. Nastier," he amended with a glance at the two men huddled back to back on the asphalt a few yards away, their hands cuffed behind their backs. Fay and another officer stood over them, reading them their rights.

"I want to stay," Sheryl insisted. "I need to see this."

"This isn't any place for civilians. We don't have time to—"

"It's okay, Ev."

Harry nodded his thanks to the medic who'd just taped a gauze bandage on his upper cheek. He crossed the asphalt to the task force command vehicle, his gaze on the woman hunched in the front seat.

"She's part of the team."

His quiet words dissolved the last of Sheryl's own secret doubts. She couldn't quite believe that she was sitting in a truck that bristled with more antennas than a porcupine on a bad-quill day, watching while an army of law enforcement agencies checked their weapons and coordinated last-minute details for the takedown of a smuggler and suspected killer. Or that she'd pulled out a .357 Magnum and squeezed a trigger herself mere moments ago. Until Harry MacMillan had charged into her life, she'd only experienced this kind of Ram-boesque excitement through movies and TV.

This wasn't a movie, though. She had the bruises and the bunched-up knot of fear in her stomach to prove it. This was real. This was life or death, and Harry was right in the middle of it. There was no way Sheryl was going to leave, as Ev insisted, while Harry calmly walked right back into the line of fire.

Besides, she and Harry had a conversation to finish. They'd tossed around a few words such as "love" and "commitment" and "prom-ises" in that dark, dirty storeroom. Sheryl wanted more than words.

She wouldn't get them any time soon, she saw. Having assured himself she'd sustained no serious injury, and having had the powder burn on his cheek attended to, the marshal was ready for action. More than ready. In the glow from the command vehicle's overhead light, his whiskey-gold eyes gleamed with barely restrained impatience. He paused before her, holding himself in check long enough to brush a knuckle down her cheek.

"I don't want to worry about you any more than I already have today. Promise me that you'll stay in the command vehicle."

"I promise."

"Ev told you that we have a U.S. Marshals Service plane standing by. If Paul Gunderson's aboard the incoming aircraft and we take him down…"

"You will!" Sheryl said fiercely. "I know you will!"

His knuckle stilled. The glint in his eyes turned feral. "Yes, I will."

She bit down her lower lip, waiting for him to come back to her. A moment later, the back of his hand resumed its slow stroke.

"I might not get a chance to talk to you after the bust. I'll have to bundle Gunderson aboard our plane and get him and his two pals back to Washington for arraignment."

"I know."

Cupping her chin, he turned her face a few more degrees into the light. He stared down at her, as if imprinting her features on his memory.

Sheryl could have wished for a better image for him to take with him. Her cheeks still carried traces of the rust and squashed bugs that had rained down on her from the overhead pipes during her desperate escape attempt. Her hair frizzed all over her head. If she'd had on a lick of makeup when she'd left her apartment so many hours ago, she'd long since chewed or rubbed or cried it off.

Harry didn't seem to mind the bugs or frizz or total lack of color on her face. His thumb traced a slow path across her lower lip.

"I'll be back. I promise."

Turning her head, Sheryl pressed a kiss to his palm. Her smile was a little ragged around the edges, but she got it into place.

"I'll be waiting."

His hand dropped. A moment later, he disappeared, one of many shadows that melted into the darkness.

Even Ev Sloan deserted Sheryl, vowing that he wasn't going to miss out on the action again. Another deputy marshal took his place in the command vehicle. He introduced himself with a nod, then gave the bank of radios mounted under the dash his total concentration.

Sheryl huddled in her borrowed windbreaker. For some foolish reason, she'd believed that she could never again experience the sick terror that had gripped her those awful hours with Broken Nose and Slick Hair. Now she realized that listening helplessly while the man she loved put his life on the line bred its own brand of terror.

Her heart in her throat, she followed every play in Harry's deadly game.

The game ended less than half an hour later.

To Sheryl's immense relief, the man subsequently identified as Richard Johnson-Paul Gunderson stepped off the cargo plane, tossed up an arm to shield his eyes from a blinding flood of light and promptly threw himself face down on the concrete parking apron.

As a jubilant Ev related to Sheryl, the bastard was brave enough with his mob connections backing him up. Without them, he wet his pants at the first warning shout.

Literally.

"Harry had to scrounge up a clean pair of jeans before he could hustle the bastard aboard our plane," Ev reported gleefully. "The government will probably have to foot the bill for them, but what the hell! We got him, Sher! We got him!''

Grinning from ear to ear, he unbuckled his body armor and tossed it into his gear bag. His webbed belt with its assortment of canisters and ammo clips followed.

''I would've left him to stew in his own juice, so to speak, but then I didn't have to handcuff myself to the man and sit next to him in a small aircraft for the next five or six hours the way Harry did.''

''I can see how that would make a difference,'' Sheryl concurred, her eyes on the twin-engine jet revving up at the end of the runway.

Ev's gear bag hit the back of the command vehicle with a thunk.

''Harry told me to take you home. Fay has to hang around until the Nuclear Regulatory folks finish decertifying the canisters. I told her I'd come back to help with the disposition. You ready to go?''

The small plane with U.S. Marshals Service markings roared down the runway. Sheryl followed its blinking red and white lights until they disappeared into a bank of black clouds.

''I'm ready.''

Ev traded places with the marshal who'd manned the command vehicle. He twisted the key in the ignition, then shoved the truck into gear.

''We have to swing by the federal building to pick up the mutt.''

''Button?''

Ev's teeth showed white in the airport exit lights. ''Harry left him with the security guards when we came chasing out here. As obnoxious as that mutt is, I wouldn't be surprised if one of the guards hasn't skinned him by now and nailed his hide over the front door.''

They soon discovered that Button was still in one piece, although the same couldn't be said for the security guards. One sported a long tear in his uniform sleeve. The other pointed out the neat pattern of teeth marks in his leather brogans.

Sheryl apologized profusely and retrieved the indignant animal from the lidded trash can where the guards had stashed him. Button huffed and snuffled and ruffled up his fur, but let himself be carried from the federal building with only a few parting snarls at the guards. After a few greeting snarls at Ev, he settled down on Sheryl's chest.

She buried her nose in his soft, silky fur. The lights of Old Town, only a few blocks from the federal building, sped by unnoticed. The bright wash of stars overhead didn't draw her eyes. Even Ev's excited recounting of the night's tumultuous events barely penetrated. In her mind, she followed the flight of a small silver jet over the Sandias and across New Mexico's wide, flat plains.

He'd be back. He'd promised.

But when?

"Looks like it's going to be next week before Gunderson's arraignment."

Turning her back on the noise of the lively group who'd just arrived at her apartment to celebrate young Master Brian Hart's christening, Sheryl strained to hear Harry's recorded message.

"You have my office number. They can reach me anytime, night or day, if you have an emergency. I'll talk to you soon."

The recorder clicked off.

Frustrated, she hit the repeat button. Except for one short call soon after Harry had arrived in D.C., he and Sheryl had been playing telephone tag for almost three days now. From what she'd gleaned through his brief messages, the man she now thought of as Richard Johnson had held out longer than anyone had expected before finally breaking his stubborn silence. Once the dam gave, the assistant DA working the case had kept Harry busy helping with the briefs for the grand jury. Now, it appeared, he'd have to stay in D.C. until next week's arraignment.

"Sheryl, where are the pretzels? I can't— Oh, I'm sorry, honey. I didn't know you were on the phone."

Replacing the receiver, Sheryl pasted on a smile and turned to face her mother. "I'm not. I was just checking my messages."

"Well? Did he call?"

"Yes, he called."

"Where is he?"

"Still in Washington."

"I want to meet this man. When is he coming back to Albuquerque?"

"He doesn't know."

Her mother's thin, still-attractive face took on the pinched look that Sheryl had seen all too often in her youth. Joan Hancock wanted to say more. That much was obvious from the way she bit down on her lower lip.

Thankfully, she refrained.

She had driven up to Albuquerque from Las Cruces three days ago, after Elise's frantic call informing her that her daughter was missing. She'd stayed through the rest of the weekend, demanding to know every detail about Sheryl's involvement in a search for a dangerous fugitive.

Needless to say, the cautious bits her daughter let drop about the deputy marshal who'd swept in and out of her life hadn't pleased Joan any more than observing Brian Mitchell's growing attachment to his namesake…and his namesake's mother.

The christening ceremony tonight had only added to her disgruntlement. Sheryl and Brian had stood as godparents to the baby. Seeing them together at the altar had rekindled Joan Hancock's grievances against Elise. She was still convinced that the new mother had schemed to steal Sheryl's boyfriend right out from under her nose.

"Just look at her," she griped, pressing the pretzel bowl against the front of the pale-gray silk dress she'd worn to the church. "The way she's making those goo-goo eyes at Brian, you'd think he'd fathered her child instead of her shiftless ex-husband."

Sheryl's gaze settled on the scene in the living room. Elise had anchored the baby's carrier in a corner of the sofa, where it couldn't be jostled by her two lively boys. They were showing off their baby brother to the assembled crowd with patented propriety. Brian leaned against the arm of the sofa, one finger unconsciously stroking the baby's feathery red curls while he chatted with Elise. Even Button had gotten into the act. Perched on the back of the sofa, he waved his silky tail back and forth and guarded the baby with the regal hauteur that had made the shih tzu so prized by the emperors of China.

It was a picture-perfect family tableau. With all her heart, Sheryl wished everyone in the picture happiness.

She'd told Elise so when the two friends had snatched a half hour alone yesterday. Even now, she had to smile at the emotions that had chased across Elise's face, one after another, like tumbleweeds blown by a high wind. Pain for Sheryl over her break with Brian. Guilty relief that he was free. Disbelief that her friend had fallen for Harry so hard, so fast. Worry that she was in for some hurting times ahead.

Like Joan, Elise couldn't quite believe that her friend had opted to settle for a life of loneliness, broken by days or weeks or even months of companionship. Sheryl couldn't quite believe it, either, but sometime in the past few days, she had.

Joan gave a long, wistful sigh. "Are you sure you and Brian can't patch things up?"

"I'm sure."

Her gaze left the group on the sofa and settled on her daughter's face. "Oh, Sherrie, I hoped you'd do better than I did."

Sheryl's smile softened. "You did fine, Mom."

A haze of tears silvered Joan's green eyes, so like her daughter's. "I wanted you to find someone steady and reliable. Someone who'd be there when you needed him to kiss away your hurts and share your laughter and fix the leaky faucets."

"You taught me to be pretty handy with a wrench," Sheryl replied gently. "And Harry was there when I needed him."

He'd been there, and he'd done more than kiss away her hurts, she acknowledged silently. After her breakup with Brian, he'd driven the hurt right out of her mind. At the airport, he'd wiped away a good measure of her terror and trauma by the simple act of acknowledging her as part of his team.

Along the way, Sheryl thought with an inner smile, he'd also taken her to dizzying heights of pleasure that she'd never dreamed of, let alone experienced. She craved the feel of his hands on her breasts, ached for the brush of his prickly mustache against her skin. She longed to curl up with him on the couch and share a pepperoni-and-pineapple pizza, and watch his face when he bit into one of New Mexico's man-sized peppers.

In short, she wanted whatever moments they could snatch and memories they could make together. Everyone else might count their time together in hours, but Sheryl measured it by the clinging, stubborn love that had taken root in her heart and refused to let go.

Her mother sighed again. "You're going to wait for this man, aren't you? Night after night, week after week?"

"Yes, I am."

Joan lifted a hand and rested a palm against her daughter's cheek. "You're stronger than I was, Sherrie. You'll…you'll make it work."

She hoped so. She sincerely hoped so.

"Come on, Mom. Let's get back to the party."

Despite her conviction that Harry was worth waiting for, Sheryl found the wait more difficult than she'd let on to her mother. The hours seemed to stretch endlessly. Thankfully, she had her job to keep her busy during the day and Button to share her nights.

According to Ev Sloan, she could expect to have the mutt's company for some time to come. He called with the news the evening after little Brian's christening. Just home from work and about to step into the shower, Sheryl ran out of the bathroom and snatched the phone up on the second ring. With some effort, she kept the fierce disappointment from her voice.

"Hi, Ev."

Clutching the towel she'd thrown around her with one hand, she listened to his gleeful news. Patrice Jörgenson/Johnson, aka Inga Gunderson, cut a deal with the federal authorities. In exchange for information about her nephew's activities, she would plead guilty to a lesser battery of charges that would give her the possibility of parole in a few years.

"We're transporting her to D.C. Got a plane standing by. She wants to say goodbye to the mutt first."

"You mean, like, now? Over the phone?"

"Yeah."

The note of disgust in Ev's voice told Sheryl he hadn't quite recovered from his initial bout with Button, when the dog had locked onto his leg.

"I'll, er, put him on."

Perching on the side of the bed, she prodded the sleeping dog awake. At the sound of his mistress's voice, he yipped into the phone once or twice before curling back into a ball and leaving Sheryl to finish the conversation. Somehow, she found herself promising to write faithfully and keep the older woman apprised of Button's health and welfare.

Sniffing, Inga provided a list of absolute essentials. "He takes B-12 and vitamin E twice a week. His vet can supply you with the coated tablets. They're easier for him to swallow. And don't forget his heartworm pills."

"How could I forget those?" Sheryl countered with a grimace.

"Make sure you keep his hair out of his eyes to prevent irritation of the lids."

"I will."

"Don't use rubber bands, though! They pull his hair."

"I won't."

"Oh, I canceled his standing appointment at the stud. You'll have to call them back and reinstate him."

"Excuse me?"

"Button's descended from a line of champions," Inga explained in a teary, quavering voice so different from the one that had shouted obscenities at Harry and Ev that her listener found it hard to believe she was the same woman. "We could charge outrageous stud fees if we wanted to, you know, but we just go there so my precious can, well, enjoy himself."

Sheryl blinked. She hadn't realized her responsibilities would include pimping for Button. She was still dealing with that mind-boggling revelation when Inga sniffed.

"He's very virile. They always offer me pick of the litter." She paused. "You may keep one of his pups in exchange for taking care of him. Or perhaps two, since you work and a pet shouldn't be left alone all day."

"Th-thank you."

Underwhelmed by the magnanimous offer, Sheryl glanced at the tight black-and-white ball on her bed. She could just imagine Harry's reaction if two or three Buttons crawled under the covers with him in the middle of the night.

Assuming Harry ever got back to Albuquerque to get under the covers.

Sighing, she copied down the last of Inga's instructions, held the phone to the dog's ear a final time and hung up. She stood beside the bed for a moment, staring down into her companion's buggy black eyes.

"What do you say, fella? Wanna share a pizza after I get out of the shower?"

Chapter 15

The glossy postcard leaped out at Sheryl from the sheaf of mail in her hand.

Tahiti.

A pristine stretch of sandy beach. A fringe of deep-green banyan trees. An aquamarine sea laced with white, lapping at the shore.

Resolutely, she fought down the urge to turn the postcard over and peek at the message on the back. She'd had enough vicarious adventures as a result of reading other people's mail to last her a while.

She won the brief struggle, but still couldn't bring herself to shove the card in the waiting post office box. For just a moment, she indulged a private fantasy and imagined herself on that empty stretch of beach with Harry. She saw him splashing toward her in the surf. The sun bronzed his lean, hard body. The breeze off the sea ruffled his dark hair. His gold-flecked eyes gleamed with—

"You okay, Sher?"

"What?" Startled out of the South Pacific, she glanced up guiltily to meet Elise's look. "Yes, I'm fine."

"You're thinking about the marshal again, aren't you? You've got that…that lost look on your face."

Sheryl flashed the postcard at her friend. "I was thinking about Tahiti."

Elise pursed her lips.

"All right, all right. I was thinking about Tahiti and Harry."

Nudging aside a stack of mail, the new mom cleared a space on the table between the banks of postal boxes and hitched a hip on the corner. She'd insisted on coming back to work, declaring that her ex-mother-in-law, her parents, her two boys and her regular baby-sitter were more than enough to care for the newest addition to the Hart family. She still hadn't fully regained the endurance required for postal work, though. Sheryl scooped up her bundle and added it to the stack in her hand.

"How long has it been now since Harry left?" Elise demanded as her friend fired the mail into the appropriate boxes. "A week? Eight days?"

"Nine, but who's counting?"

"You are! I am! Everyone in the post office is."

"Well, you can stop counting. He promised he'd come back. He will."

"Oh, Sher, he said he'd come back after the arraignment last week. Then he had to fly to Miami. I hate for you to…"

Buck Aguilar rumbled by with a full cart, drowning out the rest of her comment. Sheryl didn't need to hear it. The worry in her eyes spoke its own language.

"He'll be back, Elise. He promised."

"I believe you," the other woman grumbled. "I just don't like seeing you jump every time the phone rings, or spending your evenings walking that obnoxious little hair ball."

"Give Button time," Sheryl replied, laughing. "He grows on you."

"Ha! That'll be the day. He almost took off my hand at the wrist when I made the mistake of reaching for the baby before Butty-boo was finished checking him out. Here, give me the last stack. I'll finish it."

"I've got it. You just sit and gather your strength for the hordes waiting in the lobby. We have to open in a few minutes."

Elise swung her sneakered foot, a small frown etched on her brow. Sheryl smiled to herself. Her friend still couldn't quite believe that she would prefer the marshal—or anyone else!—over Brian Mitchell.

Despite the long talk the two women had shared, Elise had yet to work through her own feelings of guilt and secret longing.

She would. After watching her and Brian together, Sheryl didn't doubt that they'd soon reach the point she herself had come to this past week. They were meant for each other. Just as she and Harry were.

She'd wait for him. However long it took. Wherever his job sent him. She wasn't her mother, and Harry certainly wasn't her father. They'd wring every particle of happiness out of their time together and look forward to their next reunion with the same delicious anticipation that curled in Sheryl's tummy now.

After zinging the last of the box mail into its slot, she slammed the metal door. "Come on, kiddo. We'd better get our cash drawers from the safe. We've only got…"

She glanced at the clock in the central work space and felt her heart sommersault. Striding through the maze of filled mail carts was a tall, unmistakable figure in tight jeans, a blue cotton shirt and a rumpled linen gray sport coat.

"Harry!"

Sheryl flew toward him, scattering letters and advertising fliers and postcards as she went. He caught her up in his arms and whirled her around. The room had barely stopped spinning before he bent his head and covered her mouth with his. Instantly, the whole room tilted crazily again.

Flinging her arms around his neck, she drank in his kiss. It was better than she remembered. Wild. Hot. Hungry. When he lifted his head, she dragged in great, gulping breaths and let the questions tumble out.

"When did you get in? Why didn't you call? What happened in Miami?"

Grinning, he kissed her again, much to the interest of the various personnel who stopped their work to watch.

"Twenty minutes ago. I didn't want to take the time. And we nailed the arms manufacturer Gunderson was supplying."

"Good!"

Laughing at her fierce exclamation, he hefted her higher in his arms and started for the back door.

"Wait a minute!" Sheryl was more than willing to let him carry her right out of the post office, but she needed to cover her station. "I've got to get someone to take the front counter for me."

"It's all arranged," he told her, his eyes gleaming.

"What is?"

"The postmaster general got a call from the attorney general early this morning, Miss Hancock. You're being recommended for a citation for your part in apprehending an escaped fugitive and suspected killer." The gleam deepened to a wicked glint. "You've also been granted the leave you requested. There's a temp on the way down to fill in for you."

"I seem to be having some trouble recalling the fact that I asked for leave."

"I wouldn't be surprised, with all you've gone through lately." Harry wove his way through the carriers' stations. "You asked for two weeks for your honeymoon."

Sheryl opened her mouth, shut it, opened it again. A thousand questions whirled around in her head. Only one squeaked out.

"Two weeks, huh?"

"Two weeks," he confirmed. "Unless you don't have a current passport, in which case we'll have to tack on a few extra days so we can stop over in Washington to pull some strings."

He slowed, his grin softening to a smile so full of tenderness that Sheryl's throat closed.

"I want to take you to Heidelburg, sweetheart, and stand beside you on the castle ramparts when the Neckar River turns gold in the sunset. I want to watch your face the first time you see the spires of Notre Dame rising out of the morning mists. I want to make love to you in France and Italy and Germany and wherever else we happen to stop for an hour or a day or a night."

"Oh, Harry."

He eased his arm from under her knees. Sheryl's feet slid to the floor, but she didn't feel the black tiles under her sneakers. Not with

Harry's hands locked loosely around her waist and his heart thumping steadily against hers.

"I know you said it was too soon for commitments and promises, but I've had a lot of time to think this past week."

"Me, too," she breathed.

"I don't want almost, Sheryl. I want you now and forever."

He brushed back her hair with one hand. All trace of amusement left his eyes.

"The regional director's position here in the Albuquerque office comes open next month. The folks in D.C. tell me the job's mine if I want it."

Her pounding pulse stilled. She wanted Harry, as much as he wanted her. But she wouldn't try to hold him with either tears or a love that strangled.

"Do you want it, Harry?"

"Yes, sweetheart, I do. It'll mean less time on the road, although I can't guarantee I'll have anything resembling regular office hours or we'll enjoy a routine home life."

Sheryl could have told him that she'd learned her lesson with Brian. On her list of top-ten priorities, a comfortable routine now ranked about number twenty-five. All that mattered, all she cared about, was the way his touch made her blood sing, and the crinkly lines at the corners of his eyes, and his soft, silky mustache and...

"I'm a deputy marshal," he said quietly. "The service is in my blood."

"I know."

"So are you. I carried your smile and your sun-streaked hair and your little moans of delight with me day and night for the past week. I love you, Sheryl. I want to live the rest of my life with you, if you'll have me, and take you to all the places you dreamed about."

A sigh drifted on the air behind her. She didn't even glance around. She didn't care how many of her co-workers had gathered to hear Harry's soft declaration. One corner of his mustache tipped up.

"I thought about buying a ring and getting down on one knee and doing the whole romantic bit," he told her ruefully, "but I don't want to waste our time with almost-anythings. I want to go right for the real thing. Right here. Right now.''

He would, she thought with a smile.

''There's a judge waiting for us at the federal building,'' he said gruffly. ''He'll do the deed as soon as we get the license.''

An indignant sputter sounded just behind Sheryl. Elise protested vehemently. ''You have to call your mother, Sher! At least give her time to drive up from Las Cruces!''

''The judge will do the deed as soon as your mother gets here,'' Harry amended gravely, holding her gaze with his own.

Someone else spoke up. Pat Martinez, Sheryl thought.

''Hey, we want to be there, too! Wait until the shift change this afternoon. We'll shred up all that mail languishing in the dead-letter bin and come down to the courthouse armed with champagne and confetti.''

''Champagne and confetti sounds good to me.'' Harry smiled down at her. ''Well?''

''I love you, too,'' she told him mistily. ''I'll have you, Marshal, right here, right now and for the rest of our lives.''

Stretching up on her tiptoes, she slid her arms around his neck. He bent his head, and his mouth was only a breath away from hers when she murmured, ''There's only one problem. We'll have to take Button with us on this honeymoon. Unless you know someone who will take care of him while we're gone?'' she asked hopefully.

''You're kidding, right?''

When she shook her head, he closed his eyes. Sheryl closed her ears to his muttered imprecations. When he opened them again, she saw a look of wry resignation in their golden brown depths.

''All right. We'll pick up a doggie-rat carrier on our way to the airport.''

At that moment, she knew she'd never settle for almost-anything again.

* * * * *

MERLINE LOVELACE

spent twenty-three years as an air force officer, serving tours at the Pentagon and at bases all over the world before she began a new career as a novelist. When she's not tied to her keyboard, she and her own handsome hero, Al, enjoy traveling, golf and long lively dinners with friends and family.

A *USA Today* bestselling author with over five million copies of her books in print, Merline is known for her mainstream military thrillers and her historical novels for MIRA as well as her category romances. Merline is a five-time nominee for the Romance Writers of America prestigious RITA Award, and is proud to have been named the 1998 Oklahoma Author of the Year.

Merline enjoys hearing from readers and can be reached by e-mail via Internet through the Silhouette/Harlequin Web site at www.eHarlequin.com or at her own Web site www.merlinelovelace.com.

Silhouette®
Where love comes alive™

These New York Times *bestselling authors*
have created stories to capture the hearts and minds
of women everywhere.
Here are three classic tales about the power of love—
and the wonder of discovering the place
where you belong....

FINDING HOME

DUNCAN'S BRIDE
by
LINDA HOWARD

CHAIN LIGHTNING
by
ELIZABETH LOWELL

POPCORN AND KISSES
by
KASEY MICHAELS

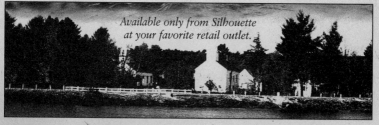

Available only from Silhouette
at your favorite retail outlet.

Silhouette®
Where love comes alive™

Coming in February 2002 from *Silhouette*®

THE FAMILY FACTOR

In **BLESSING IN DISGUISE**
by Marie Ferrarella,
a bachelor gets much-needed
lessons in fatherhood.

In **THE BABY FACTOR**
by Carolyn Zane, an assertive
TV producer humbles herself
to get mommy lessons…
from her handsome employee!

Because there's more than one way to have a family…

Available at your favorite retail outlet.

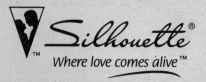

Silhouette®

Where love comes alive™

Visit Silhouette at www.eHarlequin.com   BR2TFF-TR

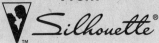

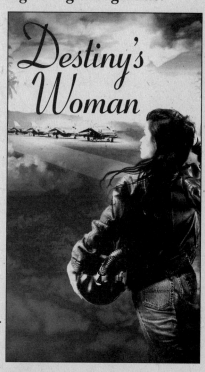
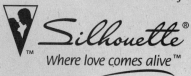

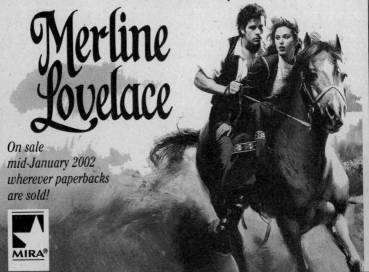